Through her marriage to Reggie Kray, Roberta Kray has a unique and authentic insight into London's East End. Roberta met Reggie in early 1996 and they married the following year; they were together until Reggie's death in 2000. Roberta is the author of many previous bestsellers including *Bad Girl, Streetwise, No Mercy* and *Dangerous Promises.*

ROBERTA KRAY

EXPOSED

sphere

SPHERE

First published in Great Britain in 2016 by Sphere

1 3 5 7 9 10 8 6 4 2

Copyright © Roberta Kray 2016

The moral right of the author has been asserted.

A CIP catalogue record for this book
is available from the British Library.

ISBN 978-0-7515-6102-9

Typeset in Garamond by M Rules
Printed and bound in Great Britain by
Clays Ltd, St Ives plc

Papers used by Sphere are from well-managed forests
and other responsible sources.

MIX
Paper from
responsible sources
FSC® C104740

Sphere
An imprint of
Little, Brown Book Group
Carmelite House
50 Victoria Embankment
London EC4Y 0DZ

An Hachette UK Company
www.hachette.co.uk

www.littlebrown.co.uk

In memory of Vernon Wells

Prologue

1966

Paddy Lynch lay dying in the back of the van. He clutched at his guts, trying to stop the life from leaking out of him. His eyes, frantic with fear, darted to the left and the right, looking at everything but focusing on nothing. A thin stream of blood trickled from the corner of his mouth.

'You'll be all right, mate. Hang on in there.'

'Yeah, we'll get you to the hospital. No worries, Pads. They'll sort you out.'

The two men who were crouched down beside him exchanged quick knowing glances. Unless Paddy got help soon, he was for it. You didn't need to be a doctor to see that. They tried to keep their voices reassuring as they watched his face turn grey.

A third man, Jack Minter, scowled and looked away. He was struggling to contain his rage. He had no sympathy for Paddy. The stupid bastard had ignored everything he'd been told, gone in like some gun-toting cowboy, managed to get himself shot with his own sawn-off and almost blown the whole job in the process. And now – the icing on the cake – someone would

1

have to take him to the hospital. And for what? The bloke was going to croak no matter where he was.

Jack glared at the row of heavy brown sacks. It was a decent haul, mainly consisting of gold, gems and jewellery, but it would have been even better if Paddy hadn't gone off half-cocked. The thought of what they'd had to leave behind made his blood boil. It had taken over a year of meticulous planning, *his* planning, hours and hours of painstaking work to get everything in place. He'd been sure that he'd covered every contingency – except for this one.

'You'll be okay, Pads. You will. Tell him, Jack.'

Jack forced a thin smile. 'Sure,' he said. 'No worries. We'll be there soon.' But he didn't look straight at Paddy – he didn't want to see those fading eyes – and focused instead on a spot to the side of his head. Jesus, he should have known better than to bring him along. The guy had been a last-minute replacement after Charlie Treen had broken his leg. A bad omen if ever there'd been one. He should have listened to the gods, postponed it and waited until Charlie was back on his feet, but it was too late for regrets now.

The van was moving rapidly along the uneven road, every bump and jolt adding to Paddy's misery. A low moan escaped from between his lips. Jack glanced at his watch, knowing they must be approaching the changeover spot. It was a quiet place where two cars were parked, where the team would separate and the haul would be split before they met up again at the house in Kellston.

'Right, we're almost there. I'll take the van and drop Paddy off at the hospital.'

'What about the gear?' Rossi asked, his expression tight and suspicious as if Jack might be trying to pull a fast one.

'Same as we planned. You divide it between you and I'll see you later.'

Rossi glanced down at Paddy, looked up again and gave a cautious nod. 'You sure?'

'It's the only way. I'll dump the van at A&E and get the Tube back.'

The van came to a halt. They heard Ned run round to open the doors. 'How is he?' he asked, staring wide-eyed at Paddy.

'Hanging on,' Jack said. 'Come on, let's get this gear shifted.'

The men unloaded the sacks in thirty seconds flat and shoved them into the boots of the waiting vehicles. The three said a few quick reassuring words to Paddy before jumping inside the cars. Jack could see they felt guilty about leaving the guy, but not guilty enough to jeopardise their own freedom. Not one of them suggested coming along.

Jack gave a snort. So much for loyalty, for standing by your buddies. When the shit hit the fan it was every man for himself. He put his foot down and went first, the others following on at the rear. At the crossroads they took three different directions, with only the van going straight ahead. The law might not be far behind and if he got stopped then at least the haul was safe. He thought about Paddy lying in the back and his lip curled. Problem was, the filth would know the idiot had been shot and they'd be watching the hospitals. That was going to make it tricky.

And there was something else to stress about too. What if by some freak chance Paddy didn't die? What if he came through the op, opened his big mouth and sang like a canary? Jack wouldn't put it past him. He didn't trust the guy, not an inch. What did he really know about Paddy Lynch? Sod all, other than the fact he couldn't follow orders. The fool might sell them all down the river.

'Stuff that!' he muttered.

Jack reached into his shirt pocket, pulled out a pack of fags, took a cigarette and lit it. He breathed in deeply, trying to

3

figure out what to do next. He expelled the smoke in a long thoughtful stream. A spatter of rain fell against the windscreen and he switched on the wipers, his gaze flicking between the road ahead and the rear-view mirror. What now? An inner voice was whispering in his ear. The answer was clear. The answer was simple. All he had to do was *nothing*.

Jack didn't think of himself as a cruel man, simply a pragmatic one. This was supposed to be his first and last job and by ten o'clock tonight – if nothing got in the way – he could be on a plane heading out of the country for good. He had no intention of ever coming back. A new life, a fresh start was what he had planned and he didn't see why he should change those plans.

It was time to get out of London, and especially the East End. Things were getting too hot. Ever since Ronnie Kray had shot Cornell back in March, there'd been tension in the area. There were going to be repercussions; there was no doubt about it. The filth would only take so much. A line had been crossed and there'd be a price to pay. Well, he didn't intend to be standing in the firing line when it all kicked off.

Jack took another long drag on his cigarette and hissed out the smoke between his teeth. 'Damn it!'

If Paddy survived and named names, they'd all be looking at a long stretch. And what if he grassed them up before he even got into the operating theatre? Not that it was likely judging by the state of him, but stranger things had happened when men were on their way to meet their maker.

Jack gave an impatient shake of his head. Sometimes important decisions had to be made, decisions for the greater good, and this was one of those occasions. After all, when push came to shove, Paddy had brought it on himself. If he hadn't been so reckless, he wouldn't be lying in the back of the van with a bullet in his guts. Why should everyone else pay the price for what he'd done? It wasn't right. It wasn't fair. It was way out of order.

He opened the window and chucked out the fag end. The cold November air snapped at his face, reminding him of why he wanted to be somewhere else, somewhere warmer, somewhere that offered better opportunities for an ambitious man with hopes and dreams. One chance, that's all you got sometimes, and he wasn't about to throw his away.

As Jack approached the junction he saw the signs for Epping town centre and the hospital. Straight on. He didn't need to think about it twice. 'Sorry, mate,' he murmured, flicking on the indicator and turning left. 'Some you win, some you lose.' He didn't view what he was doing as murder; he was simply letting nature take its course.

1

1982

Eden Chase screwed up her eyes against the bright winter sun as she stepped out of the Tube station and began to walk down James Street towards the centre of Covent Garden. It was one of those sharp, sunny afternoons that break the monotony of winter and automatically lift the spirits. Not that her spirits needed any lifting; she had never been happier in her life.

As she crossed the busy piazza, she looked towards the first-floor window of the studio on Henrietta Street, almost expecting to see the tall, fair-haired figure of her husband. He frequently stood there looking down on the hustle and bustle of the square, his hands on his hips, his expression one of deep concentration. What was he thinking? She often wondered but she never asked.

Eden liked the fact that Tom wasn't an easy person to fathom. He was the sort of man who didn't give much away. You had to peel the information from him, one layer at a time, and even then you felt like you'd barely scratched the surface. But she didn't mind that; they had years ahead of them, plenty of time to get to know each other better. Her husband was worth the effort.

She smiled as the word slid into her head. *Husband*. Even though they'd been married for a year, the word still felt new on her lips. Back when she'd first made the announcement, some of her more feminist friends had knotted their brows in disapproval. There had been a lively debate over her future nuptials. Everybody liked Tom – he was witty and clever, generous and kind – but what did she want to get hitched for? Why didn't she just live with him? In this day and age women didn't need to get married to feel fulfilled.

But Eden had discovered that she liked being married. Tom might have swept her off her feet but in many ways he grounded her too. For the first time she felt like she had direction and that she wasn't just drifting through life. Every morning and every night she counted her blessings. Meeting him was the best thing that had ever happened to her.

Her father, however, had not shared this point of view and had been vociferous in his objections to the marriage. Tom was too old for her (forty to her twenty-five) and what kind of a career was photography? There was no security in it, no solid future. And why did they have to get married right now?

'It won't last,' he'd said with his customary churlishness. 'Marry in haste, repent at leisure.'

'Can't you just be happy for me?'

'Happy about what? You've barely known him two minutes.'

'Six months,' she'd said, although it was actually closer to five.

'Six months! Exactly! It's hardly the foundation for a successful marriage. I don't see why you're rushing into things. You're young. You've got all the time in the world. Why can't you just—' He had stopped abruptly, his face paling as an obvious reason for the haste occurred to him. His eyes

8

narrowed with worry and disgust. 'Please don't tell me that you're—'

'For God's sake,' she'd snapped back. 'Of course not.' And then she'd quickly added, 'Anyhow, it's the eighties, Dad. Nobody cares about that sort of thing any more. Why would it matter if I was?' She'd known very well why it would matter – her father was staunchly conservative, rigidly middle-class and completely stuck in his ways. He regarded babies conceived out of wedlock as shameful. She had known too that it was his own reputation he was as bothered about as much as hers.

Eden sighed and lowered her gaze from the window. She loved her father but found him hard to like. Their relationship was strained and fraught with difficulty. It was fortunate that they lived so far apart. At a distance they were able to maintain some semblance of civility, avoiding the sparks that always started flying whenever they came face to face. The trouble was … Well, where to start? They both had a stubborn streak and that was never going to change.

Anyway, despite the general lack of support, Eden had gone ahead with the wedding. Her mother would have understood. Although she had no firm evidence for this assertion – Diana Shore had died when Eden was only six – she had created a picture in her head of a woman who had possessed the finest of maternal qualities, a parent who was wise and witty, sensitive and kind. Her actual memories were so vague and shadowy that she was no longer sure what was real and what wasn't.

Eden stopped as she drew alongside St Paul's church and peered around the heads of the crowd. A fire eater was in the middle of his act, plunging a torch into his mouth and spewing long hissing flames into the air. The performance held her attention for a minute or two until her thoughts drifted off again.

It was here, almost on this very spot, that she had first met

Tom. She hadn't taken much notice of him – he was just some tall blond guy, probably a tourist, with a camera in front of his face – until she realised that the Leica was pointing straight at her. She had seen his finger press down on the button and heard the smooth rapid click of the shutter opening and closing.

'Did you just take a picture of me?'

'Yes.'

For some reason, she'd expected him to deny it and his honesty had caught her off guard. Despite this she'd still glared hard at him. 'Well, you can't. You can't do that.'

He'd inclined his head as if to study her more closely. 'Sorry. It was the hair, you see, your red hair. I thought it looked kind of . . . autumnal. Captures the mood, if you know what I mean.'

Eden had continued to glower. 'I don't care what mood it captures. You can't just go around . . . I don't like complete strangers taking photos of me.'

'Why not?'

'Why do you think? Because it's rude. Because it's . . . it's weird. It's creepy.'

He'd laughed when she said that, his mouth opening to reveal a row of straight white teeth. 'It's only creepy if I'm creepy. Do you think I'm creepy?'

'How would I know? You could be.' The fact that he was so clearly amused by the exchange had only added to her irritation. 'All the evidence seems to point in that direction.'

'My self-esteem is shrinking by the second.'

'And whose fault is that?'

He'd raised his hands as if to admit defeat. 'Okay, what if I promise to destroy the negative? I won't even develop the picture.'

'And why should I believe you?'

'Because I'm a decent, honest, upstanding guy. If I say I'll do something, I'll do it. You can come and watch if you like.' He had gestured towards Henrietta Street. 'Over there, with the black door. First floor. That's my studio, the one with the blinds.'

'No, thanks,' she'd said sharply.

He had raked his fingers through his hair and grinned. 'Ah, right, no, I mean we wouldn't be alone or anything. I didn't mean that. My receptionist will be there. You don't have to worry.'

'I'm not worried.'

'Good.'

'I'm not worried because I'm not going anywhere with you. Now if you don't mind, I really have to go. I'm supposed to be—'

'So how about I buy you a coffee instead? By way of an apology. Please say yes. I feel really bad about taking that picture now. Let me make it up to you.'

Eden had intended to say no, she was in a hurry, but then she hesitated. It was that hesitation that changed her life for ever.

'Tom Chase,' he'd said, putting out his hand. 'Nice to meet you.'

Eden smiled at the memory, feeling again the touch of his long cool fingers. She remembered gazing into a pair of compelling blue eyes, of being momentarily transfixed, of feeling a sudden unexpected flicker of attraction. She wasn't sure if she believed in fate or coincidence or any of that stuff, but from that moment on there had been no going back. He had charmed his way into her life and before long they were an item. And yes, maybe they had rushed into marriage, but she didn't regret it. What was there to regret? When you knew it was right there was no point in waiting.

She moved away from the crowd and carried on walking until she reached Henrietta Street. With no lectures in the afternoon she'd decided to surprise Tom and take him out for lunch. She was supposed to be writing an essay on Caravaggio but the lure of Covent Garden had been too much for her. Although she enjoyed her art course – and was determined not to drop out again like she had when she was nineteen – she still felt an illicit thrill from bunking off for a few hours.

'London calling,' she murmured, the words from The Clash jumping into her head. It was too nice a day to be stuck in the college library, to be confined by four magnolia walls and the dry, stuffy atmosphere. Anyway, she was sure that the wild Caravaggio wouldn't have thought twice about grabbing an opportunity when it came his way.

Eden took out her key, let herself into the building and stepped into the warm hallway.

The ground floor was occupied by a theatrical agency and as she started up the stairs she glanced to her left through the open door.

'Hi,' she called out to Clara. 'Only me.'

Clara lifted her gaze from the typewriter and shot her an odd, flustered sort of look, trying for a smile but not quite achieving it. Eden didn't dwell on the response; these theatrical types could be temperamental and she didn't take it as a snub. Maybe there had been a row before she'd got there, some actor sounding off about a part they hadn't got. There was often a good deal of drama on the ground floor.

At the top of the stairs Eden turned left on the landing and walked into Tom's studio. Instantly she stopped in her tracks, her mouth falling open. What she saw there took her breath away. The waiting area, usually so smart and glamorous, looked like a hurricane had blown through it. There were photographs strewn all over the place, file drawers pulled open and furniture shifted from its usual position. The two black leather couches had been pulled out and left stranded in the centre of the room. The framed photographs had all been removed from the walls.

'Tom?' she yelled, alarm running through her.

Annabelle Keep, his assistant, came through from the studio at the back carrying a heap of glossy prints. 'Oh, it's you,' she said, dumping the photos on the desk.

'Where's Tom? Is he all right? What's happened? What's going on?' Eden continued to look wildly around the room. 'Was it a burglary?'

Annabelle's dark eyebrows arched while her face assumed its familiar supercilious expression. Unless Tom was present, she never bothered to try and disguise her dislike of his wife. 'No, it was the police.'

Eden's eyes widened. 'What?'

'They searched the place, turned it upside down. Look at the state of it. It's going to take me all day to clear up.'

'What do you mean, the police? Why? Why would they . . . I don't understand.'

Annabelle gave a long sigh, as if she was doing Eden a favour just by telling her the facts. 'About an hour ago,' she said in her cut-glass accent. 'They came with a search warrant. Six of them, for God's sake, tramping all over the carpet with their size-nine boots. Don't ask me what they were looking for because I don't have a clue. All I do know is that they made one hell of a mess.' She put a hand on her skinny hip and tossed back her long dark hair. 'You'll have to talk to Tom about it.'

'So where is he?'

'He went to the station with them.'

Eden was struggling to get her head round it all. What could the cops possibly want with Tom? He ran a perfectly legitimate business, a successful business. 'What for? He's a photographer, for Christ's sake. He's not some . . . Why did he have to go down to the station?'

Annabelle gave an elegant but unilluminating shrug. 'They wanted to ask him more questions. Tom asked me to stay in here while he took two of the officers through to the back. I tried to stop the others from trashing the place but . . .'

Eden hurried into the studio, to the large airy room where Tom's clients sat for their portraits. There was less mess in here, but everything had been moved about. She could see through the open door that led to a small kitchen that the cupboards had been emptied; there were tea bags, sugar and coffee granules scattered over the counter.

'This is crazy. It doesn't make any sense. Why would they do this?'

Annabelle came in behind her. 'They made him open the safe too.'

Eden glanced over her shoulder. 'Did they?'

'I think they found something.'

'Found what?'

Annabelle gave a shake of her head. 'I couldn't see. I was next door, wasn't I? But they took Tom away shortly after that.'

'Took him away?' Eden said, her heart missing a beat. 'But I thought . . . Do you mean they arrested him?'

'No, I don't think so. At least . . . well, they didn't put cuffs on him or anything.'

'So what did he say to you? He must have said something.'

'Only that he'd see me later – and to cancel this afternoon's clients.'

'And how did he seem?'

'Seem?'

Eden growled, her exasperation growing by the minute. She suspected the girl of being deliberately obtuse; Annabelle liked to take advantage whenever she had the upper hand and this

14

was one of those occasions. 'Was he worried, angry, what? He must have had some kind of reaction.'

'Oh, well, not overjoyed, obviously. But he was fine. You know what Tom's like: he takes everything in his stride. There's just been a stupid mix-up. He'll be back soon, I'm sure he will.'

Eden hoped that Annabelle was right. She understood now why Clara had given her such an odd look on her way in. Having the police turn up on the doorstep with a search warrant was neither a common occurrence nor a welcome one.

'What the hell were they looking for?' Eden murmured.

Her first thought, naturally, was photographs. Maybe it was the Vice Squad who'd paid a visit, thinking Tom was peddling pornography. But then she glanced back towards the kitchen and its mess. No, if they were searching in coffee jars they must have been after something small. Drugs were the next thing that sprang into her head. But Tom had never had anything to do with drugs. The odd drag on a joint maybe, but that was all.

'Do you know which station they've taken him to?'

Annabelle pulled a face. 'I've no idea. What are you going to do?'

'Try to find him, of course. I want to know what's going on.'

'They won't tell you anything. You're better off waiting here until he comes back.'

What she meant, Eden thought, was that she didn't fancy doing all the clearing up on her own. Annabelle wasn't the sort of girl who liked getting her hands dirty. 'And what if he doesn't come back?'

'Why shouldn't he?'

'Because it won't be the first time the police have made a mistake. What if they . . . I don't know, maybe they think he's done something he hasn't.'

'You'd be better off calling his solicitor then.'

Eden chewed on her lower lip. She had no idea who his solicitor was, although she wasn't about to admit this to Annabelle. 'I don't have the number with me. Is it in his address book?'

'Yes,' Annabelle said, although she didn't make any attempt to go and get it.

Eden stood and stared at her for a moment. 'I don't suppose you could do me a favour and look it up?'

Annabelle rolled her eyes as if to imply that she had enough on her plate without performing menial tasks for the likes of Eden. 'I suppose,' she said peevishly before withdrawing to the reception area.

Eden stayed in the studio for a while, gazing around. She had a sick anxious feeling in the pit of her stomach. Her legs felt unsteady too, as if she was standing on quicksand, the ground shifting beneath her. Everything would be all right. That's what she needed to keep telling herself. This was all just a terrible mistake.

2

Eden sat rigidly in the chair, staring across the desk at the solicitor. She was at Lincoln's Inn Fields in the plush offices of Wainwright, Castor & Rush. Five hours earlier, had anyone asked, she would have said that she had it all: a loving husband, a comfortable home and everything to look forward to. And now? Now she felt like a hurricane had ripped through her life, tearing up its roots and scattering all her hopes and dreams. She ran her tongue over her dry lips and said, 'I don't understand.'

Michael Castor glanced down and shuffled some papers before looking up again. 'Tom has been charged with manslaughter and armed robbery.'

Eden could feel her heart thumping in her chest. She shook her head, emitting a high-pitched almost hysterical laugh. 'But that's ridiculous. It's crazy. Tom wouldn't hurt a fly. Why would they do that? Why would they? What's wrong with them?' She took a quick breath and carried on. 'I mean, what kind of evidence have they got? Nothing! They can't have anything because he didn't do it.'

Castor's face twisted a little. 'But that's the problem, Mrs Chase. They *do* have evidence.'

Eden flinched, the reply like a kick to her guts. 'What?'

'I'm afraid so.'

'But they can't,' she said stubbornly, clenching her hands into two tight fists. It was all a nightmare, some dreadful dream she couldn't wake up from. 'What are you talking about?'

The solicitor hesitated for a moment as if trying to form the right words before speaking them out loud. 'It appears that Tom has been named by another member of the gang. And there was, unfortunately, a man who was shot during the robbery and who subsequently died.'

'What?'

'His name was Paddy Lynch.'

Eden shook her head with such vehemence that her long red hair swayed from side to side. 'But don't you see? Either they've got the wrong Tom Chase – he can't be the only one with that name – or someone's got it in for him. I mean, who is this bloke who's accusing him anyway? And why the hell should the police believe him? It isn't right. It isn't fair.'

'I don't have a name yet but . . .'

'But?'

Castor sighed. 'It seems he's turning Queen's evidence – or doing a Bertie as it's known in the trade.' Observing Eden's blank expression he added, 'Bertie Smalls was the first supergrass back in the early seventies. In exchange for immunity from prosecution, he gave up the names of numerous other criminals, all the jobs they'd done together, all the details. This guy – the one who's pointing the finger at Tom – will still serve some time, but nothing like as much as he would have done.'

Eden couldn't see the fairness or the morality in this. 'But

I still don't get why the police believe him. You could draw any name out of the hat. Maybe he doesn't like Tom for some reason. Or it's just a mistake. It has to be!'

Castor leaned forward and placed his elbows on the desk. 'Except that's not the only reason he's been charged. When the police did a search of his studio something was found in the safe: an item of jewellery that came from the robbery.'

Eden drew back, startled by this fresh piece of information. 'What . . . how . . . What do you mean?'

'It's a snake-shaped bracelet, very distinctive – gold with rubies, sapphires and diamonds. Only a few of them were made, half a dozen, and all of these were stolen from the Epping warehouse. Does it sound familiar to you? Have you ever seen it?'

'No, I don't think so. But there has to be an explanation. What does Tom say?'

'He claims he took the bracelet in lieu of a debt.'

'What sort of debt?'

Castor paused, placed his hands together and steepled his fingers. As he spoke, he stared at her closely as if gauging her reaction. 'He says a man called Jack Minter gave him the bracelet in exchange for some money he owed him. He says it was a while ago, the late sixties, when he was living in Budapest.'

Eden nodded eagerly, her head bobbing up and down. 'He *was* in Hungary! That must be it!'

'Have you ever heard Tom mention this man before?'

Eden hesitated, tempted to lie in order to back up her husband. But that might not be a smart move. She dug deep into her memory – *Jack Minter, Jack Minter* – willing it to strike a chord. But nothing came back to her. In the end she gave a simple shrug. 'I'm not sure. It's a common name, isn't it? Jack, I mean. He might have done. I can't be sure.'

The solicitor said nothing. He continued to stare at her.

Eden leaned forward. 'When was this robbery exactly?'

19

Castor glanced down at his notes. 'Fourth of November, 1966. Do you know what Tom was doing then?'

'Of course not!' she snapped. 'Do you know what you were doing? Jesus, I hadn't even met him. It was sixteen years ago!' Her eyes flew wildly around the office before coming to settle on Castor again. He was a debonair, smartly suited man with wily eyes and steel-grey hair slicked back from his forehead. She stared at him while she tried to control the panic that was rising inside her. 'Manslaughter? They're saying he *killed* this Paddy Lynch?'

'He was shot in the chest.'

Eden swallowed hard. Her lips felt dry, her tongue too large for her mouth. 'Who . . . who was he – a security guard?'

'No,' Castor said. 'He was one of the gang. Apparently he got in a tussle with the guard and was shot with his own gun.'

'So why are they accusing Tom?'

Castor glanced down at the file that was sitting on his desk. He waited a few seconds before looking up again. 'After Paddy Lynch was shot, the gang made their getaway, taking him with them. Tom, allegedly, offered to drive him to the hospital but the van was found the next day dumped in a car park – with Lynch's body in the back. The man had bled to death.'

Eden bared her teeth. 'And you think Tom could have done something like that? Jesus, he wouldn't. You *know* he wouldn't.' She shook her head again. 'And he wasn't even part of this gang. He didn't commit any robbery. You do believe that, don't you?'

Castor gave a thin smile. 'If my client says he's innocent, then of course I believe him.'

Eden hissed out a breath. 'He *is* innocent,' she insisted. 'This is all so wrong. What about the security guard? Surely he can verify that Tom wasn't there.'

'He can't say one way or the other. All the men were wearing balaclavas.'

20

'So what about the guy who gave him the bracelet? What about Jack Minter? Can't he be traced?'

Castor pulled a face. 'We'll try, but ... Well, we're talking Hungary, not London. Not to mention the fact that it was years ago. It will all take time and even then there's no guarantee we'll actually find him.'

A wave of frustration flowed over Eden. 'And in the meantime, Tom's stuck behind bars.'

'I'm afraid so.'

'I've got to see him. How can I see him?'

'He'll be up in Bow Magistrates' Court tomorrow morning, but you won't be able to talk. He'll put in his plea and that will be that. It won't take long, ten minutes at the most. Then he'll be put on remand, probably at the Scrubs or Wandsworth.'

'What about bail?'

'We'll ask, but I'm not hopeful. He'll be viewed as a flight risk. It was a big robbery, Mrs Chase. The goods taken were worth about two million. And with the manslaughter charge as well ...'

Eden put her elbows on the desk and covered her face with her hands. She thought of Tom languishing in a police cell and the despair he must be feeling. It was all wrong, a travesty of justice. How could it happen? She felt angry, horrified. She felt sick to her stomach.

Seeing her distress, Castor stretched out his hand and patted her on the arm. 'Try not to worry too much. I know it all seems a bit overwhelming at the moment but—'

'But what?' Eden snapped, recoiling from his touch. She didn't need empty words or bland reassurances. 'My husband has been locked up for something he hasn't done. He's innocent. I know he is.' Tom Chase was guilty of nothing more than being a decent, loving, hard-working man – and no matter what it took, she was going to prove it.

3

Eden moved around the Islington flat in a daze. Usually this was her sanctuary, the place she could relax, but all that had changed. The police had been here too, searching every cupboard, every nook and cranny, pulling out drawers and rooting through their belongings. Now everything felt dirty and contaminated. If she could have put the whole flat through the washing machine she would have but had to be content with the clothes she knew they had touched.

In the bedroom they had gone through her jewellery, examined it piece by piece and compared every item to a list they had. They'd found nothing of interest and the disappointment had shown on their faces. In the end the only thing they'd taken away with them was a pile of bank statements.

While Eden cleaned and tidied, putting things back where they belonged, she tried to push down the panic that was rising inside her. She wanted to believe that this would all be over in a few days, that the police would realise their mistake and release him. But that wasn't going to happen now, was it? It was too late. He was being charged in the morning. The wheels of so-called justice had already started to turn.

She thought about the bracelet that had been found in the safe. Why hadn't Tom ever told her about it? Shown it to her? She gave a quick shake of her head. God, he had probably just forgotten it was there. The safe was always full of stuff, old cameras and photos, lenses and film. And he'd had the bracelet for years. It had probably got shoved to the back and buried under all the other things.

Eden went to the window of the living room, folded her arms across her chest and gazed down on the street. It was evening now and a thin drizzle had started to fall. She could see the drops of rain sparkling in the orange glow of the street lamps. This morning the sun had been shining, the day bright and clear and full of promise. And now? Now a cold shroud of darkness had wrapped itself around her world. Despite the warmth of the flat, she shivered with fear and apprehension.

Eden yanked the curtains across, hiding her view of the outside. She couldn't bear the sight of other people passing by, people who had nothing more to worry about than what they'd be eating for their dinners or watching on TV. She started to pace back and forth, still struggling to come to terms with it all. It felt unreal, like something that was happening to somebody else.

She wondered how Tom was coping, locked up in a cell with only his thoughts for company. What was going through his head? He was a strong person, not the type to buckle under pressure, but even he must be feeling the strain. Tomorrow he'd be up in court and then . . . *Manslaughter.* The very word made her catch her breath. She had to find out who was accusing him. And she had to find Jack Minter.

The phone rang, making her jump. She darted across the

room and snatched it up, hoping it was Tom although she knew it wasn't likely. 'Hello?'

A cool voice travelled down the line. 'It's Annabelle. Any news on Tom?'

'No,' Eden said. 'The police are still talking to him.' She didn't want to admit that he'd already been charged. She couldn't say the words out loud and anyway the truth would come out soon enough.

'So what's going on? What's it all about?'

'It's just a mix-up,' Eden said. 'It'll all be sorted. It's just . . . er . . . it's taking a bit longer than we expected.'

There was a short pause before Annabelle spoke again. 'So will he be in work tomorrow?'

'I don't know. Maybe. Has he got any appointments?'

'He's got a shoot in the afternoon. Carolyn Bridges. He can't miss that, Eden. He *has* to be there.'

Eden frowned. Carolyn Bridges was a young actress, the next 'big thing' and Tom had been hired to do a spread for *Chic* magazine. It was a big job, lucrative, the kind of assignment that would help establish his reputation as a fashionable London photographer. 'You'll have to postpone it. There's nothing else we can do. Ring them up first thing in the morning.'

'I can't do that. They'll go mad. It's all organised; it's been booked for weeks.'

Eden slid the toe of her shoe across the smooth surface of the floorboards. 'You'll have to.'

'And tell them what?'

'I don't know. Anything. Say he's sick. Say he's got the flu.'

'So do I reschedule or what?'

Eden hesitated. As things stood there was slim chance of Tom being available in the near future, but what if something miraculous happened? Perhaps another Tom Chase would turn up. Perhaps the gold bracelet wouldn't be quite as rare as the police thought it was. Tom could walk out of jail in a day or two and she didn't want to have to tell him that she'd thrown away a great opportunity. 'Er ... '

'Eden?'

'Yes, sorry, I'm just thinking about it.'

Annabelle breathed out one of her long contemptuous sighs. 'Well, can you make a decision, please? I need to know what I'm doing. This isn't going to look good. They'll probably go somewhere else.'

'I'm aware of that.' Lifting her gaze, Eden stared at the framed pictures on the wall, two evocative black and white photographs of the streets of Budapest taken at dusk. Gradually, the full impact of the day's events was starting to hit her. When word got around that Tom was in prison – and what he was in prison for – his career would be in ruins. 'I'll let you know, okay? I'll call you tomorrow.'

'But—'

Eden didn't wait to hear her protestations. She said a hasty goodbye and hung up. All she could do was play for time and hope the situation changed. For a while she stood there, her eyes locked on the photographs. If Tom had never gone to Hungary he'd never have had the bracelet. If Tom had ... But *what ifs* were a waste of time. They didn't change a goddamn thing. It was all so unfair, so wrong. He had worked day and night to get where he was and now ... Jesus, everything was falling apart.

She raised a hand to her mouth and bit down on her knuckles. Tomorrow was Friday and then there was the weekend. Tomorrow was the day when Tom would be in court. Would anyone get to hear about it? There would probably be journalists hanging around, hoping for some tasty gossip, but Tom was hardly famous. With luck, nothing would be reported in the papers.

But people would get to hear about it eventually. And of all those people, it was her father's reaction she dreaded most. She could imagine the smugness, the I-told-you-so tone to his voice. He had disapproved of Tom on principle; his daughter always made bad choices, ergo Tom Chase must be a waste of space. It wouldn't even cross his mind that her husband might be innocent.

'No, you'll presume the worst like you always do,' she muttered.

The two men had only met once and that had been a strained awkward affair that she preferred to forget about. Edinburgh. Over a year ago, just before they'd married. Even the memory of it made her wince. Tom had brushed off her father's disapproval with his usual dry wit, but Eden was not so quick to forgive. A small effort was all she'd asked for and he couldn't even manage that. She'd been glad when he hadn't come to the wedding – pleading ill health but making a miraculous recovery a few days later – because his sour face would have ruined it for her.

Eden sat down, stood up again and resumed her pacing. She was unable to be still. Adrenalin was streaming through her body, urging her to act, to do something – but what? A vein throbbed in her temple. The flat felt empty without Tom and she tried not to think about how long it might be before he was back here again. She walked from one side of the living room to the other. No, the silence was too much for her. She had to talk to someone. She'd go mad if she had to spend the evening on her own. Unable to bear it, she picked up the phone and dialled.

'Hi, it's me. Can you come over? Something awful has happened.'

4

It was an hour before Caitlin Styles arrived at the flat, bringing with her a Chinese takeaway, a bottle of wine and an air of brisk efficiency. She placed the carrier bag on the floor and hugged Eden. Her old duffel coat smelled of damp. Her white-blonde hair, cropped short, was wet and sleek from the rain.

'Poor you! How are you, love?'

'I'm okay,' Eden said, although it wasn't strictly true. 'Thanks for coming. I didn't . . . It's all so weird, so awful. I don't know what to do.'

'It's the shock,' Caitlin said, stepping back and patting Eden on the arm. 'It'll take a while for it to sink in.' She bent, picked up the bag and headed for the kitchen. 'Come on, let's sort out this food before it goes cold. And while we're doing that, you can tell me all about it.'

Eden watched as Caitlin busied herself, searching out bowls and cutlery and glasses. It was a relief to have her there, a comfort, a friendly face after all the hours of hell. The two of them went way back, their friendship having begun just after Eden first arrived in London. They'd met at a women's group and instantly hit it off.

Eden explained about Tom's arrest, a faltering account as she stopped and started, still trying to get it straight in her own head. 'There's been a mistake,' she said for what felt like the fiftieth time that day. 'He could never have done anything like that.'

'Of course he couldn't.'

They went through to the living room and sat down. Caitlin perched on the edge of the sofa forking noodles into her mouth. 'I can't imagine Tom as an armed robber.'

'He *isn't* an armed robber.' Eden moved the food around her bowl, knowing that she ought to eat but not having the stomach for it. 'That's the point. It's a travesty, the whole damn thing. And how could anyone just leave a man to die like that? It's inhuman. They'd have to be a monster.'

'Or someone without a conscience.'

Eden took a gulp of wine to steady her nerves. 'And the police think it's *him*,' she said. 'They think it was Tom.'

'Only because they're thick. They've got a name and a stolen bracelet, so as far as they're concerned it's job done. Someone's put him in the frame. You're going to have to prove that the witness is deliberately lying ... or that they've got it wrong.'

'But what if I can't?' Eden put the bowl down on the coffee table and pushed it away. 'It's one man's word against another's. And I don't even know what Tom was doing sixteen years ago.'

'Surely he can remember.'

Eden gave a shrug. She'd got the impression from Castor that her husband had been vague about it. 'His brief wants me to get in touch with family and friends, anyone who knew Tom back then. But I don't know where to start. So far as I'm aware he hasn't got any family, at least none he keeps in touch with. Tom's mum died when he was young and he didn't get on with his dad.'

'What about old friends?'

Eden shook her head. 'Not that I can think of, not really. I mean, not any that go back that far.' The truth was that Tom rarely spoke about the past. While she had been more than happy to talk at length on the trials and tribulations of her early years, he'd been relatively taciturn on the subject. Why had she never pushed it, tried to draw him out? Perhaps it was because she hadn't wanted to come across as one of those women who demand to know everything about their spouses, who dig and probe until every last detail has been brought to light. 'I don't think they were happy times for him. He always said that there was no point dwelling on what couldn't be changed.'

'He must have told you something. Mind, it was the sixties; half the people who were there don't remember what they did.'

'I know he travelled a lot: Paris, Berlin, Budapest.'

'So maybe he wasn't even in the country when this robbery took place. Has he still got his old passport?'

Eden shook her head again. 'I can't remember seeing it.'

'You'll have to try and dig out everything you can – letters, cards, old bills, photographs, anything that might give you a clue. Search here and at the studio. What about his birth certificate? You might be able to track his family through that.'

But Eden couldn't recall having seen that official slip of paper either. She would have to go through all the drawers, do a thorough sweep of the flat and see what she could find.

Picking up her glass, she took another gulp of wine. 'How long do you think it will be before I'm able to see him? See him properly, I mean, on a visit?'

'I'm not sure. A few days, a week perhaps. You can ring the prison once he's got there. You won't need a VO.'

Eden looked blankly at her. 'A VO?'

'A visiting order. But you won't need one of those the first time you go. It depends on the jail, but you'll probably get a visit a week until ... unless he's convicted. Which he won't be, of course.'

The word *convicted* hit Eden like a blow to the stomach, bringing everything home to her. Her head swam with terrible thoughts: jail, a tiny cell with bars on the window, a man's life in tatters. What if Tom's innocence couldn't be proved? Her face twisted with fear.

Caitlin looked at her. 'You've got to stay positive, Eden. You're no good to him if you fall apart.'

Eden took a couple of deep breaths, trying to stop herself from spinning down into that deep abyss of panic. For hours she had been holding on to the slim hope that the truth would come out, the charges would be dropped and Tom would be a free man again. 'It doesn't feel real. None of it. I keep thinking I'm going to wake up and it was all some dreadful dream.'

'It *is* a dreadful dream, a bloody nightmare, but you have to try and hold it together. Once you can see him, face to face, you can start to get to the bottom of this mess. Be careful when you speak to the cops – they're bound to interview you at some point – and think twice before you tell them anything.'

'Tell them what? I don't know a damn thing about any of this.'

'That won't stop them, hon. They'll try and trick you into saying something incriminating, like Tom being secretive about his family or evasive about his past. And they'll ask all kinds of personal questions about money and your relationship, what you do together, where you go, who you meet. But all they'll be doing is looking for ways to blacken his character. So don't let them put words into your mouth. Stop and think before you speak.'

'Okay,' Eden murmured. It didn't surprise her that Caitlin knew so much about the police. She had trained as a solicitor and was now working with various women's groups trying to convince the cops that it wasn't okay for men to batter their wives and girlfriends. She'd had plenty of experience of the criminal system.

'From now on, they're the enemy. You have to remember that.'

For Eden, who'd been raised in the kind of middle-class home where the police were seen as a body of people who could be relied on to help, this new notion was alarming. She'd heard stories, of course, tales of bent coppers and planted evidence, but had always viewed them with scepticism – or as an example of a few bad apples. Her heart sank as it occurred to her that she was walking into a world where the law was no longer on her side and where she could no longer expect to be protected by it.

'You'll be all right,' Caitlin said. 'You're not on your own.'

Eden pushed back her shoulders and forced a smile. If she could try and look as though she was holding it together, then maybe it would actually happen. 'I know. And thanks.'

'It could all be over in a few weeks. If some new evidence comes to light and—'

The phone rang and Eden jumped at the sound. A number of possibilities ran through her head – the police, her father, Annabelle – none of which made her feel inclined to answer. The last thing she needed was even more questions.

'Do you want me to get it?' Caitlin asked.

Eden shook her head and rose to her feet. What if it was Tom? What if he'd been released? The thought sent her hurrying across the room before the machine could kick in. 'Hello?'

'Hello, Mrs Chase. It's Michael Castor. I've got a message from Tom to pass on to you.'

Eden's heart skipped a beat and she drew in a breath. 'Tell me.' As she listened, her hand gripped the phone tightly and her face dropped. 'But why? I don't get it. I don't understand.'

She listened to his reply before thanking him for the call and hanging up.

'What is it?' Caitlin asked as Eden slumped back down on the sofa.

'That was Tom's solicitor. He says Tom doesn't want me in court tomorrow.'

'Huh?'

'That it would make it worse for him, my being there. Too hard. That he'd prefer that I stayed away.' Eden rubbed her face with her hands. She reached for the glass of wine, downed what remained in one and topped up the glass from the bottle. 'Jesus, what do I do now?'

5

Archie Rudd stared across the table at his solicitor. It was two weeks since he'd been nabbed, two weeks in which he'd had plenty of time to dwell on it all. The bugger was that he'd known it was going to be a disaster right from the moment he'd woken up on the day of the job. He'd had a queasy feeling in his guts, an itch on the back of his neck. Always trust your instincts – that's what his old man had taught him – but he'd gone right ahead and done it anyway.

'So what's the option?' Archie asked morosely.

Ben Curran raised his eyebrows. 'You're not thinking of changing your mind, are you? If you do then ... well, you know the score, Arch: twelve to fifteen depending what mood the judge is in. You'll just have to hope he doesn't have a row with his missus in the morning.'

Archie, who had never been especially good at numbers, could still do the maths on this one. Even if he kept his head down and stayed out of trouble, even with a third taken off, he'd still be knocking on for sixty-five by the time he got out. 'Christ,' he groaned. 'I'll be drawing my bleedin' pension. And

Rose can't handle me being inside again.' The truth was he didn't much care for the idea of it either; he'd done plenty of bird in the past, but he was getting too old for another long stretch. 'No, I ain't changed my mind. There's no other way, is there? Unless you can conjure up some of that Curran magic.'

'It's not magic you need, it's a miracle. You went in there all guns blazing and got caught red-handed. Not much I can do about that, Arch.'

Archie gave a long sigh. 'That's what they don't get. It's safer, see, with shooters. One blast in the ceiling and it's all over. There's no one going to have a go, no one trying to play the hero. When you think about it, we're doing everyone a favour.'

'Well, it's a point of view, if not one widely held within the ranks of the English judicial system.'

Archie puffed on his fag, making the most of the free pack Curran had brought with him. The Shepperton bank job had been a big mistake. Why had he agreed to it? He wished he could turn back time four weeks and just say no. He hadn't even known three of the blokes. Billy Drake had said they were sound, said he could vouch for them, but one of the bastards must have been mouthing off, saying something he shouldn't. How else could Old Bill have known they'd be there?

Curran leaned forward, placing his hands on the table. 'One of them is talking, Arch. I've already told you. If you're going to pull out of the deal then it leaves you exposed. The police will try and do you for the Epping robbery too.'

Archie narrowed his eyes. Making a deal with the law went against the grain – he wasn't a grass – but what choice did he have? He was shafted if he didn't. Going down for the two jobs would mean he'd probably never see daylight again. 'I've said, haven't I? Said I'd do it. I ain't gonna change my mind.'

'Good,' Curran said with a look of relief on his face.

'Do you know which one of 'em opened his gob?' Not Billy,

he thought. Billy was old school, the sort who knew how to keep his mouth shut. 'Was it that Lee Barker?'

'I don't have a name, not yet.'

'I bet it was. Snivelling little toerag.'

'But all the police have at the moment is hearsay – about the Epping robbery, I mean. *You* were the one who was there. Give them the information they want and you'll be looking at a couple of years max. And not in some high-security dump either. A police station probably. Somewhere in London, somewhere Rose can visit without having to travel halfway across the country.'

Archie sighed. The thing that really pissed him off was that he'd banged the nails into his own bloody coffin. He thought back to the night, a month ago, when he'd first met the gang at Billy Drake's house. The three other blokes were young, in their mid-twenties, and he'd seen the look on their faces as Billy had introduced him: a combination of disappointment, scorn and derision. To them he was just some old geezer, a man past his prime, a possible liability on a big job like the one they had planned in Shepperton.

Archie took a slurp of lukewarm tea while he went over the meeting in his mind, step by step. He examined the surface of the table, the old wood battered and scored. He ran a finger along one of the deeper indentations, wondering how many men had done the same before him. The truth was that he'd let his mouth run away with him that night, trying to impress, trying to prove that he wasn't a has-been. The truth was he'd wanted to wipe the smirk off their faces. And now he was paying the price for his pride.

It had been a gratifying moment when he'd told them about his part in the Epping raid sixteen years ago. Yeah, their ears had pricked up then. Over two million quid's worth of jewellery and gems. And they'd got clean away – or at least most of them had. 'Audacious' was how the papers had described it, although it had been described in other ways too: 'brutal', 'callous' and 'unforgivable'. Paddy Lynch's lingering death had left a bad taste in everybody's mouth.

So he'd sat there in the armchair, swigging a can of beer and giving it the big I am. Pretending that he'd been the brains behind it all. Not thinking, not even for a second, that it was going to come back to haunt him. Stupid. And now one of the boys – yeah, he was sure it was that grinning Lee Barker – had grassed him up. He could have denied it, of course – what could the cops prove after all these years? – simply claimed that he'd made it up to impress them, but he was still looking at a long stretch. Years and years, eating away at what remained of his life.

'Archie?'

'Huh?'

'They're waiting outside. Are you ready?'

Archie wondered how it had come to this. Ten years ago, even five, he wouldn't have thought twice, but times had changed. The old ways were disappearing. Now villains were turning Queen's evidence right, left and centre. Loyalty had gone right out of the window. It went against the grain, made him feel sick to his stomach, but that's the way it was. And when push came to shove what did he owe Jack Minter anyway? The bastard had left Paddy to die, not even given the poor bugger a chance. Someone had to pay for that and he didn't see why it should be him.

6

DI Vic Banner had been in the Flying Squad for six years, waiting for the break, for a result that would give him the promotion he deserved. At forty-seven he was running out of time. So when the phone call had come through from Ben Curran's clerk, a call offering a deal on the Epping heist, he had seen his chance: a high-profile controversial case that had remained unsolved . . . until now. When it came to trial, it would be front-page news, the story on everyone's lips – and he'd be right there, standing in the limelight with a bloody big smile on his face.

'Hello, Archie,' he said as he entered the room with the constable, pulled out a chair and sat down. 'You know who I am and this is DC Steve Leigh. Good to see you again.'

'It's Mr Rudd to you.'

Banner raised an eyebrow and gave a nod. 'As you like.' He knew he had to tread carefully, that Archie was on edge, still jumpy about what he was intending to do. It didn't sit well with him and it was written all over his face. 'This is just a casual chat, yeah, another chance for us to talk things over, see where we stand.'

Archie's lip curled. 'I ain't happy about this, just so you understand.'

'Loud and clear. But you know how it works, Mr Rudd: you help us and we'll help you. Simple, really, when you think about it.' Banner flipped open the file he had brought with him and pretended to examine the contents. He left a short silence before looking up again. 'So what more can you tell us about Jack Minter?'

Archie hesitated, glancing at Curran before looking at Banner again. 'I've told you enough already. I ain't saying no more until I get it in writing. I know what you lot are like. I want it down in black and white, a proper agreement.'

'My client needs some guarantees,' Curran said.

Banner gave a patient smile. 'Sure, we understand that. And you'll get them, but not until we've covered the basics. There are just a few things we need to get clear first.' He took out a photograph and pushed it across the desk. 'Are you absolutely certain that this is the man who called himself Jack Minter?'

Archie glared at him and then down at the photograph, at the picture of the tall blond man emerging from a doorway. 'How many times? I've already told you.'

'It was sixteen years ago. People change.'

'He don't look that different. A bit older, that's all.'

'And you're positive that his real name was Tom Chase?'

'Yeah, we checked him out, didn't we? Me and Don. You don't go into a job like that without taking some care over who you're working with.'

Banner gave a nod as if to acknowledge respect for Archie's thoroughness. 'You weren't bothered by the fact he was using an alias?'

'So he used a different name, so what? Wasn't the first and he won't be the last.'

'Just trying to cover his tracks, right?'

Archie shrugged.

'And you found out he was living and working in Chigwell. A photographer, yes?'

'Yeah, he worked for Albert Shiner's: portraits and the like. It ain't there no more. Closed down years back. And he had a flat behind Brook Parade; I don't remember the exact address.'

Banner kept his eyes on Archie, watching for any signs that he might be lying. Except he didn't think he was. The guy was nervy, on edge, but that was only to be expected. Archie Rudd had form for armed robbery, lots of it, and the Epping job would have been right down his street. 'And this Tom Chase/Jack Minter – whatever we're going to call him – he first approached you in the Fox in Kellston?'

Archie's wily eyes narrowed into two thin slits. 'Not me,' he said. 'It was Don. I've told you it was Don.'

'Don West.'

'Yeah.'

'The late Don West.'

Archie gave a nod. 'Cancer,' he said. 'Couple of years back.'

Banner continued to watch him closely. Archie was a grizzled-looking man in his late fifties with grey wiry hair and skin like leather. Deep lines rippled across his forehead in waves. He was short but solid with a small round beer belly that swelled the front of his white T-shirt. 'But Don told you all about it.'

'Minter took him aside in the Fox, said he was looking to put a team together for something big, said he'd heard he was the best. Course Don didn't take the geezer serious – didn't know him from Adam, did he? Could have been one of you lot trying to stitch him up – so he told him to get lost, he wasn't interested. But Minter wouldn't give up. Kept going on at him, said at least hear him out . . . and eventually Don did.'

'And liked what he heard.'

'He reckoned the plan had legs. The geezer had done his homework, you know, planned it all out meticulous like. No loose ends. Everything neat and tidy.'

'Did he have form? Had he done anything like this before?'

'If he did, he weren't bragging about it.' Archie frowned, giving it some thought. 'To be honest he didn't talk about nothing much other than the job.'

'Single-minded,' DC Leigh said.

Archie lit another fag, pulled in the smoke and exhaled in a long thin stream. 'You could say that.'

'So how many men did he want?'

Archie gave a snort. 'No details, not until we get things sorted. And no other names either.'

'Well, we already know that Paddy Lynch was one of them.'

Vic Banner sat back and casually folded his arms across his chest. 'Yeah, shame about Paddy. That must have been a tough decision.'

'There weren't no bloody decision!' Archie retorted, rising to the bait. His cheeks burned red and his eyes blazed with indignant rage. He pointed a finger at the inspector. 'Don't go trying to pin that on me, mate. The hospital – that's where Minter said he was taking him. How were we to know any different? How were we to know that he was going to—' He stopped abruptly, his chest heaving with emotion, and took a quick angry drag on the cigarette. 'By the time we found out what he'd done it was too late. Paddy was dead and Minter had disappeared.'

'Okay, I believe you.' Banner waited a moment before reaching across the table, retrieving the photograph and holding it up. 'But what I need to know, what I need to be absolutely sure of, is that you're prepared to stand up in court and swear blind that this is the man who called himself Jack Minter, that he organised the Epping job and that he left Paddy Lynch to die like a dog in the back of a van.'

Archie didn't hesitate. 'Bring it on,' he said. 'The sooner the better. It'll be a bleedin' pleasure.'

'Good.'

'And you're going to get me out of this dump?'

Banner nodded. 'Bear with us; it might take a week or so.' He slipped the photo into the folder, snapped it shut and rose to his feet. 'Right, that's all for now. Thanks for your assistance, Mr Rudd. We'll be back in touch soon.'

Archie crushed the fag in the ashtray, put his elbow on the table and covered his mouth with his hand.

Outside in the corridor, DC Leigh looked at his boss. 'So what do you reckon, guv?'

Vic Banner slapped the file against his thigh and grinned. 'I reckon Tom Chase is well and truly fucked.'

7

On Friday morning, after a restless night, Eden was still in two
minds as to whether she should go to court. It felt disloyal not
to, even if it was what Tom wanted. But did he really know
what he wanted? His head, like hers, must be all over the
place. Maybe he regretted asking her to stay away – or maybe
he didn't. Although it hardly seemed possible, she dreaded the
thought of making things worse.

'I think you should do as he says,' Caitlin advised. 'Everyone
has their own way of dealing with stuff; perhaps it's easier for
him to face it alone. He'll just want to get it over and done
with. And it's not as though you'll be able to speak.'

'I know but . . . It feels wrong, him being there with no one
to support him.'

'He's got his solicitor.' Caitlin began to butter some toast.
'And no offence, love, but you look like hell. I bet you didn't
get a wink of sleep. Do you want him to have to start worrying
about you too? I don't see how that's going to help.'

Eden's head had a fog in it, partly down to a hangover – she
had drunk too much wine last night – and partly down to

sleep deprivation. For hours she had lain awake, overly aware of the space beside her, of the absence of Tom's breathing, of the coldness of the bed. 'I'll be all right once I've had a shower.'

'And something to eat,' Caitlin said, pushing the plate across the table. 'At least try and get some toast down you. And look, if you really want to go to court the offer's still open. I'll come along, it's not a problem.'

Eden gave a sigh. 'No, you're right. I shouldn't go. It isn't fair, not if he doesn't want me there.' Now that she had made the decision she felt a mixture of guilt and relief. 'Castor said he'd call me as soon as it's over. I'll wait here. I can start searching the flat, try and find something useful.'

'Do you want a hand?'

'No, you've done enough. I'll be fine, honestly. I'll give you a ring when I've got some news.'

It was as she was leaving that Caitlin turned and asked, 'Are you okay for money?'

Eden was startled by the question. 'Sure. Why wouldn't I be?'

'It's just that ... Well, it could be a while before Tom's earning again. And you're at college. With nothing coming in, things could get a bit tight. I mean, it could be ages before it goes to trial.'

'But it won't go to trial,' Eden insisted. 'How can it? Once we've proved that Tom isn't this Jack Minter guy they'll have to let him go.'

Caitlin gave her a reassuring smile. 'I'm sure you're right. Of course you are. It's just that the legal system doesn't move quickly and no matter what happens you'll still have the bills to pay and the mortgage, not to mention food and the rest. And solicitors don't come cheap either. All I'm saying is that you should be prepared in case it takes a bit longer than you expect.'

43

For Eden, who already had so much on her mind, this was one more unwelcome thing to worry about. 'How much longer?'

'Months, probably. And if you can't get the proof together, it could be six, perhaps even nine before the trial gets under way.'

Eden couldn't imagine being apart from Tom for that length of time. The thought made her stomach turn over. 'Jesus,' she murmured.

Caitlin bent and kissed her on the cheek. 'I'm sure it won't come to that,' she said. 'And if you need anything – it doesn't matter what – just let me know. Are you sure you'll be all right? I don't like leaving you on your own.'

'I'll be fine. I will, honestly. And thanks again for staying over.'

After Caitlin had left, Eden returned to the kitchen, sat down and put her head in her hands. She hadn't even thought about money. How much was in the joint account? About two thousand, she thought, enough for now but if it all dragged on . . . No, she wasn't going to start stressing about that. There were more important things to be worrying about at the moment.

Quickly she stood up again, found a couple of aspirin, washed them down with the rest of the coffee and began searching the flat for evidence of what Tom was really doing on 4 November 1966. She could understand his vagueness on the subject. What had *she* been doing on that particular day? Well, she had probably been at school – she'd only been ten – but as to what lessons she'd had or who she'd talked to or whether it had been dry or rainy she didn't have a clue.

Eden began with the bureau in the living room, rooting through drawers full of folders, old bills, takeaway fliers, keys, elastic bands and fluff. It didn't take her long to find his current passport. She flipped it open and looked at the picture, her heart missing a beat as she stared at the face she knew so well.

'Don't worry,' she murmured as if he could hear her. 'You'll be home soon. I promise.'

She turned over the pages, but the passport was only a couple of years old and the single stamp was the one for Italy where they had spent their belated honeymoon four months after they'd got married. Rome, Florence, Milan. The memory of those happy days swept over her. Tears rose to her eyes but she smartly brushed them away. Strength was what was needed now, a bit of courage and a lot of determination. She had things to do and drowning in self-pity wasn't one of them.

Carrying on the search she sifted through a heap of papers: mortgage statements, house insurance, car insurance, MOT, rates, guarantees and warranties. There was nothing that went back further than a couple of years. No old passports, letters, diaries or appointment books. It was possible, though, that she would find some of these at the studio.

The next thing she came across was Tom's birth certificate. She unfolded the wide narrow slip of paper and read the details. Thomas James Chase. Born in Norwich on the seventeenth of April. Father: Clive Chase. Mother: Andrea Elizabeth Chase. Clive's occupation was listed as 'Train driver' and Andrea's as 'Housewife'. Why hadn't she known their names? Because she'd never asked and he had never volunteered the information. He rarely talked about his family and when he did it was only to say there had been problems. He'd left home at fifteen, after the death of his mother, and never gone back.

Eden refolded the certificate and put it on top of the bureau. She wasn't sure what use it was – probably none – but she laid it to one side anyway. Although she wondered what had caused the rift with his family, she knew from personal experience that people couldn't always live together. She only had to be in her father's company for an hour or two before the inevitable row broke out. Chalk and cheese. They rubbed each other up the wrong way and that was the beginning and end of it. Still, for all that, she wouldn't want to be completely disconnected from him.

The phone rang and she crossed the room to answer it. 'Hello?'

It was Annabelle. She didn't bother saying who it was but just asked brusquely, 'Is Tom there?'

'No, he isn't.'

'Is he coming into work today?'

'No.'

'So can you get him to call me? I don't know what I'm supposed to be doing. I've got clients ringing up for appointments. What do I say? Do I book them in or not?'

And Eden suddenly realised that she couldn't put things off any more; she had to stop procrastinating and take control. 'No, don't take any more bookings and cancel everything that's already in the book.'

'What, *everything*?'

'Yes. Apologise and tell them that Tom's been taken ill, that we'll be in touch when he's back at work.'

There was a long pause before Annabelle asked, 'Is this to do with the police? What's going on?'

'I've just said, haven't I? Oh and there's no need to come in tomorrow. I'm afraid we'll have to close the studio for a while.'

'So what am I supposed to do?' Annabelle whined. 'You're going to pay me, yes? You can't just—'

'I'm sorry but I have to go,' Eden interrupted. 'I'll call you on Monday. Don't worry; we'll sort something out.'

As she put down the phone, she wondered if she'd done the right thing. A cancelled appointment could be a client lost for ever. But if Caitlin was right – and she usually was – then it would be a while before Tom was free to work again. In the meantime all she could aim for was damage limitation.

Eden went on with her search, checking the bedroom and

46

kitchen, but found nothing more of interest. It occurred to her as she returned to the living room that there was very little evidence that Tom had even had a past. There were no mementoes, no letters, not even a postcard from a friend. But then maybe all his memories were wrapped up in his photographs and those, apart from the two on the wall, were all at the studio. That would be her next port of call, but not until this evening after Annabelle had left.

It was a quarter past eleven before the phone rang again. This time it was Michael Castor informing her that Tom had put in his plea of 'Not guilty' and had been remanded not to the Scrubs or Wandsworth but to HMP Thornley Heath.

Eden, although she'd been expecting the news, felt a stab of disappointment. A part of her had still been hoping for a miracle, that the judge would glance at the evidence and throw the case out of court. Or if that didn't happen that Tom might at least get bail. 'Where's Thornley Heath?' she asked glumly.

'It's not that far. Near Chingford.'

Still London, then. That was a relief. She'd suddenly had visions of him being taken halfway across the country to some strange place she'd never been to before. 'How is he? Is he okay?'

'Bearing up,' Castor said.

From the glib way it fell from his tongue, Eden suspected that this was a stock reply he was used to giving. Still, what else could he say? The truth wasn't what anyone wanted to hear. 'Will he be able to call me?'

'It might take a day or two. He'll have to be processed first.'

Processed, she thought, *like a piece of meat.* 'So what happens next?'

'We get to work proving that Tom isn't an armed robber and never went under the name of Jack Minter. And he needs to start figuring out where he was and what he was doing in

November 'sixty-six.' He paused and then added, 'Can you think of anyone who Tom has fallen out with recently, anyone he might have upset?'

Eden didn't need to think twice about it. 'No, he's not that type of person. Really, he isn't. He's a photographer, for God's sake. Who is he going to fall out with?'

'Even photographers have enemies, Eden – professional jealousy, an unhappy client?'

'So unhappy they'd want to frame him for murder?'

'It's a long shot, but we have to consider every possibility. Look, maybe you could talk to some of his old friends, see if they can recall what Tom was doing back then.'

'I will,' she said.

It was only after she'd hung up that she realised how hard that was going to be. For one she wasn't sure how far back any of them went, and for two she was going to have to explain the reason for the call. And as soon as she did that it would be public knowledge that Tom had been arrested and charged with manslaughter. Not that word wouldn't get out eventually, but she dreaded having to break the news. What if they all turned their backs on him, believing he was guilty? The thought was too awful to contemplate.

Eden flicked through the address book, scanning the entries. If she'd been asked to identify Tom's best friend, she wouldn't have been able to come up with one name in particular. Denny Fielding? Andy Marsh? Jerry McClean? John Simms? Although he hung out with all of them, she'd never got the impression that he was especially close to any one of them. Denny, she decided, was probably the best bet. He owned a camera shop on Tottenham Court Road and of the four men was probably the most approachable.

Eden took a deep breath and picked up the phone.

8

As she crossed the piazza in Covent Garden, Eden was relieved to see that every floor of the building on Henrietta Street was in darkness. There hadn't been much doubt about the studio – Annabelle had probably left well before five – but the two other offices, above and below, could still have been occupied. The theatrical agency, especially, often kept late hours.

By now, of course, everyone would be talking about how the police had come and taken Tom away ... and how he had not come back. And Annabelle no doubt had been busy fuelling the gossip. How much would she have told them? Well, enough to keep the tongues wagging. She'd have enjoyed holding forth, being the centre of attention, adopting a wide-eyed expression as she embellished every detail of the story.

It was ten past seven and the piazza was full of people, some on their way to the theatre or cinema, others just heading for one of the bars. It was Friday night, the end of the week and she could feel the anticipation, the buzz in the crowd; two whole days of freedom lying ahead. Normally she'd have felt it too ... except there was no normal now.

Everything had changed. Everything was strange and wrong and scary.

Eden hurried over to the door, opened it with her key, switched on the light in the foyer and locked the door behind her. As she climbed the stairs she went over the conversation she'd had with Denny Fielding. He'd laughed out loud when she'd told him that Tom had been arrested.

'No way. You're having a laugh. You're kidding me, right?'

And it had taken her a further five minutes to explain the situation and convince him that this wasn't some bizarre and tasteless joke. 'So this guy – and we don't even know who it is yet – has named Tom as being part of the gang who did the robbery. It's completely crazy. And he says Tom was using the name Jack Minter. Does that mean anything to you?'

'Sorry, love. Not a clue. I've never heard it before.'

It turned out she'd been right about him not having known Tom for that long. They'd only become friendly four years ago when Denny first opened his shop. He hadn't been able to help when it came to mutual friends either. None of them, so far as he was aware, had been acquainted with Tom in the sixties.

'I'll have a think about it though. I'll give you a bell if anyone comes to mind.'

'Thanks.'

'Although he shouldn't have too much trouble figuring out where he was back then. At least in July.'

'Shouldn't he?' Eden asked.

'Course not. Four–two.'

'What?'

'Four–two,' he repeated.

'Is that supposed to mean something?'

'The score,' Denny said. 'The World Cup. The football. It was 1966. Anyone of a certain age knows where they were when England thrashed Germany.'

Eden had put the phone down feeling that some progress had been made. Tom, even though he wasn't an ardent football fan, must have been following the national team. It hadn't been November but it was surely close enough to jog his memory.

As Eden unlocked the studio and went inside, she recalled how she hadn't told Denny everything. She hadn't mentioned, for example, that a bracelet from the robbery was found in the safe. Why not? Because she hadn't wanted to plant a seed of doubt in his mind. Tom being accused was bad enough, but having stolen property found on his premises could be seen as damning. Sometimes it was all too easy for people to believe the worst.

The light flickered on and she gazed around. The reception area wasn't too bad – she'd helped Annabelle clear up most of the mess yesterday – but a big heap of photographs still lay on the desk. She walked over and flicked open the appointments book. A hard black line had been put through every name for the next two weeks. She winced, knowing how hard Tom had worked to build up his client list. If he didn't get out of jail soon he could lose some of his customers for good.

It had been a risk for him setting up in Covent Garden – an expensive risk – but the gamble had been starting to pay off. Gradually his popularity and his reputation were growing. Word was getting round and some of the more fashionable magazines had started to hire him. He had an extraordinary talent, an ability to get beyond the surface, to strip back and reveal. His portraits were more than just faces or poses; they had the power to capture the very essence of the person who was sitting.

Eden walked through to the studio. She had never been here on her own before and there was an odd eerie feel to the room. Like a place abandoned, she thought. The air was still, as if it was holding its breath. She had the sensation of dust gathering, dust settling, even though it was only a day since Tom had been taken away. His Leica, poised for action, was sitting on the tripod. She reached out and touched the smooth cool surface of the metal.

For a moment she sank into despair and was too over-whelmed to move. What if he was never coming back? What if the very worst happened, if the law got it wrong and he was condemned to a life behind bars? She closed her eyes, trying to block out the prospect. It couldn't happen. It wouldn't happen. Her fingers slid from the camera, her arm falling back to her side.

Before she could be defeated by fear, Eden quickly opened her eyes again. What was she doing? Wasting precious time, that was what. She had to pull herself together and stop imag-ining the worst. Evidence was what was needed if she was to get Tom out of the hole he was in. Her gaze alighted on the filing cabinets lined up along the wall. That was the place to start.

Eden began opening and closing the drawers, checking out what was inside each of them. They were mainly client files, ordered alphabetically with folders containing prints and negatives. The accounts were in one drawer with letters and invoices, advertising material in another. She continued until she came to a cabinet that seemed more promising. This one, containing a pile of shallow white boxes, envelopes and unused film, had a more haphazard feel to it, as if the contents hadn't been properly organised yet.

She pulled out all the boxes, put them on the floor, knelt down and began to rifle through them. Quickly her heart sank. There must be thousands of photos. A few of the boxes had Tom's writing on the front, a scrawled *Paris* or *Madrid*, but most were blank. She could take a guess at some locations while others were a mystery. And there were hardly any dates.

'Damn it,' she murmured.

After a while she came across a box containing photos of London: people walking through Carnaby Street, Piccadilly, Victoria station. And pictures of the East End too, black and white shots of Bethnal Green, Whitechapel and Hoxton. She thought they had a sixties feel to them, was almost sure of it as she studied the faces and the clothes. But when in the sixties? Early or late? She put the boxes to one side, intending to take them home and examine them more carefully.

It was another half hour before she found the Budapest pictures. At least she presumed they'd been taken in Budapest. Her Hungarian was non-existent but she knew the language on the street signs wasn't German. She picked up the first few photos, scrutinising the faces: five guys in a bar, a man and a woman sitting outside a café, a couple strolling along a moon-lit road. Was Jack Minter in any of the shots? How would she know? She didn't have a clue what he looked like. After putting the photos back, she closed the lid on the box and placed it beside the London one.

Eden stood up, crossed the room to the far wall and swung back the framed print to reveal the safe. She turned the dial, hoping that Tom hadn't changed the combination. It was a relief when she heard the reassuring click. Inside were three more cameras – a Nikon, a Minolta and a Polaroid – as well as spare lenses, two worn leather cases and a large amount of film, some of it waiting to be developed, some of it unused. She pushed it all aside and delved into the back, hoping to find something more useful.

There were, of course, no handy diaries or old address books. She did find, however, a couple of A4 Jiffy bags and she pulled them out to take a closer look. The first contained the original mortgage papers for the Islington flat, insurance details, solicitor's letters and the like. All dry legal stuff.

Nothing, she could see, that was of any particular interest. The second looked more promising: inside was a small bundle of handwritten letters still in their airmail envelopes and tied with an elastic band. Ah, at last! Something more personal.

A quick flick through showed her that the letters had been sent from Paris to an address in Budapest and were from a woman called Ann-Marie Allis. Her name was on the back of the envelopes. Love letters? Possibly. She felt a flicker of jealousy, resentment, even though she knew it was irrational. Everyone had a past and Tom was no exception. It was, perhaps, the fact he'd kept them, that they'd clearly meant something to him, that made her feel faintly threatened.

The dates on the envelopes were from June to December 1967. That was a shame. A year earlier could have gone some way towards proving that Tom wasn't living in London when the robbery took place. She pulled out the first sheets of paper and discovered they were written in French. Her schoolgirl grasp of the language, although enabling her to understand a sentence here or there, was by no means good enough for a proper translation. She would have to sit down with a dictionary.

Eden was aware that Tom was unlikely to be happy about her reading the letters, but decided to take them home with her anyway. There could be clues inside, important information about what he'd been doing and when. Maybe even a mention of Jack Minter. Or was she just using all that as an excuse to satisfy her own curiosity?

She was still pondering on this when she heard a noise behind her. Startled, she whirled round to find herself face to face with a stranger. She pulled in a breath, the gasp clearly audible in the quiet of the studio.

'Who are you? What do you want?'

The man was in his forties, stocky with a plump, pale face

and receding sandy-coloured hair. 'No need to panic, love. Police.' He reached into the pocket of his overcoat, took out his warrant card and held it up. 'DI Vic Banner. And I'm presuming you're the wife, yeah? Eden, is it?'

Eden continued to stare at him. 'How did you get in here?'

Banner raised his eyebrows. 'The front door was open. You should be more careful, love. Anyone could walk in.'

'I locked it. I locked the front door.'

'No, it was definitely open.'

'It was not,' she insisted, refusing to back down. She wondered if he'd used Tom's keys but didn't bother to ask. He was hardly likely to admit it. 'What do you want? Why are you here?'

'I was just passing and saw the light was on. I wouldn't have been doing my duty if I hadn't checked it out. I mean, there could have been a burglary in progress. You never know, do you?' He glanced around the studio. 'And there's some expensive kit in here. Be a shame if some thieving toerag decided to help himself.'

'Well, you don't have to worry on that score. As you can see everything's in order. So if there's nothing else? I wouldn't want to keep you.'

'And what exactly are *you* doing here, if you don't mind me asking?' A sly smile crept on to his lips. 'Not trying to dispose of evidence, I hope.'

Eden saw the way he was looking her up and down, his eyes lingering on her breasts, judging her, assessing her, and not in any professional capacity. The guy was a slimeball. 'What do you think?' she replied. 'Tidying up after you lot turned the place upside down, of course. You hardly left it like you found it. And anyway, what kind of evidence could there be? My husband is innocent. You've got it all wrong, seriously wrong, and when the truth comes out—'

Banner gave a snort. 'Shit, I wish I had a pound for every time I'd heard that. Not been married long, have you, love? What is it, a year or so? Sometimes people aren't always what they appear to be. They have dirty little secrets that their nearest and dearest know nothing about.'

Eden gave a thin smile. 'Perhaps you're right – but not in this case.' She casually placed the letters back in the safe as though she was simply tidying them away. The thought of Banner getting his hands on them sent anxious flutters through her chest. 'If you knew Tom, knew him properly, you'd realise what an awful mistake you'd made.'

'You don't know him, love. You just think you do.'

'We'll see.'

Banner shrugged, the gesture belying the glint of malice in his eyes. 'Or maybe you like the bad boys, huh? Maybe that's what attracted you in the first place. Some women get off on that kind of thing.'

Eden, aware that he was goading her, bit her lip and didn't rise to the bait. He wanted to provoke a reaction, to get under her skin, and she wasn't going to give him the satisfaction. She kept her voice clear and calm as she replied, 'Tom is a good, honest man and what you're doing to him is criminal. It's unjust. It's a travesty.'

'A travesty, huh?' Banner grinned as if the word amused him. 'Our witness doesn't think so. He reckons your husband is a murderer.'

'So I've heard. And what does your witness do for a living? A decent upstanding member of the community, is he? Reliable? Honest?'

Banner took out a pack of cigarettes, lit one and blew the smoke in her direction. 'He's a robber, just like your old man. Sometimes it takes one to know one.'

'He's a liar.'

'Maybe – but not about this. It's been on his conscience, you see, what happened all those years ago. It doesn't sit nicely with him. He wants to put things right.'

'What he wants to do is save his own skin by putting Tom in the frame. It's simple. Why can't you see that?' Eden paused before adding, 'And please don't drop ash all over the carpet. There's an ashtray on the desk.'

Banner took another drag on his cigarette, gave her a look and then went over to reception. He glanced back over his shoulder. 'You might think you're the loyal type, but you'll soon get sick of it. The prison visiting, I mean. Week in, week out. The conversation quickly runs dry. And we're not talking a few months here; it's going to be years, fifteen, twenty. How old will you be by then?'

'Why are you saying all this?'

'Just trying to be helpful, love. Truth is, I feel sorry for you. I wouldn't want to see a nice girl like you waste half her life on a scumbag like Tom Chase.'

Eden was battling to keep her anger under control. She put her hands on her hips and glared at him. 'I think I can live without your pity, thanks all the same. Has it not even entered your head that you could be completely and utterly wrong?'

Banner picked up the ashtray and walked back towards her. 'Ditto,' he said, smirking. 'How much do you really know about that husband of yours?'

'Enough to be sure he's innocent. You're chasing the wind, Inspector. You'll find that out soon enough.'

'You're just another victim, love, and the sooner you realise it the better.'

'The only victim here is Tom.'

Banner stubbed out his fag, looked at his watch and dumped the ashtray on the top of a filing cabinet. 'We should have a proper chat soon. You'll have to come down the station. I'll be in touch.'

'I'll look forward to it,' she said drily.

'And think about what I said, yeah? You've got your whole future ahead of you. Don't waste it on a man like that. He's going down, love. There's no doubt about it.' He gave her a breezy wave and walked out of the door. 'Cheerio, then. Have a nice evening.'

Eden stood very still, her hands slowly clenching into two tight fists. She remembered what Caitlin had said about the police. Well, she'd just met the enemy face to face and didn't like what she'd seen. The devil was in Vic Banner's eyes and it scared the hell out of her.

9

Rose Rudd was an old hand when it came to prison visiting. Of the thirty years she and Archie had been married, he'd spent more time banged up than on the out, but she didn't resent him for it. That was just the way it was. She'd known the deal when they'd tied the knot and there wasn't any point in complaining about it now.

An icy wind whipped around the corner and blasted her face. She dropped her chin into the collar of her coat, pushed her hands deeper into her pockets and shivered. God, she hated February: the cold, the bleakness, the sense of summer still being such a long way away. The women in the queue shuffled and sighed, impatient to be inside. And not so much for the men they were about to see, but just to get warm again.

Rose let her gaze drift along the faces. She knew the expressions, had seen them all a thousand times before: young girls who had made an effort with their hair and clothes and makeup, still with that eagerness in their eyes, still looking forward to a couple of snatched hours with the man they loved; the middle-aged women who had seen it all and done it all before but would still paint on a smile for the benefit of their spouse; the old ones with resignation etched into their features.

Over the weeks the faces would become familiar and temporary friendships would be forged. News and gossip would be exchanged: hopes of parole, forthcoming appeals, who was down the block and why, who was cheating on their old man, whose old man was having visits from other women. Stuff to pass the time while they stood out in the cold, counting off the minutes.

Rose, who was the sociable type and made friends easily, had to pull herself up short. It wouldn't be like that this time. Archie's decision – and she was still coming to terms with it – had altered everything. It was massive, life-changing. She would have to leave the place she loved and start again somewhere new. Even her name wouldn't be the same. Rose Brown? Rose Smith? Did they let you choose or did it come with the package? A new identity so nobody knew who you really were.

But the alternative was even worse: Archie banged up for the next twenty years. Watching the light go out of his eyes. Watching him grow old and fade away. No, she couldn't cope with that. And when she thought about it, the East End wasn't like it used to be. Half her neighbours had already moved out, shifting their families to Romford, to Chingford or Thetford. Everything was changing, the old life being swept away.

The queue shuffled forward as the gates were opened and a murmur of relief rippled along the line. Rose booked in and waited for her number to be called. Fifteen minutes later, after going through the search procedure, she was in the visiting room with Archie.

'You look tired, love,' he said.

'Oh, I'm all right. I'm fine. It's a bit nippy out there, though.

Still, won't be long before spring; be nice to see the sun again.' Always cheerful, always ready to look on the bright side. 'How have you been? I've left clean clothes at reception. Make sure they give them to you. You okay?'

'Old Bill was here again.'

'Yeah, well, they're not going to leave you in peace, are they, not until they get what they want.'

Archie chewed on his fingernails, glanced to the left and the right to make sure no one was earwigging and then leaned across the table. 'You got to be careful, Rosie. Don't say nothin' to no one. If word gets out that—'

'I know that!' she hissed back. 'What do you think, that I was born yesterday?' Rose understood his concerns though. If anyone caught a whisper of what he was going to do there'd be hell to pay. The cons didn't like grasses even though half of them were at it themselves. 'I know the score.'

'Course you do,' he said, rubbing his face. 'Sorry, love, it's this place. Gets you all wound up.'

'You're doing the right thing. Just remember that.'

'Am I?'

'That Minter was well out of order and you know it. Someone has to stand up and tell it like it was. Why should he get away with it?' Rose put on her indignant face, trying to gee him up. 'The bastard should be doing life, ain't no two ways about it. You're doing everyone a favour by getting him off the streets.'

Archie heaved out a sigh. 'That's not the way some will see it.'

Rose thought back to that day sixteen years ago when the news had gone round about Paddy Lynch. Shocked, that's what they'd all been. Who'd do a thing like that? Leaving him to die when the hospital was only down the road. Criminal, that's what it was, disgusting. And Archie hadn't

61

said a word – she hadn't even known that he'd been on the job. Not that living in ignorance was anything new to her; he rarely talked about his blags and, if the truth be told, she preferred it that way. But this had been different. She thought she could recall Don West coming round the house, all flushed and agitated, but it was a long time ago and her memories were sketchy.

'How come you never told me about it? All these years and I never even—'

'Because that's what we decided. Not a word. Not to anyone. It was safer that way.' Archie glanced furtively around again. 'If Vera had got to hear, she'd have had us all down the nick in five minutes flat.'

Rose pulled a face. Paddy Lynch's widow was a bolshie, quick-tempered Scouser with a tongue like a whip. 'As if I'd have said anything. You know me better than that.'

'I know you wouldn't, love. But how would you have felt when you met her in the street, when she was talking 'bout Paddy and you'd have to pretend you knew nothing? Knowing things makes you act different.'

Rose suspected that he had a point. It was all very well sympathising with the woman but when you had to look her straight in the eye and lie . . . Well, that wasn't so easy. She was glad now, relieved, that she hadn't been in on it. Vera had gone all over the neighbourhood trying to discover who'd been on the job with Paddy – but she'd never found out.

'They'll be round to see you soon,' Archie said. 'The law, I mean. Careful what you say to them.'

But Rose wasn't going to lose any sleep over that. Old Bill didn't bother her; she'd seen off more cops than she'd had hot dinners. 'I'll say the same as I always say: I don't know nothin' about it.'

'Good girl.'

Rose gazed across the table at her husband. There was something on his mind, something he was keeping back. What made her so sure? It was that shifty expression, the way his gaze kept sliding away. She'd been married to him long enough to know when he was holding out on her. 'What is it?'

'What's what?'

'Don't give me that, Archie Rudd. What ain't you telling me?'

'Huh?'

Rose shook her head. 'I'll find out eventually so you may as well come clean now.'

'What are you talking about, woman?' Archie's mouth twisted with irritation. 'Don't start, yeah? I've got enough on my plate being in this dump. I don't need you on my back too. Just leave it. Give it a rest.'

She knew better than to pursue the matter. When Archie was in one of his stubborn moods there was no getting through to him; you might as well talk to a brick wall. 'Our Davey sends his best. Says he'll be in to see you next week.'

'Don't say nothin' to him yet.'

'I wasn't planning to.' It was hard for her, keeping the truth from her own son – especially when it was something as big as this – but she had to keep quiet until it was sorted. Davey wouldn't be happy, that was for sure; no one wanted to have a snitch for a dad. When the time came she'd have to sit down with him, explain it all properly. It wasn't a conversation she was looking forward to.

'You okay for readies?'

Rose gave a nod. Whenever they were in the money, she always had the sense to squirrel some away for the leaner days. 'You don't have to worry about me. I'll cope. I always do, don't I?'

Archie reached out and gave her hand a pat, his way of

apologising for being short with her before. He was never good at saying sorry; the word stuck like glue to his lips. 'It'll be all right, love. We'll be all right.'

Rose nodded again. 'Course we will.' She said it with as much brightness as she could muster even though her instincts told her otherwise. As she smiled at her husband, she had a bad feeling in her bones, a creeping sense of dread. 'Aren't we always?'

10

The phone rang at precisely one minute past six. Max Tamer knew this because the evening news had just started as he picked up the receiver. 'Hello?' There was a series of pips followed by the sound of coins being dropped into a callbox. He waited until the line had cleared before speaking again. 'Yes?'

'Mr Tamer?'

'Speaking.'

The voice at the other end was male, low, furtive. 'It's me. It's Pym. I've got something for you.'

Max's hand tightened around the phone. 'I'm listening.'

There was a crackly pause, a long hesitation. 'What about the money? I need the money first.'

'You'll get your money . . . if the information's sound.'

'You know it will be, Mr Tamer. When have I ever let you down?'

It was true that Pym was the eyes and ears of the underworld. He was a sly, shabby little man who hung around the pubs and bars and courtrooms, listening in to conversations, gathering snippets of news and gossip which he then sold on to any interested parties. 'Just spit it out, okay? I haven't got all night.'

'It's about that Tom Chase, you know, the geezer in Covent Garden.'

Max's lips curled into a snarl as disappointment rolled through him. 'He's not the one. I've already told you that. Why the hell are you wasting my time like this?'

Pym made an unpleasant snuffling noise as if his feelings had been offended. 'Hang on, Mr Tamer. Don't go jumping to conclusions. This ain't the same. This is something different.'

'What then?'

'He's been in court, ain't he? Charged with armed robbery and manslaughter. Yesterday, it were; I tried to call but you wasn't around. Now the robbery, that was years back in the six-ties, over Epping way, but the filth have only just caught up with him. Bloke called Paddy Lynch was left for dead in the back of the getaway van. Rum sort of affair, Mr Tamer. Nasty like, if you get my drift. Thing is – and this is the interesting bit – I've heard a whisper that Chase spent some time in Budapest.'

Max's hand tightened around the phone. 'What?'

'You see what I'm getting at?'

'When?'

'When what?'

Max gritted his teeth. 'When was he in Budapest?'

The beeps went and there was a short delay while more coins were fed into the machine. 'Hello? You still there?'

'When was he in Budapest?' Max repeated sharply.

'After the job. A year or so after. I don't know all the details yet. I got his address though. Islington. Twenty-four Pope Street. First-floor flat. He's still banged up – didn't get bail – but his missus should be there.'

Max scribbled down the address on the notepad by the phone. 'You got a name for her?'

'Eden,' Pym said, and then spelled it out: 'E-D-E-N. As in Adam and Eve.'

'Right.'

'So, about the money, Mr Tamer. I was thinking a pony, yeah?'

Max gave a dry laugh. 'Twenty-five quid? I don't think so. We'll call it a tenner for now. I'll give Terry a bell and get it sent over to the Fox.'

Pym made a few grumbling noises, but bowed down to the inevitable. 'All right. But I'll stay on it, yeah? You want me to stay on it?'

'Yes. Keep me informed.'

Max thought about Tom Chase as he put down the phone. It was getting on for two years now since he'd dismissed the photographer as being of no interest. Had he made a mistake? He wasn't the man in the picture, not the guy he'd been looking for, but the Budapest connection was too much of a coincidence. That's if Pym was right. But when wasn't he? He might not be a pleasant creature but he was usually a reliable one. And if this Tom Chase had been capable of killing once, there was no reason why he couldn't have done it again.

Max made a quick call to Terry Street and arranged for Pym to be paid. As he put the receiver down again his mother's frail voice floated into the hall.

'Max?'

'Yes?'

'Who was that?'

Max walked into the living room, sat down in the arm-chair and looked over at his mother. She seemed to be getting smaller by the day, to be visibly shrinking. Her eyes, pale and rheumy, peered back at him.

'Nothing important,' he said. 'Just work.'

'Oh.'

But contained within that simple 'Oh' was something so much more. He knew that she still clung on to a slender thread of hope – a hope he had long ago relinquished – that one day there would be news. Three years of waiting and still nothing. His wife had disappeared into thin air and was never coming home again.

Max watched the television: unemployment at an all-time high, the collapse of Laker Airways leaving six thousand passengers stranded abroad, the aftermath of rioting in Bristol. None of it meant anything to him. He felt disconnected from the world he lived in, cut adrift. All that kept him going was his drive to discover the truth.

He glanced over at his mother again. 'Did you have any visitors today?'

'Father Brennan dropped by. He sends his regards.'

Max gave a thin smile. He had no time for the priest and his empty words. God had abandoned the Tamers long ago; the all-seeing, all-forgiving Lord had thrown them overboard and left them to drown in a sea of despair. He sniffed the air, sure that a lingering smell remained, a curious odour of incense and sherry.

'And what did the old crow have to say for himself?'

'You should be kinder, Max. His heart's in the right place.'

But kindness was no longer in Max's repertoire. The pain festered inside him like a wound that wouldn't heal. He had kept the bitterness alive, honing it until the edges were hard and cold and sharp as a blade. His wife was dead, he was sure of it, and one day he would have his revenge. An eye for an eye – wasn't that what it said in the Bible? – but a wife for a wife seemed a more suitable and fitting retribution.

11

Eden wasn't sure how she'd managed to get through the week. She had lurched from day to day, waking each morning with that same sick feeling in her guts, desperately trying to make sense of the senseless. She sighed as she stared down at the table. It was covered in books, paper, notes, pens, photographs and a stack of phone directories. What she needed was order, but what she had was chaos.

The phone directories, covering various parts of London, were all open at the letter C. She had made a start on ringing round but the name Chase was more common than she'd anticipated and the list of numbers was daunting. There was nothing under T. Chase and so she'd started working her way through alphabetically. To date she had made sixteen calls with every one of them drawing a blank. Not even a casual lead or two. Not even a hesitation while they thought about it.

Her cover story, after apologising for disturbing them and introducing herself as Cathy Harris, was that she was trying to track down an old friend of her husband's, a mate from the sixties, for a forthcoming birthday party. 'He was called Tom

Chase. He'd be in his forties now and I know Sam would love to see him again.'

Some people were friendlier than others, a few were downright rude, but whatever the response the final answer was always the same: they'd never heard of Tom Chase. She was about to make call seventeen, had even lifted the phone to her ear, when she changed her mind and placed the receiver back on the cradle. What was she doing? Suddenly she was sure it was all a waste of time; no matter how many calls she made she would never get the answer she was looking for.

Could there really be another Tom Chase out there, a murdering, robbing Tom Chase? At first it had seemed the most likely explanation but the more she thought about it the less convinced she became. Although she had heard of doppelgangers, what were the odds of there being two guys of the same age, similar appearance and identical name? If it was John Smith, perhaps, but it wasn't. And anyway, it didn't explain the bracelet.

No, she was sure that Jack Minter was the key to all this. He had given the stolen bracelet to Tom and had probably been part of the armed robbery back in the sixties. She could try ringing people called Minter but didn't relish the thought of starting all over again. It would be better to wait, she decided, until she'd spoken to Tom and then she might have a better idea of the person she was searching for.

Eden glanced at the clock. She would have to leave in half an hour if she was to arrive in plenty of time for her first visit to HMP Thornley Heath. Her heart gave a leap. A week, a whole week since she'd last seen Tom, and so much had changed in their lives. What state would he be in? He was the type who could cope with most situations but prison could break the toughest of men. She feared for his safety, especially if word got out as to what he'd been charged with. Paddy Lynch must

70

have had family and friends. They could be planning revenge at this very moment, unwilling to wait for the trial, deciding to take justice into their own hands.

'Stop it,' she muttered, knowing that she would send herself crazy if she continued to think along these lines. Her imagination was capable of conjuring up every kind of horror, endless nightmare scenarios that made her feel sick and scared. It was the helplessness that got to her, the thought of being able to do nothing. Which was why she was trying to do something, anything, to keep the demons at bay.

It occurred to her that Jack Minter could be the man who was trying to frame Tom. It had a sort of logic. Perhaps he'd been caught on another job and was now turning Queen's evidence – and making stuff up – in the hope of saving his own skin. He couldn't have known that Tom would still have the bracelet, not after sixteen years, but perhaps that had just been a stroke of luck. And for the police, of course, it was a damning piece of evidence.

The police. Her mouth twisted at the thought of the DI. It had been bad enough when Banner had turned up unannounced at the studio, but being interviewed by him was going to be even worse. The call had come yesterday, a summons to West End Central.

'Is that Eden?'

'Yes.'

'Hey, it's Vic, Vic Banner. How are you, love?'

As if they were old friends, as if he gave a damn how she was.

'I'm fine, thank you.' Trying to sound as cool as she could, trying to convey the impression that she wasn't worried because ultimately she had nothing to be worried about. With any success? It was doubtful. She couldn't quite keep the tremor from her voice.

'So about that little chat I mentioned. Tomorrow suit you all right? About eleven?'

'Yes, that's not a problem.'

'Good. Do you know where the station is?'

'Yes.'

'See you tomorrow then. Just ask for me at the desk.' Banner had paused and then given a chuckle. 'Looking forward to it.'

Eden, recalling that sly unpleasant laugh, pulled a face. She wondered if she should take a solicitor along, someone to support her, but then thought about the cost. Every penny counted at the moment and she couldn't afford to throw money away. Unfortunately, Caitlin wasn't around; she'd gone off for a few days to support the Women's Peace Camp at Greenham Common and wouldn't be back until Monday. As there was no way of getting in touch with her, she would have to deal with the police on her own.

'You can do it,' she muttered. 'Don't let that creep get the better of you.'

All she had to do was be careful, right? To not do anything stupid. To think before she spoke. But God alone knew what tricks Banner might have up his sleeve. She had already realised he wasn't the type to play by the rules. She'd have to be on her guard, to pay attention to every question. He'd be out to trap her, to try and make her say something that would incriminate Tom.

Eden glanced at the mess on the table, her gaze alighting on a heap of photocopies. On Monday she'd taken the Tube up to Colindale and gone to the newspaper library. Here she'd dug out everything she could on the Epping armed robbery – and there was plenty of it. The story had been widely covered in the national and the local press: an armed raid on a storage depot where the thieves had allegedly got away with over two million pounds' worth of gold, gems and jewellery.

One of the security guards, called Roger Best, had attempted to thwart the raid and a sawn-off shotgun had gone off, injuring one of the robbers. The severity of the man's injuries had been unknown at this point but an alert had been put out to local hospitals. Eden had made a note of the guard's name, wondering if there was anything useful he could recall after all this time.

The follow-up reports, with their lurid headlines, made for uncomfortable reading. It was the morning after the raid when the body of Paddy Lynch was found in the back of a locked van in an Epping car park. Dumped by the rest of the gang, he'd been left to die alone even though the hospital was only half a mile away. Eden shuddered as she contemplated the man's fate. It was hard to imagine how people could commit such a callous act; there was something brutal and chilling about it. Wasn't there a code of conduct among criminals? Didn't they always look after their own? Surely it would have been easy enough for one of them to have found a phone box and called an ambulance.

She found herself thinking about Jack Minter again. Who was he? Where was he? In jail, perhaps, trying to shift the blame for everything he'd done on to Tom. Or still walking the streets, free as a bird, while her husband was banged up and staring at a life sentence. But of course there was always the possibility that he'd had nothing to do with the raid at all. Minter could be completely innocent, having bought the bracelet from someone else, unaware of its origins. But what were the odds? No, she was sure he was behind all this.

Eden looked at the clock again. Still another fifteen minutes to go. She laid out a few of the Budapest photographs and stared at them. Black and white prints of a bustling marketplace, the sky low and grey, the crowd dressed in winter attire – heavy coats and scarves and gloves. A supermarket, houses and apartments. A stone plinth with a statue on top. Some tramps sitting by a gate, surrounded by bottles and cardboard. Meat, fruit and vegetable stalls. Men and women selling from bags and open suitcases. There was movement and life and feeling. The photographs were stunningly evocative, a heaving hotchpotch of humanity caught in a single moment and preserved for ever.

On the back of one of them, written in Tom's familiar hand, was the name *Garay Square*. The name rang a bell and when she checked the airmail letters from Ann-Marie she saw that this was the address written on the front. She still hadn't got round to trying to translate the French and now wasn't the time to start. Later, she thought, when she got back from the visit.

Eden didn't know much about Hungary, other than it was part of the Eastern bloc. She wondered what had made him go there and wished to God he hadn't. If there'd been no Budapest, there would have been no Jack Minter and no bracelet either.

She was still mulling this over when the phone rang. She reached out and picked it up. 'Hello?'

'Ah, at last!'

Eden's heart sank at the sound of her father's voice. Had he heard about Tom? Did he know anything? 'Hi, Dad. How are you?'

'I've been trying to get through for hours. Are you ever off that phone?'

'Sorry, I've been . . . I had some calls to make.'

'How come you're not at college today?'

Eden rolled her eyes, wondering why her father still felt the need to interrogate her when she was twenty-six years of age. 'I haven't got any lectures. I've got an essay to write so I'm working from home.' She glanced down at the pile of unopened art books. 'Caravaggio,' she said. 'Five thousand words, and it needs to be in by tomorrow.'

'Well, you won't get much done if you're on the phone all day.'

'I'm not on the . . . ' She pulled herself up, knowing it was pointless getting into an argument with him. 'Anyway, I've almost finished,' she lied. 'Is everything all right?'

'Why shouldn't it be?'

'You usually call in the evening.'

'I tried last night, but it was engaged.' He sighed down the line. 'I was just calling to say that I'm going to be in London next week from Wednesday to Friday. It's a work conference but I'll be free in the evenings. Perhaps we could meet up, the three of us, go for dinner somewhere.'

'Oh, right. Yes. Yes, of course.' Although Eden was relieved that he wasn't ringing about Tom's arrest, she didn't relish the prospect of having to lie to him about why her husband couldn't be there. 'I'm sure that will be fine. What night were you thinking of?'

'Friday would be best.'

'Okay. That sounds good.'

There was a short silence before her father said, 'Wasn't there something about a murder charge?'

Eden almost dropped the phone. She could feel the blood draining from her face. So he'd known all along, had just been testing her, waiting to see if she'd tell the truth. 'W-what?' she stammered.

'A murder charge,' he repeated.

'I . . . I don't . . . '

'Are you all right, Eden?'

'I'm . . . it's just . . . Sorry, I was going to tell you but—'

'Caravaggio,' he interrupted. 'Didn't he go on the run after he killed someone? I'm sure I read about it somewhere. Ended

75

up getting murdered himself, I think. Or maybe I've got the wrong man. *The Martyrdom of Saint Matthew* – wasn't that one of his?'

Eden, still in shock, hurriedly tried to regain her composure. She could feel her heart beating faster than it should, a hammering in her chest. Her mouth was dry and a thin prickle of sweat had broken out on her forehead. 'Yes, yes, that's him. Spot on. Absolutely.' Before she could start gibbering, she quickly said, 'So you'll call me when you get to London? We can make arrangements then. Or I'll book somewhere if you like. Should I do that?'

'No, don't bother. I'll make the arrangements.'

Which, roughly translated, meant he didn't trust her to choose a restaurant where the food would be to his liking. But she wasn't going to get all antsy about that. She was too relieved to be off the hook. 'I'll wait to hear from you then. I'll talk to you soon.'

As Eden hung up, her hands were shaking. She couldn't believe how close she'd come to blurting it all out. In an ideal world she would have been able to confide in him, tell him everything, but they didn't have that kind of relationship. Her father always expected the worst and this was about as bad as it got.

Perhaps, depending on how the meal went, she would come clean on Friday. Would she? Eden pulled a face. In truth, she didn't want to give him the satisfaction of thinking he'd been right all along about the marriage, and it was still possible – she clung on to the hope – that Tom's innocence could be proved before the case went to trial.

Eden picked up the London *A–Z* and opened it at the page marked with a slip of paper. She wanted to be sure of the route to the jail before she set out. It didn't look complicated but there was always the possibility of roadworks or accidents.

With her finger, she traced the roads through to HMP Thornley Heath, trying to memorise the way.

After the conversation with her father, anxious thoughts were twisting and turning in her head. While she studied the map, she sensed she was starting on a journey that went way beyond some prison walls, a journey that would test all her reserves of courage and push her to the very limit.

12

Eden's heart sank as she gazed up at the imposing grey stone walls of the prison. It was hard to think of Tom in there, to imagine exactly where he was and what he was doing. From the outside the place was bleak and depressing, and she couldn't imagine the interior being any different. Worse, probably, with its pungent smells, claustrophobic cells and barred windows. Not to mention the constant threat from other inmates.

She stood for a while, taking it all in, before crossing the road. It had started to snow half an hour ago, white flakes tumbling from the sky and settling on the ground in a thin crunchy blanket. The air was cold and sharp, pinching at her face. She shivered as she turned up the collar of her coat, passed through the gate and walked up the short path to the booking-in area.

It was busy in the room and she joined the back of a queue. She had no idea what she was supposed to do and so just stood in line watching the women in front while she tried not to look too much like a fish out of water. The room had a curious smell, a combination of bleach, damp coats and perfume.

There were a few plastic chairs lined up against the wall but not enough to seat everyone.

Most of the visitors – the ones who had already booked in – were standing around in groups, and she caught snippets of their conversations as she waited. There was talk of kids, money, bills, TV and gossip about mutual friends. There were complaints about the cold and the men inside, news of appeals and possible moves. The voices rose and fell like a wave rippling across the room.

As Eden shuffled forward in the queue, the girl behind moved too, bumping into her as they came to a halt again.

'Sorry, hon.'

Eden turned to see a slim, pretty blonde wearing jeans and a black leather jacket. She was in her mid-twenties with shoulder-length hair, kohl-rimmed eyes and a wide red mouth.

'Sorry,' the girl said again. 'God, they're slow today, aren't they? I'm sure they do it on purpose. Some of these screws are completely bloody-minded. Do you know if they've called any numbers yet?'

Eden stared blankly back at her. 'What?'

'You know, for . . . ' The girl stopped and stared at her for a moment. 'Is this your first time here?'

Eden nodded, her attempt at nonchalance having lasted all of two minutes. 'What are the numbers for?'

'They'll give you one at the desk when you book in. That's if we ever get to the front of the damn queue. Then you just have to wait for it to be called before you go through to the visiting room. There's the search first, of course, but that doesn't take long. Don't worry, you'll soon get used to it.'

'Christ, I hope not.'

The girl laughed. 'Yeah, I know the feeling. You and me both. These places really piss me off; I'm sure they make it as hard for us as they possibly can. Here to see the old man, are you?'

'Yes. How about you?'

'My brother, Pete. His girlfriend dumped him last week so he's feeling pretty sorry for himself. Not that she's much of a loss, in my opinion. Sent him a Dear John, didn't she, which is just what you need when you're banged up in here. The cow didn't even have the decency to tell him to his face.' She snorted. 'Some people are unbelievable.'

'That must be tough.'

'He'll get over it. How's your old man doing?'

'I don't know. I haven't had a chance to speak to him yet. He's only been here a week.'

'He'll be okay once he settles in. It's always hard at first.'

The thought of Tom 'settling in' served as a reminder to Eden that they could be in for a long haul, months and months, before he was finally released. That's if . . . but she refused to dwell on the alternative. It was too awful, too upsetting.

'I'm Tammy, by the way.'

'Eden.'

'Hi. So where have you come from?'

'Only Islington. How about you?'

'Shoreditch,' Tammy said. 'Two buses and I had to wait for ever. Bloody freezing it was too. Not that it's much warmer in here.' She rubbed at her arms. 'You'd think they could put some heat on, wouldn't you?'

The queue shifted forward again and eventually Eden reached the front. She gave the prison officer Tom's details and passed her driving licence through the narrow gap in the security glass. The man studied Eden's photograph for a while, glancing between her and the licence as if she might be trying to pull a fast one. He shoved a laminated cardboard square with the number nineteen on it across the counter. 'Want a locker?'

Eden shook her head, not knowing what she'd want a locker for. 'No, thanks.'

'Are you sure?' Tammy said from behind. 'You can't take your bag in with you so you'll have to leave it somewhere safe. No cash either, apart from loose change. You'll need that for tea and coffee. No notes or anything.'

'Oh,' Eden said. 'Okay. Thanks, I didn't realise.' She looked at the officer again. 'Sorry, I will, then.'

'Fifty pence deposit. You'll get it back when you hand the key in at the end of the visit.'

Eden pulled her purse out of her bag and found the necessary change. She was given a key with a tag that identified it as being for locker twenty-eight. She thanked Tammy again, and made her way through the crowd to the far wall which was lined with grey metal lockers stacked on top of each other.

A couple of minutes later Tammy joined her there. 'Twenty,' she said, holding up her visitor's card and making a grimace. 'It's usually quieter than this during the week. They'd better get a move on or we'll be waiting here for ever.'

Eden, who was staring down into her purse, glanced up. 'How much do you think I'll need in there?'

'A few quid should do it. The drinks don't cost much, but there's chocolate and crisps and the like. Depends how hungry he is. Pete scoffs everything he can lay his hands on.'

Eden put four one pound coins into her back pocket, placed her bag and coat in the locker and locked the door. Now that the time was drawing closer to seeing Tom again she felt a mixture of anxiety and anticipation. 'What's it like?' she asked suddenly. 'I don't mean the visits, I mean the prison. What's it like being here? Is it awful? Has Pete told you anything?'

Tammy gave a shrug. 'Pete's used to it. He spends half his

life in and out of the nick. This the first time your old man's been inside, then?'

Eden nodded. She had to fight against a sudden urge to let it all spill out, to tell the whole sorry story. But she caught herself in time. It wouldn't be a smart move. She had to be cautious in case word got around that Tom had been charged with the manslaughter of Paddy Lynch. 'He's never been in trouble before.'

'He'll be all right. Don't worry. He just needs to keep his head down and try to stay out of bother. Which is something Pete isn't good at. Can't help himself, can he? He's a complete idiot. I tell him over and over but he never listens to anything I say. I don't know why I waste my breath.'

'You're used to visiting, then?'

Tammy barked out a laugh. 'God, yeah. I've lost count of the number of jails he's been in. I've been all over the place. But at least he's in London for now.' She put her hands on her hips and sighed. 'And he's not really a bad person. It's the booze that does for him. He has a few pints, gets in a fight and the next thing you know he's down the nick looking at another stretch. You'd think he'd learn but he doesn't. Still, that's Pete for you.'

Eden was aware of the silence that followed this information, a space she was probably supposed to fill with something about Tom. But what? She searched her mind for an innocuous comment – and came up with nothing. In the end she settled for a nod and a sympathetic smile. 'That's a shame.'

'Yeah, it's that all right. But what can you do? He's his own worst enemy.'

They started to call the numbers, taking visitors through in small groups of three or four. Eden shifted impatiently from one foot to another, eager to get inside, each passing minute feeling like an hour.

'You're keen,' Tammy said. 'What's his name, then? Your old man.'

'Tom.'

'How long have you been married?'

'Only a year.' Eden, realising their first anniversary was still a couple of weeks away, quickly corrected herself. 'Almost a year.'

'That's a tough break. How long is he looking at?'

Eden skirted around a direct answer. 'Who knows? Anything's too long. I'm trying not to think about it.'

'It is. You're right there.' Tammy crossed her fingers and held them up. 'Here's hoping, eh?'

'Yeah, here's hoping.'

Finally their numbers were called and they went together into the search area. For Eden, the worst part of the procedure was the female officer peering into her mouth – 'Lift your tongue, please' – as if she was the subject of some bizarre examination by a prison dentist. It felt even more intrusive than the general pat-down and the inspection of the insides of her shoes.

After the search, six of them were taken through a door at the back and accompanied by a guard across an internal open courtyard. The snow was still falling, coming down in great white drifts. Their voices sounded odd, muffled in the icy air. Everyone hurried along, shivering with cold and eager to be back inside.

As Eden lifted her eyes to the sky, she saw only the high sheer walls rising on every side. For a moment she felt trapped, as if the building itself was closing in on her. She swallowed hard, her hands balling into two tight fists in her pockets. Her mouth went dry. She thought of Tom, condemned to spend God knows how long in this awful prison. A feeling, dark and menacing, wrapped itself around her body and shrouded her in dread.

13

Eden was still feeling shaky as she stepped inside the visitors' room. There were about thirty tables in all and most were already occupied. She had a fleeting impression of pale walls and bright fluorescent lights, of windows set up near the ceiling, as she quickly scanned the faces looking for Tom. When she finally saw him, her heart gave a leap. A tangle of emotions instantly wound their way through her: love, pity and sorrow battling with an indignant rage that he'd been wrongly accused and locked up in this terrible place.

Tom stood as she approached, his mouth curling into a small strained smile, his arms reaching out for her.

'Eden,' he said.

Their embrace was swift, fleeting, a brief coming together overlooked by a stern-faced prison officer.

'Take your seats, please,' the guard insisted.

They sat down and gazed at each other across the table. Eden could feel her pulse racing as she studied her husband, taking in every nuance, every change. He had a dazed look about him, she thought, as though he was still in shock. And had he lost weight? It had only been a week but already there were hollows under his cheekbones, a certain gauntness that hadn't been there before.

'How are you?' she asked, and then quickly shook her head. 'I don't know why I'm even asking that.'

'I'm all right,' he said. 'I promise. I'm coping. You don't have to worry.'

But asking Eden not to worry was like asking her not to breathe; it had become second nature over the past seven days. Every hour of every day, every restless night, was coloured by fear and anxiety.

'We'll sort this out. We will. We'll get you out of here.'

Tom placed his hand over hers and looked directly into her eyes. 'I swear I didn't do it, Eden. I swear on my life.'

Eden gave a start. 'Why are you even saying that? You don't have to say that to me. Of course you didn't. I've never doubted it, not for a second, and I never will.'

Tom bowed his head briefly, his face full of emotion, before raising his gaze again. 'I'm sorry. I shouldn't have . . . It's this place. There's too much time to think. Stuff goes round and round in your head. You start questioning everything. One minute I was in the studio and the next . . . It's mad, crazy. Nothing makes any sense. God, it's all such a bloody mess.'

'No one believes you're guilty, at least no one that matters. The police have got it wrong and we're going to prove it. You've got to believe that.' There was so much more she wanted to say, but what words could give him the hope he needed? Aware that the time they had together was limited, she knew she had to gather as much information as she could. 'So has Castor got a name yet? Does he know who's accusing you?'

'No, he reckons the cops are in the process of moving the guy, making sure he's somewhere safe before they reveal who he is.'

'Do you think it could be Jack Minter?'

Tom frowned. 'Jack?'

'Why not? It makes sense. He's the one who organised the Epping robbery, who left that bloke to die. And now he's been caught he needs to point the finger at someone else. So he's turning it around, saying that you stole his identity and that you were behind it all. And he gave you the bracelet. Obviously he couldn't have known that you'd still have it, not after sixteen years, but . . . I mean, it *could* be him, couldn't it? Perhaps he came back to London, saw you in Covent Garden, and then after he was arrested decided he could use you as a scapegoat.'

Tom listened patiently. 'So what about the rest of the crew? Why would they go along with the story? There's nothing in it for them, nothing at all. If Minter turns Queen's evidence, they'll all go down for a long stretch.'

She didn't have an immediate answer to that question, but wasn't prepared to relinquish her theory just yet. She thought about it for a moment. 'I don't know. Maybe he's not going to name the others or maybe, if he does, he thinks that the police won't be able to arrest them. They could be dead or . . . ' Eden had heard about gangsters retiring to the Costa, living a life of luxury on their ill-gotten gains. 'They could be in Spain or anywhere. And they're hardly going to turn up at court to complain about Minter telling lies.'

'And if it isn't him?'

'Then it's someone else trying to set you up. We'll find out who it is. Have you figured out where you were in July 'sixty-six yet?'

Tom shook his head. 'I'm not sure. I moved around a lot back then. I've been racking my brains but—'

'Did you watch the football, the World Cup?'

'Oh,' he said, his eyebrows shifting up. 'Yes. That was . . . Yes, I think it was Southend. Or was it Clacton? I used to hit the coast in the summer, try and make some cash by taking photos and selling them to the tourists. No, I reckon it was Southend. I can remember the pub.'

'And when the summer was over?'

'Good question,' he said. 'But I reckon I came back to London.'

Eden's heart sank at this news. She'd been hoping he'd gone abroad, far away from the capital and the robbery in Epping. 'So you would have been here in November.'

'You know, the more I think about it, I'm pretty sure I was. I was trying to get some cash together so I could take off again. Everyone was talking about Berlin. I fancied going there, seeing it for myself, but I needed some money first.' He gave a wry smile. 'And then the idea came to me that I could just pull a heist and all my troubles would be over.'

Eden pulled a face. 'Don't even joke about it.'

'Ah,' he said with mock wistfulness. 'I remember the days when you loved my sense of humour.'

'Well, I hate to break this to you, sweetheart, but—'

'Hey, hold it right there.' He grinned, raising his hands in a gesture of defence. 'Have some pity. You can't shatter the last of my illusions.'

For a few precious moments, it was as if things were perfectly natural again, a weight lifted, normality resumed. But it didn't last long. Eden was brought down to earth by the appearance of a guard patrolling up and down the aisles. The officer paused by their table, looming over them. He stared suspiciously for a while as though what they were exchanging could be contraband rather than mere banter.

Eden was relieved when he eventually moved on. 'What was all that about?' she whispered.

Tom curled his lip. 'Just to let you know you're being watched.'

'As if you could forget.' It made her uncomfortable being under constant scrutiny. She felt awkward and self-conscious, overly aware of their eyes on her. But she couldn't let it get in the way of the visit. 'So, tell me how you ended up in Budapest.'

'It must have been the following year. March or April. I stayed in Paris for a while, a few months, and then went on to Germany. I met some students in Berlin. They were planning to take the train through Czechoslovakia to Hungary and I thought it might be interesting so I tagged along.'

Eden, recalling the letters from Ann-Marie, wondered if the two of them had hooked up while he was in France. But that wasn't the question she asked. 'And that's where you met Jack Minter?'

Tom nodded. 'I was taking photos in Garay Square. He was renting an apartment there and . . . well, we got talking – he was into photography too – and we just hit it off. I liked him. He was interesting, good company. We spent a lot of time together after that. I was staying at a cheap hotel near the station, a bit of a dive, and when he offered me a room in the flat I jumped at it.' He raked his fingers through his hair, gave a brief shake of his head. 'God, he wasn't a villain, Eden. I'd swear to it. He was a straight-up guy. A bit of ducking and diving, sure, but that's the way it is out there. Nothing serious. He wasn't the type to—'

'You can't be sure. He had the bracelet, didn't he?'

'That doesn't mean anything. There's a massive black market in Hungary, lots of people trading goods. He wouldn't necessarily have known it was stolen.'

'So what did he do? I mean, how did he make a living?'

'He said he worked on the rigs, on and off. Some kind of engineer, I think. And when he wasn't working, he travelled around, visiting new places. And he hadn't lived in England for years. His parents moved to Hamburg when he was thirteen and he never went back.'

'So he said.'

Tom shrugged. 'He seemed genuine enough. I can't . . . I just can't see him as an armed robber. It doesn't add up.'

Eden thought of the photographs she'd removed from the studio. 'Did you take any pictures of him?'

'I'm not sure. Probably. I might have done.'

'What does he look like?'

'About the same age as me, brown hair, brown eyes.'

Eden arched her eyebrows. 'Anything more specific? That describes thirty per cent of the men in this room.'

Tom pondered on it for a moment before giving a wave of his hand. 'I don't know. Nothing standout. A bit taller than me, an inch or so. Ordinary. Fit – he used to go running – although he might not now. And it was sixteen years ago; people can change a lot in that time.'

'But you talked, yes? You told him about yourself?'

'I suppose so. Some.'

'Enough for him to be aware that you'd been in London the previous November?'

Tom shrugged. 'Probably.'

'So maybe he remembered that, and realised it's pretty hard to provide a convincing alibi after sixteen years. He just threw your name into the pot and hoped for the best. And then he got lucky. You still had the bracelet and—'

'No, I don't buy it. It's someone else. It has to be.'

Eden understood his reluctance to accept Jack Minter's guilt; Tom was a loyal sort of man who never thought the worst of anyone. But people weren't always what they appeared to be.

'Sometimes it's the nice guys you've got to watch out for – the sociopaths with the charming exterior. That's how they get away with it. No one thinks they can be capable of doing bad stuff.'

Tom still didn't look convinced. 'It just doesn't feel right. No, I'm sure it's not him. Anyway, we'll find out soon enough.'

'If it isn't, then we have to try and track him down. Without the stolen bracelet, all the police have got is this guy's claim that it was you who organised the robbery. His word against yours. We need Minter to testify that he gave you that bracelet in Budapest, that you didn't steal it during the raid.'

'Friendly photographer turned vicious armed robber. They've got me well and truly in the frame.'

She heard the strain in his voice and wished she could do more to help. 'Why did he even give it you in the first place? Castor said something about a debt.'

'Yeah, he borrowed some cash. It wasn't that much, just a hundred or so. He was going to Germany – he had money in the bank there – but wasn't sure how long he'd be. I was planning on leaving too so he gave me the bracelet in lieu of the debt. He said I could sell it in London, that it was gold, hallmarked, and I'd easily get my money back.'

'But you didn't sell it?'

'No, I got work pretty quickly and so I didn't bother. I just hung on to it. To be honest, I'd forgotten all about the damn thing.'

Eden became aware of other visitors going back and forth to the refreshment counter at the back of the room, carrying trays laden with plastic cups and crisps and chocolate. 'Shall I get some drinks? Would you like a coffee?'

'Yeah, sounds like a plan.'

'What about something to eat?'

'No, I'm fine. Just coffee, please.'

Eden stood up, crossed between the tables and joined the queue. While she waited she had a quick look round, making sure that her gaze didn't settle on anyone for too long. Staring was probably a cardinal sin, like on the Tube. All of the men here were in the same boat, all on remand, all killing time until their cases went to trial. Maybe some of them, like Tom, were innocent. Others – well, she didn't want to dwell on what they might have been accused of.

She saw Tammy and her brother over in the far corner, their heads bent together. Pete was a big, solid man in his early thirties, with short cropped hair, a bull neck, and tattoos covering his arms. They seemed to be in the middle of some kind of row; Tammy had an exasperated look as if she wasn't exactly hearing what she wanted to hear.

The room with all its tables and high windows had a claustrophobic air. It was warm too, the radiators going full blast. Eden pushed up the sleeves of her cardigan and took a few slow, deep breaths. She turned her attention to Tom, who was sitting staring into space. She could see the stiffness in his shoulders, the anxiety etched on his face. There was a terrible vulnerability about him, a brittle fragility that made her heart ache. He was trying his best to be strong for her, but she knew he was afraid. Who wouldn't be?

As she shifted forward in the queue, Eden recalled what Vic Banner had said at the studio. *You've got your whole future ahead of you. Don't waste it on a man like that.* But she knew, with an overwhelming certainty, that no matter how long it took she would always wait.

14

Eden placed the tray on the table and sat down. Although Tom had said he didn't want anything, she'd used her change to buy two coffees, a cheese sandwich and an apple. 'Here,' she said. 'You have to eat. I'm presuming the food in here isn't exactly Cordon Bleu.'

He looked down at the sandwich and grinned. 'As opposed to the culinary delights of the visiting room.'

'It doesn't look that bad. How about we eat half each and that way we'll both die together?'

Tom picked up the sandwich, peeled off the wrapping, and passed her half. 'Ladies first.'

'Who said the age of chivalry was dead?' She took a bite off the corner. 'Mm, it's lovely. You should try some.'

'Your acting skills leave a lot to be desired, Mrs Chase.'

Eden put down the sandwich, took a sip of coffee and widened her eyes. 'That is so untrue.'

Tom looked at her and smiled. 'So true.'

'Look, do you need anything? Clothes, books? I can bring stuff in with me, I think. Or I could post it to you. That would be quicker. I won't get to see you again until next week. Just tell me what you want and I'll sort it out.'

'Thanks, yeah, some clothes would be good. Nothing fancy, just a pair of jeans and a few shirts. And underwear and socks. Oh, and a radio. There's a spare one, isn't there, in the dresser? The little transistor, that'll do fine. There's no point having anything decent in here; it'll only get nicked or broken.'

'Are you sure there's nothing else?'

'Well, there's a library, of sorts, but I wouldn't mind a few books. Don't bother posting them, though, just bring them with you on the next visit.'

'Okay.'

'You look tired,' he said. 'Are you sleeping?'

'Yes,' she lied.

'I could be here for months, Eden. You've got to take care of yourself. Don't worry about me. Do you know what the worst thing is about this place? It's not the other guys or the food or even the bars on the windows – it's the unrelenting boredom. I've only done a week and it feels like a year. But I can deal with it, okay?'

Eden gave a nod. She didn't believe it but tried to look as though she did. 'I'm supposed to see the police tomorrow. That Banner guy. I don't like him. He's a nasty bit of work, a real creep. He turned up at the studio, said he'd like to talk to me at the station.'

'Is Castor going with you?'

'Do you think I need him? It's not a proper interview or anything.'

'I don't know. I suppose not. But he'll be looking to dig some dirt.'

'Then he's going to be disappointed. And don't worry, Caitlin's already given me the lecture on thinking before I speak. Not that there's anything to hide, but I'll be careful. Banner's the type to try and twist anything you say.'

'How is Caitlin?'

'She's good. She sends her love. She's gone to Greenham for a few days so I won't see her again until next week.'

'Ah, saving the world from nuclear disaster. I've heard there's quite a gathering there. Say hello for me.'

'I will.'

Tom's face twisted a little. 'I suppose everyone knows I'm in here now?'

'Not everyone,' Eden said, thinking of her father. 'Not at all. I've told Denny and he's probably told a few of the others, but your clients don't know anything. I got Annabelle to cancel all your appointments for the next few weeks – she's told them you're ill – but I'm not sure what to do about . . . I mean, I've said not to bother coming in for now but I'll have to let her know what's happening long-term. You don't have to decide straight away, not today or anything, but . . .'

'I'll have to let her go, won't I? There's no point in keeping her on when there's nothing to do. Tell her I'm sorry and we'll sort out some severance pay. I'll write to Elspeth or maybe I should see her. Do you think she'd come here?'

'I'm not sure.' Elspeth Coyle was Tom's accountant, a brusque Devonian woman with a sharp brain and a cool dry manner. 'And it might take a while to get organised. Perhaps I could go and see her instead.'

'You've got enough on your plate.'

'I don't mind. I'd rather keep busy.'

'You've got college, though. You won't stop going, will you?'

'No, of course not,' she said, pushing aside the thought of the essay she hadn't even started.

'Promise me. Don't let this whole mess screw things up for you too.'

94

'I won't. I swear.'

Tom buried his head in his hands for a moment. 'Jesus, you don't deserve any of this.'

'And you do?'

'It's going to be harder for you. You may not think so now but . . . you'll have all the questions to answer, people calling, and when it goes to trial . . . '

'It won't,' Eden said quickly. 'It won't go that far. We'll get you out of here before then.'

'And what about money? How are you going to manage if I'm not working? There's a couple of thousand in the current account but that's not going to last for ever. You'll have to talk to Elspeth about it; she should be able to transfer some from the business.'

'I can manage. Don't worry. You don't need to stress about that stuff. All you should be thinking about is how you ended up in here and why. Someone's stitched you up and if it isn't Jack Minter . . . I mean, who even knew the bracelet was in the safe?'

Tom sucked in a breath while he raised and dropped his hands. 'Hardly anyone. I suppose Annabelle could have seen it; she's got stuff out for me occasionally, but she's never mentioned it. And there was Denny. That was a few years back when I flogged my old Leica. Oh, and Fiona was there too, but neither of them can have anything to do with this.'

Although Eden wasn't overly fond of Denny's wife – a thin, gossipy woman who could dig up a scandal in a room full of angels – she had to agree. 'No, I guess not. But did you tell them where you got it from?'

'Yeah, I think so. In fact, Fiona took quite a fancy to it. She tried it on, even offered to buy it off me.' Tom shook his head. 'Christ, I made a big mistake there, didn't I?'

'Why didn't you sell it?'

95

'I don't know. Sentimental reasons, I suppose. It reminded me of Hungary, of Budapest. I didn't need the cash so ...' He raised his eyes to the ceiling and sighed. 'There you go, the penalties of sentiment. I'll know better in the future. Next time, remind me to take the money and run.'

'I will.'

They looked across the table at each other and smiled. Tom reached out and took her hands in his again, linking his fingers between hers. 'It isn't fair. You never signed up for all this.'

'Actually, I think I did. I believe the exact words were "For better or for worse" so I guess I'm stuck with you. And vice versa.'

The rest of the visit passed too quickly and suddenly the prison officers were announcing time. Eden looked at her watch, shocked that the allotted two hours had already run out. Their second embrace was as fleeting as the first, and made more poignant by the fact that this one meant goodbye.

'Take care,' she said, trying to keep a smile on her face. 'I'll see you soon. I'll write.'

Before she knew it, Eden was back in another queue and filing out of the room with the rest of the visitors. It broke her heart to leave. If she could have rushed back into his arms, she would, but that, apparently, was against the rules. She was allowed only one last backwards glance, another smile, a wave, before it was all over.

Eden trudged across the open courtyard, barely aware of the snow that was still falling. Weariness had descended on her. Her shoulders were hunched and a thin ache ran the length of her spine. She knew she had to remain optimistic – this was only the start of the battle – but it was impossible not to feel dispirited. How long would he be here for? She glanced up at the high walls and sighed.

Tammy caught up with her at the lockers and gave her a sympathetic smile. 'It's always tough the first time. You okay?'

Eden nodded. 'Yeah, I'm fine. It's him I'm worried about.' She took out her coat and put it on. Unable to keep her fears to herself, she suddenly blurted out, 'What if something happens to him? What if he just gives up and—'

'You can't think that way, love. You'll drive yourself mad. And he'll be all right. I've told Pete to keep an eye on him – he owes me for all these damn visits I have to make – and he'll show him the ropes, tell him what's what.'

Eden gave her a grateful smile. 'Really? Doesn't he mind?'

'Why should he? It's not as though he's got anything better to do. He knows what it's like when you first go in; it takes a while to get used to things.'

'Thanks. That's really good of you.'

Tammy gave a dismissive wave of her hand. 'We've all got to help each other, haven't we? It's the only way to get through these times.' She took her bag out of the locker, threw it over her shoulder and shut the door. 'You take care, hon. Maybe I'll see you next week.'

Eden, remembering what Tammy had told her about having to catch two buses, came to a quick decision. 'Would you like a lift home? I've got the car. It's no trouble.'

Tammy looked surprised. 'You don't have to do that.'

'I don't mind. Shoreditch isn't that far from me and it will save you having to wait around. Come on, it's the least I can do.'

'Well, if you put it like that. Thanks. You're a star. Those buses are a nightmare, especially in weather like this. A bit of snow and they all go into hiding. Can't say I was looking forward to freezing to death.'

The two women took their locker keys to the desk and retrieved their deposits. They walked out of the door and along the short path. It was as they stepped on to the street that a man suddenly appeared and planted himself directly in front of Eden.

'Excuse me. Are you Eden Chase?'

Eden stared back at him, startled. The man was in his late twenties, skinny and pale, with an almost feverish expression on his face. 'Who are you?'

'Jimmy Letts, the *Hackney Herald*. Is it true that your husband has been charged with the murder of Paddy Lynch?'

'W-what?' Eden stammered.

'Paddy Lynch,' he repeated. 'I've heard he left him to die in the back of a van. How do you feel about that?

Eden could feel the blood draining from her face. 'Tom is innocent. He didn't do it.'

'So you're standing by him? Is that the situation? Even though he's an armed robber? How do you feel about—'

Tammy shoved her face into the reporter's and snarled, 'How she feels is none of your fuckin' business. Just leave her alone, okay?'

'All I'm doing is—'

'I know what you're fuckin' doing, you filthy little creep. Just shift your skinny arse and get the hell out of our way or we'll have you for harassment.' And then before Jimmy Letts could respond, she grabbed hold of Eden's arm and started dragging her along the street. 'Don't say another word to him, hon. He's scum. Whatever you say, he'll twist it around.'

Eden's legs had gone weak at the knees and her head was spinning. The press! Christ, she hadn't even thought about the papers. Not properly. And not like this. She'd never expected to be accosted in public. As she stumbled along beside Tammy, her guts were doing somersaults. She felt sick, overwhelmed. Just when she'd thought it couldn't get any worse, it had.

15

Jimmy Letts slid into the driver's seat of the clapped-out Cortina and turned to his passenger. 'You get some decent shots of her?'

'Yeah, a few. She didn't look best pleased. Think you must be losing your charm, Jimmy. What do you reckon? Did she know what Tom Chase did before she married him?'

Jimmy shrugged as he pulled his seatbelt across. He didn't much care one way or the other. What he was after was a juicy story and this one had all the makings of a classic: an attractive redhead, a psychopathic husband, and a murder. He smacked his lips at the prospect. 'Sex and death. You can't beat it. We're on to a winner here. When do you think you can have those snaps ready?'

Colin Preston winced at the question, his lips pursing together. 'They're not snaps, Jimmy. I don't take "snaps".'

'Okay, keep your knickers on. Pictures, then, photos, works of bleedin' art – whatever you want to call them. You'll bring them round tomorrow, yeah?'

'I'll see what I can do.'

'And not a word to anyone, right? We've got a head start on this one. If we play it smart, we'll be looking at an exclusive.'

'I know the score. You don't need to spell it out.'

Jimmy started the car, but the engine immediately stalled. 'Bloody thing,' he muttered. It took another two attempts before the Cortina finally decided to cooperate.

'You should get yourself a new motor. This heap of scrap is on its last legs.'

'You prefer to walk, then? I can stop here if you like, or drop you off at the bus stop.'

Colin Preston scratched the back of his neck and grinned. 'Okay, okay, just saying, that's all. No need to be touchy. No need to bite my head off.'

Jimmy knew he was trying to rile him because of what he'd said about the snaps. Tit for tat. Preston was a pain in the arse at times. As if he needed reminding that he was driving around in a heap of junk. How the hell was he supposed to afford anything better on the salary he got? What he needed was a break, a chance to make a proper name for himself, and he wasn't going to get that working on the *Hackney Herald*.

'You need to relax, Jimmy. You're all wound up.'

'Maybe that's down to the company I'm keeping.' Jimmy tapped out a restless beat on the steering wheel. He was on edge, hyped up. What if some other reporter caught on to the story and beat him to it? He was pretty sure he was on his own at the moment, but in this game it could all change in the blink of an eye.

'You'll give yourself a heart attack, mate.'

Jimmy ignored him and stared out through the windscreen at the long line of traffic edging its way forward through the snow. The wipers swept back and forth, making an ugly scraping sound against the glass. He thought about his job at the *Herald*, seven tedious years of council meetings, summer fairs and Nativity plays. And nothing was going to change unless he made it change.

'So what next?' Colin asked.

'We sit on it for now. I've still got people to see.'

In truth, Jimmy had been hoping to get more out of Eden. Sometimes shock did that to a person; they spoke before they thought, spewing out all kinds of shit: a few good quotes to scatter through the story. He would have got more if the other girl hadn't interfered – she was a piece of work, that one – pushing her face into his, and dragging Eden away before she'd had the chance to say anything more than her husband was innocent.

Jimmy gave a snort. Innocent? That was a joke. He'd heard a whisper about a deal, about some old lag turning Queen's evidence and putting Tom Chase right in the frame. It would be a few months yet before it came to trial, but he couldn't afford to sit on his laurels.

He gave Colin a quick sideways glance. 'You ever come across this Tom Chase before, then?'

'Why should I?'

'I dunno. You're both in the business of taking photos. Don't you lot ever get together?'

'Sure,' Colin replied drily. 'All the photographers of London meet up for lunch every third Sunday of the month. We have a nice little chat and show each other our pictures.'

Jimmy raised his eyes to the heavens. 'I was only asking. Thought your paths might have crossed, that's all.'

'Well, they haven't. What he does, portraits and the like, that's a whole different ball game.'

'More upmarket, you mean?'

'Different, is what I mean. He ponces about in a studio all day; I go out and about, dealing with real life.'

'On the mean streets, huh?'

Colin gave him a look. 'You're not exactly living the high life yourself.'

'Yeah, well, I'm working on that.' To date, Jimmy hadn't made much progress with digging the dirt on Tom Chase. The guy had only been on the scene a few years, but no one seemed to know where he'd come from. Usually you could piece together someone's history without much bother, but Chase hadn't left a trail. Still, that wasn't surprising. He'd hardly had a conventional career, making the leap from armed robber to fashionable photographer. You had to give the bloke credit just for the sheer damn nerve of it all.

'He must be raking it in,' Colin said, unable to keep the envy out of his voice. 'A studio in Covent Garden. Shit. How much does that cost? I bet he earns more in a day than I do in a month.'

Jimmy sniggered. 'He's earning sod all at the moment. Stuck behind bars, isn't he? And I don't reckon he'll be coming out any time soon. That guy's going down for a long stretch.'

'If he's guilty.'

'Course he's bloody guilty. I can smell it, mate. I can feel it right here.' Jimmy took his left hand off the wheel and lightly slapped his guts. 'Christ, this is going to be one hell of a story.'

Colin lit up a fag, took a drag and gazed thoughtfully at the road ahead. 'She's a looker, his missus. When he does go down, she won't have a problem finding someone else.'

'Thinking of applying for the post, are you?'

'You'd do her if you got the chance. Don't say you wouldn't.'

'Nah, I'm more of a blonde man myself. Redheads don't float my boat.'

'From what I've heard, anything with a pulse floats *your* boat.'

Jimmy shrugged. Sadly, he hadn't had a nibble in months. It wasn't so much a dry spell as a bleeding drought. And girls like Eden Chase never gave him a second glance – even if they were single. No, she was the type to look down her nose at a bloke like him. He had no real evidence for this but chose to believe it anyway. It made it easier to justify what he was about to do: he'd rip her apart if he had to – her story, as well as her husband's, was going to hit the headlines.

16

DI Vic Banner scratched his balls with his left hand while he lifted his pint with his right. He looked up at the clock. It was a quarter past seven; she was fifteen minutes late already. What was it with women and time? They'd be late for their own bleeding funerals. He gazed around the Soho pub, one of the quieter ones of the area, taking in the shabby furniture, the dark green carpet – pitted with fag burns – and the stained flock wallpaper. Behind the bar, the landlord stared morosely into space.

'Come on,' he muttered, hoping that the tart hadn't changed her mind. She'd better not have. Tomorrow he was seeing Eden Chase, and looking forward to it. He had the larger picture when it came to Tom, but what he needed was the detail. Knowledge was power and he intended to gather every scrap of information he could.

It was another ten minutes before she finally walked through the door, had a quick look round, spotted him, walked over and plonked herself down in the seat opposite to his.

'You're late,' he said.

'You're lucky I'm here at all. Have you seen it out there? I had to wait fuckin' ages for a bus.'

'So maybe you should have set off a bit earlier.'

She glanced around, wrinkling her nose. 'And what's with this place? Jesus, I've seen condemned buildings with more charm than this dump.'

'You said you wanted quiet. This is quiet.'

'This place has died and gone to hell.'

Vic drank some more of his pint and put the glass down. 'Tammy, love, much as I'd love to listen to you whining on all night, I've actually got things to do – so can you get to the point? How did it go today? Did you talk to her?'

'I'll tell you in a minute. How about a drink first? I'm spitting feathers here.'

Vic sighed and stood up. 'What do you want, then?'

'Vodka and tonic,' she said. 'You can make it a double.'

'I could, but I won't.' Vic went over to the bar, bought the drink and placed it on the table in front of her. 'So can we get on with it now?'

Tammy took a sip of the vodka. 'It went pretty good, yeah. You're now looking at Eden Chase's new best buddy. She even gave me a lift home. Not bad, huh? Reckon I did a brilliant job, even if I do say so myself.'

'And what did your new mate tell you, then? What did she say about Tom?'

'Only that he didn't do it.' Tammy gave a smirk. 'He's innocent, ain't he, like all the rest of them poor suckers in there.'

'You reckon she really believes that?'

'Hard to say. She might. She might not. There's things people know for sure, straight up, and there's things they know in the back of their minds but which they ain't never going to admit to.'

'Very profound. I didn't realise you were so full of wisdom, babe.'

Tammy glared at him. 'There's no need to take the piss.

105

Just because I never did much school or nothin', don't mean I'm stupid.'

'Yeah, yeah, I get the message. So is that it? She says he's innocent? It's hardly news, love. I already knew that.'

'She reckons he's been framed, that this guy who's accused him is just setting him up. Something about Budapest, a guy called Jack? And you haven't heard the best bit yet.' Tammy paused for dramatic effect, lifting the glass to take another swig of her drink. 'On the way out of the jail, yeah, this shitty hack come out of nowhere, gets right in her face and starts giving her the third degree about her old man. How does she feel about him being accused of murder, blah blah blah. Jesus, you should have seen her. She was freaked out, no kidding. She didn't have a clue what to do so I jumped in and told him to sling his hook.'

'You get a name?'

'Jimmy,' she said. 'Betts or Letts, something like that. Said he worked for the *Herald*.'

Vic shook his head. 'Never heard of him.'

'Bit weird-looking, kind of sweaty. Anyway, the thing is she trusts me now. That's good, ain't it? And she says she'll pick me up next Thursday so I'll talk to her some more then. I mean, it's going to take a while, yeah? She's not the type to tell you everything straight off.'

Vic was quietly pleased, although he took care not to show it. 'You've done okay,' he said. 'It's a start. What about Pete?'

Tammy made a gagging gesture, raising two fingers to her throat. 'Where did you find that bloke? Jesus, that was the longest two hours of my life. He's not what you'd call a laugh a minute, is he? And by the way, if he wants Tom to believe I'm his sister, then staring at my tits for the entire visit probably isn't the best way to do it.'

'Give the guy a break. He hasn't seen a pair in months.'

Vic's gaze slid down to her chest and her more than adequate cleavage. 'You probably put him into shock.'

'He needs to learn some manners.'

'Has he got anything on Tom yet?'

Tammy leaned back and crossed her legs. 'He says he's working on it although I wouldn't hold your breath. Reckons Chase keeps himself to himself, that he's the quiet sort. I don't think he's too happy – Pete, that is – about pumping him for information.'

'Yeah, well, it's all relative, isn't it? I shouldn't think he'd be too happy about a three-stretch either. I mean, shit, I'm not asking him to fuck the guy, just suss out what he's thinking. I reckon that's a small price to pay for what he's getting in return.'

'You're all heart.'

'Just doing my job, love.' Vic leaned forward and gave her a look. 'Maybe the lad needs a bit more encouragement.'

'And what's that supposed to mean?'

'That you should try being nicer to him.'

Tammy barked out a laugh. 'You're kidding, right? No way. That was never part of the deal.'

'The deal is whatever I say it is, sweetheart.' Vic paused, his eyes turning cold and nasty. 'How is that kid of yours, by the way? She must be . . . what, four or five by now? Be a shame if someone called the Social, tipped them the wink about what her mother does for a living. I've heard they frown on that kind of thing. Very narrow-minded, the Social; God knows what they might do.'

Tammy flinched, her face turning pale. 'You keep her out of this.'

'Of course I will – so long as you stick to your side of the bargain. Don't get cute with me, Tammy, because you're the one with everything to lose. I need information on Tom and

Eden Chase, so you'd better get that brain into gear. I want to know what's going on inside their heads, what they're thinking, what they're doing – anything that could screw up this case when it goes to trial. I don't want any nasty surprises.'

Tammy pushed out her lower lip and pouted. 'What about my money?'

Vic pulled out a twenty from his wallet and slapped it on the table.

'A score? You said thirty. You promised I'd get thirty.'

'You'll get the rest when you give me something useful. Look on it as a down payment. Although if you don't think you're up for the job . . . '

Tammy snatched the note, shoved it in her pocket and quickly rose to her feet. She leaned down and hissed at him, 'You know what you are, Vic Banner? You're a fuckin' shit!'

Vic grinned back at her. 'I'll take that as a compliment.'

He watched as she flounced out of the pub, her bright blonde hair swinging from side to side. She'd come up with the goods – he was sure of it. Eden Chase would be putty in her hands. In truth, he wasn't holding out much hope when it came to Tom; he was too smart to spill his guts to a nobody like Pete Conway. But the wife was a different matter. Divide and rule was Vic's preferred MO. If he could drive a wedge between the couple, it would leave Tom isolated. Yeah, all he had to do was plant a few seeds of doubt and she'd work the rest out for herself.

'Eden, babe,' he murmured, 'I'm about to screw with your pretty little head.'

17

By the time Eden had dropped off Tammy and made her way back to Islington, it had been almost six o'clock. She didn't like driving in the snow at the best of times, and this certainly hadn't been one of them. It had been a treacherous stop-start journey with poor visibility and icy roads. She'd been relieved when she'd finally got home to Pope Street with the car still in one piece and only her nerves in shreds.

Now, two hours later, she was still mulling over her visit with Tom. It was what had happened afterwards, however, that was occupying most of her thoughts. The confrontation with the reporter had knocked her for six. She'd known – of course she had – that eventually it would all become public, but somehow she'd imagined that this wouldn't be until the trial began. Months and months away. And that's if there ever was a trial. She was still clinging to the hope that the police would realise their mistake, drop the charges and let Tom go.

Eden flinched as the voice of Jimmy Letts echoed in her head: *Is it true that your husband has been charged with the murder of Paddy Lynch?* She hadn't been prepared, not in the slightest. The man had come out of nowhere, firing his questions at her. *How do you feel?* How was she supposed to answer that? If it hadn't been for Tammy, she wasn't sure what she'd have done. Probably said all kinds of stupid things that could have been twisted and turned and taken out of context.

Eden had lived in London for over eight years and up until now had thought of herself as relatively worldly, relatively streetwise. But the truth was she was neither. She had no idea how to handle things. Faced with the dreadful reality of the situation – if there was one journalist on her heels, there could be a lot more following behind – her instinctive reaction was to run away and hide. But there was nowhere to run to.

Eden gazed down at her plate. After coming home, she'd opened the fridge to find nothing more than milk, eggs, cheese and butter. She couldn't face going out again to shop so, using the only ingredients available, had made herself an omelette. Knowing that she had to eat, she forced down a couple of mouthfuls, but her appetite had gone. The food was dry and tasteless. She put down the fork and pushed the plate away.

For a while she stared blankly at the black square of the window, watching the snowflakes fall against the glass. Without Tom, the flat felt empty and soulless. She didn't think she would ever get used to his absence. There was a hole in the centre of her life that couldn't be filled by anyone or anything else. Memories flooded into her head: hot sunny days in Florence, walking hand in hand along dusty streets, a cool hotel room with white tangled sheets. If only she could turn back time. She'd sell her soul to be back in Italy again.

Suddenly the front doorbell rang and Eden jumped. She might have ignored it if the lights hadn't been on. Whoever was there must know she was in. But what if it was that reporter? There was no way she was talking to him again. Jumping up, she went over to the window and looked down on to the short path.

Denny and Fiona Fielding were standing near the front door, both gazing up at the window. They gave her a wave and she waved back. Now she had no choice but to answer the door. Eden painted on a smile as she traipsed down the stairs. The last thing she wanted was company but she could hardly turn them away.

Fiona was apologetic as Eden opened the door. 'Hi there. Sorry to turn up unannounced like this, only we were just passing and . . . well, we wanted to see how you were. We've been really worried. How are you doing? Are you all right?'

As Eden stood back to let them in, she suspected that Fiona's interest was more to do with gathering gossip than any real concern for her welfare. 'I'm okay, thanks. Come on up.'

'We tried to ring earlier but you didn't answer and then we saw the light on so . . . We're not disturbing you, are we?'

'No, of course not. It's fine. I've been out all day; I went to see Tom. I just got back a while ago.'

'It's shocking all this,' Denny said. 'I still can't get my head around it.'

Back inside the flat, Eden pulled the curtains across and offered her visitors a drink. While she was making coffee, Fiona came into the kitchen, leaned against the counter and started to fire questions at her. How was Tom? How was he coping? What was the prison like? How often could she see him? What was the latest on the case? Was he likely to get out soon?

'Give her a break,' Denny said, appearing at the door. 'The poor girl doesn't need you giving her the third degree.'

Fiona threw him a look as if to tell him to shut up. 'All I'm doing is—'

'I know exactly what you're doing.'

'It's okay,' Eden said, before they got into a row. The two of them were renowned for public bickering. 'I don't mind, honestly.' This wasn't true, but she knew she wouldn't get Fiona off her back until her curiosity had been satisfied.

Once the coffee was made, they all sat down in the living room. Eden provided a quick summary of what had happened to date, told them Tom was doing as well as could be expected and that his brief was working on getting him out. 'I just want to get the name of this man and find out why he's accusing Tom.'

Denny leaned forward, placing his hands on his knees. 'This is what I don't get. How can he be put in jail when there's no evidence? I mean, yeah, you can put someone in the frame, I get that, but the police can't just bang someone up on someone else's say so. If that was the case anyone could accuse anyone and we'd all be behind bars.'

Eden took a deep breath, knowing that she couldn't keep the truth from them any longer. 'But that's the problem, they think they have got evidence. When they did a search of the studio, they found a bracelet in the safe. They claim it came from the robbery back in 'sixty-six. It was actually given to Tom when he was in Budapest – a guy called Jack Minter gave it to him in lieu of some money he owed – but the police don't believe that.'

'Minter? Isn't that the name you asked me about?'

'Yeah, that's the one. The police say Tom was using that name when he organised the robbery. For all we know the real Jack Minter could be the one making all these accusations. We haven't been told who it is yet. Tom doesn't think so, but I'm not so sure.' Eden rubbed at her face, a wave of fatigue washing over her. 'God, it's like being in the middle of some weird surreal nightmare. It doesn't make any sense. The police have built up this whole case against him, they're convinced he's guilty and . . . We've just got to find a way of proving that he isn't.'

'It's like *The Prisoner*,' Denny said. 'Do you remember that? It's the one where—'

'Denny!' Fiona said, glaring at him. 'This isn't some bloody TV show. What's the matter with you?'

'All I meant was that it *feels* like that. You know, when you don't understand what's really going on, when everything's all tangled up and confused, and someone else is pulling all the strings but you don't know exactly who that person is.'

'Well, that's clear as daylight,' Fiona said sarcastically.

Denny looked at Eden again. 'So has Tom figured out where he was in 'sixty-six yet?'

'Yes, and it's not good. He's pretty sure he was in London in November, which puts him in exactly the wrong place at exactly the wrong time.'

'Along with millions of other people,' Denny said.

'Yes, but millions of other people don't have a stolen brace-let in their possession.' Eden glanced at Fiona. 'And it's *that* bracelet. Do you remember it? The one you wanted to buy?'

Fiona stared blankly back at her. 'What?'

'You know, the gold one, shaped like a snake with gemstones in it.'

Fiona shook her head. 'I don't know what you're talking about. I've never seen any bracelet.'

'Yes, you tried it on in the studio. Tom told me. It was when he was selling the camera to Denny.'

'No,' Fiona said. 'It wasn't me. It definitely wasn't. I'd have remembered something like that.'

Eden saw the two of them exchange a glance. Something passed between them, but she wasn't sure what. 'Not recently,' she said. 'A few years ago.'

113

But Fiona continued to shake her head. Her face took on a tight, pinched expression and her voice rose by an octave. 'He must be getting mixed up. I wasn't there, Denny, was I? I don't have a clue about any bracelet.'

'No, I can't say I remember that. Tom has sold me a couple of cameras in the past but . . . No, I don't think Fiona was ever there and I can't recall seeing a bracelet. He must be thinking of someone else.'

Eden nodded. 'Okay. It doesn't really matter.' Although she wondered if it did. Fiona's reaction seemed odd and jumpy, as if she was trying to hide something. 'He must have got it wrong.'

Denny quickly changed the subject. 'This Minter guy sounds like the key to it all. You got any idea why he'd want to frame Tom like this?'

'To save his own skin?' Eden suggested. 'I don't know. All I do know is that the two of them met in Budapest in 'sixty-seven, a year after the robbery. Tom must have told him stuff about himself, information this guy is now using against him.'

Fiona cocked her head and gave her husband a thin smile. 'You were in Budapest in the sixties, weren't you, love?'

Denny gave a start and glared at her. 'What?'

'You've been to Budapest.'

'What the hell are you talking about? I've never been to Hungary in my life. Bonn, not Budapest. Jesus, woman, don't you ever listen to a word I say?'

Fiona raised her eyebrows and gave a shrug. 'If you ever said anything interesting, I might be more inclined to listen.'

'I don't know where you get these ideas.'

'I could have sworn you said Budapest.'

Eden listened to the two of them with dull resignation. Even if the world was falling in – and hers was – they would somehow find a way to have a row about it. They were both in their forties and she wondered how they'd managed to

114

stay together for so long when they never seemed to agree on anything. And Fiona wasn't the type to even try to hide her disappointment – in her life, her marriage, even in her children, who had not turned out to be quite as talented or clever as she'd once hoped they might be.

'What would I have been doing there?' Denny snapped.

'How would I know? Your reasons for doing most things are beyond me.'

Eden stepped in to try and diffuse the situation. 'I'm worried about the studio. I'm going to have to lay Annabelle off. I don't like to put anyone out of a job but there's nothing for her to do at the moment.'

'I wouldn't lose any sleep over that one,' Fiona said. 'She wouldn't think twice if the boot was on the other foot.'

'What's wrong with Annabelle?' Denny said.

Fiona raised her eyes to the ceiling. 'Well, you would defend her, wouldn't you? Anything in a skirt.'

'Oh, don't start all that again. What's wrong with being civil to people?'

'There's a difference between being civil and being a boring old lech.'

Eden sipped her coffee and hoped she could get rid of them soon. 'There was a reporter waiting when I got out of the prison today, a bloke from the *Herald*.'

Fiona and Denny stopped their mutual sniping and looked over at her.

'What did he want?' Denny asked.

'The inside story on how I feel about my husband being locked up for murder.'

'Shit,' Denny said. 'Those hacks are bloody pariahs. I hope you told him where to go.'

'Yes, but he's not going to stay away, is he? He's going to keep coming back until he gets what he wants.'

115

'How dreadful,' Fiona said, although her tone was more inquisitive than sympathetic. 'That's the last thing you need. Fancy being splashed all over the front cover of the *News of the World*. It doesn't bear thinking about.'

'It's not the bleeding *News of the World*,' Denny said. 'It's just some local rag. And you saying that kind of stuff isn't helping any.'

'It's all right,' Eden said quickly before the two of them could start up again. 'I'm just hoping they don't run with a story any time soon. With luck, we can get Tom out of jail before they go to print. I mean, it's all so ridiculous. I'm sure we'll come up with something soon, something that's going to prove he didn't do it.'

Although Denny and Fiona both smiled and nodded their encouragement, they didn't look entirely convinced. She could tell from their eyes that they thought the chances were slim and her optimism misplaced.

'You should call the police if he keeps hassling you,' Denny said. 'It's harassment, isn't it?'

Eden thought of DI Banner, her nose instantly wrinkling. 'I've had enough of the police, thank you very much.'

'Do you think this reporter knows where you live?' Fiona asked.

'I don't imagine it'll take him long to find out.'

'Maybe you should move out for a while,' Denny said. 'If they can't find you, they can't cause you grief.'

Fiona nodded her agreement. 'Yes, why don't you stay with friends for a week or two?' She paused, tugged at the hem of her skirt and then made an awkward fluttering gesture with her hand. 'I mean, we'd invite you to come to us, but there isn't really room, not with the boys and all. And not much peace and quiet either; they're in and out at all times of the day and night.'

Eden was neither surprised nor offended by the lack of an invitation – the Fieldings had always been more Tom's friends than hers – and on balance she'd rather face a horde of reporters than live in the middle of a war zone. 'That's okay. To be honest, I don't want to go anywhere else. This is my home and I'm going to stay in it.'

'Good for you,' Fiona said.

'Although you're always welcome,' Denny added, 'if you need a bolthole.'

Fiona smiled thinly. 'Of course you are.'

Ten minutes later, with the coffee drunk, Eden finally showed them out. There was a polite if slightly stiff exchange – 'Do let us know if there's anything we can do to help,' 'Thank you, I will' – before they said their goodbyes, promising to keep in touch. She heaved a sigh of relief as she closed the door and headed back upstairs.

In the flat, she walked over to the window, pushed the edge of the curtain aside and peered down at the road. The snow was still falling, although not with its earlier vigour, the pale flakes drifting through the orangey glow of the street lamps. The Fieldings were walking towards their car and she could tell from their body language that they were arguing again. Fiona's hands jerked up and down like a marionette's. Denny's shoulders were hunched, his chin set deep in the collar of his coat.

As Eden watched them, she replayed the last twenty minutes in her head. She had one of those niggling feelings that nothing had been quite as it seemed. Not so much a friendly visit as a recce, she thought. But was that down to Fiona's insatiable desire for gossip or something more sinister? Maybe she was getting paranoid, but all her instincts told her that something was wrong.

The thing about the bracelet was odd. Tom didn't usually make mistakes like that, although in his current state of mind and with everything that had happened he could have got confused. She made a mental note to ask about it next time she saw him. And then there was the stuff about Budapest. Had Denny been there or not? She would ask Tom about that too.

As the Fieldings got into their car, Eden dropped the curtain and sat down at the table. The conversation continued to revolve in her head. Were they hiding something or just trying to distance themselves from any hint of scandal? Perhaps, despite all their words of support, they had started to have doubts about Tom's innocence. She recoiled at the thought. If his close friends didn't believe in him, who would? There could come a time when his future would be decided by twelve complete strangers, a jury who might listen to the lies of a villain, who might not be able to see past the web of deceit. And what then? She closed her eyes, unwilling and unable to think about it.

18

The next morning, reluctant to brave the icy roads again, Eden left the car at home and took the Tube into the West End. At precisely five to eleven, she went into the police station, asked for DI Banner and was told to take a seat. She sat down on one of the hard plastic chairs and waited, watching the people come and go in the foyer. The minutes ticked by. The snow melted off her boots and formed a tiny puddle at her feet. Still Banner didn't show his face. It was a ploy, perhaps, to make her more nervous than she already was.

The first time she'd met the inspector – a less than pleasant experience – he'd turned up out of the blue at the studio and taken her by surprise. But this time she was prepared. She had already decided on her plan of action. Logic and reason were the only way forward; she would make him see that Tom wasn't capable of the crime he was accused of. She would be cool, clever and calmly persuasive. She wouldn't lose her rag and she wouldn't say anything she might later regret.

By the time twenty minutes had passed, Eden's resolve was starting to fray. It was hard to stay calm and collected when your nerves were strung so tight they were on the point of snapping. Every time a door opened, she jumped a little. All around her the wheels of the law were turning. She took slow, deep breaths. Her heart was beating too quickly. She felt trapped in the spokes of a giant machine, something solid and grinding and scarily relentless.

It was almost half an hour before Banner finally put in an appearance. He swaggered over to her with his hands in his pockets and a grin on his face. 'Sorry about the wait, love. Bit of a rush on this morning. You want to come this way?'

Eden followed him through a set of reinforced glass doors and along a corridor. Her impression of Banner wasn't improved by further acquaintance. The smell of sweat and fags floated in his wake, making her wonder how often he showered or even changed his clothes. The odour was partly overlain by a musky aftershave which was just as unpleasant as the smell he was probably trying to disguise.

They went into a small room, sparsely furnished with a table and four chairs, where he gestured for her to sit down.

'Grab a pew,' he said, placing a brown folder on the table. 'Can I get you a drink? Coffee, tea?'

Eden shook her head. 'No, thanks.'

Banner pulled out a chair and sat down opposite her. 'Okay. Well, I'll try not to keep you too long. This is just an informal chat, no tape or anything. You're free to leave at any time.'

Eden, who was starting to have second thoughts, was sorely tempted to take him up on the offer. Perhaps this wasn't such a good idea after all. Had she made a dreadful mistake? But no, she was here now, and nothing would be achieved by running away. She had to grab the opportunity to stand up for Tom before it was too late. She had to try and make this man see the truth.

She sat up straight, pushed her shoulders back and looked Banner directly in the eye. 'Tom is innocent,' she said. 'He's not an armed robber. He's not a criminal. You're in the process of destroying his life when he's done absolutely nothing wrong.'

Banner smiled indulgently at her. 'I respect your loyalty – and I understand it. But I'm afraid the evidence suggests otherwise.'

'And what evidence would that be? A stolen bracelet that was given to my husband and the word of a convicted criminal. Can't you see that this man is just trying to stitch Tom up?'

'And why would he do that?'

'For the obvious reason. If he can shift the blame for everything he did, he won't have to take the rap for it. He's turning Queen's evidence, right? But none of it is true. He's using Tom as a scapegoat.'

'And why pick on Tom?'

'Why not?' Eden replied. 'He obviously knows enough about him to make it all sound credible.' She leaned forward, placing her elbows on the table. 'I bet the man who's making all these accusations is the real Jack Minter.'

Banner shook his head. 'No chance.'

'And what makes you so sure?'

'Because that's not his name.'

Eden gave an exasperated sigh. 'But he could have used that name in the past.'

Banner inclined his head, a grin hovering on his lips. 'Well, he could have but he didn't. Let me explain. For one, our guy doesn't bear the slightest resemblance to the description your husband gave: he's twenty years older and six inches shorter. And for two, he's never been further than the Isle of Wight in his whole sorry life.'

Eden felt the sting of disappointment – so her theory about Minter had been wrong – but she tried not to let it show. 'How do I know you're telling the truth?'

Banner arched his eyebrows. 'I'm a cop, love. I never lie.'

Eden almost gave a snort but stopped herself just in time. 'So . . . so maybe the real Jack Minter told your guy all this stuff, told him about Tom and the bracelet and the rest. And now he's using it to frame my husband.'

'You don't think that sounds a little . . . er . . . far-fetched?'

'That doesn't mean it isn't true. And if Tom had committed this robbery and then left the country, why would he ever come back? He'd be free and clear, why take the risk?'

'You'd be surprised,' Banner said. 'Lots of them do. They get homesick. They miss the ordinary things like a decent pint of beer or a jar of Marmite. They want to see their families again or their friends or just be in familiar surroundings.' He glanced up towards the small snow-covered window set high in the wall. 'They even get tired of all that sun. Hard to believe, isn't it? But there you go. Sometimes the great escape isn't all it's cracked up to be.'

'Tom was never an armed robber,' Eden said firmly.

Banner ignored the comment. He flipped open the file, rifled through a thick sheaf of papers, pulled a couple of sheets out and laid them face down on the table. 'Let's talk about the studio.'

The change of tack took Eden by surprise. 'What about it?'

'Not cheap, is it, office space in Covent Garden? There's rent and rates, bills, wages and the rest. How can he afford it?'

'How do you think? By working hard, by putting in the hours. And by being good at what he does.'

'I wouldn't know about that. One photo looks much the same to me as another. He's had the studio for about four years, yeah?

'Yes.'

'Good, that's something we agree on. And before that he was travelling in Europe for quite a time, getting work where he could find it, flogging a few photos when he got the chance. Not exactly the way to make a fortune.' Banner scratched his forehead and assumed a puzzled expression. 'Now you see, this is what I don't get. Tom comes back to London and before you know it he's got himself a swanky studio in a prime location. How exactly do you think he managed that?'

Eden, who had never considered it before, gave what she hoped was a casual-looking shrug. 'Maybe he made more than you think.'

'Maybe he did.'

She stared at him. 'What are you suggesting? That the money came from the Epping robbery?'

'Did I say that?'

'You didn't need to. It's written all over your face.'

Banner touched his chin with his fingertips as if to check out the assertion. He smirked. 'Actually, what he told us was that he'd taken out a loan.'

Eden felt like she'd been wrong-footed and reddened slightly. But she quickly rallied, determined he wouldn't get the better of her. 'What's wrong with that? There's no law against it.'

'Of course not,' he agreed. 'Not if it comes from a reputable source.'

'What's that supposed to mean?'

'What it means is that Tom didn't go to his friendly neighbourhood bank. He claims he got the money from somewhere else – or rather someone else. A personal loan, if you like.'

'So?'

'He refused to tell us the name of his very generous benefactor. Said it was a private arrangement and none of our business.'

Eden stared at him through wary eyes. She didn't say anything.

'Did he ever discuss this with you?'

'No.'

'Really? And here was me thinking that the two of you were tight. I'd have thought he might have mentioned it.'

'Why would he? It all happened way before we even met.'

'And you're not bothered about how he funds his business or his lifestyle. Is that what you're saying?'

Eden glared at him. 'Don't put words in my mouth.'

Banner grinned. 'Just trying to get things clear.' He glanced around the room before his gaze came to rest on Eden again. 'Now the first thing that sprang into my head was some kind of loan shark. I mean, that's where people go when they haven't got good credit and need the cash in a hurry. And those guys, well, they're not keen on publicity; they prefer to keep a low profile. But then we checked through your husband's bank accounts, and guess what?'

Eden had a sinking feeling. She knew she wasn't going to like what was coming next. Her heart was beating with a dull anxious thump as she waited for the inspector to make his revelation.

Banner had a look of triumph as he turned over the top sheet of paper and slid it across the desk. 'Thirty thousand pounds,' he said. 'Transferred from an account in Munich to here.'

'So what?' Eden retorted, staring down at the statement. The relevant transaction was highlighted in yellow. She was startled by the amount but careful not to show it. 'Tom has friends all over the place. He must have borrowed the money from someone in Germany.'

'It was actually transferred from his own account in Munich. Were you aware he had an account there?'

Eden wasn't. 'He probably opened it while he was living abroad. That's not unusual, is it?'

'No, not at all. What is odd, however, is that he didn't bother to close it when he returned to London. You'd think once he was settled, once he had a business up and running, a home, a wife, there wouldn't really be a purpose for it any more.'

'He still goes abroad from time to time. I guess it's useful for that.'

Banner let a brief silence fall before continuing. 'So why would this "friend" put the money into the German account? Why not transfer it straight to England?'

Eden was beginning to feel less than comfortable. She hadn't been exactly calm when she'd entered the room and now she was more on edge than ever. She suspected that Banner was leading her into a trap and knew she had to be wary. 'I've no idea. Because it was easier? More straightforward?'

'They must have been a good friend.'

'People have them.'

'Do you have a name?' Banner asked.

'What?'

Banner sat back and folded his arms across a chest. 'Surely if this person was such a good mate – and trusting enough to lend your husband thirty grand – Tom must have mentioned him or her to you.'

Eden took a moment to think about her response. What she came out with was disingenuous but the best she could come up with. 'I don't think it's up to me to say. It's Tom's decision as to whether he tells you or not.'

'Not,' Banner said.

Eden gave a light shrug. 'Then I can't help you.'

Banner smiled at her, a snake's smile. 'Now why doesn't that surprise me?' He looked her up and down in much the same way as he'd done at the studio, his gaze lingering where it shouldn't.

Eden decided that she'd had enough. 'Well, if there's nothing else . . . ?'

'Actually, there was one other thing.' Banner flipped over the remaining sheets of paper, looked down, pretended to study them for a few seconds and then looked up at Eden again. 'We've gone through Tom's English bank accounts, personal and business, and guess what?'

Eden, who wasn't there to play guessing games, decided to keep quiet. She kept very still, her hands in her lap, her fingers tightly entwined. Only her eyebrows lifted slightly in the faintest gesture of a query.

'It's another of those oddities, but there don't seem to have been any repayments made. Not one in the last four years. Now I'm no expert or anything, but I believe the basic premise of a loan is that you eventually have to pay it back. A little or a lot, depending on the arrangement you come to, but always something. There's nothing going out of either of these accounts that could possibly be construed as any kind of repayment.'

'I'm sure there's an explanation,' Eden said, although she couldn't think of one off the top of her head. 'Maybe you've made a mistake.'

'You see, if I was an innocent man, trying to convince the police that I hadn't stashed a fortune from an armed heist sixteen years ago, I'd be doing my best to come up with a credible explanation. But your husband doesn't seem to share that point of view. In fact, if I recall correctly, his exact words were "No comment".'

'He must have his reasons.'

'And here's an even weirder thing,' Banner continued, piling on the pressure. 'A year ago, just before you got married, in fact, there was a further transfer from Munich of five grand. And hey, you know what's coming next – no repayments on

126

that either. So, either Tom has got a very generous benefactor – who doesn't care about when they get their money back – or he's not being entirely honest with us.'

'Well, I'm sorry,' Eden said, pushing back her chair and standing up, 'but I can't help you with any of that.' Her mouth felt dry, as if she hadn't had a drink in a week. She ran her tongue quickly over her lips. 'All I can say is that I know what Tom is and isn't capable of. He's a good man.'

'He's a rich man,' Banner said sneeringly.

Eden knew what he was implying, but didn't rise to the bait. She didn't care what he thought about her. It didn't matter. All she cared about was Tom. But now she had a sick feeling in the pit of her stomach because she knew there were things her husband hadn't told her.

'You need to have a good long talk with that old man of yours,' Banner said.

And with that, at least, Eden couldn't disagree. She left the room with as much dignity as she could muster, keeping her head held high even though her spirit was in tatters. She had come with the intention of putting Banner straight, of making him realise he'd got it all wrong, but was leaving with more questions than answers.

19

Max Tamer found a café down the road from the police station, bought a mug of tea, and sat down at a table by the window. There was steam on the glass and he wiped it off with the back of his hand. From here, with a good view of the entrance to West End Central, he could view everyone who went in and came out. If his own experiences were anything to go by, Eden Chase wouldn't be leaving in a hurry.

Even after three years, Max still had a bad taste in his mouth from all the hours he'd spent in those small stuffy rooms. When a wife goes missing, the number one suspect is always the husband. He understood that, but the vehemence with which they'd tried to prove his guilt had driven him almost to the edge: interviews that had been interrogations, the questions that went on and on. While he was grieving – he'd known that Anne-Marie was dead, felt it right in the depths of his soul – they had plunged in the knife and twisted it, provoking him, accusing him, challenging everything he said until all that remained was exhausted despair.

'Let's talk about Ann-Marie. She's younger than you, isn't she?'

Max had heard the underlying implication. Younger wife, jealous husband. Affairs, perhaps. Or just suspicions. 'She's thirty-three.'

The raised eyebrows above cold accusing eyes. 'Nine years. That's a bit of an age gap.'

But Max had never felt the difference. When you were older these things didn't matter so much. 'Is it?'

'And you've been married for how long?'

'Two years, just over two years.'

'And would you say it's a happy marriage?'

As if anyone under suspicion was likely to say no, that they argued and fought and hated each other. But he hadn't had to lie. 'Yes, it's happy, very happy.' The words, even as he uttered them, had seemed inadequate, too bland and overused to really describe the relationship and the strength of their feelings for each other.

'And your wife is French, yes?'

'She comes from Paris originally, but she's lived in England since she was twenty-four, twenty-five. She knows London well; she's been working here for years.'

'You don't think she could have gone back to France?'

'What?' Max had stared at the inspector with pure incredulity. 'My wife is *missing*,' he'd said with more force than he'd intended. 'She hasn't gone on holiday. She hasn't taken off on a whim. And she wouldn't have gone anywhere without telling me first.'

'Without your permission, you mean?'

'What are you talking about? Who said anything about permission?' Max had stopped to take a few deep breaths. He'd known he was being deliberately provoked, prodded and poked in the hope he'd let something slip. 'What I'm trying to explain is that we talk to each other. We call if we're going to be late home; we leave messages or write notes. She'd never want me to worry, just as I'd never want her to.'

'So would Ann-Marie normally come straight home from work?'

'There is no "normally". We both lead busy lives. Occasionally she has to stay late. Sometimes she meets up with friends for a meal or drinks. Sometimes she goes round to see my mother and sits with her for a while in the evening.'

'They get on, do they? Your wife and her mother-in-law?'

Max had experienced one of those weird, surreal, almost hysterical moments where he'd wondered what was going through the inspector's mind: was the man actually considering the possibility of a seventy-four-year-old woman disposing of her son's wife? 'They're very close,' he'd said eventually. 'They always have been.'

'But Ann-Marie hadn't mentioned any arrangements for Friday night?'

'No.'

'Okay, let's go over the day again, right from the moment you got up in the morning.'

Max stared out of the café window. With his elbows on the table and both his hands wrapped around the mug, he sipped the hot sweet tea while he revisited those interviews. They were engraved on his mind, carved so deeply into his consciousness that he could still repeat many of the exchanges word for word.

The inspector had been called Roberts, a tall stringy man with nut-brown eyes and fingernails bitten down to the quick. He'd deployed the usual technique of repeating most of his questions again and again, couching them in different words. The routine had been slick, a master class in interrogation. A less experienced suspect might have crumpled under the pressure, twisted himself into knots, stammered and stuttered and fallen apart, but Max had held his ground. He'd been army trained and with two tours of duty in Belfast under his belt, he'd learned to always be watching out for the sniper, for the bullet that could come from nowhere.

Max remembered the sheer frustration of it all. For as long as the police were focused on him, there were no other suspects and the investigation was at a dead end. Meanwhile, the man responsible was at liberty, free as a bird and with time to cover his tracks. Even when Max's alibi checked out, the law had remained reluctant to relinquish their suspicions; he might not have been physically responsible for Ann-Marie's disappearance, but that didn't mean he wasn't behind it.

Max gave a low, barely audible growl. There had been a time when he'd had respect for the police, but not any longer. The case was still open, unsolved, with nothing in the way of progress. The law had ceased to care about Ann-Marie Tamer; she'd been consigned to a file in a dusty basement. She was old news. And with nothing proved, he remained tainted by the suspicion of guilt. Not that he cared. He didn't give a damn about anything these days – other than finding out the truth.

His gaze flicked away from the station, making a fast survey of the inside of the café. There were only three other customers, two of them with their heads in newspapers, the other smoking a cigarette and gazing into space. It was one of the quieter parts of the day, that hiatus between breakfast and lunch. A song by The Jam, 'Town Called Malice', was playing on the radio. The coffee machine made a soft hissing noise.

Max put down the mug and flexed his fingers. His grey eyes narrowed as he let the memories flood back. His wife, his beautiful wife with her long, red-gold hair. He could see her as clearly as if she was standing in front of him, her head tilted back, her mouth widening into a smile. Two years of marriage. And they had been happy years, hadn't they? Occasionally doubt crept into his mind. He'd heard it said that in a relationship there is always one who loves more than the other, and if that was true then maybe he'd been that person.

It didn't matter, though. It didn't change the fact the marriage had worked. And perhaps that tiny bit of uncertainty had been what kept him on his toes and stopped him from becoming complacent. It would have been easy to start taking her for granted, but he'd never done that. Every morning, waking up beside her, he'd felt blessed.

They had met after Max left the army and set up a high-end personal security business, protection for the rich, the famous or the simply neurotic. It was surprising how many people wanted protection even if they didn't actually need it; it was a status symbol, perhaps, a self-important look-at-me kind of thing. But so long as they paid, he didn't give a toss about their motivation.

An American actor, over for a season at the Criterion Theatre in Piccadilly Circus, had been one such client. The guy was not well-known, in fact so far adrift from famous that Max could no longer recall his name. Only an impression remained of a smallish arrogant pug-faced man with tiny hands and feet. But anyway, that was how he had come to be at a West End theatre one morning, twiddling his thumbs while Mr America sat on stage and ran through his lines at an early rehearsal.

Max was used to being ignored when he was carrying out his duties, both by the client and by everyone else. The occasional nod, a vague smile, but on the whole he was made to feel invisible. That day people had been scurrying around, their hands filled with pages of dog-eared script, bits of scenery, props, plastic cups and endless bottles of water. Nobody had paid him any attention. He was like a piece of furniture, solid and immovable, not even human.

No one, that is, until Ann-Marie. She had scooted past, stopped suddenly and retraced her steps. 'Are you all right?'

she'd asked in that seductive Parisienne accent. 'It must be very tiring standing there for hours.'

Max had looked down on a slim, pretty woman with wide inquisitive eyes. 'You have no idea. Luckily, I'm in peak condition. A lesser man would probably collapse from the strain.'

'You don't get bored?'

'It depends on the company.'

She had peered around him, looking towards the American on stage. 'Is he in much danger, do you think?'

Max had grinned at her. 'Only from the audience. When the play opens.'

She had smiled too and put out her hand in a sweetly formal gesture. 'I'm Ann-Marie Allis, costume department.'

'Max Tamer. Guardian angel, protector of the good and righteous.'

She had shaken his hand, her gaze fixed on his face. 'Are you sure you're in the right place?'

'Oh, yeah,' he'd replied. 'Believe me, I've never been more sure.'

Max winced as he recalled that moment, the chance meeting that had changed his life for ever. It was painful to revisit the past, but that was why he did it. He had to keep the agony alive, to keep scratching away at any healing wounds. It gave him the impetus to carry on. Without the rage and bitterness, he would have no reason to get up in the morning.

He glanced over towards the door of the police station. How long had Eden been in there now? About half an hour, he reckoned. When he had driven over to Islington this morning, it had only been to check out the address, to take a look at the place where Tom and Eden Chase lived. He'd had no intention of following her.

After parking on the corner, Max had walked slowly down the street, his shoes crunching on the crisp white blanket of snow. He'd counted off the numbers until he came to twenty-four, a three-storey Victorian terrace conversion, red brick with a smart white trim. His gaze had shifted up to the first-floor flat with its wide window and dark blue curtains. He'd almost expected to see someone there, a face behind the glass, but there had been no one.

Not wanting to be spotted, Max hadn't lingered long. He had walked to the end of the street, where he turned around and retraced his steps. It was as he was approaching the house again that the front door opened and the girl with the long red hair stepped out. She was wearing a cream woollen coat, a pale green scarf and boots. Was it Eden Chase? He couldn't know for certain – all three flats must share the same entranceway – but he felt in his bones that it was.

Max had followed her on to Upper Street and from there to Angel Tube. She had bought a return ticket to Oxford Circus from the machine, and he had done the same. There had only been a short wait on the platform before the train roared in. He had sat at the far end of the carriage, well away from her, and had taken care not to look at her too much. It was odd how you could tell when someone's eyes were on you, a sixth sense that you were being watched.

At King's Cross, she'd changed on to the Victoria line and travelled a couple of stops to Oxford Circus. He had wondered if he was on a wild goose chase, tailing some random girl who had decided to go up West and spend the day shopping. It was only after she'd turned into Savile Row and walked into the police station that he had been sure of her identity.

Max sat back, let out a sigh, glanced at his watch and considered buying another mug of tea. But then he'd need to take a slash and it would be just his luck if she came out of the station at the precise moment he was emptying his bladder. Not that it really mattered. Chances were that she'd be going straight home again. But he wanted to see her face, her expression, after the police had put her through the wringer. He wanted to know how bad things were looking for her husband.

Tom Chase. The man was a pathological liar. Max cursed under his breath, thinking of all the time he had wasted. But Chase had been credible, convincing, he'd give him that. And Max hadn't taken much persuading; from the moment he'd set eyes on him, he'd been sure that this wasn't the bloke he was searching for. Now, looking back, he could see how easily he'd been fooled, and how he'd been blindsided by that bloody photograph.

But he was getting ahead of himself. With nothing else to do but wait, he may as well go through events in a methodical fashion. It was important, necessary, to keep everything in order, for it all to be perfectly clear. No more mistakes. He would put the pieces together like a jigsaw until the picture was complete.

It had been two months after his wife's disappearance when the woman had called out of the blue, a former colleague of Ann-Marie's who had been working abroad and only just heard the news. Her name was Katherine Standish. She'd been flustered, apologetic.

'It's probably nothing. I wasn't even sure I should ring. I don't want to ... I mean, you've got enough to deal with without ... '

It had taken Max a while to get the information out of her. 'Please. Anything could be useful.'

'It's just one of those things that stuck in my mind. It was my last day at work, the Friday, the same day Ann-Marie went missing. She went out at lunchtime to get a sandwich and when she came back she said ... Well, she told me that she'd bumped into an old friend from Budapest. She was saying what a coincidence it was, after all the years, strange, you know, that they should meet again like that.'

'Did she give you a name?'

'No, I don't think so. I've been racking my brains, but ... We were really busy and it was just one of those quick conversations.'

'What is a man or a woman?'

'I'm pretty sure it was a man. Yes, she definitely said "he".'

'And did she say whether she was going to see him again?'

'No, no, nothing like that. But they'd gone for a coffee together, for a catch-up, you know? She was a bit late back and ... she didn't say much more than that. I don't think so. We were rushing around trying to get the costumes sorted for the evening. She just seemed amazed, amused, to have bumped into him again.'

The first name that had sprung into Max's head was Tom Chase. The man Ann-Marie had fallen for at the age of twenty-one. The man she'd followed to Budapest from Paris. The man she'd described as 'the type who you know is bad for you but who you fall in love with anyway'.

By this time, having lost all faith in the police, Max was conducting his own investigation into Ann-Marie's disappearance. He had turned his back on the law and sought help from another source. Terry Street was a villain, a gangster, a man who operated outside the normal moral boundaries; he was part of the dark underbelly of London, a place of violence and shadows. If the good guys couldn't help, Max was more than prepared to do business with the bad.

It was Street who had put the word out, requesting information on Ann-Marie or Tom Chase. And it was Pym who had come up with the photographer in Covent Garden. With Drury Lane being within spitting distance of the piazza, Max was convinced that this must be the same Tom Chase that

Ann-Marie had bumped into, the same Tom Chase she had been in love with all those years ago.

He had gone through all her photographs and found the three black-and-whites from Hungary. Two of the pictures were of her with a couple of hippy-looking girls in the middle of a crowded market, the third of her sitting outside a café with a man. The guy was broad-shouldered, dark-haired with a rather arrogant expression. His head was inclined to one side, his arm around Ann-Marie's shoulder. On the back of the picture she had written simply: *Budapest*.

Max had stared at the photograph for a long time. He had stamped the image of the man on his brain. But he still hadn't come close to understanding. It had crossed his mind – of course it had – that after Chase and Ann-Marie had met again, something had been rekindled between them, a spark, a fire, and then ... But then what? She'd agreed to meet him that evening, had run off with him without a word? Decided to ditch her marriage, to throw away everything they'd built up?

No sooner had the thought entered his head than he was engulfed by shame. To even think about her doing such a thing was a betrayal of their whole relationship. No, it would have been Chase who had wanted more, who had wanted her back, and when she'd refused to go along with it ...

Max had stood for a long time in the piazza at Covent Garden, staring up at the studio window. He'd craved a drink, something to take the edge off, but had resisted the urge. He needed to be lucid, to be thinking straight. One foot in front of the other. Stay calm and in control. Think. Breathe. Preparation was everything. Across the square, past the church. Eleven more steps until he reached the door. As he pressed the buzzer, he knew he could be on the brink of coming face to face with his wife's murderer.

A woman's voice, smooth, upper-class. 'Hello?'

'I'm here to see Tom Chase.'

'Come on up. It's the first floor.'

A click as the door opened. Max had walked through the red-carpeted hallway and climbed the stairs with grim determination. He could have passed the information about Chase on to the police, but his trust in them had long since been destroyed. No, this was something he had to do himself. He wanted to look into the man's eyes, into his soul, and see the darkness that was there.

The receptionist was a sultry brunette. She smiled as Max approached the desk, a professional smile that didn't stretch further than her red-lipped mouth. 'Good afternoon. How can I help?'

'You can't,' he'd replied abruptly. 'I want to see Tom Chase.'

The smile had faded at his tone. 'Do you have an appointment?'

Max had ignored the question. 'Where is he?' Glancing around, he'd spotted the closed door that must lead through to the studio and made a beeline for it. By now the adrenalin was streaming through his body. He was pumped up and ready to beat the truth out of Chase if he had to.

The receptionist was instantly on her feet. 'Hold on. You can't go in there. You can't just—'

But Max was already through the door, only seconds away from a confrontation that could change everything. He was coiled, ready to pounce. What he saw, however, pulled him up short. The only other man in the room, currently in the process of setting up a camera, was definitely not the man in the photograph. He was a sleek, fair-haired bloke, a completely different physical type. Max stared at him. 'Are you Tom Chase?'

The man gave a nod. 'That's me.'

The receptionist barged in behind Max, her high heels clicking angrily on the wood floor. 'I'm sorry, Tom. He wouldn't wait. I tried to stop him but—'

'It's all right, Annabelle. I'll deal with it.'

And after Annabelle had retreated, throwing a withering scowl in the direction of the intruder, Tom Chase had dealt with it. Not even a flicker when Max mentioned Ann-Marie's name. A small shake of his head. A swift but calm denial that he'd ever known her. And when it came to Budapest . . .

'Ah, is that in Romania or Hungary? I always get those two mixed up. Budapest and Bucharest. But no, I've never been to either.'

By this time, Max had been convinced that he had the wrong man anyway. The disappointment had been almost too much to bear. He had left the studio, apologising for the interruption. Chase had been pleasant, even charming about it.

'Don't worry. I understand the confusion with the same name and everything. I hope you find her.'

Max's hands curled into two tight fists on the café table. It was all down to that damn photograph. Ann-Marie had never told him that the man in the picture was Chase, but he had simply made the presumption. Now he realised he'd been wrong. Tom Chase, perhaps, was the one who'd actually taken the photograph.

He wondered how Pym had found out about Chase and the Budapest connection, but there was no point in asking. Street's lackey guarded his sources with fervour, keen to keep his contacts to himself. Someone in the Force, perhaps? But at least Max knew now that Tom Chase had lied to him. And there could only be one reason for that.

Max's biggest regret was that he hadn't done some further digging. He was still cursing his stupidity when the door to West End Central opened and Eden Chase walked out. Quickly he rose to his feet and left the café. He kept her in his sights, but at a distance, knowing she was probably going to the Tube station. Her head was bowed, her shoulders slumped. Clearly things had not gone well with the boys in blue.

On the train, Eden stared at the floor for the entire journey. Her long red hair fell around her face like a curtain, preventing him from reading her expression. What was she thinking? That she had married a no-good murdering bastard – or that the cops had got it wrong? No matter how damning the evidence, some women would go on defending their men until hell froze over.

Max looked away but then glanced along the length of the carriage again. Despite himself, he couldn't keep his eyes off her. It was the hair, he thought, the hair that was almost the same colour as Ann-Marie's. But that was the only similarity. Eden – it was a strange kind of name. The garden where Eve tempted Adam, where a single bite of an apple proved to be a snack too far when it came to the fate of the human race.

Max gave a quick shake of his head. He wasn't going to think about Eden Chase, not as a person anyway. To him, she was only an object, a means to an end. And when the time came, he would do what he had to do.

20

Rose Rudd looked over at her son and felt tears prick her eyes. She turned away, not wanting him to see. She was doing her best to put on a brave front, but the expression on his face was killing her. No mother wants to see her child hurt or disappointed. Her hopes of protecting him from the truth, at least for a while, had been dashed at ten o'clock that morning when Archie's brief had called to say her husband had been ghosted out of jail and was now at Chiswick nick.

'Christ,' Davey said again.

Rose busied herself with the mugs and the kettle. 'You know he wouldn't be doing this if there was any other way. He's got no choice. It's this or a life sentence, Davey.'

'They'll call him a squealer, a grass. He will be a bloody grass.'

'They can call him what they like, but they'd do the same if they were in his shoes. And this isn't down to him. He wasn't the one who went shouting his mouth off after Shepperton. They pushed him into a corner, didn't they? One of those lads went blabbing to the law about the Epping job. If they hadn't done that, your dad wouldn't have said a word.'

'He's going to have to stand up in court and name names, Mum.'

'Yeah, well, not any names that matter.' She was trying to sound calm and matter-of-fact, but inside she was all churned up. 'There's no one left round here. I mean, it don't make no difference to Don now – God bless him – he's long gone. And Rossi's out in Spain. The only one who'll be going down is the bastard who left Paddy to die. I can't see no one complaining too much about that.'

Davey gazed at her. 'And what the hell are you going to do in Chiswick? Have you even been there before?'

'Oh, I'll manage. And it'll only be for a year or two. Once your dad gets out, we can move somewhere new.'

'But you've lived here all your life.'

'So? Time for a change, I reckon.'

'It ain't fair, Mum. You shouldn't have to . . . I mean, it's your home, ain't it?'

'So what's more important, a few old bricks or your dad being free to smell the fresh air? It's no competition so far as I'm concerned.'

'And what are you going to tell everyone?'

'I've already told them. Said I'm going to stay at Lil's for a while.' Her sister lived in Ashford, and Rose often spent time there, especially when Archie was banged up. 'There's nothing unusual about it, nothing for them to think twice about. I'll just take the one suitcase with me so it looks right. They'll shift out the rest of the stuff nearer the trial.'

'Why don't you go to Aunt Lil's?'

'I don't want her getting involved in all this. She'd guess something was wrong and I'd end up telling her everything – you know what I'm like – and then she'd tell Jocky and . . . well, he can't keep his mouth shut for more than five minutes. It would be all over the county before the sun went down. No,

142

I'm better off doing it this way. Careless talk costs lives and all that.'

Davey gave her a look. 'It ain't the war, Mum.'

Rose put a mug of hot sweet tea in front of him and let out a sigh. 'No, course it ain't. And you don't have to worry. No one's going to have a go at you.'

'I ain't worried.'

But Rose could see by his frown that he was. 'No one's going to blame you, love. You'd best keep your head down for a while, mind, when the trial's on the go.' She felt bad for him. Although he lived over Romford way now, he still had mates in the area, boys he'd grown up with, and it was never easy to face the judgement of others. 'It'll all blow over in time.'

Davey shook his head. 'There won't be no blowing over, Mum, and you know it. None of us are going to be able to show our faces round here again.'

'Your dad had no choice,' Rose repeated.

'Yeah, he did. He had a choice not to go out on the bloody Shepperton job. What the hell was he thinking? He promised you, Mum – no more shooters, no more bank jobs. If he hadn't—'

'I know, I know. But there's no point going over it all. It's done and dusted. We just have to deal with it now.'

Davey sat back and drank his tea. He was quiet for a while as he thought things over. 'How come he's never mentioned that job in Epping? Not a word in all these years?'

'You know why. With what happened to Paddy . . . If the law had got wind, they'd all have gone down for murder.'

'Pat's going to do his nut when he finds out Dad knew all along.'

Rose pulled a face at the mention of Paddy's crazy son. He'd gone off the rails after his father's untimely death, and never got back on them again. He was a cruel, vicious man with a black heart. 'Pat's inside. He can't do nothing.'

'He's not going to be inside for ever.'

'Long enough. Another ten at least,' she said. 'They ain't going to let him out in a hurry, not after what he did to that poor girl.'

'Yeah, well, being inside doesn't always stop people from—'

'Just drink your tea, Davey. I can't be worrying about that on top of everything else.'

'Sorry,' he said.

Rose smiled at her son. She was proud of him for making his own way – he had a steady job and a flat of his own – and not following in his father's footsteps. And that wasn't because she had any respect for law and order, but simply for the reason that she didn't want to see him languishing behind bars. She'd seen too many kids round here go to the bad and was grateful that he wasn't one of them. 'We'll be okay. We'll get through this.'

'Sure we will. We always get through, you and me.'

Rose felt the tears filling her eyes again. It had been just the two of them for so much of Davey's life with Archie in and out of prison all the time. She couldn't have asked for a better son. He was good and kind and deserved more than she'd ever been able to give him. 'I know it's not fair on you, none of it is. You shouldn't have to—'

Rose's apology was interrupted by a knock on the back door. No one came to the front door round here unless they were rent collectors or bailiffs. She quickly crossed the kitchen to answer it. She thought it was probably Margie, who popped in most days for a brew and a gossip. Her stomach dropped like a stone when she saw Vera Lynch standing there.

'Oh, hello.'

'Hello, love. Not disturbing you, am I? Can I have a word?'

Rose drew in a breath. Christ, did she know? Could she? 'Er . . . yeah, course. Come on in. Davey's here. Look who it is, Davey. How are you? I haven't seen you for a while. You're looking well. Would you like a brew? I've just made a pot.' She knew she was rambling, but she couldn't stop herself. Fear was rattling her nerves and she couldn't control them. 'Why don't you sit yourself down and I'll bring you one over.'

'Ta, love, I wouldn't say no.'

Vera was a big imposing woman with wide jutting hips and a bosom that looked like it was made of concrete. She said hello to Davey and lowered herself down into one of the kitchen chairs. 'I heard about Archie,' she said.

Rose gave a start. 'W-what?'

'Back inside, yeah?'

'Oh, yes, yes that's right.'

'In the Scrubs,' Davey said. 'But he's doing okay. Mum's going to stay with Aunt Lil for a while. Aren't you, Mum?'

'Just for a while.' Rose's hand was shaking as she poured out the tea. 'The house is too quiet when he's away.' She took the mug over and placed it on the table. 'Help yourself to sugar.'

'Ta, love.' Vera shovelled in three large spoonfuls and gave the tea a brisk stir.

'And how's Pat?' Davey asked. 'He still on the island?'

'Yeah, still there.'

'Bugger of a journey,' he said.

'You're telling me. That ferry is like a bloody rollercoaster in winter. Last time I went I was sick as a dog. And how are you supposed to face a visit after that? It's a bloody joke.'

Rose pulled out a chair and sat down beside Davey. Archie had done a stretch in Parkhurst and she'd made many a journey to the Isle of Wight herself. 'A nightmare,' she said. But that wasn't really the nightmare she was thinking of. 'So was there something . . . '

Vera slurped her tea and nodded. 'It's about my Paddy.'

Rose stiffened, the breath catching in the back of her throat. 'Paddy?' she said hoarsely.

'There's word going around that the filth have got one of the guys who done it. I've not heard nothing, mind, not from the law I mean. But then the shits wouldn't bother telling me, would they? Too much effort to pick up the bleedin' phone.'

'Well, it's good they've got him,' Davey said. 'If it's true.'

'*If* it's true. That's what I'm saying. I still don't know one way or the other. I was wondering if you'd heard owt?'

'Me?' Rose asked, the word coming out almost as a squeak. 'I . . . er . . . '

Davey quickly came to her rescue. 'No, we ain't, have we, Mum?' He threw her a glance, a warning to pull herself together before Vera smelled a rat. 'Not a whisper. Nothing at all. We'll let you know if we do, though. How long is it now? Must be over ten years?'

'Nearer sixteen,' Vera said.

'Sixteen,' Davey repeated. 'I can't believe it's that long. I hope they have got him, whoever he is. The bastard deserves life for what he did.'

Rose vehemently nodded her agreement. 'He does. He really does.'

Vera pulled a face. 'I'd pretty much given up, to be honest. After a while, you stop expecting anything. The whole fuckin' lot of them got clear away. Makes me sick to my stomach what they done. It really does.' She paused and then added, 'What about your Archie?'

'What? What do you mean?' Rose asked, her heart missing a beat.

146

'Do you think he could have heard anything before he went inside?'

'I don't reckon so,' Davey interjected, coming to the rescue again. 'He'd have said, wouldn't he, Mum?'

'Yes, of course he would. He wouldn't keep something like that to himself.'

Vera finished her tea and slammed the mug down on the table. 'If I ever catch those scumbag bastards, I'll string 'em up myself. And as for our Pat . . . '

Rose shuddered, knowing exactly what her Pat would do. 'I'd be the same,' she said. 'It weren't right. They shouldn't get away with it.' She wasn't a two-faced person by nature, but when it came to protecting her own, she'd lie through her teeth if she had to. 'Who's been telling you this stuff, anyhow?'

'I heard it down the Fox,' Vera said. 'Just a rumour, you know. No names or nothing. Maybe I should go to Cowan Road and ask them straight out.'

'If they'd tell you anything,' Davey said. 'You know what the law are like. Tight-lipped fuckers when it suits them. I'd hang on a day or two, see if anything else comes to light.'

Vera rubbed at her nose with the back of her hand and made a loud sniffing noise. It was hard to tell if she was upset or just suffering from a cold. 'Yeah, I might. I've been looking for that Pym – he always knows what's going down – but no one's seen hide nor hair of him for the past few days. Typical, ain't it? Usually you can't get rid of the little creep, and then when you do want to talk to him, he's nowhere to be found.'

Davey stared across the table at her. 'Pym? You know, I reckon I saw him going into the Hope about twenty minutes ago. I'm pretty sure it was him.'

'The Hope, you say?'

'Yeah. I was on my way here and . . . Well, it looked like him. You should give it a try. He might still be there.'

'I'll do that,' Vera said, hauling herself to her feet with a series of grunts. She glanced at Rose and smiled. 'Ta for the brew. I'll see you when you get back.'

Rose stood up too. 'Yes, I'll see you then. I hope you ... hope you find out something.'

'You and me both, love. You and me both.'

Rose opened the back door, showed her visitor out, and closed it again. She leaned against the wooden frame for a moment, letting the relief flow through her. 'Did you really see Pym?' she asked Davey.

'Course not. I just wanted to get rid of her.'

Rose put a hand to her chest, feeling the fast beat of her heart. 'I'll be glad to be gone. Christ, I thought I was going to have a stroke when I saw her standing there. My nerves can't take much more of this.'

'What time are they coming?'

'They're sending a taxi at five. Just to make it look normal. Like I'm on the way to the station.'

'Do you want me to come with you?'

Rose shook her head. 'Best not. I'll give you a ring when I get there, let you know the address.'

'I'll drive over and see you during the week. Are you sure you'll be okay?'

'I'll be just fine.'

'You shouldn't have to do this.'

Rose walked around the table and laid her hand gently on his shoulder. She knew it would be the last time they were ever together in this house. Everything was changing. All the things that had anchored her – her home, her friends, her place in the community – were about to be swept away. Even her name would be different. Rose Rudd was about to disappear for ever. Her heart was breaking and there was nothing she could do about it.

21

The first thing Eden did after getting back from West End Central was to call Elspeth Coyle's office and make an appointment. The earliest the accountant could do was Tuesday and she knew it would be a long four days before she could ask the all-important questions about the money that had come from Munich. There had to be a logical explanation, a *legal* explanation.

Frustrated by the fact it would be almost another week before she could see Tom again, she thought about writing to him. But what could she actually put in a letter? No, she was better off waiting until after she'd seen Elspeth. She didn't want to come across as making accusations or doubting his innocence. And wasn't all correspondence read by the prison censor? There was every chance that Banner would have any interesting information passed on to him.

Eden hadn't needed to think much about money since getting married, but she knew this comfortable state of affairs was now at an end. Without Tom's income it was only a matter of time before the cash ran out. She would have to leave college and get a job. And sooner rather than later. It didn't take a genius to do the maths.

She sat down at the table and stared at the mess, at the jumble of paper and books and photographs. She should tidy up but didn't know where to start. She picked up the letters from Ann-Marie, the airmail envelopes pale blue and light as a feather, the handwriting neat and sloping. She scanned through them again, searching for the name Jack or Jacques, but couldn't find a mention. There were some words she recognised from her French lessons but not enough for her to properly translate most of the sentences.

Eden sighed at her own ineptitude. She should have worked harder at school and paid more attention. Tom's skill with languages was something she'd always envied. He was fluent in German and had enough Italian and Spanish to get by. Clearly he could speak French too – or at least read it.

She flipped over one of the envelopes and read the Paris address on the back. Rue Bezout. Was there any chance, after all these years, that Ann-Marie was still living there? It seemed a long shot but perhaps it had been the family home – in which case a relative, her mum or dad, might still be around.

Ann-Marie's evidence could be the key to the whole case. If she could confirm that Jack Minter had existed, that she'd actually met him, Tom's story would hold up in court. But would the girl be prepared to help? Eden had no idea how the relationship had ended or if there was any bad feeling on either side.

Well, she couldn't just sit around waiting for things to happen – she had to *make* them happen. This thought was enough to galvanise her into action. She knew she should probably ask Tom first, but he might not want her to get in contact with his ex. Male pride was a complicated thing and if he refused his permission she could hardly go behind his back. This way, if Ann-Marie didn't reply or wasn't prepared to get involved, he would never need to know about it. Eden didn't feel entirely comfortable with what she was doing, but the alternative of doing nothing was even worse.

She stood up, went over to the dresser, opened the drawer and took out a pad of Basildon Bond. She returned to the table and sat down again. For the next ten minutes she made numerous drafts, trying to keep it simple – she didn't know how good Ann-Marie's English was – while at the same time attempting to get across the message that Tom was in desperate need of help. The final result, although less than perfect, was the best she could manage.

Dear Ann-Marie,

I am sorry to contact you out of the blue. I am writing about my husband, Tom Chase, who I believe you were friendly with many years back. I'm afraid Tom is in serious trouble due to something that happened in Budapest in the late 60s. Do you remember meeting a man called Jack Minter? If you do, I would be very grateful if you could contact me at the above address or give me a call and I will ring you back.

Best regards,
Eden Chase

Eden read it through again before folding the crisp white sheet of paper and putting it in an envelope. She wrote the address on the front and propped up the letter against the base of the lamp. Now all she had to do was post it. But something was niggling at the back of her mind. If Ann-Marie had met Jack Minter, why hadn't Tom mentioned it? It could be his way out of this mess.

She wished that Caitlin was around so she could ask her

advice, but unless she got in the car and drove to Greenham there was no way of speaking to her. And really, the sooner the letter was sent, the better. It would probably take four or five days to get to France and then might have to be forwarded to another address. Surely there was no point in waiting? No, she would send it off today and have done with it.

Before she could change her mind, Eden jumped up, pulled on her coat, grabbed her bag and the envelope and rushed out of the flat. Outside, she walked at a brisk pace, feeling the cold sting her face. The temperature had to be close to zero and the breath escaped from her mouth in white steamy clouds.

Eden joined the long queue at the Post Office, impatiently shifting from one foot to the other. While the minutes slowly passed, she kept telling herself that she was doing the right thing. Someone had to try and find a way to dismantle the case the police were building up before it was too late. She thought of DI Banner – he reckoned he had it in the bag – and was determined to wipe that smug expression off his face.

Eden finally reached the front of the queue and passed the letter over. 'Airmail please, to France.'

After leaving the post office, she walked to the market and bought some provisions – the cupboards were almost bare – before going to the small supermarket on the corner and adding milk, coffee, bread and pasta. With a carrier bag in each hand, she started to walk home.

Eden had just crossed Upper Street when the reporter, Jimmy Letts, appeared from nowhere and fell into step beside her. 'Hey, how are you doing?' he asked, as if they were old friends. 'Bit chilly, isn't it?'

Eden stared at him, her heart sinking. 'Go away.'

'How's Tom?'

Eden carried on walking, trying to pick up speed to get away from him, although this wasn't easy when the ground was slippery and she was weighed down by groceries. 'I've got nothing to say so just leave me alone.'

But Letts was sticking to her like glue. 'As it happens, I've got news. I've got something to tell you.'

'I don't want to hear it.'

Letts threw her a sly glance. 'Really? I'd want to if I was in your position.'

Eden stared at him. She knew what he was trying to do and wasn't falling for it. 'What don't you understand about "Leave me alone"?'

'I'm here to help. You might not think so, but it's true.'

Eden, stymied by the traffic lights, was forced to wait on the edge of the pavement until they turned red again. She twisted her face away, refusing to be drawn. If she ignored him for long enough, he might eventually get the message.

But Letts wasn't the sensitive sort. 'I've heard they've moved the squealer, put him somewhere safe. And already there's rumours flying round the East End that the police have nabbed the guy who did for Paddy Lynch. It won't be long before Pat gets to hear about it. That's the son, in case you're wondering. He's doing life at Parkhurst – shoved some poor cow out of a moving car – but that won't stop him from . . . well, let's just say he's not what you'd call the forgiving sort.' He left a short pause before adding menacingly, 'Maybe you should think about getting some protection.'

Eden gave him a glare. 'And maybe you should think about not trying to scare the shit out of people.'

'Just saying it how it is. You've got caught in the middle of something nasty here, Eden. You've got to look after yourself, take precautions. Now I could organise a great deal for you with one of the nationals, safe house, nice cash payment, the whole caboodle. And a chance to put your side of the story.' He dug into his pocket, pulled out a business card and held it out to her. 'Look, you don't have to make your mind up right now. Have a think about it, mull it over. Isn't it better that you're in control, in charge? Otherwise they'll just write whatever they like.'

Eden ignored the proffered card. 'I'm not interested, okay? I'm not talking to you; I'm not talking to anyone.' The lights finally changed and she set off across the road. She was hoping he'd get the message, but he continued to trot along beside her like a stray yappy dog she couldn't shake off.

'Bit of a mystery, your old man, isn't he?'

Eden didn't reply.

'No one seems to know much about him. Odd that, don't you think? Makes you wonder.'

When they reached the other side of the road, Eden turned to him and said, 'If you don't clear off right now, I'm going to report you to the police for harassment.'

Jimmy Letts smirked. 'I'd have thought you'd had enough of the police for one day.'

Eden gave a start, surprised that he knew. 'So what have you been doing? Following me around?'

'No, love. I've got my sources, that's all.'

Eden wasn't sure if she believed him. She'd be looking over her shoulder from now on, checking to see if he was on her tail. It gave her the creeps even to think about it. 'This conversation is over.'

Jimmy Letts held out the card again. 'Just take it,' he said. 'In case you change your mind. You can call me anytime.'

Deciding that this was probably the only way to get rid of him, Eden transferred the carrier bag in her right hand to her left, plucked the card from between his fingers and shoved it in her pocket. It was going straight in the bin as soon as she got home. 'Happy now?'

'Take care,' he said. 'And you know where I am if—'

Eden walked off before he could finish the sentence. She resisted the urge to look back and kept her gaze fixed firmly ahead until she reached the corner of Pope Street. Only then did she turn to see if he was still around, but there was no sign of him. As she hurried towards the flat, she tried to dismiss what he'd said about Paddy Lynch's son.

Eden's hand shook as she put the key in the lock. The creep had just been trying to shake her up, to scare her. The trouble was, he'd succeeded.

22

DI Vic Banner looked around and nodded. It wasn't exactly the Ritz, but it was ten times the size of a normal cell and had a sofa, table, two chairs, kettle, TV and radio. There was carpet on the floor and curtains on the barred windows. There was even a separate bedroom with bathroom facilities. He'd stayed in worse hotel rooms in his life. 'Not bad, eh?' he said. 'A bit more comfortable than your previous accommodation.'

Archie gave a shrug. 'It'll do.'

Vic settled himself on one of the chairs, reached into the carrier bag and took out a bottle of Scotch. He held it up for Archie to see. 'Fancy one?'

'I'd prefer a pint,' Archie grumbled, but he went and got two plastic cups and put them on the table.

Vic poured out a couple of stiff ones. He could tell from Archie's demeanour that he had the jitters – hardly surprising as he was in the process of breaking that eleventh commandment, *Thou shalt not grass* – and needed a drink to take the edge off things. It was too late for the old villain to change his mind, but Vic didn't want him holding back. He wanted every little detail of what had gone down in 1966.

Although this case was never going to be in the supergrass league, nothing like the Bertie Smalls revelations which had resulted in twenty-eight men being convicted, it was important in a different way. With the number of armed robberies in London being at an all-time high, the police needed some good publicity and a high-profile result to show that no matter how many years went by they always got their man. And the Epping heist, ending as it had in the gruesome and possibly unnecessary death of Paddy Lynch, was emotive enough to hit the headlines.

Vic had been passed an opportunity to shine and he wasn't going to squander it. Over the next few weeks he'd be going over all the details, but today he was going to start with some names. Delving into the carrier bag again, he took out a notebook, a pen and forty John Players. He slid the two packs of fags over to Archie along with a box of matches. 'You ready, then?'

Archie looked about as ready as a man on his way to the gallows. 'How's my Rose?' he asked. 'She still at home?'

'No, she'll be out of there by now. She's perfectly safe.' In truth, she wasn't being picked up until five, but he didn't want to give Archie an excuse to stop talking. 'Have a drink, relax. Everything's going to be fine.'

Archie took a few fast gulps of the whisky. 'You reckon? Only the way I see it, nothing's ever going to be fuckin' fine again.'

Vic had come on his own today, deciding that this first meet at Chiswick might go better if it was just the two of them so he could try and build up a rapport. They were never going to be best mates, but some kind of connection was necessary if he was going to get the right result. 'Ah, c'mon, Arch, don't be

157

like that. It's better than spending the next twenty years at Her Majesty's Pleasure – and your Rose having to traipse halfway across the country every time she wants to see your ugly mug.'

Archie drank some more whisky. Already a red flush was creeping across his cheeks as the alcohol entered his bloodstream. He lit up a fag and puffed on it hard. 'No going back now, I suppose,' he said dolefully.

'No,' Vic agreed. 'The rumour machine's already started up. You know what the East End's like.'

Archie's face grew tight and angry. 'What? They know about me already?'

'Course not,' Vic said quickly. 'No one's got a clue about this. There are no bloody leaks in my department. So far as your neighbours are concerned, you're banged up for the Shepperton job, end of story. No, what I mean is that word's got out about the guy who left Paddy Lynch for dead. Some poor constable at Cowan Road had Paddy's missus on the blower this afternoon, screaming blue murder about not being told anything.'

'You sure Rose is out of Kellston?'

'I said, didn't I?'

Archie curled his lip. 'Your lot say anything that suits you.'

'Yeah, well, I'm not lying, okay? We're taking good care of her, I promise.'

'And your promises are worth fuck all.'

Vic shook his head. 'Not these ones. You can trust me.' He picked up the pen and looked at Archie. 'It's up to you. If you want to pull out, just say the word, but . . . You know what the deal is. If you don't cooperate, someone else will. This way you get to call the shots. Those shitbags you worked with on the Shepperton job are queuing up to sell you down the river. They're not thinking twice about it, Arch. Not what you'd call old school, huh?'

'They don't know nothin'.'

'They know enough to fuck you over.'

Archie gave a dismissive wave of his hand, but his face said something different. 'Let's get on with it.'

'How about we start with the names of the other members of the crew? We've got you, Don, Paddy and Jack Minter. What about the others? How many were there in all?'

Archie hesitated for a moment. 'Five.'

'And who was the other one?'

Another long hesitation. Another drink. 'Paul Rossi.'

Vic wrote the name down in his notepad. 'The last I heard, he was in Spain.'

'I wouldn't know.'

'And that was it, just the five of you?'

Archie stared at him over the rim of his glass. 'I'd have gone for more myself, six or seven, but Minter wanted to keep it tight. He reckoned the more people who knew about it, the bigger the chance of something getting out. Paddy wasn't first choice, that was Charlie Treen, but Charlie broke his leg and so we had to get someone else. We didn't have much time and Paddy was up for it so . . . '

'And Minter was all right with that?'

'I wouldn't say he was all right. Nah, he wasn't happy, but it was either that or wait around for Charlie to get back on his feet again. And we're talking months here, by which time they could have changed all their routines at the warehouse and we'd have to start from scratch.'

'So tell me about this Minter guy.'

'What do you want to know?'

'Anything. Everything. You said Don met him in the Fox. When did you first meet him?'

Archie stared down at the table and swirled the whisky around in his glass. 'I dunno. A few days later, two or three? It was the middle of the week, I think.' He looked up at Banner. 'Yeah, Don came round and asked what I thought. Well, I wasn't so sure – I've never liked working with strangers – but Don was keen and him and me go way back so I agreed to a meet. The three of us got together at Don's house. Can't say I took to the geezer, but the plans were sound. He'd done the legwork, checked out the place, all the comings and goings. He said it was a one-off, that we were talking big money, maybe four or five million.'

Vic raised his eyebrows. 'Not to be sniffed at.'

'Yeah, gold and jewellery mainly.'

'When you say you didn't take to him, what do you mean by that exactly?'

Archie frowned and pursed his lips. 'Just that he wasn't one of us, not from the East End. He wasn't what you'd call posh or nothin', but he weren't local.'

'Did he say where he came from?'

'Said he'd lived all over, that he preferred to move around. I didn't like that he had no one to vouch for him, you know? Made me wonder. Could have been anyone, couldn't he? Could have been one of you lot. That's why me and Don decided to do some digging of our own. Make sure he was kosher.'

'And that's when you found out he was working for Albert Shiner.'

'Yeah, the photo place in Chigwell. Followed him, didn't we? Being careful like, so he wouldn't spot us. He'd told us his address and that checked out so we drove over there one morning, early, about half seven. The guy comes out about quarter to nine, walks to Shiner's and goes inside. Three hours we were sitting there, waiting for him to come out again. And it don't take three bleedin' hours to have your photo taken so we reckoned he had to be on the staff.'

'And then?'

Archie took another long drag on his cigarette and blew the smoke towards the ceiling. 'It was about quarter past twelve before he showed again and took off down the high street. So Don waits a minute or two and then goes inside the shop. There's a girl behind the desk. "Is Mr Minter around?" he asks, all innocent like. And she shakes her head. "Who?" And Don says, "Jack Minter." But she reckons there's no one by that name working there so Don gives her a description and she says, "Ah, do you mean Tom Chase?" So that's how we found out his real name.'

'Did you ever confront him about it?'

Archie shook his head. 'Nah, we reckoned he was just trying to cover his tracks so no one knew his real identity. That way if any of us got picked up after the job, we couldn't grass him up to you lot.'

'Not very trusting of him.'

'Yeah, well, to hear him speak you'd think he was doing us a favour just by asking us to come along. And I'm not saying he wasn't smart – the geezer had brains, there's no denying it – but it takes a team to pull off a job like that.'

'Describe him to me,' Vic said. 'Everything you can remember.'

Archie gave a shrug. 'Tallish, taller than me anyhow, in his mid-twenties, fair hair, natty dresser.'

'What build?'

'Normal. Average. Slim but not skinny.'

'And his eyes? What colour were they?'

Archie tapped the ash off his cigarette. 'Shit, it's been years. I can't remember what colour his eyes were. Doubt I even noticed.'

'What about distinguishing marks, scars, tattoos, anything like that?'

'Nah, I don't think so. Nothin' obvious anyway.'

'Wedding ring?'

Archie shrugged. 'Don't recall seeing one, but I couldn't swear to it either way.'

'Any unusual mannerisms?'

'Huh?'

'You know,' Vic explained, 'any tics or nervous gestures, odd ways of doing things.'

Archie pondered on this for a moment, but then shook his head again. 'Nah, can't think of anything.'

'You didn't notice much.'

'Maybe that's 'cause there weren't much to notice. He was ... I dunno, like anyone else.'

'Come on, there must have been something.'

'I'm trying my best. I only met the bloke a few times.'

'You did a bleedin' armed robbery with him!'

Archie knocked back the last of his Scotch, picked up the bottle and poured another hefty slug into the cup. 'But that's the thing, see? When you're on a job, all you're thinking about is that. There's sod all else on your mind. You're fixed on it, concentrating. You've got all that adrenalin running through you.'

'Okay,' Vic said. 'We'll go through the details of the job another time, but tell me what happened after Paddy got shot.'

Archie lowered his head and dived into his drink again. 'Fuck, I didn't even see what happened, not really. One minute he's goading this security guard, right up in his face, waving the shooter round like he's John bloody Wayne, and the next ... '

'Wasn't the guard tied up?'

'Supposed to have been, but that was Paddy's job and I don't think he was with it that day. Me and Don, we both had a snifter before the job, just something to steady the nerves, but

I reckon he went overboard. So there he is lying on the floor with a bloody big hole in his guts. Fuck knows how we got him in the van, but somehow we did. And then we couldn't hang about, not with him being in that state. We weren't even halfway through the loading – it was a bloody disaster.'

'And how did Minter react?'

Archie gave a dry laugh. 'How do you think? All those months of planning and now everything had gone tits up. I mean, he wasn't going to be best pleased, was he?'

'He was angry?'

'Course he was fuckin' angry. He didn't say much, but he had this look on his face, like if Paddy hadn't already been shot he'd have been more than happy to do the honours.'

Vic grinned. This was more like it. He could already hear Archie's words resounding around the courtroom, a damning indictment of Tom Chase's frame of mind on the day that Paddy Lynch had gone to meet his maker. 'Go on,' he said. 'Tell me more.'

23

Eden woke up on Tuesday morning with a hangover headache, a queasy gut, dry mouth and a fervent intention to never touch alcohol again. Just what she needed when she had a ten o'clock appointment with Elspeth Coyle. She groaned, rolled out of bed and staggered to the bathroom. As she went through the automatic processes of brushing her teeth, showering, dressing and putting on make-up, she reflected on the actions that had led her to this sorry state.

It had all begun yesterday afternoon when she'd called Tammy, ostensibly to check if she still wanted a lift to the jail on Thursday, but really to pick her brains about Pat Lynch. After her encounter with the reporter, Eden's nerves had started to fray. And what Tammy had said hadn't exactly put her mind at rest.

'Oh, yeah, I've heard of him. Everyone round here knows Pat. The guy's a psycho, love. You don't want anything to do with him. Keep well clear. I mean it. He's the kind of trouble you never want to see coming your way.'

'Well, that's a relief,' she'd tried to joke. 'I thought you might say something bad about him.'

'Is this to do with your old man?'

'In a way. Sort of. I mean, it's complicated.'

'It always is, hon. Look, do you fancy coming over later? I'm a bit tied up right now, but I can get my mum to babysit for a couple of hours this evening. We can grab a drink and you can tell me all about it. Or not, if you don't want to. To be honest, I'd just be glad to get out of the flat for a while.'

Eden had hesitated, but suddenly the idea of company – especially the company of someone who could relate to what she was going through – had been an appealing one. And maybe she could find out more about Pat Lynch, although she wasn't entirely sure she wanted to. 'Okay. Why not? Shall we say half seven?'

'That's good for me. See you then.'

Eden had gone over to Shoreditch with the firm intention of only telling Tammy the bare minimum, but by the time she'd embarked on her third glass of wine, most of the story had already tumbled out. Still, it had been a relief to get things off her chest. Tammy had listened, wide-eyed, asking questions when Eden paused for breath.

'So you reckon this Minter bloke is out to stitch him up, then?'

'Who else can it be?'

Tammy had nodded. 'Exactly.' She'd had the good grace not to point out the obvious – that Tom could be the one who was lying – but instead had been kind and sympathetic. 'And if this French girl gets back to you ... What did you say her name was?'

'Ann-Marie.'

'Yeah, well that could make a real difference, couldn't it?'

Now, in the cold light of day, Eden wondered if she'd said too much. But where was the harm? And sometimes you just had to trust people. She'd asked Tammy not to say anything to anyone else and she'd promised she wouldn't.

'Don't worry. I won't say a word, I swear.' Then Tammy had grinned at her over the rim of her glass. 'What did you say that reporter's number was again?'

'Don't even joke about it.'

'Sometimes you've got to laugh, hon. Otherwise it drives you crazy.'

It had been late by the time Eden got back. She'd caught a cab, although she couldn't remember much about the journey. Drinking on an empty stomach was never a good idea. She had only a few blurry memories of white streets, of cars blanketed in snow, of the tinny sound of the driver's radio. And then, after getting home, she'd rolled straight into bed without even brushing her teeth.

Eden forced herself to eat a slice of toast, downed a cup of coffee, and headed out for her meeting with Elspeth. She was in no fit state to drive and so walked instead to Angel Tube where she waited for a 73 bus that would take her to Victoria. By the time it arrived, twenty minutes later, her fingers and toes were turning to ice.

She went upstairs on the double-decker, found a seat and began trying to get her thoughts in order. What did she need to ask? What did she need to know? All she really wanted to do was go back to bed and sleep for the next ten hours. She felt groggy and vague and in no fit state to be discussing finances.

Eden kept glancing at her watch as the bus trundled along. Had she left enough time? She didn't want to be late. Elspeth Coyle wasn't the type to appreciate lateness. In fact she was more than likely to cancel the appointment. 'Come on, come on,' she urged as the bus stopped at yet another red light. What was it with the stupid lights today? They seemed to be conspiring against her.

By the time Victoria Station came into view, Eden had

only minutes to spare. She shot off the bus as it was pulling into the stop, hurried across the busy forecourt and legged it along Wilton Road. As she entered the office, red-faced and out of breath, she could feel the heavy, aching rhythm of the hangover throbbing in her head.

The receptionist gave her a dubious look. 'Yes?'

'Eden Chase. Hi. I've got a ten o'clock with Elspeth Coyle.'

The woman checked her book and gave a nod. 'If you'd like to take a seat.'

Eden had no sooner sat down than the receptionist picked up the phone, tapped in a number, had a brief exchange with the person on the other end, and then looked over at Eden. 'Ms Coyle will see you now. Up the stairs, second door on your right.'

Eden stood up again. 'Thank you.'

A minute later she was in the office, shaking hands with Tom's accountant. Elspeth Coyle was in her fifties, one of those stern-looking women with cropped iron-grey hair, shrewd eyes and a forbidding expression. She reminded Eden of her former headmistress.

'Sorry to hear about Tom's troubles. How is he?'

'Still in shock, I think.'

Elspeth gestured for her to sit down. 'Well, that's understandable. And how are you?'

'I'm okay, thanks. Well, you know, trying to make sense of it all.'

Elspeth offered her a drink, but Eden declined. Her headache was growing more intense and she just wanted to get on with things. She watched as the older woman flipped open a file and began to peruse the contents.

'Mm, where to start?'

Eden, unsure as to whether this was a rhetorical question, said nothing.

Elspeth looked up. 'I'm presuming Tom could be on remand for quite a while?'

'About six months, I think, before it comes to trial. Unless we can ... Obviously we're trying to prove his innocence, get the evidence together and ... '

'And in the meantime you've still got all the expenses of the studio, but with none of the income.'

'Yes.'

Elspeth gave a thin smile. 'A state of affairs that can't go on indefinitely.'

'No.'

'And looking at these figures, the business will be in the red sooner rather than later – unless you have other funds you can transfer into it?'

'Not really,' Eden said. 'There's a couple of thousand in our current account, but the mortgage needs paying, and the bills and all the rest. I'm at college at the moment so I'm not earning anything.'

Elspeth's eyebrows shifted up. 'That could be a problem.'

'I know. I'll have to start looking for a job.'

'A well-paid job if you want to keep the studio on for any length of time.'

Eden, who had never had a well-paid job in her life, gave a sigh. 'What are the chances?'

Elspeth shook her head. 'You've got rent, rates, utilities, not to mention salaries. Is it still just the one employee?'

'Yes, Annabelle.'

'I presume you're going to let her go?'

'I guess so.'

'Do it soon, then. The longer you wait, the more you'll have to pay. And you'll have to give notice on the studio, so I'd suggest you make a fairly quick decision on that too.'

'But everything could change in a month or two. Tom could

168

be out. I don't want to get rid of the studio if I don't have to. It's his business. He's spent years building it up. That place means everything to him.'

'There are plenty of other studios.'

'Not like this one.'

'Well, obviously you'll need to discuss it with Tom, but sometimes you need to be practical about these things and not let your heart rule your head. I'm sure he doesn't want you living in penury just to keep hold of it.'

Eden's headache continued to beat in her temples. 'Actually, there was something I wanted to ask. Do you know anything about the money that was transferred from Munich into the business account? There were two payments, thirty thousand about five years ago, and another five last year.'

Elspeth gave her a wary glance. 'What does Tom say about it?'

'I haven't had the chance to ask. It was some kind of loan, I think. The police mentioned it on Friday.'

'Right.'

'So?'

'As you say, I believe it was a loan.'

'But from whom?'

'I have no idea. Surely Tom is in a better position to answer that than me?'

Eden bristled at the response. She had a feeling Elspeth knew a damn sight more than she was letting on. 'Tom's locked up. He isn't in a position to say anything.'

There was a brief silence while the two women eyed each other across the table. 'I'm sorry,' Elspeth said, 'but I really can't help.'

'The police think it came from the robbery.'

'So Tom should be able to put them right.'

Eden spoke through gritted teeth. 'Except Tom won't tell them anything.'

'Sometimes that's the best way.'

169

'Meaning what, exactly?'

'Meaning it isn't always wise to show your cards before you have to.' Elspeth leaned forward and, despite the fact they were alone, lowered her voice. 'Sometimes it's smarter to play them close to your chest. If the police think they know something for a fact, and that fact can later be proved to be a falsehood, then . . . well, would you rather the mistake was revealed now or when Tom was standing in front of a jury?'

Eden could see her point. 'So you do know where the money came from?'

'Absolutely not. I'm speaking purely hypothetically. All I'm saying is that he could have his reasons for keeping quiet at the moment.'

Eden put her elbows on the desk and rubbed her face with her hands. She didn't like being kept in the dark; it made her feel tense and anxious. In a couple of days she could ask Tom about it, but until then she'd have to be patient. 'Okay,' she said wearily. Unable to think of anything else to discuss, she unhooked the strap of her bag from the back of the chair and prepared to leave. 'Thanks for your time.'

Elspeth sat back and looked at her. 'There is another option, if you really want to hang on to the studio.'

Eden, who was halfway to her feet, sat back down again. 'Really?'

'It's just an idea, but have you thought about selling the flat?'

'The flat?'

'Why not?'

'Because it's our home. Where am I going to live if—'

'No, no,' Elspeth interrupted. 'Not the Islington flat, the one in Kellston. It's empty at the moment, isn't it? I'm sure it is. The tenant moved out a few months ago.'

Eden stared at her, bewildered. 'What flat? What are you talking about?'

Elspeth's mouth slipped into a grimace. There was a short, awkward pause before she said, 'Ah, you didn't know about it.'

'What flat?' Eden repeated. 'He's got another flat? I don't understand.' She felt her stomach heave at this sudden unexpected revelation. She couldn't comprehend how Tom could own a property she didn't even know about. 'Why . . . what . . . why didn't he tell me?'

Elspeth Coyle shifted on her chair, obviously wishing she'd said nothing. 'Er, maybe it just—'

'What? Slipped his mind? For God's sake, you don't forget something like that!'

'I think he bought it quite a while ago. He lived there for a few years before he moved to Pope Street.'

Eden could feel the shock sinking into her bones, a heavy sludge of astonishment, anger and suspicion. Why had he kept it hidden from her? A bolthole in case the marriage went wrong? An investment she wouldn't be aware of? Or even a place for secret liaisons?

She swallowed hard and stared at the accountant. 'What's the address?'

Elspeth glanced away. 'I don't think I should—'

'It's too late for that now,' Eden snapped. 'I'm not leaving here until I have it.' As if to press home the point, she placed her elbows firmly on the desk. In truth, she didn't think she could stand up even if she wanted to. Her head was spinning and her legs had turned to jelly.

24

It was getting on for twelve by the time Eden got back to Islington from Victoria. She'd spent the entire bus journey going over and over what Elspeth Coyle had told her. Another flat, for Christ's sake! That wasn't something you didn't tell your wife about. Not if you loved her. Not if you trusted her. She had never professed to know Tom Chase inside out, but now she was starting to wonder if she knew him at all.

It was this thought, as much as the cold, that caused Eden to shiver as she climbed the stairs. She unlocked the door, went through to the living room, took off her coat and threw it over the back of the sofa. Her gaze fell on the wedding photo standing on the mantelpiece. She went over to it and traced her husband's face with her fingertips, trying by sheer force of will to make a connection to him.

'What the hell is going on?' she muttered.

He stared back at her, silent and smiling, a man who looked happy. But was he? Perhaps everything she believed in, their life together, their marriage, was built on a lie. The moment the thought crossed her mind, she hated herself for it. What about the benefit of the doubt? She hadn't even given him the opportunity to explain. Although, off the top of her head, Eden couldn't think of any reasons – other than bad ones – for keeping it a secret, she knew better than to judge too soon. If she stopped believing in him, then he'd have no one. The law, already baying for his blood, would throw him to the wolves.

Still, there were things she needed to know.

Eden lowered her hand, turned and went over to the dresser. She pulled out the drawers and started rooting through them. It didn't take her long to find the keys. There were four in all, each with a small plastic tag that had been neatly initialled in black felt tip pen. Two were spares for the studio, the front door and upstairs – CG; one for Pope Street – PS; and the other . . . Eden held it up, feeling a weird nervous flutter in her chest as she read the letters aloud, 'KHS.'

She knew now what those letters stood for – Kellston High Street. After the threat of a sit-in, it had only been seconds before Elspeth Coyle had scribbled down the address on a piece of paper, ripped it from the pad and pushed it across the desk. With other clients to see, she couldn't afford to have Eden littering up the office.

'Here,' she'd said, with a curt nod.

'And the flat's empty at the moment?'

'I believe so.'

Eden had folded the sheet of paper and put it in her pocket. She had left the office with as much dignity as she could muster, feeling the older woman's gaze on her back. What was in the accountant's eyes – pity or contempt? By that point she'd been past caring.

The paperback London A–Z was on the living room table. Eden flicked through the pages until she found the one she was looking for. She had a rough idea where Kellston was – hadn't she noticed a sign when she was taking Tammy home? – but

173

wanted to be sure. Yes, just as she thought, an East End borough lying between Shoreditch and Bethnal Green. The high street ran in a long straight line through the centre.

Eden put the *A–Z* in her bag along with the address. Although the latter was already firmly imprinted on her memory – 192B Kellston High Street – she had a dread of her mind going blank the minute she got there. She put on her coat, picked up the car keys and set off on her second journey of the day.

Eden drove carefully, keeping a close eye on the road and the traffic around her. Conditions were still bad, icy and treacherous, and the sky threatened more snow. She hoped by now the alcohol levels in her blood were under the limit; the last thing she needed was to be involved in a collision and end up being breathalysed.

As she made her way towards the East End, she could feel her stomach churning again. Once – and it wasn't so long ago – it had been the things she didn't know about Tom that had excited her, but now they only caused her fear and panic. What else would be revealed? The closer she got to Kellston, the more anxious she became.

She turned on the radio – 'Don't You Want Me', by the Human League, floated into the car – and she tried to keep calm by tapping out the rhythm on the steering wheel. Why hadn't he told her about the flat? It was a question that wouldn't go away. She thought of all the evenings he had worked late at the studio and began to wonder if that was where he had actually been. She wished now that she'd asked Elspeth about that tenant – had they been male or female? But it was a big leap from an unknown flat to infidelity. She was overreacting; she had to be.

The first thing Eden noticed when she got to Kellston High Street was the three tall concrete towers on the horizon. They loomed over the area, a trio of monstrous nineteen sixties constructions devoid of any charm and, for the tenants forced to live in them, probably of any hope either. The high street was run-down and shabby, with many of the shops boarded up. She peered through the windscreen, searching for numbers on doors, and soon realised that she was at the wrong end.

Eden carried on driving for a couple of minutes and then began looking for a place to pull in. By the time she found one, she'd overshot 192 and had to walk back. The door to the flat was squashed between a bakery and an off-licence. Bread and wine. What more did anyone need? But despite the flippant thought, her hand was shaking as she put the key in the lock and turned it.

Inside, the place smelled musty and abandoned. There was a tiny square of hallway and a narrow flight of stairs leading up to the flat. A few fliers littered the floor, but there was no mail. She ascended slowly, wondering what she was about to find. A disturbing notion suddenly occurred to her: what if the flat wasn't empty at all? The tenant might have moved out, but someone else could have moved in. A squatter, perhaps, or a tramp. Her hand tightened around the rail as she stopped, held her breath and listened.

No, not a sound.

Eden carried on. At the top another door led straight into the living room. She went in and looked around. The room was light, a reasonable size and overlooked the high street. The walls were painted cream and had oblongs of a darker shade from where someone had hung pictures. The furnishings were basic but not too shabby: a brown corduroy sofa, matching chair, a table, and one of those old-fashioned standing lamps with a pink fringed shade. There was a worn beige carpet and a pair of brightly coloured patterned curtains.

She made a quick tour of the other rooms. The bedroom at the back contained a double bed with a bare mattress, a wardrobe and a chest of drawers. The kitchen was small but serviceable, and the bathroom had a bath but no shower. She opened and closed cupboards, peering into every corner. There was nothing remaining of the former tenant, no old bills, no newspapers, not even an empty bottle of shampoo. Either they'd been the tidy sort or a cleaner had been in after the flat was vacated.

Eden returned to the living room, where she stood by the sofa and looked around again. What had she expected to find? Some hint of Tom, perhaps, an indication that he might have been here recently, but there was nothing. She was relieved there was no trace of him. It didn't allay her concerns over his failure to inform her of the flat's existence, but at least there was no evidence of a squalid love nest. It was a terrible thing to suspect your own husband, especially when you'd only been married a year, but these were terrible times and somehow she had reached a stage where anything and everything seemed possible.

Eden wondered how much the flat was worth. Would there be enough profit to keep the studio going for a while and to pay Castor's legal bills? And how long would it take to sell? There probably wasn't a huge demand for properties in Kellston. She crossed over to the window and took in the view. Grim was the first word that sprang to mind. Even a blanket of snow couldn't make the dilapidated high street look pretty.

She shifted her gaze and it came to rest on a building diagonally opposite, an undertaker by the name of Tobias Grand. Like a bad omen, the sight of it made her feel uneasy. She thought of her mother, dead at twenty-nine. She thought of Paddy Lynch, left to bleed to death in the back of a van. She wrapped her arms around her chest, a defence not just against the cold but all the bad feelings that were crowding in on her.

Eden briefly closed her eyes and then opened them again.

Standing just to the right of the doorway of Tobias Grand was a tall, dark-haired man in a black overcoat. He was smoking a cigarette and idly flicking the ash on to the pavement. She wasn't sure why he held her attention although there was, she thought, something vaguely familiar about him. Where had she seen him before? She racked her brains but nothing came to her.

She was still staring when he abruptly raised his face and looked up towards the window. His gaze was so hard and cold that Eden instinctively took a step back. She felt afraid, threatened by him. The breath caught in the back of her throat and her pulse started to race. For the next thirty seconds she stood firmly rooted to the spot.

When she eventually plucked up the courage to return to the window, the man had disappeared. She looked up and down the street but there was no sign. Was she overreacting, letting her imagination run away with her? Perhaps. But she still couldn't shake off the bad feeling she had. Those eyes. That look. It had been so dark, so menacing, she could have been staring into the face of Lucifer himself.

25

It took Max Tamer by surprise when he looked up and saw her standing there. Their eyes locked for a moment before she stepped back out of sight. What had he seen on her face in those few fleeting seconds? Fear, confusion? Certainly something that had shaken her. It had been reckless of him to wait so close to the flat and in clear view, but in truth he had no sense of caution these days. He was caught up in the moment, making impulsive decisions, following his gut rather than his head.

Quickly he crossed the road, keeping in by the shops, and started walking towards the station. It was too risky to hang about. She'd already registered his presence and if she saw him again she would realise he was on her tail. Anyway, he'd had enough of playing shadow for now.

Unable to sleep, he'd been parked on the corner of Pope Street from seven o'clock this morning, watching the world wake up, the darkness gradually lifting, the lights going on in the houses. No one had taken any notice of him. He was just a bloke sitting in a car, blankly gazing through the windscreen. He'd smoked half a pack of cigarettes while he was waiting.

Eden Chase hadn't emerged until after nine, when she'd walked to Upper Street and caught a number 73 bus. He'd followed her on, but had stayed downstairs while she'd gone up, and had taken a seat by the rear platform so he'd see when she got off. Unsure as to where she was heading, he'd paid the full fare to the final destination, Victoria, and as it happened, hadn't wasted any money.

Max had no idea what the accountant, Elspeth Coyle, had said, but whatever it was hadn't been pleasant. Eden had stormed out of the building, her face pale and pinched as if she'd just been punched in the stomach. Still, any news on the financial front wasn't likely to be good when your old man was banged up for murder.

Max hadn't chanced catching the same bus back to Islington and had taken the Tube instead, intending to retrieve his car and go into the office. He had long ago ceased to have any interest in the business, but felt obliged to show up occasionally to prove, if nothing else, that he was still alive.

It was just as he'd been starting up the motor that Eden had appeared in Pope Street, walking quickly towards number twenty-four. A girl on a mission. A girl with something on her mind. And just out of curiosity he'd held off leaving for a while. Which was how he'd ended up in Kellston, watching her cross the road, watching her nervously glance around as if someone was about to mug her, watching her let herself into the flat between the baker's and the off-licence.

Max was bemused by this latest turn of events. With her stylish clothes and somewhat superior air, Eden Chase was like a fish out of water in Kellston. What was she doing here? Planning a move? A lunchtime tryst with a secret lover? He still didn't know, but one way or another he was going to find out. In his heart, he wanted to think the worst of her. It would make what he intended to do so much easier.

When he reached Station Road, Max crossed at the lights and went into the Fox. He was in need of a drink and was also hoping to find Terry Street in there. The latter wish was granted as soon as he walked in: Terry was in his usual spot, the table in the corner where he had a clear view of everyone who entered the pub. He was in conversation with his right-hand man Vinnie Keane, a great bear of a bloke who must have been over six foot five, but he glanced up, nodded at Max and beckoned him over.

As Max walked to the table, Vinnie rose to his feet and went to the bar.

'How are you?' Max asked as he sat down.

Terry gave another nod. 'Good, thanks. More to the point, how are you?'

There had been a time, and it wasn't so long ago, when Max had despised the likes of Terry Street – a violent man who lived outside the law, who lied and cheated and used brute force to get what he wanted – but he had laid aside all those black and white opinions since Ann-Marie had disappeared. When he'd needed help the police had responded with nothing but suspicion. When he'd despaired, when he'd been on his knees, Terry was the only one who had neither judged nor accused, but simply offered him some hope.

Max took a tenner out of his wallet and held it out. 'For Pym,' he said. 'I owe you.'

Terry waved the note away. 'Have it on me.'

But Max shook his head and pressed the tenner into his hand. 'Take it.'

'What's up? You scared of owing me?'

'Yes,' Max replied drily. 'Shouldn't I be?'

Terry grinned.

Vinnie came back, put a couple of glasses on the table, and then took himself off again.

'You'll have a drink at least,' Terry said. 'Or would that be a threat to your integrity too?'

Max lifted the glass of whisky and toasted him. 'Cheers. As it happens, I have no integrity left, but thanks for suggesting that I might.'

'That's bullshit and you know it.'

Max shrugged, sat back and looked around. The Fox was always busy, no matter what time you came. It had an atmosphere, a buzz, which was missing from other places. A log fire burned in the grate, sending out waves of heat. The clientele was mixed, from bankers to blaggers and a few whores too. Everyone was welcome at Terry's pub as long as they spent their cash and behaved themselves.

'You found out any more about this Chase guy?' Terry asked.

'I know he's a fucking liar. Do I need to know any more?'

'I've heard he could be in Thornley Heath. If you want, I can arrange for someone to have a word.'

Which was, Max presumed, villain-speak for getting the crap beaten out of him. 'No thanks,' he said. 'I'm dealing with it.'

'Meaning?'

'Meaning you don't have to worry.'

Terry grinned again. 'You sure?'

Max looked back. 'Completely sure.'

Max's unexpected friendship with Terry Street felt fragile and tenuous, a connection that he didn't entirely understand and which, he suspected, could be easily broken. Terry was younger than him, still in his thirties. There were rumours of how he'd risen to the top, of how he'd usurped the late Joe Quinn by smashing in his skull with a baseball bat. It was a crime he'd never been convicted of but it didn't stop the talk.

'You know where I am if you change your mind.'

Max nodded. He could understand why Terry was so

181

successful. The guy might not be educated, probably hadn't even spent much time at school, but he had an instinctive intelligence, an ability to read people, to anticipate, to make the right call at the right time. And he also had charm. It was all these things combined that had given him power and control over the East End.

'So what's the plan?' Terry asked.

'I'm still thinking about it. No rush, is there? Chase isn't going anywhere in a hurry.'

'Be careful, Max, or you'll end up in the slammer too.'

Max drank the whisky slowly. It was good stuff, the best. He rolled it around his mouth before he swallowed. 'You got anything more on him?'

'Only that he's in the frame for the Epping job. There's a squealer, but we ain't got no name yet. The filth are keeping a tight hold on this one. Pym's got his ear to the ground, though. It'll leak out sooner or later. Oh, and there's a reporter hassling the wife, local hack by the name of Jimmy Letts.'

'Is she talking to him?'

'Not so you'd notice. Not yet, at least.'

Max made a mental note of the name. It wasn't good news having a journalist sniffing around. It could get in the way of things. 'I need something,' he said, lowering his voice. He glanced around, making sure no one was earwigging before he completed the request. 'A revolver. Something decent. Any chance of that?'

Terry didn't ask why. 'I'll see what I can do. It shouldn't be a problem.'

'Good.'

'So this Budapest stuff, this link between Chase and Ann-Marie – you're not taking it to the law, then?'

Max shook his head. 'What's the point? The bastard isn't going to admit it, is he?'

Terry was quiet for a moment, and then he asked, 'Do you think Ann-Marie could have known about the robbery, about what happened to Paddy Lynch?'

'No.'

'Are you sure? It would explain why he . . . She'd have been a threat to him, wouldn't she? He might not have trusted her to keep quiet.' Terry narrowed his eyes. 'Pillow talk. People say all kinds when they've got the love blinkers on. Maybe, back then, he admitted what he'd done, confided in her and . . .'

But Max refused to believe that Ann-Marie could have known such a thing and not told him about it. 'No, it isn't possible.'

'So where's your motive? Why would Chase—'

'Maybe the shit doesn't need a motive. Maybe he just gets off on hurting people, destroying them.' Max could hear his voice rising, the rage bubbling up from his chest. 'Maybe he just couldn't bear to see her happy.'

Terry laid a restraining hand on his arm. 'Take it easy, mate. Pym isn't the only one with ears, if you get my drift.'

Max took a breath and tried to calm down. He was weary of the anger, of the bitterness that never stopped gnawing at his soul. He wanted to be ice, to feel nothing, to move through the great Arctic waste of his life with no emotion at all.

Terry finished his drink and placed the glass on the table. He knew, without being told, what Max was planning on doing. He gave him a sidelong glance. 'You sure this guy even likes his wife? It's been a year. The honeymoon could be over by now.'

Max stared straight ahead. The sounds of the pub washed over him, the chink of the glasses, the scuff of feet against smooth wooden boards, the rise and fall of conversation. He ran his tongue across his lips, dry from the cold outside. 'I'll take the chance,' he murmured.

26

Jimmy Letts' breath escaped from his mouth in white steamy clouds as he jaywalked across Station Road trying to dodge the traffic. He was in a hurry and couldn't afford to wait for the lights to change. Now he'd made up his mind, he felt the need to get there as quickly as he could. An irate cabbie honked his horn. Jimmy raised a hand as he swerved around the bonnet and finally made it to the other side.

Ten minutes earlier, he'd gone into the Hope to have a pint and listen out for rumours. It was a villain's pub, all spit and sawdust, and frequented mainly by old lags who gathered there to plan their next job or to reminisce over past ones. Fashionable London magazines would have described it as 'authentic', but in reality it was simply a dive. The chairs were worn and shabby, the floor littered with fag ends. But no one went there for the decor.

Jimmy had paid for his pint and was just lifting the glass to his lips when the door had opened and Bob Rich from the *Evening News* walked in. Bob was in his sixties, an experienced and crafty hack who would steal a story out from under your nose if you were careless enough to let him. They'd spent the next few minutes playing out that game familiar to all fellow journalists, sidestepping questions, making small talk, ducking and diving while they both tried to figure out what the other one was doing there.

Jimmy's worst fears had been confirmed when Bob had eventually asked in an overly casual tone, 'So have you heard about this Lynch business?'

'Lynch?'

'Bit before your time, I suppose.'

Jimmy had adjusted his face into an expression he hoped was suitably blank. 'Something I should know about?'

'Nah, no big deal, just some blag from years back. I heard they might have caught the blokes who did it. Don't reckon there's much in it, though. You know what it's like round here; there's a new rumour every five minutes.'

Jimmy had given a nod. 'True enough.' What he was really thinking was: *shit, shit, shit.* He'd known it was only a matter of time before someone else latched on to the Paddy Lynch story, but he'd been hoping for a few weeks' grace. What now? He still hadn't got the background on Tom Chase – the guy, it seemed, had materialised from nowhere – and Eden was being less than cooperative. 'Big job was it, then?' he asked, just to keep the conversation going.

But Bob Rich wasn't playing ball. If the gossip had legs, he didn't want the likes of Jimmy muscling in. 'Nah, nothing special. I hear there was trouble on the Mansfield last night. The law were out again.'

Jimmy went along with the change of subject. 'When isn't there trouble? That place is a powder keg.' It was less than a year since the Brixton riots and last summer there had also been disturbances in Dalston and Stoke Newington. The

185

three tall towers of the Mansfield estate, high-rise prisons for the poor and the unemployed, were a breeding ground for criminality, resentment and racial tension. 'It won't be long before someone lights the fuse and the whole bloody lot goes up in smoke.'

'Something's brewing. You going to take a look?'

Jimmy, who preferred not to put himself in the line of fire, had no intention of going near the place. 'Yeah, I might head over there.'

Bob leaned against the bar, his shrewd eyes making a fast survey of the other customers. 'Be a shame to miss out on the action.'

Which had given Jimmy exactly the excuse he needed to exit the Hope without arousing the other man's suspicions. Now he walked quickly with his hands in his pockets and his head bent against the cold. There was no way he could hold off any longer. With Bob Rich sniffing around, he had no choice but to take a chance and go for it. He glanced over his shoulder, making sure that no one was on his tail, before turning to the right.

St Mary's was a street of two-up, two-down red-brick terraces that ran parallel to the railway. The houses were small and dilapidated, council properties that should have been condemned years ago, but which – either through oversight or sheer indifference – still remained standing. The trains roared by every fifteen minutes, bringing a rumble like thunder, throwing up dust and shaking the foundations.

Jimmy, knowing better than to knock on any front door round here, veered down the alleyway that ran along the rear and counted off the houses until he came to number eighteen.

He took a moment to gather his thoughts before striding through the gateway and rapping on the back door.

It was opened by a large thickset woman with black hair scraped into a ponytail and dark suspicious eyes. 'Yeah?'

'Mrs Lynch? I'm sorry to disturb you, but I was wondering if I could have a word as regards your late husband.'

Vera Lynch looked him up and down and clearly didn't like what she saw. 'And who the hell are you?'

'I'm Jimmy Letts. I'm a reporter with—'

'Shove off!' She waved her arms and tried to shoo him away like he was some flea-ridden mutt she'd found in the yard. 'I've got nothin' to say. Just fuck off and leave me alone.'

But Jimmy, who was used to such welcomes, wasn't deterred. Before she had time to slam the door in his face, he quickly offered the bait, the juicy morsel that might make her think again. 'You know that one of the robbers has been charged, yeah? Charged with the murder of your old man, I mean.'

Vera suddenly became still, her arms dropping back to her sides. 'I might have heard a whisper,' she said cautiously.

'Not from Old Bill, I'll bet. They're playing their cards close to their chests.'

'No, not the filth. They've told me nothin'.'

'Typical,' Jimmy said. 'And you're the one person who has a right to know. All these years of waiting and then when they do catch the bastard ... Well, you'd think they'd be straight round, wouldn't you?'

'Fat chance.' Vera raised her arms again and crossed them over her ample chest. Her hands were red and callused, as rough as a labourer's. 'So what have you found out? You got a name? Is that it?'

Jimmy stamped his feet on the ground and rubbed his hands together. 'Bit chilly out here, isn't it? How about we go inside and have a proper chat?' He glanced at the houses either side as if the neighbours might be listening. 'Somewhere a bit more private.'

Vera hesitated, torn between her desire to know and a basic suspicion of the press. But eventually, grudgingly, she stood aside and let him in.

As soon as he was over the threshold, Jimmy knew he'd got his story. It wasn't the one he really wanted – the Eden Chase angle would have to wait – but it would do for now. A good local tale of crime and betrayal, of a grieving widow, of a community ripped apart by secrets and suspicion.

27

On the way to the prison, Eden didn't mention the Kellston flat to Tammy. She'd said too much, she thought, the last time they'd met, when the wine had loosened her tongue and all her fears had spilled out. Now she was trying to keep a lid on it. Tammy could tell something was wrong – something in addition, that was, to Tom staring down the barrel of a life sentence – and wasn't letting it rest.

'You sure you're okay, hon? You still worried about Pat Lynch?'

Eden kept her eyes on the icy road. 'Only the odd sleepless night,' she said drily. 'But to be honest, I'm trying not to think about him.'

'Yeah, I'd be the same. You've got enough to deal with, huh?'

'More than enough.'

'So did you find out anything about the money?'

Eden gave her a quick sideways glance, trying to remember how much she'd said about the Munich transfers. 'The money?'

'You know, the cash in the business account, the money the law was going on about.'

'Oh, that. I need to ask Tom about it today.'

'Did you not see his accountant, then?'

'No, something came up. We had to reschedule.' The lie slipped out before she'd even thought about it. She didn't want to admit that Elspeth Coyle couldn't or wouldn't tell her where the money had come from. It would look dodgy, would make Tom look dodgy, and she didn't want Tammy to view him that way. 'We're doing it next week instead.'

'I'm sure Tom can explain.'

Eden glanced at her again, wondering if she was being sarcastic, but her expression appeared open and straightforward, devoid of any cynicism. 'Yes.'

'Bet you can't wait to see that cop's face when he finds out the cash didn't come from the Epping job.'

'I'd rather see it when Tom walks out of jail.'

Eden felt her stomach tighten as she thought about the conversation she was about to have with him: the money from the account in Germany, the flat in Kellston, the reporter who was probably going to splash his name across the front cover of the local rag. None of it was good. All of it made her feel like she was heading for the kind of confrontation that could rock the very foundations of her marriage.

'Are you sure you're okay?' Tammy asked again. 'You look kind of pale.'

Eden forced a smile. 'I'm all right. It's just ... you know ... '

'Everything?'

'That pretty well sums it up.'

'You've got to try and stay positive, hon. I know it's easier said than done, but ... You don't want the filth putting doubts in your head.'

Eden opened her mouth, about to claim that she didn't have any doubts, but the words caught in her throat. Who would she be trying to convince – Tammy or herself?

'They like playing mind games,' Tammy continued. 'They get off on it. Don't let them get to you.'

'I won't.'

'And I'm always here if you need to talk or anything. I know I've got a big gob, but I can keep it shut when I have to. You don't have to worry on that score.'

Eden nodded, hoping this was true. 'Thanks.'

Fifteen minutes later they arrived at HMP Thornley Heath. They found a place to park, tramped back through the snow to the jail and signed in. As Eden was going through the search procedure – the walk through the metal detector, the pat down, the examination of the inside of her mouth – she realised that although it still felt intrusive, it wasn't as bad as the first time. She wondered how long it would take before the process didn't bother her at all, before it became as routine as eating or drinking or brushing her hair.

Knowing that the visit wasn't going to be an easy one, Eden took slow deep breaths as she crossed the courtyard. She thought of what she'd learned over the past week – all of it disturbing – and prayed that Tom would give her the answers she wanted to hear. *Please, God.*

She saw him the moment she entered the visiting room and quickly went over, reaching up to put her arms around his neck. In that instant, feeling his body against hers, inhaling his comforting familiar smell, everything felt right again. Hope resurfaced and her doubts retreated. This was her husband, the man she loved, her other half. She had to believe in him. Being faithful was about more than sexual fidelity – it went to the very core of loyalty and trust.

'How are you?' she asked as they separated and sat down.

'Getting used to it.' He gave a wry smile. 'I'll be an old lag in no time at all.'

'Now there's an attractive prospect.'

'And thanks for the clothes and the radio. It's good to be wearing my own stuff again.'

Eden had sent a parcel through the post. She had intended to write a letter to go with it, but after three attempts had given up – she couldn't find the right words – and had settled for a card instead. 'Let me know if you need anything else.'

Tom looked at her. 'What's wrong?'

'What do you mean?'

He raised his eyebrows. 'Eden?'

She stared back at him, wondering where to start. He had chosen to wear a white shirt today, a colour that brought out the blue of his eyes. She gazed into those eyes, trying to hold on to the faith while she made a choice. 'I saw Banner,' she said finally. 'He was going on about some thirty grand that came from an account in Munich. He seemed to think . . . well, he was implying that . . . '

'It might have been from the proceeds of an armed robbery?'

'I think that was the gist.'

'And what did you say?'

'What could I say? Other than whatever he thought, he was wrong.'

Tom nodded and leaned forward, lowering his voice. 'He is wrong. It was a loan from a man called Lukas Albrecht, thirty-five grand in all – well, more of an investment really. I wanted to shift the studio into the West End and I needed some capital. The banks here wouldn't touch me – too much of a risk – and so I went over to Munich. I knew Lukas from years back, and he offered me the money in exchange for a share in the business. Forty per cent is what he wanted, and I wasn't in a position to argue.'

'So this Lukas is actually your business partner?' Eden felt bemused by the fact Tom had never even mentioned him. Then she remembered something else the DI had said. 'But Banner reckons that no repayments have been made. They've been through your business accounts and . . . '

'Banner is believing what he wants to believe. I've got a copy of the agreement showing exactly where the money came from. And there's a reason why no profits were paid out. Lukas died three weeks after we made the contract, dropped dead of a heart attack. He has no surviving family, no kids or anything. He wasn't the marrying type, if you get my drift.'

'So you just get to keep the money?'

'There's no one to pay it back to.'

Eden gave a tiny shake of her head, wondering if this was entirely legal. 'How come you didn't tell me?'

'It was four years ago, before we even met.'

Which wasn't exactly the answer she was looking for. Eden realised he'd never really talked much about the nuts and bolts of the business. He'd mention new clients or shoots he had planned for the week ahead but the financial side of things had never been discussed. Maybe he'd have confided in her if she'd asked, but she hadn't.

Tom carried on explaining. 'I could have told Banner about Lukas Albrecht, but Castor decided I should keep it under wraps. It might be useful during the trial. You see, even if I can prove the money was legit, it's not going to get me out of here. The cops have gone too far down the road to turn back now.'

'So why didn't Elspeth tell me about Lukas? I mean, I was right there in her office and . . . '

Tom gave a shrug. 'I don't know. She should have done. Maybe she thought it was down to me to explain.'

'So why didn't you? Before now, I mean.'

'Like I said, it was a long time ago. You have to trust me. You do trust me, don't you?'

'I'd just like to be kept in the loop, that's all. I need to know what's going on.' Eden laid her hands in her lap, her fingers curling together as she prepared to cover the next bit of tricky ground. She watched him closely as she said, 'Elspeth suggested that if you wanted to hold on to the studio, you should consider selling the Kellston flat.'

He didn't even flinch. 'It's an idea, I suppose. What do you think?'

Eden sighed with exasperation. 'God, Tom, I didn't even know you had a flat in Kellston. How come I didn't know that?'

'Of course you knew. I told you.'

'You didn't.'

Tom's forehead crunched into a frown. 'I must have. It's where I used to live before Pope Street.'

'You've never said a word about it.'

'No way,' he said. 'Really? Are you sure?'

'It's hardly the sort of thing you forget.'

'No, sorry, I suppose I just . . . I don't have anything much to do with it now. An agent deals with the letting and the maintenance. I haven't been there for years.'

Eden didn't feel especially reassured by any of this, but she didn't want to get into a major row about it. For some reason, he had chosen not to tell her and she would have to form her own conclusions as to why that was. 'So do you want me to put it on the market?'

'You're mad at me.'

'I'm not. I'm just confused. How do you expect me to feel? I've suddenly found out that you own a flat in the East End of London and—'

'It wasn't a secret,' he said. 'I thought I'd told you. I don't know how . . . Anyway, the spare keys are in the top drawer of

194

the bureau. The flat's empty at the moment. Why don't you go and take a look at the place, see what state it's in? It might need a lick of paint before we try and sell.'

Eden didn't say that she'd already been there. 'Yes, I will. I'll go at the weekend.'

'It's pretty basic, just a one-bed over a shop. I needed something cheap until I got the business up and running. To be honest, I don't think we'll get that much for it. Kellston isn't exactly a hotspot when it comes to the property market.'

'Are you sure you want to sell?'

'It makes sense, doesn't it?'

'I suppose so.' Then, because there seemed little left to say on the subject of the flat – at least nothing that wouldn't turn the atmosphere even more frosty – she asked, 'So what's happening with Castor? Is there any news on Jack Minter yet?'

'He's still trying to track him down. Trouble is, the guy could be anywhere by now. Castor's contacted the embassies in Hungary and Germany, but the chances of him being found are slim.'

'He has to find him,' Eden insisted. 'It's the only way of proving that you didn't steal that bracelet, that you didn't have anything to do with the Epping robbery.' She remembered then that she'd forgotten to bring the Budapest photo. Damn it! The picture was still lying on the table at Pope Street. 'I was going through some of the Hungary photographs. There's one of a man and woman sitting outside a café. I was wondering if the guy could be Jack Minter.'

Tom shook his head. 'I took lots of pictures. I haven't looked at them in ages.'

Eden did her best to describe it. 'The man has his arm around her shoulder. She's young, pretty, long light-coloured hair. He's a bit older, mid-twenties maybe, wearing jeans, kind of cocky-looking.'

Tom thought for a while, but then gave a shrug. 'No, it doesn't ring any bells. They were probably just some couple I noticed, not anyone I actually knew.'

But Eden wasn't convinced. There was something about the relaxed way the pair were staring into the camera that made her sure they had known the photographer. It was just a hunch, a feeling. 'I'll post it to you.'

'They might not let me have it. They've got weird rules about photographs here.'

'Okay, so what if I give it to Castor? Would he be able to show it to you on your next legal visit?'

'I guess so, but I really don't think it is Minter.'

Suddenly an idea came into Eden's head. 'Maybe I should go to Budapest and look for him myself.'

Tom seemed taken aback. 'What?'

'Why not? I could go to where he used to live – Garay Square, wasn't it? – and ask around. Someone might remember him. They may even know where he is now.'

'Christ, Eden, you can't go wandering around Budapest on your own. You don't speak Hungarian; you don't even speak German. How do you expect to make yourself understood?'

But now that she'd thought of it, Eden wasn't going to let a few minor problems get in the way. 'I'll find someone who speaks English. It can't be that hard. There must be interpreters, guides, that kind of thing. I can pay someone to translate for me. I mean, God, it's better than sitting around doing nothing all day. And Castor isn't getting anywhere, is he?'

'Give him a chance. These things take time.'

'And meanwhile you're stuck in here. I might be able to find Jack Minter or at least get a lead on where he went. It's worth a go, isn't it?'

'No,' Tom said firmly. 'You can't go out there. It isn't safe.'

'I can take care of myself.'

'I'm not saying you can't, but what if I'm wrong about him?'

Eden stared across the table. 'What do you mean?'

'I mean, what if Jack *was* an armed robber? What if he did leave Paddy Lynch to die? He's not going to be happy when you turn up looking for him.'

'A week ago you were saying he wasn't capable of anything like that.'

Tom raked his fingers through his hair, his mouth turning down at the corners. 'Yeah, well, a week's a long time in jail. Plenty of empty hours to mull things over. Maybe I did get him wrong. Maybe he was smarter than I thought. It's just not worth the risk, Eden. It's way too dangerous. You can disappear without trace in a place like Budapest.'

Eden had gone from hope to disappointment in a matter of minutes. 'But there has to be a way of tracking him down.'

'Not this way. Promise me you won't go there.'

'I won't. I promise.' As Eden gazed into his eyes she saw the relief in them and a terrible thought crossed her mind. Perhaps it wasn't just her safety he was worried about. Perhaps he had another reason for not wanting Jack Minter to be found.

28

Pat Lynch flexed the muscles in his arms as he paced from one end of the cell to the other, muttering under his breath. He'd suspected something was wrong when his mother had turned up on a visit yesterday – she wouldn't usually brave the Solent in weather like this – and he'd been spot on. She'd looked green in the gills when he'd seen her, although that might have been partly down to the ferry crossing. Bad news, he'd thought. It had to be. Someone was dead or dying. And it hadn't taken her long to spit it out. No sooner had she sat down than the words were spilling out.

'One of the fuckers, the ones who did for your dad, they've finally got him.'

Pat had stiffened, narrowed his eyes. 'What? Are you sure?'

'No, I've just come all the way out here 'cause I heard a bleedin' rumour. Course I'm sure.'

'Okay, okay, no need to go off on one. I'm only asking.' And he'd taken a breath, steadying himself, because he'd waited sixteen years to find out who the murdering bastards were. 'Who was it? Tell me.'

His mother had leaned in close enough for him to smell the sweat on her, the fags, the cloying scent of cheap perfume – but she didn't come straight out with it. First she had a story to tell about a reporter called Jimmy Letts who'd been round to the house, what he'd said to her and what she'd said to him, an interminable saga that made him want to slap her.

'For fuck's sake,' he'd hissed. 'Just tell me who it was.'

'I'm getting to it, ain't I?'

'Well, get to it a bit fuckin' quicker.' What was it with women? They could never give a straight answer to a straight question; they had to fanny around for half an hour, saying twice as much as they needed to as if they were getting paid by the word. 'Before the end of the visit would be good.'

She had given him one of her disappointed looks, pissed off because this was her big moment and she wanted to savour it. 'The name won't mean nothin' to you. I was sure it was going to be someone Paddy knew, one of the old crowd, but . . . ' The sentence had trailed off as she'd seen the cold expression on his face. 'Tom Chase,' she'd said smartly. 'That's the bastard's name.'

'Huh?'

'Tom Chase,' she'd repeated. 'Jimmy says he's a photographer, that he's got a studio in Covent Garden. They pulled him in a couple of weeks back. He's been charged with the Epping job and manslaughter.'

'It was bloody murder not manslaughter. The shitheads left him to die.'

'Jimmy reckons there's a squealer, that someone's grassed him up. He doesn't know who it is yet. I've called the filth but they won't tell me nothin'.'

'A photographer?' Pat had said as if this piece of information had only just sunk in. Villains didn't run around with

199

cameras; they had car lots or scrapyards or clubs and pubs. It didn't make any sense. 'Who the fuck is this guy?'

Pat stopped pacing the cell, sat down on the bunk and immediately stood up again. He was still processing the information she'd given him yesterday. At the time of the Epping heist, he'd only been fifteen. Dad had gone out in the morning and never come back. Even after all the years that memory was still sharp, raw enough to make him flinch. *Tom Chase.* He rolled the name over his tongue, trying to think back, to dig it out from some shadowy corner of his mind. Had his father ever mentioned him? He must have. Paddy Lynch never worked with strangers. He must have known the bloke – or someone he trusted must have vouched for him.

Pat was still sifting through his memory – and getting nowhere – when there was a knock on the door. Gonzo came in and nodded. 'You okay, mate?'

Sammy Gonzales was the prison fixer, a lean, sinewy guy with a jutting chin and dark hooded eyes. If you needed something doing, inside or out, he was the man to go to.

Pat nodded back. 'You got anything? You know where he is yet?'

'Give us a chance, mate. I've only just put the word out. But I'm thinking one of the London nicks – Wandsworth, maybe, or the Ville. Could be down the block, though. We'll have to wait and see.'

Pat sent up a prayer that the bastard wasn't in solitary confinement for his own protection. It was a shame the sodding reporter hadn't known where Chase was being held – or maybe he did and just wasn't saying. 'It could be quicker to ask that Jimmy Letts.'

'Yeah, if you want the whole world to know what you're planning. What if he goes to the law? The screws will have Chase off the wing before you can bleedin' blink.'

200

Pat hadn't thought of that. He was in a hurry to get things done, to get the ball rolling. All his anger and frustration was bubbling to the surface. 'And that other bit of business. You got it sorted?'

'No problem.'

'When?'

'Soon as. A few days probably.'

'And he's sound?' Pat asked. 'He ain't going to fuck up or nothin'?'

'He's good as gold, Pat. There's no worries on that score.'

'He'd better be.'

After Gonzo left, Pat lay down on the bed and put his hands behind his head. If he hadn't been stuck in this dump, he could have sorted things himself. And whose fault was it that he was here? That bloody bitch, Mariah's. His face contorted with irritation. If she hadn't been winding him up, yapping in his ear, he'd never have shoved her out of the car in the first place. Women were nothing but trouble.

Pat had no regrets about the others either, the ones nobody knew about, those superior girls with their long straight hair and cool judgemental eyes. Even the way they walked was like a taunt – *Look at what you can't have.* Except he could have it, and he'd taken it. He could still see their faces, their pale skin and bruised mouths. He'd buried them in shallow graves right in the heart of the forest, ripe peaches left to rot in the ground.

He thought about that other bit of business with Gonzo and smiled. He'd have liked to have done Eden Chase himself, to have leaned in close and whispered in her ear: 'Think of your husband, babe. This is what he's done to you.'

29

While Eden went through the wardrobe searching for something to wear, her thoughts were still with the visit she'd had with Tom the day before. 'I mean, you don't just forget about owning a flat, do you? It's not the kind of thing that slips your mind.'

Caitlin was perched on the edge of the bed. 'Not unless you're made of money. So what are you thinking? Some kind of safety net, perhaps?'

'What, in case the marriage didn't work out? It's hardly romantic.' Eden held up a tailored black suit and asked, 'How about this?'

'Lovely – if you're going to a funeral.'

'The mood will be fairly similar.' When she was meeting her father, Eden usually tried to wear something he would disapprove of, like skin-tight jeans or a shocking-pink dress that clashed with her hair, but tonight was going to be difficult enough without winding him up before the conversation even began.

'Are you going to come clean about Tom?'

'That's the plan. I haven't really got a choice. It's going to come out eventually; better he hears it from me than reads about it in the papers. Can't say I'm looking forward to it, though. It's going to be a whole evening of "I told you so" . . . and worse.'

'Maybe it won't be as bad as you think.'

'Hey, Dad, guess what? Your son-in-law is currently at Her Majesty's Pleasure, charged with manslaughter and armed robbery.' Eden pulled a face. 'Somehow I can't see it going down that well.'

'You're still his daughter. And you're going through a shitty time. He might surprise you.'

'Don't hold your breath. You know what he's like.' Eden put the black dress back in the wardrobe and took out a cream cashmere sweater and a pair of beige trousers. 'How about these?'

'Thoroughly respectable.'

'Good,' Eden said, dropping the clothes on the bed. 'At least that's one thing he won't be able to complain about.' She went over to the mirror, pulled back her hair and started twisting it into a knot at the nape of her neck. 'So tell me about Greenham. How's it going there?'

'It's amazing, and there are more women arriving every day. It's turning into something big. You'll have to come down one weekend.'

The protest, against the siting of nuclear missiles at RAF Greenham Common, was a cause that Eden would have once embraced with enthusiasm. Women were uniting and standing up for what they believed in, challenging male dominance in a way that had not been seen before. Of course the press didn't see it like that – she had taken to reading the papers more closely since Tom's arrest – and were already making jibes about how the protestors would be better employed staying home and taking care of their children. 'I will . . . you know, once things have calmed down a bit here.'

Caitlin nodded. 'Yeah, you don't need any more trouble at the moment.'

Eden looked at her in the mirror. 'Is there going to be trouble?'

'There's bound to be. You can't go trampling over male sensibilities – or their army bases – without there being some kind of backlash. Men don't like their decisions being questioned. I reckon they'll try and break up the camp before too long. You don't want to end up being arrested.'

Eden gave a wry smile. 'Or you,' she said. 'I couldn't face visiting both of you in prison.'

Caitlin laughed. 'They'll have to catch me first.' She glanced at her watch. 'So when are you meeting your dad?'

'Seven.'

'You'd better get a wriggle on if you want to get there on time.'

'I don't want to get there at all.'

'Are you taking the car?'

Eden shook her head. 'The Tube. I'll need a drink, lots of drinks, to get through this evening.'

'Come on, then. Get your glad rags on and I'll drop you off at Angel. I'm going past there anyway.'

The Fitzpatrick was one of those old-fashioned hotels, full of wide gilt mirrors and overstuffed sofas, which wouldn't have looked out of place in the nineteen fifties. It had a quiet, almost reverential, air. Eden braced herself as she walked through the foyer, trying to prepare for what lay ahead. Just how did you tell your father that your husband was in jail? On the Tube, she'd rehearsed several different methods, all of which seemed equally inappropriate now that she was here. Tell him straight away or wait until they were eating dinner? Just blurt it out or build up to it slowly? She still had no idea.

Eden hesitated at the door to the bar, almost tempted to turn on her heel and make a run for it. It was that look in his eyes she dreaded most, the unspoken disappointment she had lived with all her life. 'Get a grip,' she murmured. What she had to do was stand up for Tom and protest his innocence. It didn't matter what her father said, or even what he thought. She just had to bite the bullet and get it over and done with before he heard the news from someone else.

She painted on a smile as she walked into the bar. It wasn't busy and she saw him straight away, sitting at a table over to the right. For a brief moment she saw him as a stranger might – grey-haired, middle-aged, a solitary man, perhaps even a lonely one, staring wistfully into a glass of malt whisky – before he lifted his head, rose to his feet and became the person she was more familiar with.

'Eden,' he said, leaning down to kiss her cheek. 'I thought you might have forgotten.'

'I'm not that late. It's only five minutes.'

'Ten,' he said.

'Sorry, there was a hold-up on the Tube.'

'No Tom?' he asked, looking over her shoulder.

'Er . . . no . . . I'm afraid he can't make it. He sends his apologies.'

Her father's eyebrows shifted up a notch, disapproval etched into their curves. 'I booked the table for three.'

'Yes, well, there was . . . something came up. Anyway, it'll be nice, just the two of us.' And before he could ask any more probing questions about Tom's absence, she quickly went on, 'How was the conference? Was it interesting?'

'Moderately.'

Eden turned towards the bar. 'I'll get a drink and then we'll go on in, shall we?'

The dining room was as quiet as the bar, with only half a

dozen customers, none of whom would ever see sixty again. They were seated in the centre of the room where, surrounded by a sea of white tablecloths, Eden had the sense of being stranded. The waiters came and went, soft-footed, solemn, quietly spoken, as if they were dealing with the terminally ill rather than a few hungry diners wanting to fill their stomachs.

Eden sipped on the wine, trying not to gulp, as she perused the menu. The contents were bland, typical British fare – lamb chops, steak and kidney pie, cod in parsley sauce – with none of the 'fancy foreign muck' that her father couldn't stand. She ordered the fish, hoping she'd be able to eat it when it came. Her stomach was fizzing with nervous anxiety. A part of her wanted to get the confession over and done with, but the greater part preferred to put it off for as long as possible.

While they waited for dinner, Eden made slightly manic small talk about everything from the state of the underground to the weather. She figured that while she was talking, he wasn't – which had to be good when it came to the avoidance of awkward questions.

'So how's college?' her father asked when she finally paused for breath. 'Did you ever finish that essay on Caravaggio?'

'Yes,' she lied, thinking of the books lying unopened on the table, 'all done and dusted.'

'And so what will you do with this degree when you finally get it?'

Eden knew her father thought all arts degrees were a waste of time, a frivolous accessory like a pair of expensive shoes or a handbag. 'I don't know. I haven't decided yet. Maybe some kind of restoration work.'

'Is there money in that?'

'I shouldn't think so.'

Her father pursed his lips. 'Well, so long as you're happy.'

Unsure as to whether he was being sarcastic or not, Eden

gave him a probing look. She was used to his disapproval, which to some extent she had nurtured through the years, negative attention being better than no attention at all. As a teenager she had learned which buttons to push – wrong clothes, wrong friends, wrong attitude – and had never really got out of the habit. And now, of course, she was about to deliver the cruellest blow of all, the news that she was married to a would-be murderer.

He met her gaze. 'Is everything all right? You're looking a little tired. Not been burning the candle at both ends, have you?'

Eden bristled at the question, hurt and annoyed by the presumption that her weariness must be self-inflicted. 'Of course,' she said. 'You know me. Life's one big party.' And as if to underline the statement she beckoned the waiter over and ordered another glass of wine. 'A large one, please.'

Her father stared at her. 'You're not driving, I hope.'

'No, I'm not driving. I've already told you I came on the Tube.'

While they ate, she watched him surreptitiously, trying to figure out what he was thinking. They were like two snipers standing on opposite sides of a river, waiting for the opportunity to take a shot. It was ironic that her father made a living out of building bridges and yet there seemed no way to bridge the gulf between them. And now, very soon, everything was going to get a whole lot worse.

That moment came when her father had almost cleared his plate. As he gathered the final mouthful on to his fork, he asked, 'So how is Tom? Hard at work, I presume?'

Eden swallowed hard. Her mouth was dry and she felt her heart start to hammer in her chest. 'Er . . . actually there was something I wanted to—'

'Oh,' he said, interrupting her. 'I almost forgot to tell you the good news. Your brother has got engaged! It's about time, but he finally got round to popping the question.'

'To Alison?' she asked rather stupidly. The interruption had thrown her off balance and she said the first thing that came into her head.

'I can't think of anyone else he'd be likely to propose to.'

'No, of course not.' Iain had been dating Alison since university. She was a clever, sensible, practical girl who would, no doubt, be an excellent wife and mother. Not to mention daughter-in-law. This marriage, unlike her own, was one her father thoroughly approved of.

'Well, pass on my congratulations to them both.'

'Or you could pick up the phone and do it yourself.'

'Yes,' Eden said. 'I'll do that.'

'It won't be until next year. The wedding, I mean. They're thinking April or May.'

'Lovely,' Eden murmured.

'And it's going to be a proper church wedding, one with all the trimmings.'

Eden felt the bullet whiz through the air. A *proper* wedding, rather than an improper one at a registry office. He just couldn't resist. He couldn't help himself. And Eden's response was as predictable. 'Let's hope you manage to make it this time.'

A thin brittle silence fell over the table.

Eden drank the rest of her wine. When had it started, this tension between them? Or had it always been there? She was reminded of that experiment she'd done at school where if you put the north pole of a magnet near the south pole of another, the two of them were attracted. But if it was north to north or south to south, the magnets repelled each other. They were like the latter, always pulling away as if ordered by a natural force they had no control over.

'Perhaps you and Tom will come up to Edinburgh this summer,' he said. 'If you're not too busy.'

And Eden knew in that moment that she wouldn't tell him, *couldn't* tell him, at least not face to face like this. It would have to wait. She would write a letter, perhaps. Yes, that would be better. She would put it all down on paper and send it through the post. 'We'll try.'

The meal finally came to an end and – although it was only half past nine – neither of them made any attempt to prolong the evening. Her father muttered about having to be up early in the morning to catch the train, and Eden said she understood, she had things to do too. Now that it was over, they both made the effort to be pleasant, to smile, to part in a manner that if not exactly loving was at least civil.

He insisted on walking her out of the hotel and hailing a black cab despite her protests that she'd be fine on the Tube.

'Just humour me,' he said, pushing a ten-pound note into her hand. 'This way, I'll know for sure that you got home safely.'

Eden hesitated, battling with that familiar knee-jerk reaction to do exactly the opposite of whatever he wanted. But she was too tired to argue, and too downhearted. 'Thank you,' she said, leaning across to kiss his cheek. She caught a light lemony whiff of aftershave. 'And thanks for dinner.'

As the cab pulled away, Eden glanced over her shoulder. Her father was still standing on the pavement outside the hotel. She felt a sudden urge to stop the taxi, to get out, rush back to him and say, 'Dad, something terrible has happened.' But even as she turned her head towards the driver, she knew she wouldn't do it; the words stuck in her throat. She couldn't run to her father. She never had. She was too proud, too wary, too afraid of rejection. With a sigh she sat back in the seat, defeated by her own history.

30

Teddy Gill had been obsessed by fire since the age of seven when he'd stood with his mother and watched, wide-eyed, while the Albany pub burned down. To this day he could still recall it vividly, the flames raging through the building, the heat and the smoke, the crackling, splintering, destructive thrill of it all. And while he was watching, nothing else had mattered. He had been as consumed by the fire as the building itself.

His first attempts, a few years later, had been minor, tentative affairs – a pile of timber stacked up in a yard, a garden shed, an old garage with its doors hanging off – but gradually he'd grown more ambitious. It was the drama he craved, the spectacle. Fire shouldn't be contained to a few mouldering planks of wood; he had to set it free and let it run wild.

The church had been his finest success to date – and worth the time he'd spent in jail for it. God's house. Grey brick, solid, the place of holy secrets. He had watched the flames grow and spread. He had seen the stained-glass windows illuminated for one last time before they exploded into fragments, blown out into the night air, showering the grass like glass confetti.

And when the shrink had asked him why he'd done it, he'd said, 'Why not? If God wanted it saved, he should have called the fire brigade.'

Teddy was still pleased by that retort. He smirked as he turned the corner into Pope Street, lit a fag, and began checking out the numbers on the houses. Already he was feeling the buzz of anticipation, the sense of exhilaration that never faded no matter how many matches he struck.

The street was quiet, residential, two rows of smart three-storey terraces with big windows. Behind the drawn curtains, lights were blazing. It was early, half past nine, and he was only here to do a recce, to make sure he knew exactly which house it was before coming back later.

Teddy found number twenty-four. He didn't stop but strolled casually past, his gaze taking in everything he needed to know without appearing overly curious. You could never tell who might be watching. The whole house was in darkness. He liked the look of the letter box – a decent size – and was pleased to see that the door was set back, creating a small porch area where his activities could go unobserved by everyone but the occupants of the houses opposite. Hopefully, by the time he returned they would all be asleep.

His feet made a cracking noise as he tramped down the snow-covered street. He pushed his cold hands deep into the pockets of his anorak. The handles of the carrier bag were looped around his right wrist, and inside the bag was a litre bottle of petrol, a rubber hose and some old rags. The bottle knocked against his leg as he walked.

Teddy always worked at night, never in daylight. This was partly for practical reasons – he was less likely to be noticed – but also because he preferred the look of fire against a dark background. It was more intense, more dramatic, more satisfying. He raised his left hand to his neck and scratched. Already the itch was with him, the longing to be getting on with it. But he knew he had to wait.

He would walk to Upper Street, to one of the pubs, and hang out there until they closed. A few pints would hardly make a dent in the thirty quid CJ had given him. The six crisp five-pound notes were neatly folded in his wallet.

'Just torch the place,' CJ had said. 'Send it up in smoke. Reckon you can manage that?'

Which was like asking if Pelé could kick a ball around. 'What do you think?'

'Don't fuck it up.'

Teddy hadn't enquired why he wanted the house burned. It was none of his business. His only questions were where and when. 'Consider it done, mate.'

'And don't hang about, huh? Don't wait for those big shiny fire engines to turn up.'

When he reached the corner of Pope Street, Teddy glanced back over his shoulder towards number twenty-four. A smile tugged at the corners of his lips. Ashes to ashes, he thought, dust to dust.

31

It was ten past ten by the time Eden got home. She toyed with the idea of ringing Iain, but decided it was too late. Her brother, if he was in, wouldn't welcome a call at this time of night. Although they now had an amicable relationship, they were not especially close. He was five years her senior and the gap meant they'd had little in common while they were growing up. She had always been the annoying kid sister and, to some extent, this was probably still the case.

Eden went through to the kitchen, made a weak coffee and took it back to the living room. The light was blinking on the answer machine. She pressed the button and sat down at the table. There was a message from her tutor requesting that she get in touch. Eden grimaced. It was two weeks now since she'd last graced college with her presence and she suspected she was never going back. The next message was from Denny, asking after Tom. The third and final message consisted of one of those long silences while someone made up their minds as to whether they were going to speak or not. They didn't.

Eden sipped her coffee while she thought back over the evening. She felt the same things she always felt after seeing her father – disappointment, irritation and a faint sense of regret. Snatches of their conversation drifted into her head and she turned them over, examining them from different angles, wondering what he'd meant by this or that. There had been no full-on battle tonight, only a few minor skirmishes from which she'd emerged relatively unscathed. Had she given him the ammunition – the truth about Tom – the outcome would have been very different.

But the confrontation couldn't be put off for ever. She should write the letter now, perhaps, and get it over and done with. She opened the pad of Basildon Bond and picked up a pen. *Dear Dad.* She paused, unsure as to how to continue. There was no good way to break the news that his son-in-law was currently languishing in prison . . . or that she'd failed to tell him when she had the opportunity.

Eden tried to think of the right words, but they just wouldn't come. She chewed on the end of the pen. The seconds ticked by. Her mind remained blank. Maybe what she needed was a good night's sleep before she even attempted to climb this particular mountain. She pushed aside the pad, intending to go to bed, but still didn't move from the table.

Her gaze strayed towards the pile of photographs and she began to sift through them again: faces in crowds, outside bars, on streets and in markets, nameless men and women she would never know, never meet. And it suddenly occurred to her that, had things been different, she could have been one of these anonymous people herself. Just a girl with long red hair, walking through the piazza in Covent Garden. If she hadn't heard the shutter on the camera, hadn't reacted, hadn't challenged him . . .

A chance encounter. That's all it had been. Was that how

life worked? Your destiny decided by a single stroke of fate. Five minutes earlier, five minutes later, and their paths might never have crossed. That was an odd thought. To have never met Tom, never fallen in love, never bound her life to his.

Despite the recent revelations, she still didn't doubt his innocence. What she did doubt, however, was how well she actually knew him. While she had thrown open the doors to her past, her feelings, her emotions, her triumphs and failures, he had given away very little. If he had opened the door at all, it was only by a fraction. Aware that he was self-contained, cautious – certainly not the type to wear his heart on his sleeve – she had, nevertheless, believed they shared an instinctive understanding. Now she was even starting to question that.

This thought didn't sit easily with her. She put down the photographs, pushed back her chair, rose to her feet and went over to the window. The street was empty. Couples didn't tell each other everything, not every little detail, but they usually shared the important stuff. That Tom had deliberately hidden the existence of the flat from her – and she was sure this was the case – made her feel ... What did she feel, exactly? Excluded, angry, offended, even betrayed to some extent. If the flat had been a safety net, then he couldn't have felt that their relationship would last for ever.

She wondered if this was a naive way of looking at things. He was older than her, more experienced, less inclined per-haps towards romantic notions. Was she overreacting? No, she damn well wasn't. What he'd done was completely out of order. Eden yawned and stretched out her arms. She was too tired for all this. What she needed was sleep.

She took a quick shower, wrapped herself in a towel and dried off in the bedroom. She put on one of Tom's T-shirts, a navy blue crew neck with short sleeves, and got into bed.

There was a book on the bedside table, *The Hotel New Hampshire* by John Irving. She picked it up, meaning to read for a while, but the words danced in front of her eyes. She gave up, switched off the lamp, lay down and five minutes later was fast asleep.

Eden dreamed she was on her way to meet Tom. She was late and was attempting to run but her legs were like lead; it took every ounce of effort just to put one foot in front of the other. She realised that wherever she was going, she wasn't going to get there in time. He would go away thinking she didn't care, and she'd never see him again. Panic rose in her chest, a tight suffocating sensation as if all the hope was being squeezed out of her lungs.

Eden woke suddenly, but not to the darkness she expected. There was a grey misty wash to the room, a lightness similar to dawn but not quite the same. With her brain still dulled by sleep, she blinked hard, unable to process what she was seeing. It only came to her gradually: first the smell – burning, was it burning? – and then the odd crackling sound. Jesus Christ, it was smoke. The flat was on fire!

Eden leapt out of bed and rushed barefoot to the door. She yelped as her fingers made contact with the hot metal handle and instantly jumped back. Grabbing the damp towel from the chair, she wrapped it round her hand and tried again. As soon as she opened the door, terror swept through her. She could see it was hopeless – the flames had taken hold and the living room was ablaze. There was no path through to the hallway and the stairs. She was trapped.

Horrified, Eden slammed the door shut. Her heart was pounding. The heat was coming through the wall, the smoke still drifting into the room. She could feel her chest growing tight, the panic rising inside her. What now? She had to act fast. She had to *do* something. Quickly she dragged the quilt off the bed and crammed it along the foot of the door. It wouldn't prevent all the smoke from getting in, but it might hold back the worst of it. For a while, at least.

She dashed over to the window, her only way out, and looked down on the dark patch of garden. It was a twenty-foot drop. Could she survive that? But it wasn't as if she had a choice – it was either jump or burn to death. She'd have to take her chances. And where the hell was everyone? The goddamn house was on fire and no one was doing anything.

Eden flipped the lock across and pushed up on the central bar of the window with her palms. It didn't budge. She tried harder, but still couldn't shift it. The sash was stuck. It was always sticking. Tom usually had to open it, but . . . 'For fuck's sake!' she cried out in frustration.

Frantically she looked around, searching for something, anything, to break the glass. She could feel the fire growing closer, hear the flames licking at the door. She plundered the dressing table, picking up and discarding perfume bottles, aerosols, hairbrushes, even her jewellery box. No, there was nothing heavy enough. She rushed back to the window and tried again, putting all her strength into it, pushing and push-ing. By now the smoke was getting denser, filling the room, wrapping itself around her. She was coughing and spluttering, finding it hard to breathe.

Eden slammed on the glass with the palm of her hands. She had to get the damn thing open. Her whole body was shaking, her legs like jelly. She was running out of time. She grabbed the towel and wrapped it around her hand again, picked up a can of hairspray from the floor and hammered it over and over against the top right corner of the window. The corners – they were the weak spots, weren't they? She was sure she'd read that somewhere.

'Jesus! Come on, come on!'

Finally she heard a reassuring splintering sound and a long crack appeared in the window. By now her breath was coming in short fast pants and she could barely stand. Just a few more blows, one final effort, and she could ... but the strength had suddenly drained out of her. Her arm dropped down by her side, the can slipping out of her grasp. Her head was swimming, her eyes seeing only murky grey. So was this it? Was this the end? She fought to stay conscious, to hold on to life, but the darkness was already descending. 'No,' she protested, the word barely audible. She swayed on her feet before her knees buckled and she crumpled to the floor.

32

Max Tamer often drove around at night, aimless journeys that could take him anywhere. Sometimes it was the West End, the Strand, Drury Lane, revisiting the places where Ann-Marie had worked. Other times he went further afield, deep into the heart of Essex or Kent. Tonight, however, he had only got as far as Islington.

It was true that the city never slept, but it dozed a little in the early hours. Once the pubs and clubs had emptied, only the strays remained on the streets: the dazed party-goers, the insomniacs, the lost and lonely, and those who had no home to go to.

Max was thinking about Tom Chase as he made his way along Essex Road and on to Upper Street. Was the man asleep in his cell, untroubled by conscience, dreaming of his days in Budapest? His fingers tightened around the wheel. He knew the bastard would never confess to Ann-Marie's murder. And so what choice did he have? Sometimes, if you wanted justice, you had to take the law into your own hands.

It was after three o'clock when he turned into Pope Street and pulled up ten yards away from number twenty-four. When he glanced towards the house, he was aware that something was wrong, but it took a moment to convert what he was seeing – a dark orange glow – into the knowledge that the building was actually on fire.

For a few seconds, Max didn't move. Was Eden Chase still inside? It was more than likely. There was no sign of her on the street, no sign of anyone, in fact. While the house burned, the neighbours were sleeping. The easiest thing in the world would be to drive away. It was what he wanted, wasn't it? Eden Chase dead and her husband left to grieve. A wife for a wife. A fair exchange.

There was only one problem. This revenge wasn't his; it was somebody else's. He'd been beaten to it, had the opportunity snatched away. And there was no satisfaction in that. He felt a sudden stab of resentment – nobody had the right to take away *his* retribution – and it was this thought that propelled him into action.

Max jumped out of the car and ran over to the house. It was clear, even as he approached, that there wasn't a hope of getting through the front door. He could see the flames through the glass panel at the top, a roaring inferno. He stared up at the first-floor window. More flames, more smoke. If Eden was in the flat, she wouldn't have long to get out. She might already be unconscious, stifled by carbon monoxide, oblivious to what was happening.

He went to number twenty-six and rang the bell, three long rings, keeping his hand on the button. And then, in case there could be any doubt as to the urgency of the situation, he hammered hard on the door and rattled the letter box. 'Fire!' he shouted.

It was less than thirty seconds before he was face to face with a middle-aged man dressed in pyjamas and slippers. His hair was mussed, his eyes bleary with sleep.

'What's going on? What is it?'

'There's a fire next door,' Max said. 'You need to call the fire brigade.'

The man stepped outside, looked across, caught sight of the flames and retreated back inside again. 'Shit,' he said. 'Sandra!' he shouted. 'Next door's on fire! Twenty-four. Call 999.'

A woman appeared at the top of the stairs, her hair in rollers. 'Is anyone in there?'

'I think so,' Max said.

She stood for a moment, her eyes growing wide, and then disappeared from view. A few seconds later, she called out, 'And you be careful, Geoff. Wait for the fire brigade to get here.'

Now, suddenly, there was a lot of activity from the neighbours with doors and windows opening, and people gathering on the street. They bunched together in groups, staring at the burning building.

'Can we get round the back?' Max asked. 'Is there another way in?'

'Yes, yes. Come through.' Geoff beckoned him into the house and grabbed a coat as they hurried along the hallway. 'Christ, I can't believe this is happening.'

'Next door. Is there anyone on the ground floor?'

'They're away on holiday. And the top flat's empty. But Tom and Eden ... they're on the first.'

Max noted that the news about Tom being in jail hadn't got around yet. 'I'm sure I saw a face at the window.' He needed the lie to explain his certainty that someone was still in the flat. 'I was just driving past and ... '

'It's a good thing you were.' Geoff took him through the kitchen, quickly unlocked the back door and stepped out into a long narrow garden covered in snow. 'The fence isn't too high. We'll get over easily enough.'

'Have you got a ladder?'

'In the shed.'

Max helped him get it out, picking up a hammer at the same time, and then clambered over the fence. Between them they got the ladder into the garden and, when Geoff had joined him, put it up against the wall. 'Hold it steady for me.'

Max stared up at the rear window of Eden's flat. It had a grey smoky look but he couldn't see any flames. There was a diagonal crack running from one corner to the other, evidence perhaps that she'd been trying to break the glass. He tucked the hammer into his belt and started climbing.

He could feel the heat radiating from the house and wondered what the hell he was doing. This was no act of heroism. You couldn't call a man courageous if he didn't care whether he lived or died. No, he'd been prompted by something far less noble than bravery, by a desire to reclaim his revenge, to not let someone else take away what was rightfully his. It was perverse, but then nothing in his life was normal any more.

He heard the sound of a siren in the distance – the fire brigade was on its way – but he couldn't afford to hang about. Every second counted. By the time they got here it might be too late. Max reached the top of the ladder but the room was too smoky to see anything. In case Eden was still conscious and huddled by the window, he shouted out a warning, 'Stay back!' before waiting a few seconds and then smashing the glass with the hammer.

The smoke billowed out and Max put his arm over his face. Once the worst of it had cleared he peered into the room. He saw her almost immediately, collapsed on the floor. He slipped the hammer back inside his belt, crawled inside and knelt down beside her, putting his fingers to her neck. There was still a faint pulse. He had a moment when he knew he could finish her off, right then, right there. No one would be any the wiser. But it wasn't the way he'd decided to do things.

By now the bedroom door was on fire, the flames devouring the wood. It wouldn't be long before the whole room was consumed. Max dragged Eden up and flung her over his shoulder. She wasn't heavy. She weighed about the same as Ann-Marie. Her long red hair fell in a stream down his back.

Getting a foothold on the ladder was going to be the trickiest bit and as he grabbed the edge of the window his hand pressed into the broken jagged glass. He cursed, instinctively lifting the bleeding palm to his mouth. At almost the very same moment flames shot across the bedroom. He could feel the extreme heat on his face, the burning, melting force of the fire.

Max quickly swung out on to the ladder. It shifted under the combined weight of the two of them and for a moment he thought he was going to lose his balance. He took hold of the sill until he'd steadied himself, glanced down at Geoff, gave a nod and began the descent. He could feel the smoke wafting into his lungs, the sweat pouring off him. Every step was an effort. As he neared the ground, he gritted his teeth and prayed. All he needed now was for one of the ground-floor windows to blow out and they'd both be dead meat.

Eventually, after what felt like a lifetime, he made it safely on to terra firma.

'Is she all right?' Geoff asked.

Max carried her down to the end of the garden, away from the house. 'Still breathing . . . just about.'

'What about Tom? Did you see him?'

'He's not there.'

'How do you know?'

Max didn't want the guy doing something stupid, like trying to save someone who wasn't even in the flat. 'She told me, yeah? She was still conscious when I got to her. She said there was no one else in there.'

Max lay Eden down on the ground and shifted her into the recovery position. The blood from his cut hand left a red smear on her arm. 'Stay with her. I'll go and get some help.' He climbed over the fence, ran through the house and on to the street. A fire engine, its blue lights flashing, was already in Pope Street. An ambulance was just pulling up.

He went to the ambulance first and explained about Eden. Then he went to speak to the fire crew, repeating the lie he'd told Geoff. 'She said her husband wasn't there. And there's no one in the other flats either.'

'You'd better stick around; the police are going to want to talk to you.'

'Of course.' Max gave his good-citizen nod and walked away. He waited until he was sure no one was paying him any attention before he hurried down the street, got in his car and drove off.

33

It was thirty-six hours before Eden was finally discharged from hospital on Sunday afternoon. She had a few minor burns but no permanent damage. The doctors told her she'd been lucky, but she didn't feel that way as she sat in the passenger seat of Caitlin's car and thought about everything that was lost: their home, their clothes, so many possessions and, last but not least, the chance of any peace of mind. She had a tight feeling in her chest that was not all down to the smoke she'd inhaled. Someone had tried to kill her. The thought was terrifying.

'What did the police say?' Caitlin asked.

'That it was deliberate. They reckon there were rags shoved through the letter box before they were doused in petrol.'

'Shit.'

'Yeah, it's that all right.' She tried to force a smile. 'I guess someone doesn't like me too much.'

'I'm pretty sure it's Tom they don't like. Have the police got any leads?'

'Nothing they're prepared to share with me.'

'What about the guy who got you out? Have they found out who he is yet?'

Eden shook her head. 'He disappeared before the police got there.'

Caitlin frowned. 'I wonder why. A modest hero or . . . '

'Or?'

'Someone who had something to hide.'

'I know,' Eden said with a sigh. 'I've been wondering about that too. But why set fire to the place and then rescue me? It doesn't make any sense.'

'Unless he didn't realise you were inside.'

'It was the middle of the night. Where else would I be? And it was only chance the other two flats were empty. I'll have to have a chat with Geoff and Sandra, see what they can remember. The police said Geoff helped the guy get me out.'

'What do *you* remember about it? Anything?'

Eden shook her head. 'Not much. I woke up and there was smoke pouring into the bedroom. I couldn't get out through the living room and so I tried to break the window. That's about it, really. When I came round I was in the ambulance.'

'Christ, it must have been awful.'

'The doctor said if I'd stayed in there much longer . . . It's a scary thought. A few more minutes and I'd have been on my way to meet my maker. I could have been knocking on those pearly gates.'

Caitlin grinned at her. 'Yes, well, be grateful for small mercies. God clearly doesn't want your company right now.'

'Is that supposed to make me feel better?'

'Doesn't it?'

'Oh yeah, loads. Even God doesn't want me. That's a real confidence boost.'

Caitlin laughed, but then her expression grew more serious. 'Has Tom been told yet?'

'I think so. I didn't want them to at first. I mean, I didn't want the prison to tell him. I thought it would be better if it came from me, face to face, so he could see I was okay. He's got enough on his plate without having to worry about all this. And then I started thinking that he could be in danger. Maybe someone's out to get him too.'

'They can move him if they think he's at risk, put him in the segregation unit. He'll be safe there. No one can get to him.'

Eden felt slightly reassured by this. 'Good. That's something, I suppose.' She glanced over her shoulder at the cars behind, the third time she'd done so in as many minutes.

'What's the matter?'

Eden turned back to face the front. 'What if we're being followed? They could have been waiting at the hospital.'

'There's no one following us.'

'There could be. They'll know by now that I got out of the fire. What if they try again?' She could feel the panic rising inside her. 'Maybe I shouldn't stay with you. It's not fair. I don't want to put you in danger.'

Caitlin flicked on the indicator and pulled in by a row of shops. The traffic behind flowed on past them. 'See?' she said. 'No one else is stopping. It's fine. We're on our own.'

'Am I being paranoid?'

'Yes, and you've got every right to be after what's happened. But I don't think they'll try the same thing again. Even if they know where you are – which they can't – they've already made their point. And they'll probably presume you're under some kind of police protection by now.'

Eden wasn't convinced, but she gave a nod. 'Let's hope so.'

'Anyway, there are fire alarms in the block, lots of them. And fire extinguishers. You don't have to worry.'

Eden was quiet for a while. She stared through the windscreen at the streets of Finchley. Too many thoughts were tumbling through her head, all battling for attention, clashing and colliding, falling apart before she had the chance to address any of them properly.

She sighed. 'There's so much to do. I don't know where to start.'

'You can start by taking it easy for the next few days.'

'I'm fine. The doctors gave me the all-clear.'

'Only to leave hospital. Not to dash around like a blue-arsed fly.'

'I've got the insurance to sort out, and the bank, and the car – the keys were in the flat – and I haven't even got any clothes.' She glanced down at the grey tracksuit Caitlin had brought to the hospital. 'I can't wear this for ever. And I'm going to have to find somewhere else to live.'

'There's no rush. You can stay as long as you like.'

'Thanks, but you don't need me cluttering up the place. It's going to be months, maybe longer, before the flat's fit to live in again.' Eden wasn't even sure if she was brave enough to move back in. The thought of returning, of being there on her own, was enough to make her stomach turn over. 'I've got to get organised.'

'So we'll take it one step at a time. Don't worry, we'll get everything sorted. I know a mechanic who can deal with the car. He'll be able to get you some new keys. And I can give you a lift to the bank in the morning, drop you off on my way to work. That's if you feel up to it. Don't worry if you don't: I can lend you some money to tide you over.'

Eden looked at her gratefully. 'You're a lifesaver. I don't know what I'd do without you.'

'That's what friends are for. You'd do the same for me – although hopefully you'll never have to.'

Eden successfully fought against the urge to look over her shoulder again, but continued to surreptitiously check the wing mirror. She couldn't help herself. The knowledge that someone had tried to kill her – and had almost succeeded – was always on her mind. The police hadn't offered much in the way of support, merely suggesting she leave London for a while, maybe go and stay with her father, but that was the last thing she wanted to do. If she was going to help Tom, if she was going to clear his name, she had to be here.

It was a few more minutes before Caitlin drew up outside a small, square, modern block of flats. As they got out of the car, Eden's gaze swept over the surrounding area, taking in the other vehicles, the people passing by, everything and everyone. It wasn't just the cold that made her shiver. Suddenly the world had become a very frightening place.

34

On Monday morning, Eden began the arduous task of trying to sort out her life. She started with the bank where she handed over the crime number she'd got from the police, and then endured a long cross-examination in order to establish her identity. Eventually she was able to withdraw a hundred pounds and left the branch feeling tired but elated. At least she now had the cash to buy some new clothes and start replacing all the other things she'd lost.

She yawned as she walked along Upper Street. Caitlin had offered her the bed, but she'd refused point-blank – she was imposing enough on her as it was – and spent a restless night on the sofa instead. Her broken sleep was entirely down to being in a strange place with too many frightening thoughts running through her head. She had found herself jumping at every sound: the ticking of the radiators as they cooled, the gurgle of water running through the pipes, a creak from the ceiling. Three times she'd got up and gone over to the window to look down on the forecourt, checking that nobody was lurking there.

Eden glanced at the watch she had borrowed off Caitlin.

It was just after eleven. She hurried round the corner to Pope Street where a man in oil-smeared overalls was already waiting by the Audi with his elbow on the roof.

'Sorry I'm late,' she said. 'Mr Harris, is it?'

'Call me Snakey.'

Snakey Harris was a tall man in his twenties with a long, narrow face, brown eyes and brown hair. His most distinguishing feature, however, was the snake tattoo that wound around his right wrist, the head coming to rest on the back of his hand between his thumb and index finger. Eden, who had found herself temporarily transfixed by it, dragged her gaze away.

'Thanks for coming out. I appreciate it, especially at such short notice.'

'It's no trouble.'

'So what's the verdict?' she asked. 'Will you be able to get new keys?'

Snakey shifted his arm off the car, dug into his pocket and took out a couple of keys on a ring. He passed them over to her. 'Here. These should do the job.'

She unlocked the door without any trouble, climbed in the car, checked that the ignition key was working and then turned off the engine and got out again.

'That's great, fantastic.' She delved into her bag (another loan from Caitlin) and unzipped the inner pocket. 'How much do I owe you?'

'No worries,' he said. 'I'll send Caitlin the bill. You can square up with her.'

'Oh, okay. If you're sure.'

'And if you want the bodywork sorted, just bring it into the garage. I'm down in Dalston, behind the station.'

Eden stared at him blankly. 'What?'

'Dalston,' he repeated.

231

'No, I meant the bodywork. What's wrong with it?'

'You haven't noticed?' Snakey stood to one side and gestured towards a long ragged scratch running from the passenger door all the way to the rear. 'Not too pretty, huh?'

'Shit!' she exclaimed. The first thought that came into her head was that Tom wouldn't be happy, but then realised how stupid her reaction was. He had more important things to worry about. She ran a fingertip along part of the scratch. 'Look at the state of it.'

'Some little scrote, probably. I can fix it, though. Good as new.'

'Right. Yes, okay. I'll bring it in when I've got time.'

'Caitlin's got my number.' He gave a nod. 'Take care of yourself.'

Eden watched him get in his van and drive away. She returned her gaze to the side of the car, wondering if the culprit was her arsonist. Maybe setting fire to the house hadn't been enough for him. Or maybe it was someone else entirely, someone like the reporter Jimmy Letts, pissed off that she'd refused to talk, and taking out his frustration in some mindless vandalism.

Eden turned away and began walking along the street towards number twenty-four. As she approached, she could feel her heart beginning to thump. She stopped at the gate and stared up at the building. The door and windows were all boarded up, the brickwork blackened by smoke. She felt light-headed, slightly nauseous, as memories of the fire crowded in on her. She heard the crackle of the flames, felt the intense suffocating heat. What she remembered most clearly were those final few seconds as she tried to smash the bedroom window. Suddenly she was back inside again, fighting for breath, full of panic and fear and desperation.

Quickly she took a step back, her borrowed trainers

crunching on the snow. She shook her head, trying to shake off the horror. She breathed in deeply. *Calm down.* It was over, she told herself. By a miracle she'd survived. But she still had to find out how that miracle had come about. With this is mind, she went next door, hurried up the path and rang the bell.

It was Sandra Holmes who answered the door, her face lighting up as she saw Eden. 'Sweetheart! It's so good to see you. What a relief. We've been so worried. Are you all right? Come in, come in. Don't stand out there in the cold.'

Eden smiled and stepped inside. 'I'm fine. They let me out of hospital yesterday.'

Sandra took her through to the kitchen and waved a hand towards the big oak table. 'Ah, right. We did call but they wouldn't say much with us not being relatives or anything. Sit down and I'll get you a coffee. I've just made a pot. Is coffee okay? I can make tea if you'd prefer.'

'No, coffee's great, thank you.' Eden pulled out a chair. 'I just wanted to say thanks to Geoff for helping to get me out of the flat. Is he in?'

'He's at work, I'm afraid. But he'll be glad to know you're up and about again.'

Eden watched as Sandra filled two mugs from the percolator. Her neighbour was a middle-aged woman with ash-blonde hair and soft brown eyes. Eden didn't know her that well but they'd had the occasional chat when their paths happened to cross. Tom, who had lived here longer, was better acquainted with the couple.

'It's such a terrible thing,' Sandra said, bringing the coffees over to the table. 'Do they know how it started yet?'

'We're still waiting for the reports. I think it was downstairs, though.'

'Faulty electrics, perhaps.'

Eden shrugged. She didn't want to lie but didn't want to say it had been deliberate either. That would only lead to a shocked response and a lot of awkward questions, and she hadn't got the strength to deal with either at the moment. 'We'll have to wait and see.'

'Is everything gone or do you think you might be able to salvage some of it?'

Eden thought back to the blazing living room, sure that nothing could have survived the intensity of the fire. The furniture would have been destroyed, the stereo, the TV, not to mention everything that had been on the table. All the Budapest photographs would have been destroyed too, including the one that may have been of Jack Minter. Damn it! Her heart sank even further as she remembered the letters from Ann-Marie. Now she'd never know what had been written in them; any information there could have been about Minter was gone for ever.

'Sorry,' Sandra said, leaning across the table to pat her hand. 'I don't suppose you need reminding. Poor you. But the most important thing is you're safe. Everything else can be replaced.'

Not quite everything, Eden thought, but she murmured her agreement. 'Yes, of course.'

'And what about Tom? Is he not here with you?'

'He's working abroad,' Eden said. How could she admit he was in jail? It was too long a story and she had no desire to share it. 'In the States, in New York. He's been trying to get a flight. He should be home tomorrow.' She could feel her face growing redder the more she embellished the tale. Would Sandra guess she wasn't telling the truth? But if her neighbour did have any suspicions, she kept them to herself.

'You'll be glad to have him home.'

'Yes, I will.'

'I was just thinking this morning how lucky it was you were still conscious when the chap got to you. We told him there

234

were two of you in the flat, you see, you and Tom. If you hadn't put him straight he may have gone in again. God knows what would have happened.'

Eden stared at her. 'Is that what he said?'

Sandra nodded. 'Do you not remember?'

Eden was certain she hadn't come round until she was in the ambulance. She had no recollection at all of the man getting her out of the flat. 'To be honest, it's all a bit blurry. I wanted to ask you about the bloke, though. I don't even know what his name is. The police say he disappeared before they got a chance to talk to him. I don't suppose you remember anything, do you? I'd like to thank him if I can find him.'

'Well, I only saw him briefly.' Sandra screwed up her face while she thought back. 'Let me see. He was tall, broad-shouldered, in his forties, grey hair. I think it was grey . . . I'm not sure. Oh, that's not very useful, is it? I wasn't really paying much attention.'

'That's all right,' Eden said. 'You had more important things on your mind. There was a lot going on.'

'Hang on, though. Geoff did say something. He thought he might have been military or ex-military.'

'Why was that?'

'Just a hunch, I think. Something about the way he held himself, the way he took control. Geoff was in the army for a while – National Service – although that was years ago. Still, it doesn't help much, does it? Maybe he's just the kind of man who doesn't like a fuss.'

'Maybe,' Eden said. 'It's a shame, though. If it hadn't been for him, I'd never have got out of there alive.' She drank some of the coffee and put the mug down on the table. 'Look, this is probably a long shot but if you see him around, could you give me a ring? He might be local. I'm staying with a friend for now until I . . . until we find somewhere else to live.'

'I'm not even sure if I'd recognise him again.' Sandra got up, fetched a piece of paper and a pen, and gave them to Eden. 'Write down the number, though, just in case. And I'll tell Geoff to keep an eye out.'

'Thanks.'

'I'll let you know if he remembers anything else. He was with him, you see, so something might spring to mind. And do let us know if there's anything, anything at all, we can do to help.'

Eden finished the coffee, reiterated her heartfelt thanks for Geoff's contribution to her rescue, and left. It was starting to rain and as she jogged along the pavement to the car her thoughts were preoccupied by the mystery man. She was still sure she hadn't spoken to him, sure she hadn't come round, and if that was the case then how could he have known Tom wasn't in the flat?

It had to be someone who knew Tom was in jail. Either that or someone who'd been watching the house all evening. And the military angle – if it was true – ruled out the likes of the reporter Jimmy Letts. Not that he'd really crossed her mind as a likely candidate. Letts was more likely to get out his notebook than climb up a ladder.

'Who are you?' she muttered as she got into the car.

Her problem was she didn't know what to feel, what to think. She was torn between gratitude and suspicion. On the one hand she was indebted to the man for saving her life, but on the other couldn't help wondering if he was the one who'd put her life in danger in the first place. Why hadn't he stuck around to talk to the police? There was something odd about that.

Eden sighed and turned her mind to more immediate concerns. She took out the list she had made and studied it, wondering where to start. Clothes were the most pressing requirement: jeans, trousers, tops, sweaters, coat, socks, tights, underwear and shoes. And these were just the basics. She also needed a handbag and a purse. Not to mention a watch if she was ever going to get anywhere on time. Caitlin had bought her a new toothbrush, but she still needed make-up, cleanser, moisturiser, cotton wool, shampoo, conditioner and a comb. Eden knew she had to buy carefully, thriftily, if she was going to make her cash last. It would be a while before any insurance money came through and with limited funds in the bank she couldn't afford to splash out on anything that wasn't strictly necessary. She thought of Chapel Street market but then remembered it was closed on Mondays. Still, there were other cheap places to shop in Islington. She stared through the windscreen at the rain – and mentally added an umbrella to her list.

Two hours later, tired, wet and hungry, Eden was making her way back to the car laden with carrier bags. There was nothing much to excite her about the purchases she'd made, but at least she'd got the essentials. And she'd struck it lucky at one of the charity shops, managing to buy a new-looking black wool coat and a pair of slightly scuffed but still service-able leather ankle boots for less than a tenner.

Eden was passing the Tube station when a solution to her housing problem suddenly occurred to her. Why hadn't she thought of it before? The Kellston flat was empty and there was no reason why she shouldn't move into it. She dived into a phone box, dumped the carrier bags at her feet and dialled Directory Enquiries. Thirty seconds later, having got the number she wanted, she was talking to Elspeth Coyle.

'So you see,' Eden said, after having explained about the fire, 'I need somewhere to stay, but I haven't got any keys. The spares were in the flat in Pope Street.'

'You can pick some up from the letting agents: Weston's.

They're on Kellston High Street, about halfway down. I'll give them a call, explain the circumstances and tell them to expect you. What time do you think you'll be there?'

Eden glanced at her watch. 'About half an hour? Say two o'clock?'

'Okay, that should be fine. Have you had any more thoughts on the studio?'

'I think we're going to hold on to it for now. I'll let you know if anything changes.'

After Eden had expressed her thanks, said her goodbyes and hung up, she started thinking about the studio. There had to be a negative of the lost 'Jack Minter' photograph sitting somewhere in the filing cabinets. But it could take for ever to find it. Still, it was worth a go if it meant she could finally put a face to the man who had given Tom the bracelet.

Eden returned to the car, piled the bags into the boot and set off for Kellston. When it came to places to live, the East End wasn't exactly top of her list, but it was better than nowhere. Although she knew Caitlin wouldn't mind her staying on, the flat was really too small for two. Plus there was always the nagging fear that just by being there she might be putting Caitlin in danger.

By the time Eden was driving down Kellston High Street, however, she was beginning to have second thoughts. There was something menacing about the area, something dreary and grey and depressing. She had to fight against the impulse to drive straight through and head back to Finchley.

Eventually she pulled herself together, found the office for the letting agent and picked up the keys. Then she drove up towards the top of the high street and found a place to park. She sat for a while gazing up at the three concrete towers before getting out, crossing the road and unlocking the door to the flat.

It was icy inside and she rubbed her hands together as she ran up the stairs. She went into the living room and gazed round. It's not so bad, she told herself. With a bit of effort – and a lot of imagination – she could make it nice enough. And anyway, it wouldn't be for ever. If Tom could cope with a prison cell, she could cope with this.

Eden walked over to the window and gazed down at the funeral parlour. She almost expected the man to be there again – was he the undertaker? – but the space to the side of the door was empty. She turned away, faced the room again and sighed.

'Home sweet home,' she murmured into the emptiness.

35

DI Banner needed his star witness to be word perfect by the time the trial came round, all the wrinkles and inconsistencies in his story ironed out so there was nothing for the defence to jump on, but sometimes Archie wasn't as cooperative as he might be. There were occasions when he'd hardly speak at all, when he'd stare at the floor with a stubborn, almost sly expression on his face. It was the kind of expression Banner didn't want a jury to see.

'You think he's getting cold feet?' DC Steve Leigh asked.

'No, it's too late for that. He's just pissing about, trying to make sure he gets the best deal he can.'

'Let's hope you're right.'

Vic glared at him. 'Lesson number one, son. I'm *always* fuckin' right.' He lit up a fag, puffed on it and thought some more about Archie. 'You got anything on that Albert Shiner yet?'

'Still dead,' Leigh said drily. 'The Shiners didn't have any kids, but I managed to track down a niece. The studio was sold after Albert passed on. Unfortunately, she doesn't know what happened to the books so there's no way of proving that Tom Chase was actually working there in 'sixty-six.'

'Or that he wasn't.' Vic didn't care whether they could prove it or not, so long as the defence was in the same situation. What he didn't want were any nasty surprises when the trial was in progress. 'Check out the surrounding shops, see if any of the owners were trading at the same time as Shiner. Someone might remember Chase. Take a photo with you, show it around.'

'Yes, guv.'

Vic waited, but the constable didn't move. 'Today would be good, if you're not too busy. And don't bother coming back until you've found out something useful.'

After Leigh had left, Vic opened the *Hackney Herald* and flicked through the pages until he came to the story about Vera Lynch and her long-dead husband. He grinned at the picture; despite the photographer's best attempt to take a sympathetic portrait, she still looked capable of ripping the head off any poor sod who happened to cross her.

He read through the article, noting that it didn't mention Tom Chase by name; he was referred to only as a man from Islington who had been charged with the manslaughter of Paddy Lynch. There were a few choice quotes from Vera, one of them accusing the police of failing to properly investigate her husband's death at the time because he'd 'occasionally' been in trouble with the law. Vic gave a snort. Paddy had never been out of trouble from the moment he left his mother's tit.

It was the last part of the story that really pissed off Vic, in particular the reference to a suspected 'squealer' currently being held at a London police station. Where the fuck had that come from? A lucky guess or a tip-off? He'd had the whole case on lockdown ever since Archie had agreed to spill his guts.

There were only half a dozen people who knew about it apart from Rudd's immediate family – and the latter were hardly likely to be shouting their mouths off.

It wouldn't be long now before it became common knowledge that Archie Rudd was turning Queen's evidence. The East End rumour mill would already be in full swing, the local villains rapidly putting two and two together. The squealer had to be someone who was active back in the sixties, someone who knew Paddy, someone who had recently been caught on another job. Word would soon get around that Archie had been ghosted out of the Scrubs and hadn't been seen since. The fact that Rose had left the area would only add fuel to the fire.

Vic pondered on how this development would affect the case. Archie wouldn't be best pleased that the cat was out of the bag – for as long as it remained a secret he'd always had the choice of changing his mind, but now that option would be closed to him. On the one hand this was a good thing. It might help focus Archie's mind if he understood there was no going back. On the other hand, there was every chance that Tom Chase would get to hear the name of his accuser sooner than Vic would have liked. The defence now had more time to try and discredit whatever Archie Rudd was going to claim in court.

Vic stubbed out his fag in the ashtray and immediately lit another. He pushed the paper to one side, picked up a brown folder and flipped it open. Inside was the original statement from the security guard, Roger Best, who'd been at the Epping warehouse during the raid. His description of the robbers was too vague to make a direct link to Tom Chase. All of them had been wearing balaclavas, their faces obscured. The only thing he could say for sure was that the guy in charge hadn't been Cockney. That was something, but it wasn't enough. Vic would have to interview him again, try and jog his memory as to what he'd really seen and heard that day.

'Guv?'

Vic looked up to see DC Steve Leigh standing in front of him. 'Jesus, what are you still doing here? I thought I said—'

'You're going to want to hear this, guv. There was a phone message left yesterday from a DS Nicholls over at Islington. It was supposed to be passed on but . . . Anyway, here it is.' He dropped the slip of paper on to Vic's desk. 'There was a fire in Pope Street in the early hours of Saturday morning, Tom Chase's place. Arson, they reckon. No fatalities, but Eden Chase was taken to hospital.'

Vic glared at him. 'Yesterday? For fuck's sake. Why have I only just got it?'

'I think there was some confusion over who it should go to. Apparently the desk wasn't sure who was dealing with the Tom Chase case so—'

'She still there?' Vic interrupted. 'Is she still in hospital?'

Leigh shook his head. 'I dunno, guv.'

'So find out. Do something fuckin' useful for once.'

Vic picked up the phone, dialled the number on the slip of paper and asked to be put through to DS Nicholls. 'Hey,' he said when the officer finally came on the line. 'DI Vic Banner, West End Central. I just got your message.'

'Thanks for calling me back.'

Vic listened carefully while Nicholls gave him the low-down on the fire. 'So it was definitely arson, yeah, no doubt about it?'

'No doubt at all.'

'You got any suspects?'

'I was kind of hoping you could help me out there. I spoke to Eden Chase at the hospital and she told me her husband, Tom, was on remand.'

'Armed robbery and manslaughter. It's an old case.'

'Who was the victim?'

Vic hesitated, not wanting to say too much over the phone.

'Bit of a sensitive one, is it?'

'You could put it that way,' Vic said. 'How about we meet up later? I'll come over to Islington. The Cat and Whistle, the small bar at the back? Six o'clock any good for you?'

'I'll see you there.'

Vic hung up. He hadn't decided yet how much he was going to tell the guy. He still wanted to try and keep things under wraps for as long as he could. His eyes darted towards the *Hackney Herald*. Had the reporter tipped off Vera Lynch, given her the name of the man accused of leaving Paddy to die? It seemed more than likely. And it seemed likely too that Vera had passed on the information to her son.

Vic hissed out a breath as he thought about Pat Lynch. The bloke was a fully paid-up member of the psychopath club, a vicious monster who preyed on women. And he wouldn't let the minor inconvenience of being banged up stop him from wreaking revenge. Although Lynch would be unaware of what jail Chase was in at the moment, it was only a matter of time before he found out. The prison grapevine stretched far and wide.

Vic sucked on his cigarette. He was pretty sure the fire was down to Lynch. The psycho had probably decided that if he couldn't get to Chase then his wife and home would do instead. No, not instead. Just in the meantime. It wouldn't be long before word got back as to Tom Chase's whereabouts, and then Lynch would exact a more direct form of retribution. There'd be a bounty on Chase's head. He'd be dead meat within the month.

Vic couldn't allow this to happen. If Chase was topped, there would be no trial, no publicity, no triumph and no bloody promotion. All his hard work with Archie would have been for nothing. Well, he wasn't having it. No way. He wasn't going to sit back and let Pat Lynch ruin all his plans. He had to keep Chase safe until the trial.

Vic opened his address book, picked up the phone and dialled. 'Hey, Tammy. How are you doing, sweetheart?'

'Oh, it's you.'

'Yeah, try not to sound so happy about it.'

'What's there to be happy about?'

Vic rolled his eyes. 'I need to see you.'

'When?'

'Soon as. Half an hour.'

'I can't. I'm busy.'

'It's not a request, darling.'

But Tammy was still resistant. 'Look, I've got Mia to take care of. I haven't got anyone to leave her with and I can't drag her out to some shithole pub in Soho.'

'Fine. I'll come over to your place, then.'

'No way! I'm not having that. Are you mad? What are you trying to do? If anyone sees you here, I'll be for it.'

Vic grinned, aware that the idea wouldn't be appealing to her. 'So tell me where, then. Only make it snappy 'cause I haven't got all day.'

'All right, let me think.'

There was a long pause on the other end of the line. Vic smoked his fag, small impatient tugs while he waited for her to make a suggestion. 'Jesus, Tammy, just name a place.'

'I'm trying to think, ain't I?' She sighed and said, 'Okay, I'll meet you at Malt Street. On the corner, where they've pulled those old houses down.'

'Malt Street,' he repeated. 'Half an hour. Don't keep me waiting.'

Tammy hung up.

Vic put the phone down, still grinning. He looked across the

245

incident room to where DC Leigh was just finishing a call of his own. The constable stood up and came over to him.

'Well?' Vic asked.

'Nothing serious. Some smoke inhalation, but she got the all-clear. They let her out of hospital yesterday afternoon. She's staying with a woman called Caitlin Styles.' He dropped a slip of paper on to Vic's desk. 'Finchley. Here's the address.'

'Right. Good. Now get your arse out to Essex and sort out that Shiner business.'

Vic watched him leave and then stubbed out the fag, grabbed his jacket off the back of the chair and set off for Shoreditch. While he drove he went over the whole Pat Lynch problem, figuring out the best way to deal with it. Come what may, he wasn't going to let some no-good lowlife get the better of him.

The traffic was bad – an accident blocking the roundabout at Old Street – and by the time he got to Malt Street, Tammy was already there. She was standing on the corner, shuffling from foot to foot. The hood was up on her coat and she had the hunched, furtive look of a dealer. He pulled up next to her. She hesitated, having a quick glance round before climbing into the passenger seat.

'You're late,' she whined. 'I've been here for ages.'

'So where's the kid?' he asked, coming straight back at her. 'You've not left her on her own, have you?'

Tammy glared at him. 'She's with a neighbour. I haven't got long. What is it? What do you want?'

'We've got a bit of a situation as regards Eden Chase.'

'What sort of situation?'

'A tricky one. I need you to do something.'

Tammy wrinkled her nose as if there was a bad smell in the car. 'Like what?'

'Can we skip the attitude, babe? I'm really not in the mood.'

Vic paused, gave her a hard stare and continued. 'When you see Eden on Thursday, I want you to say you've heard Pat Lynch is out to get her husband. Tell her Tom has to get off the wing or someone's going to have a go. Tell her that he's in real danger. And make her listen, right? She has to persuade him to go down the block.'

'Is that true? About Lynch, I mean?'

'Yeah, it's true. So make sure she does it or the next time she sees her old man will be when he's laid out in the morgue.'

Tammy thought about it for a moment and then gave a nod. 'Okay. I'll try.'

Before she had time to realise what was happening, Vic leaned across, grabbed her wrist and squeezed until she yelped. 'Trying isn't good enough, babe. You do it, yeah? You do whatever you have to. You make it crystal clear. You scare the fuck out of her. And if he's not in seg by Friday morning, I'd hold you fuckin' responsible.' He let go of her and sat back. 'Do we understand each other?'

Tammy rubbed at her wrist, her eyes full of tears. 'You didn't have to do that. Fuck. What did you have to do that for?'

Vic stared at her coldly. 'Don't let me down.'

36

Eden's move to the flat in Kellston was scheduled for Friday when the phone was due to be connected. With only two days to go, she was still trying to sort out everything she needed, from a supply of fifty pence coins for the gas and electricity meters, through bedding and towels, to crockery, cutlery and glasses. She had managed to buy a cheap second-hand TV and a small radio. A record player would have to wait. As all her records had gone up in smoke, she'd have nothing to play on it anyway. She mourned the loss of her music – a collection that went back to her teens – but knew she had to keep things in perspective. Unlike flesh and bone, vinyl could always be replaced.

'Are you sure you want to do this?' Caitlin asked.

Eden looked up from the list she was ticking off. 'Huh?'

'You know you can stay here for as long as you want. There's no need to rush into anything.'

'Thanks, but I'll have to move eventually.'

'You don't have to move to Kellston. What about Vera Lynch?'

Eden glanced at the copy of the *Hackney Herald* lying on

the arm of the chair. Jimmy Letts had run with his story, but fortunately it hadn't mentioned her or Tom by name. It had, however, revealed that Paddy Lynch's widow lived in Kellston. 'It's a big place. She won't know I'm there. My name isn't even in the article.'

'But what if she finds out?'

Eden gave a shrug. 'She could find me wherever I went.' If the truth be told, she didn't relish the thought of being in close vicinity to any member of the Lynch family but it was too late now to start changing her plans. 'My only other option is to try and find a tenant for the Kellston flat – which could take months – and for me to rent another property. It just seems like a waste of time when I can move straight into this one. Anyway, it needs to be decorated if we're going to sell, so I may as well live there while I'm doing it.'

Caitlin didn't look convinced. 'I don't like the thought of you being on your own, not after everything that's happened.'

'Well, I'm going to have to get used to it. It doesn't look like Tom's coming out in a hurry.'

'Any news from Michael Castor?'

'Nothing encouraging. I called him this morning, but there's still no lead on Jack Minter. They've drawn a blank in Budapest, no trace of him. Now they're checking out the oil companies – Tom said he used to work on the rigs – but no joy yet.' Eden shook her head, frustrated by the lack of progress. 'I mean, someone must know where he is. The bloke can't have just disappeared.'

'It's a big world. And it's fifteen years since Tom last saw him. The guy could be anywhere by now. If he is your armed robber, he's going to make damn sure he isn't found in a hurry. He could easily have changed his name again.'

Eden placed a bar of soap into the toiletries box, packing it neatly between a bottle of shampoo and some cotton wool.

'I know. It's like looking for a needle in a haystack.' Her only hope now was that her letter might somehow reach Ann-Marie and that the woman would get back to her. She'd been to the Post Office and arranged for her mail to be redirected to the Kellston address. Now all she could do was wait.

'Maybe you need to concentrate on whoever it is who's accusing Tom. Doesn't Castor have a name yet?'

'If he does, he isn't telling me. Mind, that's nothing new. It's hard work getting anything out of him.'

'Perhaps he's just being cautious.'

'But I'm Tom's wife, for God's sake. Castor shouldn't be keeping stuff from me.'

Caitlin nodded. 'In an ideal world. Trouble is, wives can sometimes turn against their husbands. In a high-profile case like this, he has to try and protect his client. But you're seeing Tom tomorrow, aren't you? If he has heard, he'll be able to tell you himself.'

Eden was reminded that she hadn't rung Tammy about a lift to the jail. She'd lost her phone number in the fire and hadn't been able to get it through Directory Enquiries. She would either have to call round early – in case Tammy presumed she wasn't coming and set off on the bus – or put a note through her door later this evening.

Eden looked at her watch. It was half past six. She had arranged to meet Annabelle at the studio in an hour, a meeting that was bound to be less than cordial. 'I'd better go. I don't want to keep the delightful Ms Keep waiting.'

'Would you like some company? I don't mind riding shotgun.'

Eden was tempted – safety in numbers and all that – but decided against it. After dealing with Annabelle, she wanted to have a good root through the studio to see if she could find the negatives for the Budapest photographs. 'Thanks, but I might be a while.'

'See you later, then. Good luck.'

Eden was halfway to the door when the phone rang. Caitlin answered it and said, 'Ah, she's just gone out. Hang on, I'll see if I can catch her.' She put her hand over the mouthpiece of the receiver and said softly, 'It's Geoff Holmes. Shall I tell him you'll call back later?'

But Eden was too curious to wait. She hurried over and took the phone off her. 'Geoff, hi. How are you? Thanks for ringing. And thanks for everything you did. I can't tell you how grateful I am.'

'Oh, I didn't do much. Honestly. I was just the ladder-holder. You gave us quite a fright, though. For a moment we thought ... Are you all right now? Fully recovered?'

'I'm fine. I'm good, thanks.'

'That's a relief. Sandra told me you were after some information about the man who got you out.'

'Yes. I don't even know what his name is. Or have much of a description.'

'Well, I can't help you with the name – there wasn't time for introductions – but he was in his forties, about six foot, grey hair, smartly dressed. I'd say his accent was southern but not Cockney. And I'll stick to my guess he's spent time in the military. I'm sure he's army or some section of the armed forces. Just the way he held himself. And he was used to organising, in control; there wasn't any sense of panic about him. He was very calm.'

'Right, okay. And you've definitely never seen him before? I was thinking he could be local.'

'No, never.'

'Oh,' Eden said, disappointed. 'I feel bad that I can't even say thank you to him. He seems to have disappeared without a trace.'

'I wish I could be more help, but he was there one minute and

251

gone the next. I've asked a few of the neighbours but they can't remember seeing him. By the time the fire brigade arrived, there was quite a crowd. He must have just slipped away.'

'Never mind,' Eden said. 'Thanks anyway. I guess I'll never know who he was.' She paused and then thought of something else. 'Sandra mentioned . . . she said he told you Tom wasn't inside.'

'That's right. After he brought you down from the flat. I was worried, of course, so it was quite a relief to know he wasn't there.'

'I don't remember telling him that. It's all a bit of a blur.'

'That's not surprising. It's lucky the bloke was passing when he was. If he hadn't noticed the fire and seen you at the window, then—'

'What?' Eden said, feeling a jolt run through her. 'Hang on. He told you he saw me at the window? The *front* window, is that what you mean?'

'Yes, of course.'

'But I—' Eden stopped abruptly before her mouth ran away with her. There was *no way* the guy could have seen her there. The living room was already on fire when she opened the bedroom door. She hadn't been able to get near the window.

'I'm sorry I can't be of more help. I've been racking my brains but I just . . . well, there is one other thing but I don't imagine it's going to help much.'

'Go on,' Eden said, desperate for any extra snippet of information.

'The bloke cut his hand while he was getting you out. His right hand, the palm. I think he must have caught it on the glass from the window. It was bleeding quite badly. He might have gone to A&E. Perhaps they could help. I don't suppose they'd give you his name, but they might pass on a message if you explained the circumstances.'

252

'Okay, that's an idea. I might give it a go.' Eden thanked him again for everything he'd done, said her goodbyes and hung up. She turned to look at Caitlin. 'That's weird. Geoff says my mystery rescuer saw me at the window.'

'What's weird about that? You were at the window.'

'No, not the bedroom window – the one at the front.'

'Ah,' Caitlin said. 'Now that is weird.'

Eden frowned and sat down. 'I'm not even sure what it means. He lied, right, about seeing me? Why would he do that?'

'Maybe he didn't lie. With all the fire and smoke, he could have thought he'd seen something he didn't.'

'Except he also claimed that when he found me I was conscious and told him Tom wasn't in the flat. I'm sure that's not true either.'

'So he knew you were there and Tom wasn't. Maybe he's a cop. They could have been keeping an eye on the house.'

'What for?'

Caitlin shrugged. 'In case something like this happened? They may have guessed there'd be a backlash after Tom was charged.'

'So why not tell Geoff he was a cop? And why not hang around? What's with the big disappearing act?'

'All good questions, but when it comes to the law, who knows what goes on in their pretty little heads.'

Eden continued to ponder on it. 'I don't think he was a cop. And he clearly wasn't some random guy just passing by. And I don't think he was the arsonist either. If he knew I was inside, why would he set fire to the place and then go to the trouble of saving me? Especially if he's not going to stick around to play the hero.'

'Which leaves?'

Eden sighed. 'I don't know.'

Caitlin glanced at her watch. 'Shouldn't you be on your way to see Annabelle?'

Eden leapt to her feet. 'Oh God, yes. I'm going to be late.'

By the time Eden had driven to Covent Garden, found a place to park, fed the meter and legged it over to Henrietta Street, a disgruntled Annabelle was already waiting outside the studio. The girl glared at her.

'You're late!' she snapped. 'It's freezing out here.'

Eden nodded, forcing a fake apologetic smile on to her lips. 'Sorry, the traffic was awful. Anyway, I thought you had a key.'

'Only for upstairs.'

Eden unlocked the main door and switched on the light. There was a small heap of mail for the studio on the hall table, and she picked it up hoping there would be cheques inside some of the envelopes.

'So what's going on?' Annabelle asked. 'What's happening with Tom?'

Eden walked up the stairs. 'I wish I knew,' she replied, unwilling to say any more than she had to. 'Some nonsense over a bracelet the police found in the safe. It's all got a bit complicated.'

'I don't understand.'

'The whole thing is ridiculous.'

'Daddy says if the police haven't released him yet then he must have been charged.'

Eden didn't reply. She walked along the landing, opened the door, flicked on the light and looked around. The breath caught in the back of her throat. There was so much of Tom here it made her heart ache. She glanced towards the studio, a part of her still expecting him to appear at any moment.

'So has he?' Annabelle persisted.

'Huh?'

'Has he been charged?'

Eden could hardly deny it. 'Yes.'

'I thought as much. Daddy said—'

'To be honest, Annabelle, I really don't care what your father says. Does he know anything about this case? Is he in possession of anything more than rumour and gossip? If not, then I suggest you keep your opinions – and his – to yourself. I'm really not interested in them.'

Annabelle glowered and her mouth took on a pouting look. 'I was only saying.'

'Well, don't, okay?' Eden went over to the desk, sat down and laid the mail beside her. 'Have you ever even seen the bracelet?'

'No.'

'It was in the safe.'

'No,' Annabelle repeated. 'I've never set eyes on the damn thing. I've already told the police that. I don't know anything about it.'

Eden heard the agitation in her voice and wondered whether it was down to the fact she was lying or a more general irritation at being dragged into the inquiry in the first place. 'What else did they ask you about?'

'Nothing much. How long I'd worked here, what kind of a boss Tom is, that sort of thing.'

'Did they mention Budapest?'

Annabelle hesitated, frowning before she shook her head. 'Why would they?'

'I just wondered.'

Annabelle pushed back the cuff of her fur coat and glanced at her watch. 'Look, can we just get on with it? I have to be somewhere and I'm already running late.'

'Sure.' Eden opened a drawer and took out the cheque book. With Tom's permission, Elspeth had arranged with the bank for her to be able to write cheques for the business while he was in jail. There were bills to be paid if she was going to keep things ticking over.

'What exactly has he been charged with?' Annabelle asked while she waited. 'Or aren't I allowed to ask?'

'The police think the bracelet was stolen. Tom didn't realise that of course but ...' Eden gave a shrug. 'It could be a while before he's released.' She quickly wrote out the cheque and passed it to over. 'He sends his apologies, but obviously we can't keep you on when the business isn't bringing in any money.'

Annabelle stared down at the cheque, pulling a face. 'Is this it?'

Eden, who thought she'd been relatively generous considering the circumstances – and the fact the girl had never shown her anything but contempt – gave a nod. 'If you need a reference, let me know.'

Annabelle folded the cheque and put it in her purse. 'That won't be necessary,' she said. 'I hardly think a reference from a man in jail is going to help my career prospects.'

Eden stared at her, unable to resist the dig. 'I wasn't aware you had any.' She held out her hand. 'And if I could have the key back?'

Annabelle's mouth twisted, her eyes flashing with anger. She took out a key ring, found the right key and threw it on the desk. Then she turned on her heel and flounced out of the studio. When she was on the landing, she looked back over her shoulder and said, 'You think you can trust him, but you can't. He's a liar and a cheat. The two of you deserve each other.'

Eden didn't have time to make a retort, even if she'd been able to think of a suitable one. Annabelle was already flying down the stairs as though she feared Eden might be in hot pursuit. The front door slammed and then there was silence.

A liar and a cheat. The words seemed to hang in the air

long after they'd been spoken. Eden could almost taste them, nasty and sour. Just malice and spite. That's all it was. Wasn't it? Annabelle lashing out because she was angry. Leaving her with something to think about. Planting a seed of doubt in her mind.

Eden stood up and went through to the studio. There wouldn't have been any doubt, she thought, if Tom had been straight with her, if he'd been open and honest from the start. But she didn't believe he'd ever cheated on her. She couldn't. If she started to suspect his fidelity, there'd be nothing left. No trust. No love. No future.

'Get a grip,' she muttered.

This was exactly what Annabelle wanted, to provoke and torment her, to leave her with unanswered questions. She wouldn't give her the satisfaction. Quickly she knelt down, pulled out the lowest drawer of the filing cabinet and began rooting through the contents, searching for the negatives of the Budapest pictures. She wasn't going to let the likes of Annabelle – or Vic Banner, come to that – start messing with her head. In her heart she knew what she knew – her husband was innocent of the crimes he'd been charged with. All she had to do was find a way to prove it.

37

It was almost midday by the time Eden reached Shoreditch. Rain was falling heavily, lashing down on the road, the ice turning to slush as it was churned up by the car tyres. The sky was still full of cloud. Last night, after a long and fruitless search for the Budapest negatives, she had taken a detour on her way home and dropped a note through Tammy's door saying she'd pick her up around twelve if she didn't hear from her before. Caitlin's number had been on the note but Tammy hadn't called.

Now as she drew up near the house, Tammy came hurrying out. The girl dashed down the path and along the road, opened the door, jumped into the passenger seat and shook herself like a wet dog. Even over the short distance she'd come, the rain was so torrential that her hair was dripping.

'Jesus, can you believe this bloody weather? If it's not snowing, it's pissing it down.'

'The great British winter,' Eden said.

'Well, you can keep it. Thanks for the note by the way. I

tried to ring you on Tuesday but I couldn't get through. Is there something wrong with your phone?'

'There is no phone.'

'Oh, shit, they haven't cut you off, have they?'

Eden indicated and pulled out. 'Not exactly. There was a fire at the flat so I've had to move out. I'm staying with a friend, Caitlin, at the moment.'

'A fire? Christ. How did that happen?'

'With a can of petrol and a match. Some bastard set fire to the place in the middle of the night.'

Tammy sucked in a breath. 'What? No way! God, that's awful. Are you okay? I mean, you're here so you must be, but . . . How bad was it? Have you lost much?'

'Pretty well everything. I may be able to salvage some stuff from the bedroom – a few clothes and the like – but I can't get in until they make sure the flat's safe. Caitlin's been brilliant. I don't know what I'd've done without her.'

'Oh, Eden, I'm so sorry. I can't imagine . . . What do the police say? Do they know who did it yet?'

'I haven't heard anything so I'm guessing not.'

'Do you think . . .' Tammy stopped, lifted a hand to her mouth and chewed on her fingernails. 'Do you think it could have been . . .'

'Who?'

'I saw the story in the paper, the one with Vera Lynch.' Tammy gave her a sidelong glance. 'I don't know. Could the fire have been something to do with that?'

'With Pat Lynch, you mean.'

'Your name wasn't mentioned but it was the same reporter who's been hassling you, that toerag, Jimmy Letts. And he knows where you live. Maybe he told Vera, and Vera told Pat. He could have, couldn't he?'

'I wouldn't put it past him.'

Tammy shifted in her seat, crossing and uncrossing her legs. 'And that means Pat also knows that Tom's been charged with the robbery and . . . and with what happened to his dad. Jesus, that's not good! I hope Tom's down the block. He is, isn't he?'

Eden knew from Caitlin that being 'down the block' meant in segregation, away from all the other inmates. 'I don't think so.'

'Well, he should be. I mean it, Eden. For his own sake. He has to have a word with the screws and get himself shifted off the wing. As soon as possible. If Pat arranged to have your flat torched, he could easily . . . Tom isn't safe.'

'We can't be sure it was Lynch who arranged the fire.'

Tammy's brows shot up. 'Got any other suspects?'

'Not exactly.'

'So there you go. Who else could have done it? Who else could have *wanted* to do it? Believe me, men like Pat Lynch aren't bothered about trials and evidence. They don't wait around to see what a jury says. If he thinks Tom left his dad to die, then . . . Do you have any idea how many blokes are attacked in jail every day? The screws can't protect them; they can't be everywhere at once. All it takes is . . . ' Tammy stopped, seeing Eden's face. 'Sorry, hon, I don't mean to scare the hell out of you, but you have to do something. I've heard a lot of stuff about Pat Lynch and all of it's bad. He's psycho, crazy. Tom has to protect himself before it's too late.'

Eden felt her stomach turn over. Her fingers tightened around the wheel. 'I'll talk to him.'

'Good. And make sure he listens. He probably won't want to go down the block – it's not much fun being on your own all the time – but it's better than . . . well, you know what I mean.'

Eden did know. It could be months before the case came to trial. Plenty of time for Pat Lynch to attempt to wreak his revenge. How would she cope with being worried sick about

Tom twenty-four hours a day? Not that she wasn't already, but this made it all ten times worse. 'Do you think I should talk to Vera too, try explaining that the police have got it wrong? If I explained everything, told her about Jack Minter and—'

'Are you kidding me?' Tammy screeched. 'No way! You don't want to go near that woman. I mean it, Eden. Don't even *think* about it. For starters, she's not going to believe a word you say, and for seconds she'll tell her psycho son that you've been harassing her. She might even report you to the law, say you were trying to . . . what's the word? *Intimidate* her or something.'

Eden hadn't thought of that. She wasn't thinking clearly about anything much these days. 'That would be a no, then.'

'That would be the biggest no ever.'

Eden sighed, a reflection of the frustration that came from feeling helpless. How was she supposed to stop the madness if she couldn't speak about the causes of it? For as long as Pat Lynch continued to believe in Tom's guilt, the possibility – or perhaps more accurately, the probability – remained of another revenge attack. And this time the target would be Tom.

Tammy began chewing her fingernails again. Her face took on a nervous, panicky expression. 'Look, you won't tell anyone what I said, will you? If Pat Lynch ever finds out I warned you about what he might do, then . . . '

'I won't.'

'Not even Tom,' Tammy said. 'Because if you tell him, he might tell someone else and . . . I don't want any of this coming back on Pete. I've got Mia to think of too. That shit wouldn't think twice about hurting a kid.'

'I promise,' Eden said. 'I won't mention your name.'

'Ta.'

Eden understood Tammy's concerns; the girl had a child and a brother to think about as well as herself. 'Don't worry.'

She glanced over and it was then she noticed the bruises, dark ochre and purple, on the girl's wrist. 'That looks nasty.'

Tammy quickly dropped her left hand, covering her right wrist with it. 'Oh, it's nothing. I fell over. I slipped on the ice. It's fine. It looks worse than it is.'

What it looked like, Eden thought, was that someone had squeezed the flesh so hard it had left an imprint of their fingers. A violent boyfriend, perhaps? Tammy hadn't mentioned anyone – Mia's father had disappeared years ago – but there could be some guy on the scene. 'It must be painful.'

'It isn't.' Tammy rubbed at her wrist as if she could wipe the marks away. 'Not at all.'

Eden could tell Tammy didn't want to talk about it and so she dropped the subject. Instead she turned her mind to Tom and what she'd say to him. Hopefully she could persuade him to get off the wing. How would he be today? How would he be feeling? She had no good news, nothing to lift his spirits. Things were just going from bad to worse.

38

Tom leapt up from his chair as soon as Eden came into the visiting room and started walking towards her, an action that caused one of the screws to intervene and order him back to the table. She saw his expression, a combination of anger and frustration, and hurried forward before he said or did something he'd regret.

Tom held her at arm's length for a few seconds, gazing into her eyes, as if to reassure himself that she was actually there. 'Are you all right? God, I'm glad to see you. I didn't know if you'd come. I thought . . . '

Eden smiled, standing on her toes so she could reach up and kiss him. 'I'm okay. I really am. I told them to tell you.'

Tom sat down and shook his head. 'You can't trust anyone here. They didn't even say there'd been a fire until you were out of hospital.'

'That was down to me,' Eden said quickly. 'I didn't want you getting stressed out. I was going to wait until I came on a visit so you could see for yourself, see that I was fine, but then I thought you might hear about it from someone else so . . . But I'm okay. I'm dealing with things.'

'You shouldn't have to. How did it start? Was it an accident or . . .'

'No, not an accident. Someone set fire to the hall.'

'Christ,' he said, pushing his fingers through his hair. 'I knew it, I bloody knew it. This is all my fault.'

'How is it your fault? You didn't light the damn thing. Don't think like that.'

Tom covered his face with his hands for a moment. 'You could have been killed.'

'But I wasn't, so there's no point in . . . I mean, I'm here, I'm fine.' And then, not wanting him to feel any worse than he already did, she provided an edited version of events. 'Geoff and some other guy helped me get out. They put a ladder up. It was over in minutes. And I was only in hospital for observation; it wasn't anything serious.'

Tom glanced away from her and then looked back. 'Do the police know who's responsible?'

Eden shook her head. 'Not the person who actually did it, but I'm pretty certain they think there's a link to Paddy Lynch's son, Pat. He's in Parkhurst and . . . There was a story in the paper, the *Hackney Herald*, last week. It didn't mention you by name, but the reporter knows who you are; he must have been in court the day you were charged. Most of it was an interview with Paddy's widow, Vera.'

Tom's fingers curled into two tight fists on the table. 'You have to get out of London, Eden. It's not safe.'

'I'm all right. I'm staying with Caitlin. No one knows where I am.'

'But they can find out. Why don't you go up to Edinburgh and stay with your dad for a while?'

Eden stared at him. 'I can't do that. I'll never see you. Anyway, I've got the flat to sort out. I can't do it from up there.' She didn't mention the other reason – her father didn't even know what was going on yet. 'And I reckon you're in more danger than I am. You should be protected. Can't you ask to be taken off the wing?'

'And go down the block?'

'Why not? God, Tom, if this Lynch bloke can organise a fire from inside prison, there's no saying what else he can do. *You're* the one who isn't safe.'

'I'm okay. I can take care of myself.'

'You think?' Eden's eyes quickly scanned the room. 'There could be someone here, right now, who's just waiting to ...' She stopped and swallowed hard. 'I've heard all sorts about him. He's evil. And he thinks you killed his dad. He's going to do everything he can to make you pay for that.'

'Who's been talking to you?'

'What does it matter?'

Tom shrugged. 'You can't believe everything you hear.'

Eden frowned at him. 'There's that reporter, for one – Jimmy Letts, the *Herald* guy. He had plenty to say on the subject. I told him to push off, but he wouldn't go until he'd told me all about Lynch.' She hesitated, not wanting to get caught out in a lie, but determined to make her point. 'And then there are the police. When they came to see me at the hospital, they actually asked if you were on protection. I mean, why would they do that unless they thought you were in danger?'

'They don't know anything.'

'And nor do you, not for sure. It isn't worth the risk.'

'I've heard what it's like down the block. Basic isn't the word for it. And you're in solitary confinement twenty-four hours a day. What am I supposed to do? Stay there for the next six months until the case comes to trial?'

'Yes, if you have to. It's better than being dead!'

'That's not going to happen. I'll watch my back. I'll be careful, I promise.'

'It doesn't matter how careful you are. If someone wants to ... How can you stop them? I'll be worried about you all the time. Won't you think about the block? Just for a while, and then if you can't stand it ... I mean, it might only be for a few weeks. Castor could find Jack Minter and that's going to change everything.'

'It's not going to happen.'

'You don't know that.'

Tom gave a wry smile. 'I don't think we're going to find Jack. And even if we do, he's not going to admit to ever having been in possession of that bracelet. Not if it links him to the robbery.'

Eden gazed at her husband, aware that his mood was a dark one. It was hardly surprising, considering the fire, but there was a pessimistic tone to his voice she hadn't heard before. 'We'll see. Do you know where the negatives are for the Budapest photos? I'm afraid the picture of Jack – if it was him – went up in smoke.'

'They're somewhere in the studio.' He raised his hands and dropped them again. 'Sorry, that's not very helpful. I can't remember. In one of the cabinets, probably.'

'Okay. I'll take another look.'

'I wouldn't bother. It's not Jack you have to worry about, it's Archie Rudd.'

'Who?'

'He's the man who's accusing me. Castor told me yesterday.'

Eden's eyes widened. 'And who the hell is Archie Rudd?'

'Some old lag from the East End. He's got form for armed robbery, lots of it. He's the one who's going to stand up in court and swear blind I organised the Epping job, and that I dumped Paddy Lynch in a car park and left the guy to die.'

'And how is he going to do that when you weren't even there?'

Tom smiled thinly. 'By lying through his teeth.'

'What does Castor say? What he's going to do about it?'

'All he can do – try to find a way to discredit the bloke. Try and figure out why he's putting the finger on me.'

'There has to be a connection between the two of you, something you haven't thought of.'

'I'm telling you, I've never met the guy. I'm sure of it. Why's he doing this to me?'

Eden repeated the words she'd said so many times before. 'To get himself off the hook. To shift the blame on to someone else.'

'But why *me*?' Tom persisted. 'Where did he get my name from?'

Eden's eyes flashed with grim determination. 'I don't know, but I'm going to find out.'

Tom sighed, his mouth turning down at the corners. 'I don't want you to even try, Eden. Please don't. Just leave it to Castor. All I want is for you to get out of London.'

'I've already told you. There's the flat and—'

'The flat can wait. It's just bricks and mortar; it doesn't matter. All that matters is that you're safe.'

Eden was about to protest when she had a change of heart. A better idea had suddenly occurred to her. 'If I go to Edinburgh, will you go down the block? That's fair, isn't it? Then we'll both be . . . How about it?' Eden extended her hand. 'Is it a deal?'

Tom hesitated, but then extended his hand too. 'It's a deal. You drive a hard bargain, Mrs Chase.'

As they shook hands, Eden knew she was going nowhere. She didn't like lying, but if that's what it took to keep him out of danger it was a small price to pay. Getting the answers she needed meant staying in London. They had an enemy and now they had a name. She was going to find out everything she could about Archie Rudd.

267

39

Archie was struggling to keep his story straight. It was easy to forget stuff, especially when he'd had a drink or two. Things became blurry, soft around the edges, and the detail was lost. Sixteen years was a long time. That's what he kept telling Banner, but the inspector only curled his lip.

'Try harder, Arch. A jury isn't going to want to hear how crap your memory is.'

It was the number five Archie had to keep in his head. Yes, there were only five of them on the job: Jack Minter, Don West, Paul Rossi, Paddy Lynch and himself. He'd decided to keep Ned Shepherd out of it. He might be turning Queen's evidence but he wasn't about to screw over a mate. He still had some decency left, some honour. There was no need for the law to know that Ned had been the driver.

Archie wondered if his old pal knew what was going on. He must. After that *Herald* piece, the East End would be buzzing. And Vera Lynch wouldn't be slow in spreading the word; there was a squealer, a grass, a lowlife rat spilling his guts about the Epping warehouse robbery – and all the sordid details of her husband's death. Ned would be shitting himself, waiting for the knock on the door.

'That fuckin' Minter,' Archie muttered.

Banner looked at him, his eyes sly and narrow. 'You want him to go down, Arch, you've got to make sure you nail the bastard.'

Archie stared at the floor. He hadn't seen much of Ned in recent years, not since he and the missus had moved out to Thetford, but they'd been tight once. The three of them – Don, Ned and himself – had grown up together, gone to school together, drunk their first pint together, even started thieving together. Don had died a few years back – nothing could hurt him now – but Ned was still alive and kicking. Although his old mate might not be living in the East End, he still had family there. Word would have got to him by now. It must have. And the word would be that Archie Rudd was squealing like a pig.

'What are you thinking?' Banner asked.

Archie didn't reply. He was wondering if he should get Rose to tip Ned the wink, let him know he was safe, he didn't have to worry. But that was tricky. She wouldn't be able to use the blower in the Chiswick flat – it was bound to be tapped (Banner would be keeping tabs on her, making sure her old man wasn't planning any nasty surprises) – which meant she'd have to use a phone box. And if the law were keeping an eye on her, they'd wonder what the hell was going on.

'Archie?'

'What?'

'What's on your mind?'

Archie shook his head. This problem wasn't one to be shared. Maybe he could get Davey to call Ned instead. But the moment the idea entered his head, he instantly dismissed it. There'd be questions, accusations, all kinds of grief. No, he didn't want to drag his son into it. Perhaps it was best to let sleeping dogs lie. Ned would realise soon enough that he wasn't in the frame. The poor bloke would have a few sleepless nights between now and then, but it couldn't be helped.

Banner tried again. 'Is everything all right here? Is there anything you need?'

What Archie needed was to be able to turn the clock back, to have never accepted a place on the Shepperton job, to have never opened his big mouth, to be home where he belonged and not stuck in a three-star jail with everything he needed but his liberty and dignity. There was no denying the Chiswick set-up was good – comfortable living space, decent food, booze, plenty of fags and lots of visits from Rose – but none of it made him feel any better about the choices he'd made.

Archie lit a fag while he contemplated the miserable truth – that he actually *missed* mainstream prison. Everything was clear in there, black and white; you knew who you were and which side you were on. He missed the camaraderie, the banter and the gossip. He missed waking up every morning with a clear conscience. Now, when he looked in the mirror, he didn't even know who he was. It was as though his very identity had become distorted, a twisted reflection of his former self.

'If something's bothering you—' Banner began.

Archie waved a hand, dismissively. The ash from his fag dropped on to the floor, a tiny cylinder of grey. He gazed at it, wondering why he'd made the choices he had. What did the likes of Banner know when it came to what he was going through? Fuck all. For him, it was all about getting results, getting names, getting a foot on the next rung of the ladder. The pig pretended to care, but he didn't really give a damn.

'Talk to me, Arch. I need to know what's going on.'

The edges of Archie's thoughts had no straight lines; they

dipped and curved, drifting off to some distant horizon. What was the word on the street? What were people saying about him? His chest tightened as he visualised faces, people he'd known all his life, and heard the scorn in their voices. There was the man he'd been – good old Archie, loyal, reliable, salt of the earth – and the man he was now. He had crossed the line and there was no going back. He was a Judas, a turncoat, the lowest of the low.

Vic didn't like it when Archie went all quiet on him; it made him suspect the old lag was hiding something. Or maybe the guy was just depressed. He'd seen it before when men decided to turn Queen's evidence. There was all the bravado at first, the self-justification, before the doubt began to set in. Perhaps he should call the doctor to sort out some happy pills. There were still months to go before the trial and he couldn't afford to let Archie slide into the pit.

'Let's talk about the money from the Epping heist,' he said. 'Two million, yeah? That was quite a haul.'

Archie barked out a laugh. 'Two million? I wish.'

'That's what the company claimed.'

'Well, they would, wouldn't they?'

'What are you saying?'

'It weren't nothin' like that much,' Archie said. 'Shit, we didn't have time to clear the place, not even half, before Paddy got shot. We took what we could but . . . those shysters were just conning the insurance, saying they'd lost more than they had.'

Vic shrugged, knowing this was probably true. It was easy money for the company involved. They claimed on the insurance and then sold on the allegedly stolen goods, making twice the amount of profit. 'So how much are we talking about, then?'

'Less than a million, a good bit less, and by the time the fence had taken his share ... I don't know, we only came out with about a hundred grand each. I mean, it ain't to be sniffed at but it ain't a fortune neither.'

Vic did some mental calculations. It was probable that the money in Tom Chase's Munich account had come from the raid but there wasn't any way of proving it. And if Chase had been living off the proceeds he must have been living pretty thriftily to have still had thirty-five grand left four years ago. But then he could have done other jobs, topping up the cash from different sources.

Vic wasn't making much progress with the bank in Munich. The bloody Krauts were being less than helpful when it came to giving out information about Tom Chase's account. So much for European cooperation. He needed to know exactly when the money had been deposited and where it had come from, but all he was getting was a pile of bureaucratic bullshit.

The information Tammy had passed to him was worrying too. She reckoned Tom Chase could prove where the cash had come from – and that it was a legitimate loan. At least that's what Eden had told her. If it was true, it could put a spanner in the works. Although it couldn't explain what the bracelet was doing in his safe.

Vic folded his arms and looked over at Archie. 'What about this snake bracelet? How come Chase ended up with it if all the haul was sold on to the fence?'

'Because the cheating bastard stashed some things away, didn't he? Kept them back, shoved them in his pocket instead of in the sacks.'

Vic grinned. 'And you didn't?'

'A few rings, a couple of gold chains, but nothin' flashy, nothin' that could be traced directly to the warehouse. He was an amateur, see, a greedy fuckin' amateur.' Archie touched the side of his head with his right index finger. 'You've got to think when you're on a job. You've got to use some smarts.'

'Whatever happened to honour among thieves?'

Archie gave a derisory snort. 'I didn't owe that bastard a thing. Me and Don split the extras we got; it weren't that much, just a bit on the side. What kind of twat holds on to a piece like that? It's asking for trouble.'

Vic wondered why Chase hadn't got rid of the bracelet when he was abroad. Maybe he'd kept it as a souvenir, something to remind him of the job. Except who in their right minds would want to be reminded of a job that had gone so spectacularly wrong? Perhaps it had just been down to carelessness.

Everything was resting on Archie's testimony. It had to be right. It had to be solid and convincing. Apart from Chase, Paul Rossi was the only other surviving member of the gang. And, if the rumours were to be believed, he was currently sunning himself on the Costa del Sol. As there was no extradition treaty with Spain, there was sod all chance of bringing him to justice.

Vic's thoughts skipped on to the fire at the Chase flat. He'd met up with the Islington cop, DS Nicholls, but hadn't learned more than he already knew – that the fire had been deliberate and that whoever had started it didn't give a damn about the people inside. He wondered what state Eden was in now. She had to be scared. She had to be bloody terrified. And who was to blame for that? Her no-good, lying, murdering husband. When would she see him for what he really was? It was time the stupid bitch woke up and smelled the coffee.

40

Jimmy Letts had one decent article under his belt, but it wasn't enough. There was something bigger out there, an exclusive that had his name all over it. How had Tom Chase, an apparently respectable photographer, got away with murder? It was sixteen years since Paddy Lynch had met his miserable end and no one had been charged until now. Chase had somehow managed to slip under the net, to evade justice, for all this time.

He stood and stared up at the blackened exterior walls of the house on Pope Street. There was little doubt it had been a revenge attack, payback for what Chase had done. Jimmy didn't feel guilty about being the cause of that – the truth was the truth and if he hadn't told Vera, someone else would. His conscience was clear. It was unfortunate, of course, that Eden Chase had got caught in the blaze, but she hadn't been seriously hurt. What bothered him more was he had no idea where she was staying now.

Still, that was a problem soon to be solved. Hopefully Eden would be at the jail today, and Maurie Post would be waiting for her. Jimmy had bunged him a score plus some petrol money, and given him the details of the car and a photo of Eden.

'I just want you to follow her home, yeah? Wherever she goes. Think you can manage that without being spotted?'

Maurie was in his early twenties, a small-time dealer, a thief and a snout. He was the kind of lowlife who'd sell his granny for a fiver and not think twice about it. 'Sure, man. Just leave it to me.'

'Don't get too close, right? Keep your distance, but not so far off you lose her.'

Maurie had given him a look. 'I'm not stupid, man. I know what I'm doing.'

'And I want the address as soon as you get back. Not next bloody week or whenever you decide it's convenient. This afternoon. Bring it to the office and if I'm not there leave it with the woman on reception. Think you can manage that?'

'The woman on reception,' Maurie had dutifully repeated in a bored monotone. Then he'd looked at the photo and grinned. 'A redhead, huh? She'll be hard to miss.'

Jimmy lowered his gaze from the house and glanced at his watch. It was twenty past two. Maurie should be on his way to the jail by now – so long as everything had gone to plan. If Eden had changed the day of her visit, or decided for some reason or another not to go, then he'd just chucked a score down the pan. It would probably have been easier, and certainly cheaper, to do it himself, but he hadn't wanted to take the risk of being recognised. One look in the mirror and she could have easily clocked him.

Anyway, he had better things to do than hang around outside jails. One of these things had involved a trip to Somerset House to try and dig out Tom Chase's birth certificate. Three bleeding hours he'd been leafing through those ledgers before finally hitting pay dirt. He took the slip of paper from his pocket and studied the details he'd copied down: *Thomas James Chase, born 17 April 1940 in Norwich, Norfolk. Parents – Clive and Andrea Chase.*

It had to be him, surely? The date would make him forty-two this year which sounded about right, and the full name was the same as the one given in court. What were the odds of two different men having the same name and age? Pretty slim, he reckoned. The address of the parents at the time of the birth had been recorded as 23 Lester Street. Jimmy had gone to the library and checked out the Norfolk phone book, but there had only been three Chases listed. None of these had tallied with the address he'd got, but a number in Norwich – Sadler Street – had been listed under C. Chase.

Jimmy had called and a man had answered after a couple of rings. 'Hello, is that Mr Clive Chase?'

'Yes, speaking. How can I help you?'

But Jimmy hadn't wanted to give him advance warning of his visit or give him time to concoct a story about his murderous son. An element of surprise was always useful in situations like these. He wanted to speak to the parents directly, to look into their eyes when he asked how they felt about their son being charged. 'Oh, I'm really sorry, Mr Chase. My apologies but something important has just come up. I'll have to call you back.'

So the good news was he'd found Tom Chase's father, the bad that he'd have a three-hour drive to get to him. Jimmy slipped the piece of paper back into his pocket, walked over to the Cortina and got in. He pulled the door closed and sat for a while staring along the street. Earlier, he'd gone knocking on doors, hoping for some neighbourhood gossip on Tom and Eden Chase, but no one had been prepared to talk. People round here were suspicious of the press;

middle-class lefties, most of them, the sort who only ever read the *Guardian*.

Jimmy's knees jerked up and down as he tried to decide whether to set off for Norfolk straight away. His editor was going to kill him if he went AWOL. He was supposed to be over at Kellston this afternoon, chatting to the residents of the Mansfield estate and getting some copy on the recent troubles. Still, he could probably cobble something together this evening, the usual shit, a few fake interviews and the like.

Jimmy mulled it over. It would mean missing Maurie too, but that didn't really matter. There was no point in having Eden's address if he didn't have something solid to confront her with. A thin prickle of sweat broke out on his forehead. It was nerve-racking being so close and yet so far. Every morning he woke up dreading that some other reporter had beaten him to it, and that the inside story of Tom Chase was already splashed across one of the nationals.

Yes, it made sense to head for Norfolk right now. If he wanted the low-down on Chase, he had to talk to the family. He needed to know about the bloke's past, his childhood, his history, if he was ever going to fathom why he'd become what he had – a vicious armed robber who had heartlessly left a man to die. He needed background, colour and plenty of quotes. At the moment all he had was a vague grey outline.

Jimmy put the key in the ignition and started the engine. 'Tom Chase,' he muttered. 'Who the fuck are you?'

It was a long drive and by the time Jimmy reached Norwich, darkness had fallen. He'd spent most of the journey trying to figure out his approach. The parents were going to be defensive and he needed an 'in', a way to ingratiate himself. The best method, he decided, was to say he believed Tom was innocent. That way they might be willing to talk. Yes, something along the lines of a miscarriage of justice could do the trick.

Jimmy knew he'd only get one chance and he couldn't afford to blow it. Hope was the gift he would offer the Chases, an opportunity for their son to get a fair hearing. Unless they already knew he was guilty, in which case he'd have to go down a completely different road. Sympathy, an understanding ear, might be what was required in those circumstances. Well, he could do that. He could do sympathy in buckets.

Until he got there, Jimmy wouldn't know for sure how to play it. He had to be prepared for all eventualities – including getting the door slammed in his face. That would be a bummer after driving all this way. Shit, no, he had to make sure that didn't happen. He was close enough to smell the exclusive, to breathe in its glory. To fall at the last hurdle would be a goddamn disaster.

Sadler Street was to the west of the city and he had to stop several times to study the map. The traffic was heavy with everyone heading home after work, and the rain was lashing down. It was another half hour before he found the address, a small bungalow in a winding street of identical properties, with a garage to the side and a square of grass out front.

He pulled up outside and gazed along the drive. There was a light on in the front room behind drawn curtains. Good, someone was in. He hoped it was the mother, Andrea. Women were more emotional, more likely to blurt out what they really felt. Jimmy checked his face in the rear-view mirror, ran a comb through his hair and adjusted his expression to one of righteous indignation.

'You can do this,' he said, as he got out of the car. He slapped his fist against his leg. 'Don't mess it up, Jimmy. Don't mess it up.'

He walked briskly up the drive and pressed the bell. A ding-dong sound came from inside and seconds later the light went on in the hall. Jimmy saw the silhouette of a man through the opaque glass in the door. He took a couple of deep breaths and prepared for what could be the most important exchange of his life.

The man opened the door and raised his eyebrows. 'Yes?'

'Mr Clive Chase?' Jimmy asked.

'That's me.'

'Good evening. My name's Jimmy Letts. I'm a reporter from the *Herald* in London. I'm sorry to disturb you. I realise this is a very difficult time, but I was hoping I could have a word about your son.'

Clive Chase was a short, thickset man in his late sixties. He looked bemused. 'Aidan?'

Jimmy shook his head. He hadn't thought about the fact there could be a brother. 'No,' he said quickly. 'I meant Tom, Tom Chase. He is your son, isn't he?'

The man flinched as if he'd just received a blow. Then his eyes grew dark and menacing. He took a step forward and pushed his face into Jimmy's. 'What's your fucking game? What are you playing at?'

Jimmy moved back and raised his hands, palms out. 'I'm sorry. I didn't mean to ... I think there may have been a misunderstanding.'

'Is that what you call it?'

From inside the house there was another voice, a female's. 'Who is it, Clive? Who's there?'

'No one,' Clive called back. 'Fuck off,' he hissed to Jimmy. 'Get the fuck out of my sight.'

The woman appeared at the door and looked at them both. 'What's going on?'

Jimmy knew he was seconds away from losing everything.

His brain was rapidly trying to process what was happening. So the bloke didn't want to discuss his boy – that was understandable, bearing in mind what he'd done – but why had he jumped to the conclusion it was Aidan they were talking about? There was something weird about it, something off. Unless he didn't know Tom was in jail . . . Jimmy stared at the wife – she was about the same age as Clive, thin, with cropped grey hair and glasses – and addressed his question only to her. 'I'm here about Tom. He is your son, isn't he? Tom Chase?'

There was shock on the woman's face. Her mouth dropped open. 'W-what?'

Clive made a move as if to lunge at the unwelcome visitor, but she grabbed his arm and held him back. 'No!' Then she peered at Jimmy, swallowed hard and said, 'Why are you asking about Tom?'

'You do know he's in prison, don't you? He's been charged with murder and armed robbery.'

Mrs Chase visibly paled. Even in the artificial light from the hall, Jimmy could see the blood draining from her face. Her gaze jumped from him to her husband. 'Clive? What does he mean?'

'He doesn't mean anything, love. He doesn't know what he's talking about.'

'But he's saying that—'

'I know what he's saying. I'm standing here, aren't I? I can hear him.'

The rain was seeping under Jimmy's collar. It was cold, bloody freezing, but that wasn't the only reason he was shivering. He was balanced on the edge of something big and had to find the right words to tip the situation in his favour. 'Look, I'm sorry. I'm really sorry. I didn't mean to cause any upset. It must be hard for you. I understand that. That's why

I'm here. I don't think Tom's guilty, not at all. I want to help if you'll let me.'

There was a long, strange silence. Jimmy was aware of two pairs of eyes boring into him. 'Ten minutes of your time,' he added. 'That's all I'm asking.'

'There's been a mistake,' Mrs Chase said, shaking her head. 'I think you'd better come in. Don't you think so, Clive?'

Clive didn't look keen. 'He's a reporter, love.'

'We need to sort this out.'

Eventually Clive gave a shrug. 'If that's what you want.'

And so the decision was made. Jimmy smiled as he followed them into the bungalow, taking care to wipe his feet on the mat.

Jimmy was still smiling when he emerged half an hour later. In fact, there was an almost euphoric expression on his face. He had come to Norwich in the hope of getting background information on Tom Chase, but was leaving with something else entirely. What he had in his possession was dynamite. As he climbed into the Cortina, his pulse was racing. A new story was already taking shape in his head, an explosive tale of lies and deceit, love and betrayal. Did Eden Chase know about her husband? If she didn't, she was about to be confronted with a truth that would blow her life apart.

41

Tom Chase lay on the bunk with his hands behind his head and stared up at the ceiling. There were fine cracks, like spiders' webs, running across the plaster. He traced them with his eyes while he tried not to think about the fire, but the harder he tried the less successful he was. Horrifying visions came to him: flames roaring through the flat, thick black suffocating smoke, the burning heat of Hell. What if Eden hadn't woken up? It was pointless to torment himself in such a way, but he couldn't stop. He was haunted by what might have been.

She could have died and it would have been his fault. His heart missed a beat. It was too awful to think about. It was all he could think about. Without her, he was done for, finished. She was his rock, his other half, his one point of sanity in a world that had gone mad. But how long before she stopped believing in his innocence? Already the foundations of her trust were starting to crumble – he could see it in her eyes – after the revelations of the Kellston flat, the Munich loan and, most damning of all, the bracelet found in the safe.

Tom couldn't blame her for wondering. When you stacked

up the 'evidence', things didn't look good. The trouble was he had got in the habit over the years of never saying more than he had to. It was a defence mechanism, a shield. The past was too painful to talk about and so he'd put it in a strongbox, locked it up and thrown away the key. Would he have told her the truth if she'd pressed him for it? Perhaps. Except one of the reasons he loved her so much was her capacity to let things lie. She wasn't the type of woman who had to open the doors to every room in your head and poke around inside.

Tom had known within a few days of meeting her – or was it within a few hours? – that she was the one. The perfect fit. His other half. People talked a lot of crap about love, when all they really meant was lust. True love was something entirely different. What he felt for Eden went beyond physical desire; it was a deep connection, pure and instinctive. To lose her would be to lose everything.

Tom's thoughts were interrupted by the arrival of Pete Conway. He gave a light knock, came into the cell, and sauntered over to the bunk. 'Fancy a game of pool?'

'No, thanks.'

'What are you doing?'

'Thinking.'

Pete pushed his hands into his pockets and rocked back on his heels. 'That ain't good for you, man. Screws with your head. The less thinking you do in here, the better.'

'Thanks for the advice.'

'I mean it. You just end up crazy, going over it all again and again. You got to keep busy, at least as busy as you can in this godforsaken shithole.'

'Maybe later, huh?'

Pete, who was not the most sensitive of blokes and couldn't quite grasp when he wasn't wanted, continued to linger. 'So what's on your mind?'

'Eden wants me to get off the wing, go down the block for a while.'

'Maybe she's right.'

Tom turned his head to look at him. 'Why? Have you heard something?'

'Nah, I ain't heard nothin'. I'm just saying, that's all. That Pat Lynch, the one you told me about, sounds like he's got a screw loose, man. You might be better off on the seg, least for a while.'

Tom raised his eyebrows. 'I thought you didn't approve of thinking. There's not much else to do in that place.'

'Yeah, well, you got to take care of yourself in here. No one else is gonna do it for you. Your missus could have a point. All you have to do is turn your back for a second and . . .' Pete pulled a face. 'I ain't saying it *will* happen, but sometimes you've got to take . . . er . . . what's the word?'

'Precautions?'

'Yeah, that's it. Precautions, man. You've got to do the smart thing even if it ain't exactly what you want.'

Tom had already made up his mind – he'd promised Eden, made a deal, and wasn't going to let her down again – but was putting it off for as long as possible. In solitary, the past would come crowding in on him. With no distractions, he'd be forced to face some uncomfortable truths. Long-buried secrets would rise to the surface like cold bones drawn up from the bottom of the ocean.

'Sure you don't fancy that game of pool?'

'Some other time, yeah?'

Pete looked at him for a moment, opened his mouth as if to say something, shrugged and walked out of the cell.

Tom went back to studying the ceiling. It was odd how quickly you grew used to prison, to the sounds, the smells, the tedious routine. After the shock and disbelief had subsided, there was nothing left but the need for acceptance. It didn't pay to fight against the system, even if you were innocent. You had to roll with it, tell yourself it wasn't for ever, live in the present and not in the future.

What he missed most, apart from Eden, was his camera. The only time he felt truly at ease with the world was when he was viewing it through a lens. He still hadn't figured out why that was. Something to hide behind? Or something that enabled him to focus, to close off everything else? Maybe it was both. The camera was so much a part of him that even now he would sometimes reach for it, forgetting where he was.

He thought of the Leica perched on the tripod in his studio. He'd been using that camera when he first saw Eden walking across Covent Garden piazza. The autumn sun had caught her hair, making it gleam like burnished coppery gold. Yeah, okay, it was a cliché, but it was still true. The decision to capture the moment was a split-second one, an impulse that had changed his life for ever.

'Did you just take a picture of me?'

Tom could remember the expression on her face, still hear the chagrin in her voice. He smiled. He'd liked the way she stood up to him, how her eyes flashed with irritation. A girl who wasn't afraid to speak her mind. A girl who wasn't easily impressed. It had not, perhaps, been the most auspicious of starts, and yet there had been a connection between them. It had been a fateful meeting like that earlier one in Budapest, the one that had led him, ultimately, to be languishing in this prison cell right now.

Tom knew he should regret ever having clapped eyes on Jack Minter. Wasn't he the cause of all his troubles? And yet if their paths hadn't crossed, he might never have met Eden. It was Jack who had provided the means for his escape, a way out of the old life, an opportunity to cut the ties for good.

Their friendship, based partly on a shared nationality – in Budapest there were hardly any other British residents – was cemented by their interest in photography. Jack, who claimed to be an enthusiastic amateur, was in fact highly talented. He had an extraordinary eye, a way of looking at things that was quite unique. Tom had learned from him as they meandered through the city, and not just about photography. Jack was a drinker, a womaniser and a gambler, a charismatic man who was thoroughly intriguing. He was also as secretive about his past as Tom was himself.

Who could have guessed at the truth? Jack's claim that he'd left Britain as a teenager was enough to throw anyone off the scent. And anyway, you'd hardly expect to meet an armed robber from London when you were hanging out in Garay Square. He'd realised quickly enough, however, that not everything Jack did was legal. His friend was involved in the black market, in the buying and selling of illicit goods, although that wasn't so unusual in Budapest at the time. Struggling under the yoke of the Soviet Union, there were often shortages of food and booze, of fashionable clothes and household appliances. If you wanted something – and had the money to pay for it – Jack could usually procure it for you.

Tom had been thinking a lot about his old friend recently. It wasn't so much the armed robbery that shocked him – although that was disturbing enough – but what had happened after. Why had he left Paddy Lynch to die like that? Panic, perhaps. Or maybe he thought the bloke was already dead. What Tom didn't want to believe, *couldn't* believe, was that Jack Minter had been involved in an act of cold-hearted brutality.

But that was what Archie Rudd was claiming. The old lag had been arrested on some other heist, decided to turn Queen's evidence and thrown Tom's name into the mix for the Epping job, alleging that Tom and Jack Minter were one and the same.

It might not have gone any further than a police interview if it hadn't been for the bracelet. Having that piece of damning evidence sitting in his safe had given credibility to the accusation.

Tom moved his arms from under his head and rubbed his face in frustration. He was hoping Castor could find a way of discrediting Archie Rudd before the case ever went to court, but what were the odds? The man was a squealer, a grass, and he wasn't going to let a small matter like the truth get in the way of a tasty deal.

'Christ,' he muttered.

He was like a rat in a trap, going round in circles. He had got himself involved in one big lie, so twisted and complex he couldn't find a way out of it. To tell the truth would probably mean losing Eden. Jesus, of course it would. But if he didn't, he could be spending the next twenty years rotting in jail. And that would mean losing her anyway.

The cold, hard truth was that he was in a no-win situation. When the trial started it would be Archie Rudd's word against his. Who would the jury believe? In order to sway the verdict in his favour he would need to produce the real Jack Minter. And that was never going to happen.

Tom knew what he had to do. The longer he waited, the more dangerous it was for Eden. It might be difficult but it wouldn't be impossible for Pat Lynch to track her down to Edinburgh. She wasn't safe. She would never be safe while this was hanging over them. He had to come clean before it was too late.

42

'And how exactly are you going to pull that one off?' Caitlin asked, as she helped Eden to unpack her meagre possessions. 'I mean, I presume you've no intention of going to your dad's, seeing as you're moving in here. So what happens when you write to Tom? He's going to notice that the letters aren't coming from Edinburgh.'

Eden opened the fridge, put in a pint of milk and a carton of eggs, and closed the door again. 'I've no idea. I'll figure something out. I just wanted to make sure he got off the wing and the only way I could do that was to promise I'd go to Scotland.'

'And now you're going to break your promise.'

'Of course I am. I'm not going to be able to do anything from up there, am I? And you know what Dad's like; he'll realise something's wrong and give me the third degree until I give in and tell him. I can't cope with his attitude on top of everything else. Not right now.'

Caitlin laid a box of tea bags on the counter. She filled the kettle and put it on to boil. 'Have you told him about the fire?'

'No. I said there was a damp problem in the flat and we've had to move out for a while. Of course he then started asking all sorts of questions about what *sort* of damp it was, rising or penetrating or condensation, and naturally I didn't have a clue so ... ' Eden put her hands on her hips and sighed. 'It probably confirms all his worst suspicions about his daughter's intelligence – or lack of it.'

'It might be easier to tell him the truth.'

'Oh, believe me, it wouldn't. I know I'll have to tell him eventually, but after the fire and everything ... I just want a bit of time to try and get my head straight.'

'I get that. But don't leave it too long. It'll be worse if he hears from someone else.'

They took their tea through to the living room and sat down on the sofa. Eden sipped from the mug and gazed around the living room. 'It's not so bad, is it? I could get some new curtains and cushions, jazz it up a bit. There's a market down the road – they'll have some cheap stuff there. Anyway, it doesn't matter. It'll only be for a while.'

Caitlin looked at her. 'Are you sure you're okay? You don't have to move in right now. You can stay with me for as long as you like. Why not leave it for another week or two?'

'Thanks, but I need to be settled somewhere. I've got to sort myself out and start getting on with things.'

'What kind of things?'

'Well, there's Archie Rudd for starters.' Eden put the mug down on the coffee table, picked up a carrier bag from the floor and took out a stack of photocopies. 'I went to Colindale newspaper library again and did a search through the records. You wouldn't believe how much form this guy has got. He's been in and out of prison all his life.'

'That's why he's turning Queen's evidence. He doesn't fancy another long stretch.'

'I need to figure out why he's accusing Tom.'

Caitlin glanced towards the heap of paper. 'And you think the answer's in there?'

'I've no idea, but there could be something. He couldn't have just plucked Tom's name from thin air. Jack Minter must have given it to him.'

'But I thought Minter didn't meet Tom until after the robbery?'

'He didn't. But Rudd and Jack Minter could have seen each other since. Minter could have mentioned Tom's name and . . . I don't know. I can't make any sense of it. Not yet. But there has to be an explanation.'

'Maybe you need to find out who else was on the Epping job. There must have been what, half a dozen of them? If Rudd's naming names, he'll have to provide those too. And they're not going to be happy about it. You should call Castor, see if he knows anything about the other members of the gang.'

'If he'll tell me.' Eden sighed and put the papers down. She was quiet for a moment. The sound of traffic came through the closed windows, a perpetual roar she would have to get used to. 'Annabelle said Tom was a liar and a cheat.'

'Well, she would, wouldn't she? She's just trying to stir it. She's hardly going to say anything nice after you just got rid of her.'

'Unless she knows something I don't.'

'Do you think he has lied to you?'

Eden screwed up her face. 'Not lied, exactly, but he hasn't been what you'd call open and honest. I didn't even know this flat existed until recently. It's not normal to keep something like that from your own wife. And I only have to mention his family and he instantly clams up. He won't tell me anything about them, not really.'

'But that's Tom, I guess. He's always come across as a private sort of guy.'

'Private or secretive?'

'It's a thin line,' Caitlin said. 'But don't let that bitch get under your skin. She's out to cause trouble. Don't give her the satisfaction.'

'I'll try, but . . . '

'But?'

Eden wouldn't have been so honest with anyone other than Caitlin. 'I don't think he's guilty, not for a second, but I'm starting to wonder if I actually know him at all. The things I've been finding out . . . not just the flat, but the Munich money, the way he started his business, his friendship with Jack Minter . . . I just . . . sometimes he feels more like a stranger than a husband. Is that a terrible thing to say?'

Caitlin reached out and pressed her hand. 'No, it's not terrible. Of course it isn't. For whatever reason, he hasn't been straight with you. Maybe that's something the two of you need to talk about.'

'Only I won't be seeing him for ages. And God, what am I going to do about writing? I'm supposed to be in Edinburgh in a few days.'

'What about your brother? Would he help you out, forward on your mail to Tom?'

Eden shook her head. 'No, I don't want him involved in all this. He'd have to lie to Dad and that isn't fair on him. I'll think of something else. Maybe I could tell Tom that Dad's going abroad on business, that I don't want to be alone in the house and so I'm staying with a friend instead, someone who lives outside London. Kent, perhaps. That's not too far away, is it? Straight through the Blackwall Tunnel and I'm almost there.'

'Expensive letters,' Caitlin said. 'Are you sure you want to lie to him like this?'

'I know it makes me sound like a hypocrite. I complain about him not being straight and then . . . but I don't have any choice. If I want him to stick to his side of the bargain, I've got to make him believe I'm sticking to mine.'

'And what about his accountant – Elspeth, is it? – what if she tells him that you've moved in here?'

'I'll have to take the chance. I shouldn't think he's got that much contact with her at the moment. I could always say I thought about it and then changed my mind.'

Caitlin gave a small shake of her head. 'I'm worried about you staying in London.'

'Don't be. No one's going to know I'm here. I'll be careful.'

'Make sure you are. Don't tell anyone else. I mean it, Eden.'

'I won't.'

'Not even Denny. That Fiona can't keep her mouth shut for more than five minutes.'

Eden nodded. 'Especially not Denny and Fiona.'

'Or that girl you've been giving a lift to.'

'Tammy?'

'Yeah, Tammy. Stick to the story and tell her you're going up to Edinburgh.'

'Tammy's okay. She won't say anything.'

'I'm sure she won't – not deliberately – but she's going to the prison every week. She might let something slip. Tom's not going to be too happy if he finds out you're still in London.'

Eden wasn't sure how Tom could find out if he was down the block, but it was probably better to be safe than sorry. However, she did feel guilty about abandoning Tammy. Having seen the bruises, she suspected the girl needed all the friends she could get at the moment. 'All right. I promise.'

'What about money?' Caitlin asked. 'Are you all right? It could be a while before the insurance comes through.'

'I'll be okay. Most of the mortgage is paid off on this place so there's not much to pay every month. I reckon I can manage it now I've got a job.'

Caitlin looked surprised. 'A job? What job? You didn't tell me about that.'

'I only got it this morning. It's nothing much, just some shifts in the café down the road. I was walking past and there was a card in the window so I went in and . . . well, you're now looking at the newest waitress in Connolly's.'

'Do you think that's a good idea?'

'If I want to eat and pay the bills, then yes.'

'But working round here. Don't you think it's kind of risky? That Vera Lynch doesn't live far away. What if she comes into the café and realises who you are?'

'Why would she? Realise who I am, I mean. I won't be wearing a name tag and no one takes much notice of waitresses. Anyway, I used my maiden name, so as far as John Connolly and anyone else who works there are concerned I'm Edie Shore.'

Caitlin grinned. 'Edie?'

'I know. It's awful. But I don't care so long as no one guesses who I really am. And I'll be paid in cash. It's not much but I get to keep any tips I make.'

'Have you ever done waitressing before?'

'No, but it can't be that hard.'

'Famous last words. Just make sure you've got some comfy shoes. It's not easy being on your feet for hours.' Caitlin paused before adding, 'And for God's sake be careful. I don't know if it's a smart idea working as well as living round here.'

'It saves on travelling costs. I've only got to walk down the road and I'm there. There's no point wasting money on bus fares or petrol. I've got to save every penny I can.'

Caitlin opened her mouth to say something else but was interrupted by the ringing of the phone.

Eden rose to her feet and quickly crossed the room. The only people who had the new number were Caitlin, her dad and Tom's lawyer. She hadn't given it to the police. So far as they were concerned, she was still in Finchley and that's the way she wanted to keep it. She could do without any unannounced visits from the despicable Vic Banner. However, she had left a message for Castor, saying she was staying with a friend after the fire, and provided the Kellston number as the one she could currently be contacted on.

'Hello?'

'Is that Mrs Chase?'

'Yes.'

'It's Michael Castor here. I'm glad I caught you.'

Eden felt a sudden jolt of alarm. Castor had barely been in touch since Tom's appearance in court and immediately she presumed the news must be bad. 'Has something happened? Is Tom all right?'

'Yes, yes, he's fine. It's nothing like that. Only I've just come out from a legal visit with him and . . . well, there have been some developments.'

'What sort of developments?'

'He wants to see you. Could you go to the prison on Monday? I've been able to arrange a special visit.'

'What do you mean? What's going on?'

'If you turn up at the usual time and—'

Eden's mouth had gone dry. 'What developments?' she repeated.

There was a brief hesitation from the other end of the line. 'I'm afraid I can't tell you that. Tom wishes to talk to you himself. But if there's anything you want to ask afterwards, please feel free to give me a call.'

'You *have* to tell me,' Eden insisted, her voice rising up an octave as a heady cocktail of fear and panic rushed to her head.

'You can't just . . . You can't leave it like this. What's it about? Please, tell me something.'

'I'm sorry. I wish I could help but—'

'You can help. It's another two days until Monday. How am I supposed to get through the weekend? I have to know.'

'I'm afraid there's nothing more I can say. I'm under strict instructions from my client. I know this is difficult, but Tom will explain everything when he sees you.' And then, before she had the chance to make any more pleas, he said a formal goodbye and hung up.

Eden could feel the thumping in her chest as she put the phone down. She turned to look at Caitlin. 'That was Castor. Tom wants to see me on Monday.'

'What about?'

'I wish I knew. He says there have been some developments, but wouldn't tell me anything more. They can't be good ones, can they? I mean, if it was good news he'd have told me straight out. Anyway, I could tell from the tone of his voice. Something seriously bad is going on.'

'You can't be sure of that, not yet.'

Eden walked back across the room and slumped down on the sofa. She covered her face with her hands and took long deep breaths, trying to calm down. 'I am sure of it.'

Caitlin put an arm around her. 'What are you thinking?'

But Eden couldn't bring herself to say the words out loud. Even having them in her head made her feel cold and treacherous. Was it possible that Tom had *confessed*? Instantly, she stamped on the thought. No, it couldn't be that. He was innocent. He'd sworn to her. Her husband wasn't an armed robber, not the type of man to leave someone to die. He wasn't. He couldn't be. She closed and eyes and prayed. *Please, God, don't let it be that.*

43

Max Tamer bent down and collected the mail, a heap of fliers and the free local paper, and put it all on the hall table. It was only then that he noticed the pale blue airmail envelope lying half hidden between a couple of bills. He picked up the letter and turned it over, looking at the address on the back even though he already knew it was from Ann-Marie's mother, Juliette. Her letters came less often now. What was there left for her to say? He hesitated, almost tore it open, but then changed his mind.

After putting the letter and bills to one side, he took the junk through to the kitchen where he dropped it into the bin. Then he made a rapid tour of the flat, checking that everything was in order after the recent bad weather – no burst pipes, leaks or other emergencies that needed his attention.

The place smelled musty and abandoned. A fine film of dust covered every surface. He rarely slept here these days. He couldn't bear the silence or the constant reminders of Ann-Marie. In the bedroom, her clothes still hung in the wardrobe, coats and dresses, blouses and jackets that would never be worn again. There was make-up, a hairbrush and bottles of perfume on the dressing table. He winced and quickly looked away.

Max couldn't live in the flat but he couldn't get rid of it either. It was all he had left of her. Sometimes, if he stood very still, held his breath and listened, he could hear the sound of her voice echoing though the empty rooms. He would imagine her walking barefoot across the pale green carpet, her tread as soft and sure as a cat's. And then ... surely, if he waited long enough, she would once again appear in the doorway with her beautiful smile and her long red-gold hair tumbling over her shoulders. Ann-Marie: his wife, his lover, his other half. Just for a moment, he would be whole again.

But the pain of such desire, such empty hopes, was always too much to bear. Cold reality would slice through him like a blade, bleeding him dry, emptying his heart of everything but pain. Max cleared his throat, just to make some noise in the silence. Then he walked rapidly back to the hall, swept up the mail, shoved it into his pocket and left the flat.

Outside, the rain was still falling. The cars swished past, their headlights striping the road, their tyres kicking up water from the gutter in long sideways sprays. He bowed his head, keeping in to the wall to avoid getting soaked. He breathed in the damp evening air, feeling a faint rasp in his lungs. Too many cigarettes. He smoked heavily these days, careless of his health, indifferent to the consequences.

It was only a short walk to his mother's house. He didn't call it home, even though he had spent his childhood there. Home was the flat he and Ann-Marie had bought together, decorating the rooms one by one, carefully painting the walls, scouring the flea markets at weekends for interesting pieces of furniture, for old Persian rugs and fabrics to make curtains and cushions. Her tastes were quirky, his more traditional. It had been an eclectic mix, but somehow it had come together. Now he paid the mortgage for a place he never used, unable to live in it, unable to let go.

The lights were on in his mother's house, his car parked on the drive. He had taken the Tube into the office this morning. He paused on the doorstep, gathering himself in, giving the mask time to settle over his features. The mask was as much for his benefit as hers, something civilised to hide behind, something to disguise his cold, primitive rage. She wasn't fooled by it, of course, but went along with the pretence, hoping perhaps that one day what was acted would become real, that he would eventually be healed and find a way to move on.

As he put the key in the door, Max felt a sharp, stabbing pain in his palm. He had a fleeting flashback to the night of the fire, the smoke and confusion, the weight of Eden Chase across his shoulder. He blinked a couple of times, trying to clear his mind of the memory. He didn't want to think about her. The cut had been cleaned, stitched and bandaged at A&E, but still made him flinch if he curled his fingers too quickly.

It was warm inside and the smell of cooking floated on the air. One of his mother's better days, then. Sometimes she barely ate at all. She would shake her head at everything he offered, saying she wasn't hungry, claiming she'd eaten earlier although he knew she hadn't. He would have to coax her with soft boiled eggs and soldiers – as if she were the child and he the parent.

Max found her in the kitchen, stirring a pot of beef stew. 'That smells good. Can I do anything?'

'There are bowls in the oven. Be a love and get them out, will you?'

He put the warmed bowls on the counter and got the cutlery from the drawer. They chatted as she dished out the food, keeping to safe and mundane subjects like the dismal weather and how crowded the Tube had been. Simple, soothing conversation, the actual words less important than the comfort they provided.

It was only after they'd eaten that Max remembered the post he'd picked up from the flat. While his mother watched television, he collected the mail from his overcoat pocket, returned to the living room and began going through it. He opened the bills first, water rates and electricity, the latter for so small an amount it had barely been worth the cost of the invoice.

He saved the airmail letter to last, girding himself, for although Juliette tried her best not to burden him with her grief, no artfully constructed sentences could even begin to disguise that dreadful sense of loss, the awful yearning of a mother for her daughter.

What he found inside the envelope, however, was completely unexpected. There was only a short note from Juliette, written in English and explaining that a letter – enclosed – had recently arrived for Ann-Marie. The tone was flustered, bewildered. *Do you know anything about this woman? Does this mean anything to you?*

Max briefly studied the outside of the second airmail envelope, already opened by a neat slice across the top. Although he didn't recognise the writing, the return address was familiar to him. He frowned as he pulled out the single sheet of crisp white notepaper and began to read.

Dear Ann-Marie,

I am sorry to contact you out of the blue. I am writing about my husband, Tom Chase, who I believe you were friendly with many years back. I'm afraid Tom is in serious trouble due to something that happened in Budapest in the late 60s. Do you remember meeting

a man called Jack Minter? If you do, I would be very
grateful if you could contact me at the above address or
give me a call and I will ring you back.
  Best regards,
  Eden Chase

Max's hands had started to shake even before he reached the end. He had waited two long years but here it was, finally, in black and white – irrefutable proof that the Tom Chase he had confronted in Covent Garden had known Ann-Marie. Although he hadn't been in doubt, having it confirmed in this way was a bonus he hadn't expected. But what the hell was Eden Chase playing at writing to Juliette? Shock and surprise at the content of the letter yielded quickly to fury. He leapt to his feet. He needed answers and he needed them now.

'I have to go out.'

His mother stared up at him. 'What is it? What's wrong?'

'Nothing, nothing at all.' Max pushed the letters into his jacket pocket. 'I just remembered. I'm supposed to meet a client at seven.'

'Where do you have to go?'

'What?'

'Where are you meeting them?'

Max flapped a hand, plucking a location out of the air. 'Leicester Square.'

'You look pale. Are you sure you're all right?'

He nodded, forcing a smile. 'I'd better go. I don't want to be late.'

She continued to gaze at him, knowing something was amiss, but not probing any further. 'I'll see you later, then.'

Max hurried through to the hall, grabbed his car keys and left the house. It was only when he was sitting in the car, about to switch on the ignition, that he realised he no longer had an address for Eden Chase. She wouldn't be at Pope Street. Damn it! Where had she gone after the fire? How could he find out?

He remembered the place in Kellston, the flat she'd let herself into after being interviewed by the law. It was a long shot. There was no saying she'd be there, but someone might be, someone who could – with the right kind of persuasion – point him in the right direction.

Max's face was grim as he started the engine and pulled out. However long it took, *whatever* it took, he was going to find her. He wouldn't sleep until he'd hunted her down.

44

Eden wasn't sure what she was searching for as she trawled through the pile of old press cuttings with their reports of trials and convictions. What was she hoping to achieve? She was working on the premise that she'd know it when she found it: a clue, a tiny detail, something to shed light on why Archie Rudd was accusing Tom. But she didn't seem to be learning much other than Rudd clearly wasn't the most successful criminal in the world. When all his sentences were added together, he had probably spent as much of his life in prison as he had out of it.

Although her gaze remained fixed on the pages, she couldn't stop her mind from wandering. The phone call from Castor loomed so large in her thoughts it overwhelmed everything else. She was desperate to hear what Tom had to say, and at the same time dreading it. There was no doubt it was important. She screwed up her face. God, more than important. Life-changing, perhaps. Earth-shattering. Her stomach shifted with fear and foreboding. She couldn't bear to think the worst, but what if—

The sound of the doorbell cut across her angst, making her

jump. Who could that be? Other than Caitlin and Elspeth, no one knew she'd moved in – and Caitlin had left hours ago. She'd be at Greenham Common by now, giving support to the cause and offering legal advice to those who needed it. There was no reason either why the accountant would be calling round at seven o'clock in the evening. No, she wasn't going to answer it. She sat very still, holding her breath, as though whoever was at the door – even though they were a floor down – might sense any movement from inside.

The bell was pressed again, three long insistent rings. Eden remained motionless. Whoever it was would be able to see the light on behind the curtains, but she didn't care. Hopefully they'd give up and go away. But no sooner had the thought crossed her mind than the bell started up again. More long rings, one after another. She flinched at the noise. Like a full-on bombardment, it was impossible to ignore.

Eden held her ground for a couple of minutes but it soon became clear that her visitor would not concede defeat. Could it be DI Banner? Perhaps he had tracked her down and wanted another of his 'chats'. Eventually, unable to bear the noise any longer, she pushed back her chair, went out into the hall, put on the light and stomped downstairs. She was so annoyed by the disturbance that it didn't even occur to her, until she was opening the door, that it might not be the brightest idea in the world. By then it was too late.

For a moment she didn't recognise the man who was standing out in the pouring rain. He was tall, over six foot, and broad across the shoulders. He was also soaked. His hair was slicked down to his head and the front of his shirt was almost transparent. She frowned. But then it suddenly came to her. She started and shrank back, realising it was the undertaker from across the road, the man who had scared her so much when she'd first come to look at the flat.

'I'm Max Tamer,' he said.

Eden's fingers curled nervously around the side of the door, ready to slam it shut if he took a step closer. She stared at him, nonplussed. 'Sorry?'

He stared right back, his face tight and grim. 'Max Tamer,' he repeated, as if the name should mean something to her.

Eden gave a small shake of her head. 'I don't—'

'I'm Ann-Marie's husband.'

The announcement took Eden completely by surprise. It was the last thing she'd expected to come out of his mouth. She sucked in a breath. 'What?'

Tamer reached into his pocket, pulled out a blue airmail envelope and held it up. 'I think we need to talk. Can I come in?'

Eden now understood what he was doing here, but she still hesitated. There was so much she wanted to know, but the guy scared her. She peered around him. 'Is your wife with you?'

'No. She couldn't come.'

Eden wasn't sure what to do next. On the one hand, she didn't want to be alone with him, but on the other, he could have some important information as regards Jack Minter. In the end this outweighed any concerns for her personal safety. She nodded and stood aside.

They walked up the stairs in silence. Eden studied his back as they ascended, noting the tightness in his shoulders. The guy was tense, coiled. She could see the stiff straining muscles of his neck above the collar of his jacket. Had she done the right thing by inviting him in? Well, it was too late to change her mind now.

They went into the living room and she gestured towards the sofa. 'You'd better sit down.' She thought about offering coffee, but quickly dismissed the idea. This was hardly a social visit. Instead she said, 'I've seen you before, haven't I?'

Tamer sat down and gave a shrug.

'Yes,' she insisted. 'You were here. You were standing across the road. I was at the window and . . .'

'I was following you,' he said.

Eden blinked at the admission and the matter-of-fact way in which it was delivered. She felt her anxiety ratchet up several notches. 'You were what?'

Tamer gave a thin, unapologetic smile. 'Don't worry, I'm not some crazy stalker. I suppose you could say I was choosing my moment. I wanted to talk to you but . . . There's always a right time for everything, isn't there?'

Eden couldn't think of any useful response to this explanation. There probably wasn't one. And as for not being worried, it was way too late for that. 'I thought you were the undertaker,' she murmured.

This time he was the one who was startled. He stared up at her, glanced away and then looked back. A red flush spread across his cheeks. 'Huh?'

Eden didn't bother to explain. Instead she tried to steer the conversation in a more productive direction. She wanted to get to the point. The sooner she did that, the sooner she could get rid of him. 'So Ann-Marie got the letter.'

'Her parents got the letter.'

'Right.' Eden sat down in the armchair, perched on the edge and waited, but Tamer didn't go on. She saw his gaze slide around the room, taking in the shabby furniture and the brightly patterned curtains, the worn carpet and the table covered in photocopied pages from the newspaper library. 'So does she remember meeting Jack Minter?'

Tamer answered her question with another. 'How long have you known?' he asked.

'Known what?'

'About the relationship between my wife and your husband.'

Eden gave a mirthless laugh. 'You make it sound like they were having an affair. I mean, it was years ago, wasn't it?'

'When did he tell you about her?'

Now it was Eden's turn to blush. She felt the heat rise and spread over her face. Did she tell the truth, that Tom hadn't told her anything at all, or did she lie and pretend she knew more about the relationship than she actually did? In the end, she settled on vagueness as the best way forward. 'I don't know. I'm not sure. I think he might have mentioned her in passing.'

'In passing,' he echoed softly, raising his eyebrows.

Eden stared at him. She wondered if he was one of those jealous, possessive husbands who couldn't bear the thought of his wife having slept with anyone else – even if it had been before they'd even met. 'Yes. And then I found her address on the letters and thought she might—'

'What letters?' he interrupted, quickly sitting forward.

'Just some letters she wrote to Tom when he was in Budapest.'

'Do you have them?'

'No. There was a fire where I used to live. They were all destroyed.'

Tamer hissed out a breath. 'But you read them, right? You know what they said?'

Eden shook her head. 'They were in French. I couldn't . . . I only went through them hoping to find a mention of Jack Minter, but there was nothing.'

Tamer thought about this for a while, his gaze fixed on his feet, and then slowly raised his head. 'Maybe that's because Jack Minter doesn't exist,' he said provocatively.

'How would you know?' she snapped back.

'How do you think?'

Eden had a sudden disturbing thought that made her guts

twist. 'Is that what Ann-Marie says?' She raised a hand to her mouth and worried on her fingernails. 'Is it?'

Max Tamer sat back and crossed his legs. 'Your husband's a liar.'

Eden was reminded of her meeting with Annabelle at the studio. *You think you can trust him, but you can't. He's a liar and a cheat.* But she wouldn't be swayed by what other people told her. Everyone had an agenda. She wasn't exactly sure of Tamer's yet, but she figured they were getting there. 'Meaning?'

'Meaning he doesn't tell the truth.'

'Perhaps you could be more specific.' Eden spoke with a confidence she didn't feel. All the time, in the back of her mind, Castor's phone call was niggling away. The summons from Tom had put her on edge; she felt uneasy and fearful, as if what remained of her fragile world was about to come crashing down.

'Okay,' he said. 'How about this for starters: I paid a visit to your husband's studio two years ago and he denied ever having known Ann-Marie. I showed him a picture. He lied through his teeth. He even claimed he'd never been to Budapest.'

Eden pulled a face. 'I don't understand. Why would you be asking him about Ann-Marie? It's old news. It all happened ages ago, back in the sixties.'

'Surely the more important question is why he lied about knowing her?'

'Not really,' Eden retorted. 'It depends on how you asked. If you stormed in there, all guns blazing, he may have presumed you were about to accuse him of something – like having an affair with your wife, for example.'

'Why? Did he make a habit of it?'

Eden glared at him. 'No,' she said. 'I'm just trying to make a point. He may have thought . . . well, that you were itching for a fight. Perhaps he felt threatened. Perhaps he took the easy way out. I'm not saying it was the right thing to do, but . . . '

'Ah, so that's the line he's going to take.'

'There isn't any "line".' Eden gave a sigh of exasperation. 'I'm just providing you with a different interpretation. Anyway, I still don't understand why you went to see him in the first place.'

'Because I was looking for my wife.'

'Ah,' Eden said, believing that she'd finally caught on. His wife must have left him, done a bunk. 'And you thought she might be with Tom? Why would you think that?'

'Because one of her work colleagues told me she'd bumped into an old friend from Budapest. What can I say? He seemed the most likely candidate.'

'She could have met lots of people in Budapest.'

'At the time she was working round the corner from your husband. A bit of a coincidence, don't you think?'

'There are millions of people in London.'

'But not so many who used to live in Hungary.'

A silence fell over the room and the two of them watched each other warily. Eden wasn't sure what he wanted from her, what he was actually doing here. 'I didn't even know Tom back then,' she said.

'Do you know him now?'

The jibe hit home and Eden scowled at him. Hadn't she been asking herself the same question recently? 'Well enough.'

'I could almost feel sorry for you.'

Eden bristled. 'Don't waste your pity. I don't want it. Just get to the point. I take it there is one?'

Max Tamer briefly closed his eyes and opened them again. 'My wife – Ann-Marie – went missing three years ago. She went out to lunch, bumped into a friend from Budapest, went for a coffee, returned to work and never came home.' He paused before adding, 'Is that direct enough for you?'

'You're saying that she left you?'

'Not voluntarily.'

'What exactly are you insinuating?'

'Oh, I'm not insinuating anything,' he said. 'I think your husband killed her.'

Eden's response, a reflex born of pure shock, was to bark out a laugh. 'What? Are you mad?' Instantly, she saw his face darken. 'Tom wouldn't. He could never do anything like that. Why would he?'

'Didn't you hear what I said? On the same day she met your husband, she disappeared for good.'

'You don't know she met Tom. And even if she did, it doesn't mean that he ... For God's sake!' Eden jumped up, went over to the table and leaned against it with her arms wrapped around her chest. She stared across the room at Tamer, her heart racing. The guy *was* mad. He had to be. 'You said she went back to work *after* seeing this friend so even if it was him, how could he have done anything?'

'I think they made arrangements to meet again after work.'

Eden swallowed hard and tried to keep her voice calm. 'Or maybe she just left. People do. They do it all the time.'

'What? Leaving everything behind – her home, her family, her job, her clothes, her passport?' Tamer shook his head. 'From that day, nothing, not a penny, has been taken out of her bank account. No, it didn't happen like that. We were happy. We had a good marriage. Your husband took that away. He murdered my wife.'

'Why would he? Why would Tom do that?'

'Why did he leave Paddy Lynch to die?'

'He didn't,' she snapped. 'That was a man called Jack

309

Minter. Why do you think I wrote that letter? Ann-Marie spent time in Budapest, and Tom shared a flat with Minter; she must have met him.'

Tamer's voice was cold and ugly. 'Well, we'll never know now, will we?'

'If you're so sure Tom killed her, why haven't you told the police?'

'There's no rush. It's not as though he's going anywhere.' He kept his eyes fixed on Eden. 'And anyway, they weren't much use first time round. As I'm sure you've already gathered, the law isn't always on your side. No, I figured I'd sort things out myself.'

Eden stiffened at the words, hearing the menace behind them. Max Tamer's methods of sorting things out were unlikely to be pleasant. She tried to read his face, but it was closed down, impenetrable. Fear prickled her scalp. The best course of action, she decided, was to try and placate him

'I'm sorry about your wife. I really am. And I apologise if my letter caused any upset. If I'd had any idea that Ann-Marie—'

'Sorry doesn't bring my wife back.'

'No.'

'All I want is the truth.'

'I understand that.'

A silence fell between them again. Outside, the traffic went by, tailing off now after the evening rush. Inside, there was only the soft ticking of the radiators. Eden, scared of where this exchange was going – and where it would finally end up – struggled to think of anything to say. Her gaze nervously swept the room before returning to her unwanted visitor. It was only then, as her eyes fell upon the bandage on his right hand, that she suddenly recalled what Geoff had told her: the man who'd saved her had cut his hand on glass from the window. But it couldn't be Tamer. Why would he? Not the way he felt about Tom. He was more likely to have set the fire than to have rescued her from it.

'What happened to your hand?'

Tamer glanced down, studied the hand for a moment, and looked back up again. 'An accident at work.'

'What kind of work do you do?' Eden wasn't interested, she didn't give a damn, but she wanted to make some kind of connection with him. It was harder to hurt someone when they weren't a complete stranger. At least this was the premise she was working on, and as she didn't have a better one it was what she'd have to run with.

'Personal security.'

'Like a bodyguard, that kind of thing?'

'Yes, that kind of thing.'

Eden racked her brains and came up with something else Geoff had mentioned. 'Were you in the army?'

Her question clearly took him by surprise. He shifted on the sofa and frowned. 'Why do you ask that?'

Eden gave a shrug. 'I don't know. You look like you may have been. The army or the police.'

'The police?' he snorted. 'I'd rather work down the sewers.'

There wasn't much Eden could say to that and so she said nothing.

Tamer stared hard at her, as if he was trying to fix her face in his mind. Something flickered in his eyes, but she still couldn't read them. She could feel the danger, though, the anger rising off his body like steam. She felt as vulnerable as a tethered goat waiting for a tiger to pounce.

'When are you next seeing your husband?' he asked.

'On Monday.'

'Ask him about Ann-Marie.'

Eden gave a nod. 'I will.'

Tamer stood up suddenly, making her jump. She instinctively tried to shift back but the base of her spine was pressed against the table. The hair stood up on the back of her neck. Adrenalin washed through her veins. Her mouth opened in preparation for a cry, a scream, but he didn't approach. Instead, he headed for the door.

'Is ... is that it?' she stammered.

Tamer glanced over his shoulder. His lips slid into a thin, sinister smile. 'For now.'

Eden watched him leave. She listened to his heavy footsteps on the stairs. When the front door had closed, she ran out to the landing to make sure he'd gone. A long breath of relief rushed out of her lungs. But she wasn't stupid enough to think it was over. This was just a temporary reprieve, a stay of execution. She knew, without a shadow of a doubt, that Max Tamer would be back.

45

Vic Banner was in the kind of mood that could best be described as black. Ever since his contact at HMP Thornley Heath – a screw by the name of Rakes – had called, he'd been trying to find out what was going on. The information had set off alarm bells in his head. Tom Chase had, apparently, seen his lawyer this morning. A special meeting had then been arranged between Chase and his wife for Monday. That meant developments – and probably not good ones.

Vic finished his third pint and ordered another. He lit a cigarette, inhaled and puffed out the smoke. He didn't like being out of the loop. He didn't like surprises. Jesus, what if Chase was about to confess? That would be a disaster. If Vic was going to make a name for himself, he needed a nice long trial with a blaze of publicity that would last for longer than a day. He needed the whole sensational story to come out, piece by piece, covered by all the national newspapers. He wanted Chase convicted by a jury, not by his own lips.

Vic paid for the drink, picked up the glass and took a couple of long, deep draughts. The bastard was definitely up to something. He thought of all the hard work he'd put in with Archie Rudd and bristled at the idea of it going to waste. Chase was maybe planning on a plea of diminished responsibility or some other pile of shit. Already he and his lawyer would be cooking up some cock-and-bull story, a tissue of lies, in a cynical attempt to defend the indefensible.

The Shoreditch pub was heaving. It wasn't the sort of place Vic would normally have chosen, full of brash City types in suits, but his need for a drink had outweighed the vexatious nature of the company. He'd been in search of Tammy for the past couple of hours, but she was nowhere to be found. At least not for now. He knew where she'd be later on – plying her trade on Albert Road. It was Friday night, pay day, and her regular punters had money in their pockets.

A customer came to the crowded bar, jostling his way to the front. In the process he knocked Vic's elbow, spilling some of the beer from his glass.

'Hey! Watch what you're doing!'

The guy – a cocky-looking bloke in his early twenties – gave Vic a defiant, dirty look, but then saw something in his eyes that made him think twice. He quickly raised his hands in apology. 'Sorry, mate.'

Vic clocked the gold Rolex on the younger man's skinny wrist. It didn't do anything to improve his mood. How come he worked his bollocks off so people could sleep safely in their beds at night but had sod all to show for it at the end of every month, while this flash git got paid a fortune for waving his arms around at the Stock Exchange spending other people's cash? He was in the wrong bloody job, no doubt about it. 'So just look where you're going, yeah? You've got eyes. Try using them once in a while.'

'I've said sorry, haven't I?'

Although Vic was itching for a fight, he managed to restrain himself. He was already on a warning and couldn't afford to get into any more trouble before the Tom Chase trial. 'Yeah, right. Maybe say it like you mean it, huh?'

The guy shifted along the bar, annoyed but still sober enough to realise that Vic was trouble.

Vic went on glaring at him, transferring his frustration about Chase and Tammy and everything else that had been winding him up on to the stranger. The little shit deserved to be taught a lesson. No one had any bloody manners these days. No respect, either. He continued to dwell on the episode, even after the bloke had gone, turning it over in his mind while he studied the incriminating puddle of beer on the counter.

Half an hour later Vic walked out of the pub and got in his car. By now his festering resentment had shifted into a simmering rage. His nerves were stretched tight like thin metal wires ready to snap. What was wrong with people? Everyone was out to thwart him, to wind him up. He was sick of it.

The journey from Shoreditch to Kellston took less than ten minutes. He kept his speed down, aware that he was over the alcohol limit and not wanting a pull from the local plod. He drove up Station Road, passing the Fox on his right and the Hope and Anchor on his left, both pubs owned by Terry Street. There, that was something else to make his blood boil. Street was an out-and-out villain, a dangerous manipulator who had the East End neatly tied up to his own advantage. Drugs, girls, protection rackets; you name it, he ran it.

The rain was pissing down but Vic knew that wouldn't keep the toms off the streets. Nothing short of the apocalypse would stop the whores from plying their trade. He indicated left and turned into Albert Road, the centre of the red light district of Kellston. Many years ago, it had been an affluent part of the district but all that remained of that wealth now were the crumbling Victorian mansions, their floors divided and sub-divided into flats, bedsits and sparsely furnished rooms which the girls could rent out for fifteen-minute intervals, paying a nominal fee for the pleasure of being fucked by a punter somewhere slightly more comfortable than a dark alley or the back of a car.

The smarter toms worked out of the brothels where they had some protection from those customers of a more psychopathic persuasion. The has-beens, the addicts and the part-timers like Tammy took their chances on the street. He cruised slowly along Albert Road, keeping his eyes peeled for that shock of blonde hair, until he finally spotted her sheltering in a doorway to his left. Wearing a short red minidress, a black leather jacket and fishnets, she seemed more like the cliché of a prostitute than the real thing, a girl dressed up for a tarts and vicars party.

Vic pulled up to the kerb and flashed his lights. He wasn't driving his own car and it was too dark for her to see him clearly. He knew, as she tottered through the rain in her high heels, that she had no idea who it was. As she leaned down to look through the open window on the passenger side, her painted-on smile quickly disappeared.

'Jesus,' she hissed. 'What the fuck are you doing here?'

'Looking for you, babe. Get in the car.'

Tammy glanced around to see if anyone was watching. A couple of toms were standing fifty yards away, their eyes fixed hungrily on Vic's motor, their expressions cold and resentful. A pair of junkies, he reckoned. They had that sick, craving look about them, that desperation for the next fix.

'For Christ's sake, Tammy, just get the fuck in. I haven't got all night.'

She hesitated, but only for a second. The longer she waited, the more suspicious it would look. 'Do a U-turn,' she said, as she closed the door. 'Don't go past those two. They can smell the filth a mile off.'

'Jesus,' he muttered, but did what she said. He was prepared to indulge her, to try and keep her happy until he got what we wanted. After executing a less than perfect three-point turn, he headed back on to Station Road.

'So what's the problem now?' she asked peevishly, her gaze flicking towards the clock on the dashboard. In Tammy's world, time was money and she couldn't afford to waste any of it.

'Hey, come on. It's not as though you're rushed off your feet.'

'It'll pick up.'

'If you say so.'

Vic circled round to the old abandoned railway arches, made sure there was no else about, and pulled up by one of the black gaping holes in the wall. He left the engine running, the head-lamps illuminating sparkling arrows of rain, before switching off the lights and plunging them into darkness.

'What are you doing?' Tammy asked.

'A bit of privacy. I thought that's what you wanted.'

'Put the lights on.' She started shifting in her seat, nervously wriggling, crossing her legs and uncrossing them again. 'I don't like this place. It's creepy.'

Vic shrugged and turned on the lights again. 'There's no pleasing some people.'

'So what is it? What are you after?'

He rolled down the window a fraction and lit a fag. 'I want to know what's going on with Tom Chase.'

Tammy frowned. 'I talked to Eden, didn't I? Like you said. I told her to make sure he went down the block. I laid it on thick, said he weren't safe on the wing, that Pat Lynch was out to get him. After the visit, she reckoned he'd agreed and . . .

but I already told you all this. I told you Thursday night when I rang, remember?'

'I need to know what's happened since then.'

'What do you mean?'

Vic glared at her. He couldn't figure out whether the tart was being deliberately obtuse or if she was just plain stupid. 'What's not to understand?' he said sharply. 'Chase saw his solicitor this morning. Something's going down and I want to know what. Have you heard from her since you last called me?'

Tammy hesitated just long enough for him to know that a lie was about to come out of her mouth. 'No.'

'Don't fuck me about, love. I've had enough bullshit for one day.'

Tammy's face took on a sulky expression. 'I don't want to do this no more,' she whined. 'What if someone finds out I've been talking to you? You ain't paying me enough to take the risk. It ain't fair.'

Vic felt the anger bubbling up inside him, a culmination of the night's frustrations. He answered her through gritted teeth. 'You know what's not fair, Tammy? Holding out on me. We've got a deal and you can't back out whenever you feel like it. So just tell me what you know, yeah, and make it snappy.'

'I don't know nothin'.'

'Jesus, do I have to—'

'What I mean is she didn't say nothin' when she rang this morning, nothin' important, only that she was going away for a while and wouldn't be able to give me a lift to the jail no more. She didn't mention no solicitor. She said she was going up to see her dad and wasn't sure when she'd be back.' Tammy stared at him. 'That's it. I swear.'

'And you didn't think to let me know?'

'I was going to. I've had things to do, ain't I?'

Vic curled his lip, hearing the attitude in her voice and not liking it one little bit. 'Where's she living at the moment?'

'With that Caitlin, over in Finchley. I've got the number but I ain't got no address.'

'Well, she's not going anywhere before Monday – she's got a visit booked with her scumbag of a husband – so in the meantime you can find out what's going on. She must have some idea.'

'And how am I supposed to do that?'

'How do you think? Talk to her, for God's sake. Get on the blower, have a chat. Go for a drink. I thought you two were supposed to be mates.'

'And what if she won't tell me? I can't force her, can I?'

Vic felt those wires in his head stretch even tighter. He pulled on the cigarette and deliberately blew smoke in her face. 'Bad things, love. That's what going to happen. So don't disappoint me, right?'

Tammy coughed and flapped her hand. 'Leave it out. What d'ya do that for?'

Vic gave a thin smile. 'A bit of smoke is the last thing you need to worry about. Now get out of the car.'

'What?'

'You heard. I'm sick of the sight of your slutty little face.'

Tammy's eyes widened. 'You can't leave me here.'

'Watch me.'

'What for?'

'To teach you a lesson, love. Next time don't keep me in the dark. If Eden Chase so much as farts, I want to know about it.' Vic glared at her. He'd had enough of being wound up, of people taking the piss. 'I'm waiting. Get the fuck out before I throw you out.'

Tammy stared at the gaping, black mouths of the arches and shrank back into her seat. He knew she was thinking about the girl who'd been killed here a few years back, another tom who'd made a bad decision. Her voice instantly slipped into a pleading tone. 'Ah, come on, Vic, don't be like that. Just drop me off at the station. It ain't safe here, you know it ain't. There's all sorts hanging about.'

'You should have thought about that before you decided you had more important things to do than keep me up to date.'

'I told you. I was going to call. I *was*.'

'Too little, too late.'

Tammy opened her mouth as if about to protest, but then clearly decided not to bother. The battle, so far as she was concerned, had already been lost. She opened the door and stepped out into the rain. It was then she made her big mistake. 'Bastard!' she spat, as she slammed the car door shut.

Vic wasn't exactly sure what happened next, but something snapped and a red mist descended. It was one thing being disrespected by a jumped-up tosser in the pub, but when some slut of a whore decided to join in too, he knew the line had been well and truly crossed. The bitch needed teaching a lesson.

He was out of the car and on to her before she fully realised what was happening. Grabbing her round the neck, he dragged her over to the arches and slammed her up against the wall. There was a satisfying thud as her spine made contact with the old grey brick. 'What did you say, you fucking whore?'

'N-nothin',' she stammered, trying to get her breath back.

'It didn't sound like fucking nothing.'

'Don't hurt me,' she begged, clawing at his left arm, which pressed against her throat. 'I'm sorry. I'm sorry.'

Vic slapped her hard across the face, enjoying the power he had over her. He pushed his face into hers, smelling the fear on her breath. 'Shut it!' he snarled. 'You think I want to listen to your bloody whining?'

With the light from the car headlamps, he could see the panic in her eyes. He had done enough to scare the hell out of her, but the rage was still inside him. Someone had to pay for all the shit he'd put up with today and why shouldn't it be her? The tramp deserved it.

'Please,' she continued to plead. 'I won't do it again. I won't. I swear it.'

'What's the matter with you? Are you deaf as well as stupid? What did I say? What did I just say?' Vic slapped her again. 'Just shut the fuck up!' He swung her away from the wall and sent her sprawling down on to the muddy ground. Bending over, he grabbed the back of her neck and pushed her face into the dirt, into the wet soil and gravel and short stumpy weeds. She struggled for a while but then seemed to give up. A small mewling noise came from her mouth like the sound of a drowning kitten.

46

Eden sat on the edge of the bed, rubbing her feet. She had worked two shifts at Connolly's over the weekend and had the blisters on her heels to prove it. How many miles had she covered going back and forth to the counter? It felt like a hundred. Saturday afternoon had been so busy she'd barely had time to pause for breath. Still, at least it had kept her occupied and given her something to think about other than the meeting with Tom.

There was no escaping those thoughts now, however. In less than a couple of hours she'd be at HMP Thornley Heath. Eden felt a fluttering, panicky sensation in her chest as if a trapped bird was desperately beating its wings against her ribcage. She was certain that when she returned from the prison everything would be different. As yet she didn't know how or why, but she was certain the change was coming. Her world was about to undergo another shift and there was no good way of preparing for it.

She stood up and opened the wardrobe doors. Since the fire, the dilemma of wondering what to wear no longer existed.

Her choice was limited and it didn't take long to make up her mind. She reached out and plucked a pair of black trousers and a pale grey jumper from their hangers.

After changing, she went through to the kitchen and made a strong black coffee. It was almost lunchtime but she had no appetite. She had spent most of the morning going through the Archie Rudd press cuttings again, but hadn't learned anything new. She drank the coffee standing by the living room window, looking down on the high street. Her gaze was drawn towards the door of the undertakers, where she almost expected to see Max Tamer. How long would it be before he came back? Tonight? Tomorrow? His words still echoed in her head: *Ask him about Ann-Marie.*

The rain was easing off as Eden walked round to Violet Road where the car was parked. She stared for a moment at the long scratches on the paintwork, wondering if Tamer had been responsible. He'd been following her, that's what he'd said, so he'd have known which car was hers. The thought of him tracking her every move was more than disturbing. What kind of a man did that? And why hadn't she noticed? She looked up and down the road, wary and watchful. From now on she'd be paying more attention.

As Eden drove towards Chingford, her eyes constantly flicked towards the rear-view mirror, taking in not just the car behind her but the cars behind that. Even though she knew Tamer was unlikely to be on her tail – he'd hardly have told her if he was planning to continue – she still couldn't stop checking.

During the journey, she tried to hold on to the slim and improbable hope that Tom's news could be good rather than bad. Maybe a piece of evidence had finally come to light, something that put him in the clear, and he'd wanted to be the one to break the news to her rather than leaving it to Castor.

What were the odds? Small, very small. But still she preferred to cling on to the chance than to let go completely and drown in fear and panic.

Despite Eden's best attempts to keep calm, the closer she got to the prison the more anxious she became. By the time she arrived she was struggling to keep her composure. There was a knot in her stomach, a sick feeling that wouldn't go away. She parked the car, locked it, and took a deep breath before skirting back along the high stone wall and walking through the gate.

The waiting room was quiet and there was no one in the queue. Monday clearly wasn't a popular day for visiting. She went up to the counter and slid her driving licence through the gap in the reinforced glass.

'Eden Chase,' she said to the officer. 'I've ... er, I think I've got some kind of special visit?'

He glanced at her ID, checked his book and looked back up. 'Take a seat and someone will be over to collect you. You want a locker?'

'Yes, please.'

Eden paid the deposit, got her key and went to stash her coat and bag. Then she sat down and waited. There were seven other women in the room, but no one spoke to her. She stared at the wall, at the floor, at the ceiling. The time passed slowly. It was another ten minutes before a female officer finally turned up and called out her name.

'Yes,' Eden said, jumping to her feet.

'This way.'

Eden followed her through the usual door at the back. As she left, she was aware of the other women's eyes on her, part curious, part disapproving at this blatant display of queue jumping. Inside the search area, she went through the usual procedure, too distracted to be even slightly bothered by the hands sliding quickly over her body. Her heart had started to beat faster. Her mouth had gone dry.

She was escorted across the courtyard, but when they reached the other side, instead of going into the visiting room she was taken along a corridor to a door marked *Legal Visits*. The officer opened it, stood aside and waved Eden in.

'You've got an hour.'

Tom was already there. He stood up as she entered, but made no attempt to approach her. His face looked grey and drawn, as though he hadn't slept for several nights.

As she went over, Eden's meagre hopes were already draining away. She stood on her toes and kissed him. His lips felt as dry as hers. Usually his arms would go around her, but not today. His body seemed stiff and unyielding. His hand briefly touched the back of her head before his arm dropped back to his side again.

'How come we're on our own?' she asked.

'Castor arranged it. Special circumstances.'

'Is that another term for bad news?'

Tom moved away from her and sat down. 'Of a kind.'

The room was small, furnished with three large chairs upholstered in a blue flecked material and arranged around a circular table. There was a window set high in the wall and a bright overhead light. She could see a square of grey through the window. A part of her wanted to run away right now, to turn her back on what was coming, to refuse to listen. If she didn't hear it, it couldn't be true. But she didn't run. How could she? There was nowhere to go. Instead she sat down and looked at him. 'Of a kind?' she repeated dully.

Tom placed his palms on his thighs and stared down at the floor for a moment. When he lifted his head, there was a tight, grim expression on his face. 'There's something you need to know before anything else. I haven't lied to you about the robbery, about Paddy Lynch. I had nothing to do with that. I swear.'

Eden felt relief wash over her. She almost said, 'Of course not. I never doubted you,' but it would have been a lie. It had been there in her mind, a terrible possibility. And this, surely, was the time for truth, for honesty. 'So what is it?'

Tom's face twisted a little. She could see a small pulse beating in his temples, a prickle of sweat on his brow. He lifted his right hand as if he might be about to reach out and take hers. It hung in the air for a second but then dropped back on to his thigh. 'Okay,' he said, but then seemed unable to speak. A few seconds passed. He swallowed hard, his Adam's apple bobbing in his throat. 'Okay,' he said again. 'There's something I should have told you. I meant to but somehow . . . Look, what I didn't mention is that I've been married before, a long time ago. When I was nineteen I got hitched to a girl called Jackie Blake.'

Eden frowned, confused. 'So why the big secret? Why didn't you tell me? It wouldn't have made any difference.'

'It's what came later that makes the difference.'

'Oh.'

'We were . . . well, she was my first proper girlfriend, the first girl I'd slept with. Anyway, we'd been together about four months when she fell pregnant. She came from a staunch Catholic family so there wasn't any question about what would happen next. We were marched straight up the aisle as soon as the banns could be read.'

Eden drew in her breath, shocked. 'You've got a child?'

Tom shook his head. 'No, she lost the baby a few weeks after we were married. If she hadn't . . . I don't know, I suppose I'd have tried harder, for the kid's sake if nothing else. But once the honeymoon period was over, it was pretty clear we didn't have much in common. Everything happened too quickly and

326

by the time the dust settled we were stuck with trying to make the best of it.'

'So how long did you stay together for?'

'About five years. It was the small-town thing as much as anything else. I wanted some excitement. I wanted to get out there, travel, see the world, but Jackie was happy where she was. She liked being near her family and friends. Don't get me wrong, she's a nice girl, decent; we were just . . . incompatible. We wanted different things.'

Eden still wasn't sure where all this was leading. 'So you left her?'

'Not exactly. I got a job here in London, in a camera shop on Tottenham Court Road. Close to where Denny's place is now, as it happens, although he wasn't around back then. The idea was that once I was settled, she'd come down and join me, give it a go and see how she liked it. Except she never did – give it a proper go, that is. She spent a couple of weeks here, decided the big city wasn't for her and went back home.'

Eden shifted in the chair, wanting to urge him on, wanting to beg him to get to the point. She knew he hadn't brought her here to discuss a failed first marriage. There was something else, something much worse, waiting in the sidelines. She didn't want to hear it, but she had to. She wanted it over and done with. The suspense was killing her. 'Where's all this going, Tom?'

He leaned forward, rubbing his face with his hands. 'Okay, well you know most of the next part. I didn't stay long at the camera shop. I travelled around the south coast in the summer months, taking pictures, working in bars. Then during the winter I came back to London. In 1967 I bought a ferry ticket, went over to France and started working my way through Europe. That's how I ended up in Budapest. That's how I met Jack Minter.' He left a short pause, cleared his throat. 'Although he wasn't using that name at the time.'

327

'What was he calling himself?'

There was another hesitation, an intake of breath. 'He was going under the name of Tom Chase.'

Eden gave a start. 'What?' She stared at him, bewildered. 'How could he be? I don't understand. I mean, it doesn't . . . How could he have been using your name?'

'But that's the point, Eden – it wasn't mine. It never was. I stole it from him.'

47

Eden felt as though all the breath had been sucked from her lungs. While her brain tried to process the information, she stared at Tom, dumbstruck. Her heart started pounding, a fast heavy thump. This couldn't be happening. She traced his face with her eyes, examining everything that had once seemed so familiar. But her husband has ceased to be the same person. Everything she'd believed to be true had suddenly been turned on its head. Out of the blue, he'd become a stranger to her.

'I did something stupid,' he said. 'I don't expect you to forgive me, but I'd like to explain.'

'Tom Chase isn't your real name,' she said, finally finding her voice.

He shook his head. 'Laurence. That was the name I was christened with. Larry to my friends, Larry Hewitt.'

Eden ran her tongue over her dry lips. 'Larry,' she murmured.

'It's a long story.'

Eden waited. She kept her gaze on him, feeling her guts turn over. She wanted time to stop, to rewind, to go back to that bright February morning when she crossed the Covent

Garden piazza on her way to the studio. Nothing that had happened since then had been good. And now it was about to get a whole lot worse.

'It was when I was living with Jack – I'll keep on calling him that for now – in Budapest. I'd been there about three months when Jack went out one morning and didn't come back. I wasn't worried. Sometimes he'd disappear for days at a time. I just presumed he'd met some mates or a girl and that he'd turn up again when he got bored of whatever he was doing.'

Eden's hands moved restlessly in her lap. She listened, letting the words wash over her. Tom looked at her and she nodded, encouraging him to go on. The story had to be told and she had no choice but to hear it.

'Anyway, I was in the flat the following morning when the bell rang. I went to answer the door and there were two police officers standing there. One of them spoke some English and he asked if this was Larry Hewitt's address.' A long sigh escaped from Tom's mouth. 'To be honest, I panicked. The day before I'd been taking pictures near some government buildings and I thought I might have been reported. Back then, there was a mass of paranoia, a lot of activity by the secret police. It was the Cold War and foreigners, especially ones with cameras, weren't exactly trusted. So I said the first stupid thing that came into my head: I told them Larry was out. They asked me who I was and I came out with the first name I thought of: Tom Chase.'

Tom gazed down at his shoes. It was a few seconds before he continued. 'And then they told me something awful. They said a body had been recovered from the river and they believed it was Larry's. They wanted me to go with them to the morgue and identify the corpse. I asked why they thought it was him and they said they'd found some papers with his name and address in a rucksack left on the bank. I knew then it was Jack.

It had to be. He'd borrowed my rucksack the day before and the papers must have been in one of the pockets.'

'So Jack Minter's dead?'

Tom glanced at her and nodded. 'Yes, it was him. They didn't know exactly what had happened. There was some damage to the back of his head, but it could have been caused by a fall before he went into the water. The path was icy, slippery. I couldn't take it in at first, seeing him lying there. It didn't seem possible. He was one of those people who … he was always full of life, full of plans and now … It was awful, shocking. I couldn't believe he was gone.'

Eden saw the distress on his face. Instinctively, she wanted to reach out, to offer comfort, but she fought against the urge and her hands remained in her lap. 'So you went ahead and identified him as Larry Hewitt?'

'I didn't know what else to do. I'd already lied to the police about who I was. I was scared, shaken up. I just wanted to get out of that place, but the questions went on and on. They wanted to know what he did, how he lived, about his family, who to contact, and I told them there was no one. They wanted to know if his passport was in the flat. I said I'd look for it, but that he usually carried it around with him. I couldn't hand it over, could I? Not with the wrong picture on it. I was hoping they'd think it had been stolen from the rucksack.' Tom gave a hollow laugh. 'All the time I was just digging a bigger and bigger hole for myself. But I couldn't stop. I didn't know how. By the time I got back to Garay Square, my only thought was to make a run for it, pick up my stuff and get the first train out of there. I even started to pack, but then I realised that could be an even worse mistake. It would make me look suspicious, guilty even. What if they arrested me? And then found out I'd lied about a dead man's identity? I could spend the next twenty years in a Hungarian jail. If I was going to get out of Budapest, I had to come up with a better idea.'

Eden could see how he'd got in a fix, could even understand why he'd done what he'd done, but that didn't explain why he'd kept it from her. 'So what next?'

'I did the only thing I could – I brazened it out. I looked in Jack's room and found his passport. Well, two passports, in fact. He had one in the name of Tom Chase, another in the name of Jack Minter. There was a birth certificate for Tom as well. I was worried the police might search the flat so I destroyed all the passports, mine included. I burned them in the sink. And then I went to the British Embassy, introduced myself as Tom Chase, told them about the death of "Larry Hewitt", and asked for their help in sorting things out. I said that both our passports had gone missing from the borrowed rucksack and I had no way of getting home to England.'

'That must have taken some nerve,' Eden said.

'I was shit scared, to be honest. I was sure they'd see right through me – or it would turn out someone there had known the real Tom Chase. It was a gamble. But I was more afraid of the police than I was of them. I reckoned if the worst came to the worst, I could come clean and explain who I really was. But I think they took my nerves for shock. I used the details from the birth certificate to fill in a form for a temporary passport.

'The next few days were the hardest. I didn't know many people – the students I'd come with had gone back to Paris – but there was always the danger of running into an acquaintance or one of Jack's friends. I had no idea if the police would release my name to the newspapers or if anyone would link that name to me, so I holed up in the flat as much as I could and didn't go out unless I had to.

'Eventually, the results of the post-mortem came

through – accidental death – and the inquiry came to an end. Shortly after that, I was free to leave. Through the embassy, I made arrangements for Jack be buried in Kerepesi cemetery.' Tom's hands balled into two tight fists. 'I wouldn't have gone through with it, Eden, if he'd had any family, anyone close, but he'd always said there was no one. I packed up everything, including all his stuff – it wasn't much, he travelled light – and got out of Hungary as fast as I could.'

Eden had a hundred questions she wanted to ask and didn't know where to start. She still wasn't happy, far from it, about being kept in the dark, but was beginning to see how this confession could eventually lead to his release. Surely the trial couldn't proceed once the facts were known about Tom's real identity. 'So when you say you took Jack's stuff, does that include the bracelet?'

Tom nodded. 'Another big mistake, but I didn't want to leave anything behind in the flat and didn't know what else to do. I had no idea it had come from a robbery. Back in England, I couldn't bring myself to sell the bracelet – it was Jack's, not mine – and so I just put it away and forgot about it.'

'God, Tom,' she said, exasperated. 'Why didn't you tell the police all this before they charged you?'

Tom pulled a face. His shoulders lifted and fell. 'I kept on hoping I could prove I wasn't Jack Minter. I was sure I could find a way. Or that Castor could. And then I thought ... I thought if it all came out, you'd walk away, you wouldn't want anything more to do with me.'

'Jesus, you just did something stupid, a spur-of-the-moment thing. You made a mistake; you didn't kill anyone. I'm pissed off that you kept it a secret, it makes me feel you can't trust me, but ... I mean, how could you think that risking prison was a better move than telling the truth?'

'What I did was illegal. I stole another man's identity.'

'But you didn't rob a bank. You didn't leave Paddy Lynch to die. They might charge you with something but it can't be anything like as bad as that.' Eden felt buoyed by relief. The truth, now it had emerged, was startling, unpleasant even, but not grotesque. She had feared the worst and instead, suddenly, there was a faint light at the end of the tunnel. Another comforting thought occurred to her. 'There was a bundle of letters in your safe from Ann-Marie. She was Jack's girlfriend, wasn't she, not yours?'

'What made you think ... Oh, right, of course, they're addressed to Tom. Yes, the two of them were together for a while, a few years, I think. But they'd already split up before I got to know Jack. I never met her. I don't even know what she looks like. I took the letters with the rest of his belongings – something else I didn't know what to do with once I was back home. It didn't feel right to throw them away so—'

'Max Tamer paid me a visit.'

'Who?'

'Max Tamer. Her husband. He came to see you too, didn't he, at the studio? A couple of years ago.'

'Was that his name? I don't remember. I lied to him, though. I presume he told you that.' Tom leaned back his head, closed his eyes for a few seconds and then looked at her again. 'Another moment of sheer panic. He stormed in like a man possessed. He was sure I was *the* Tom Chase, his wife's ex-boyfriend. At least until we came face to face and then he seemed to get confused. I think Ann-Marie must have kept some photographs and when he realised I wasn't the man in the pictures, he didn't know what to do next.'

'What did you say?'

'What could I say? All I could do was politely deny it, claim I'd never heard of her and tell him I'd never been to Budapest. He calmed down and left. I spent the next few weeks convinced he'd come back but that was the last I ever heard of him.'

'Until now.'

Tom gazed at her, his eyes full of concern. 'He didn't threaten you, did you? He didn't—'

Eden shook her head. 'No, not exactly, but he's kind of weird. And he knows you lied to him. He's put two and two together and come up with five.'

'Like Annabelle,' he said.

'What do you mean?'

'Well, she saw the state of him when he arrived. One angry man. And no one gets that worked up unless it's something personal and something important. I dare say she was trying to listen in at the door and caught a few words here and there, the most interesting being "my wife". After he left, she came in and asked, "What was all that about?" I told her it was nothing, a misunderstanding, but she'd already jumped to her own conclusions. She thought I was seeing some other guy's wife.'

'So? What difference did it make to her?'

'I was dating one of her friends at the time, nothing serious but . . . I suppose she thought I was screwing around behind her mate's back.'

Eden understood now why Annabelle had said what she had about Tom being a liar and a cheat. 'And you'd rather she believed that than start to wonder what Tamer's visit had really been about.'

'Got it in one.'

Eden stared up at the rain-spattered window, a small square of grey. Then she looked back at her husband. *Larry Hewitt.* He'd kept his secret well. Mistaking his reticence for a natural reserve, she'd never suspected a thing. 'Weren't you always afraid of the truth coming out? Always looking over your shoulder?'

'Only at the beginning. After a while, you stop thinking about it. You'd go mad if you didn't.'

Eden sighed. Despite everything, he was still the man she loved. So he'd messed up, done something stupid, reckless, but it didn't change the way she felt about him. There would be some bridges to build, but they could get through it.

'Don't,' he said.

'Don't what?'

'Don't try and justify my actions to yourself. You think you can forgive me but you can't.'

Eden frowned. 'Isn't that up to me to decide?'

'You haven't heard the whole story yet. You don't know the half of it.'

Eden's heart sank. She saw how pale his face was, how his eyes refused to meet hers. What was coming next? She wanted to put her hands over her ears, to refuse to listen. A moment ago she'd had hope, but now it was starting to crumble.

'You'd better tell me, then.'

48

Tom stood up and paced around the room for a while, as if trying to get his thoughts in order. He put his hands in his pockets, took them out, put them back in. Eventually, he spoke again. 'What you have to understand is that I never intended to keep on being Tom Chase once I came back to London. The minute I was back on British soil, I thought I could put it all behind me. I'd return to being Larry Hewitt, normal service resumed. It took me a few days to figure out it wouldn't be that easy. How was I going to get a new passport, for starters? If I applied for one in my real name, it could be on record that Larry Hewitt had died in Hungary. I presumed the embassy would pass on that kind of information. And then there was tax and national insurance – if I was flagged as dead, how was I going to explain my miraculous resurrection? I could see a whole lot of trouble coming my way.'

Eden watched him as he paced, following him with her eyes. Back and forth from one side of the room to the other. There was a heaviness centred in her chest, a dread of what was coming next. 'And so you decided to make the change more permanent.'

'I didn't have a choice,' he said. 'There was nothing else I could do.'

'But weren't there people in London who knew you as Larry Hewitt?'

'A few, but they were acquaintances rather than friends – other photographers mainly. I didn't see it as a major problem. People often change their names for professional reasons – actors, singers and the like, so why not photographers? I reckoned I could get away with it. And if someone started asking too many questions, I could always leave, move to another city or go abroad. As it happened, no one ever did ask. I doubt if anyone cared. I opened the studio and work gradually began coming in.'

As he mentioned the studio, Eden was reminded of DI Vic Banner and what he'd implied about the way it had been financed. And the truth suddenly dawned on her. 'There was no loan, was there? No Lukas Albrecht. The money belonged to Jack.'

Tom gave a wry smile. 'Although, strictly speaking, it didn't belong to him either.'

'But you took it from his bank account?'

Tom shrugged again. 'I had no idea he had money – not *that* kind of money – until I started sorting through the things I'd brought back from Budapest. Along with the letters and bracelet, there was a Munich bank book and a couple of statements. I found the pass code in the back of his address book.'

'So you just opened a bank account over here and transferred the money.'

'Not immediately,' he said. 'I thought about it for a while. But yes, eventually.'

'Isn't that theft?'

338

'Is it?' he asked, frowning. 'I mean, who was I actually stealing from? Jack had no family. The money was just going to sit in the bank for ever – or until someone figured out he was no longer alive. It seemed to me that it didn't really belong to anyone so I may as well use it myself.'

Eden could see there was a twisted kind of logic to the argument, but it still didn't sit well with her. Taking money from the dead was neither decent nor moral. It was one thing to take a man's identity, quite another to empty his bank account. There was something cold and greedy about it.

'You're shocked,' Tom said, standing over her.

Eden looked up at him. She couldn't deny it and so she said nothing.

Tom shifted from one foot to the other, raised his hand and pulled at his right ear. 'But I never set out to take his name or his money. None of it was planned. One thing led to another and . . . '

'Here we are,' she said.

'Yes, here we are.'

It was only now that Eden thought to ask the question she should have asked much earlier. 'What about Jackie? How did you explain all this to her?'

Tom flinched, screwed up his face and looked away.

'Tom?'

'It was as much for her sake as mine. We were both trapped, stuck in a loveless marriage we couldn't escape from. Good Catholic girls don't get divorced. She couldn't move on and neither could I.'

'What are you saying?'

Tom let out a breath, a long hissing sound like a tyre deflating. His eyes still refused to meet hers. 'I sent a letter from Tom Chase informing her of Larry's accidental death in Budapest – and a copy of the death certificate. It was for the best. I set her free. She could get married again, go on and have the family she really wanted.'

Eden gasped. She shifted forward, clutching her stomach, his words like an unexpected thump to her guts. 'You told her you were *dead*?'

'Why not? To all intents and purposes, Larry Hewitt *was* dead. Once she'd got over the initial shock, it was probably a relief to her. We hadn't lived together in years. It was a marriage only in name; she didn't love me any more than I loved her. I was a millstone round her neck.'

Eden's eyes grew wide. 'How did you think you'd get away with it? What if Jackie or someone she knew came to London and saw you?'

'It was a risk, but a slim one. Jackie hates London. And most of her friends never stray further than Manchester.' He flapped a hand dismissively. 'They're small-town people with small ambitions.'

'And your family,' she croaked. 'What about them?'

'What about them? We never got on. I doubt they did much grieving.'

Eden swallowed hard, barely able to look at him. 'Has anything you've told me about your life been true? Is your mother even dead?'

'She is to me.'

Who was this man? He looked like Tom, spoke in his voice, but underneath the familiar wrapping was someone Eden had never met before. And then, suddenly, the full meaning of what he was saying sank in. Her jaw dropped open. 'Christ, we're not even legally married, are we?'

Tom inclined his head, his mouth twisting at the question. 'I never meant to hurt you. You have to believe it. That day in Budapest, the morning those police officers came to the door – if I could go back and change what I said to them, I would.'

340

But Eden didn't believe a word of it. Being Tom Chase had, until now, worked out pretty well for him. He'd managed to dump an unwanted wife, get a new one, grab a large amount of cash and build a successful business. His only regret, she suspected, was that it was all coming to an end. Suddenly she couldn't breathe. The walls were closing in on her. She leapt to her feet, panic rising in her chest. 'I have to get out of here. How do I get out?'

'The door's open. You can leave any time you want.'

Eden walked quickly across the room and pulled open the door. Outside, in the corridor, two prison officers were waiting. 'I want to go,' she said. 'I want to go now.' She glanced back over her shoulder, one last look at the man she had loved.

'I'm sorry,' he said. 'It was never meant to end like this.'

Eden couldn't speak. Her throat had closed up. A bitter, cold despair swept over her. She turned away, not wanting him to see the tears in her eyes. So this is it, she thought: the last goodbye. It took every ounce of her willpower just to keep it all together as she was escorted across the courtyard and out of the prison.

Eden walked slowly along the street, got into the car and leaned over the wheel. A low moan escaped from her lips. There was nothing left. All her hopes and dreams were in tatters. Everything she'd thought real was just an illusion. Tom Chase wasn't her husband. She wasn't a wife. Nothing about her life was real. Even her name was fake. She felt lost, bereft, empty, as though her very soul had shrivelled up and died. She closed her eyes and wept.

49

Jimmy Letts was climbing the walls with frustration. He'd been sitting on the story since Thursday and it was now Monday afternoon. But he couldn't do anything until he found Eden Chase. Where the hell was she? On Thursday, Maurie Post had followed her from the prison, to Tammy's place and then on to a block of flats in Finchley, but no one was answering the bell to number four. He was starting to wonder if the little shit had given him the right address or if he'd even gone to HMP Thornley Heath.

Jimmy had camped outside the flats for most of the weekend, but to no avail. There wasn't a sign of Eden's car on the forecourt reserved for residents or in the surrounding streets. He'd had a good scout round, checking everywhere within reasonable walking distance. The flat was definitely empty; no one came or went and the lights remained out when it got dark.

It had been too late for him to come round after he'd got back from Norwich on Thursday evening. Then, on the Friday, he'd got a bollocking from his editor, Lipton, who was less than pleased about him going AWOL and had sent him out on as many menial jobs as he could think of. It had been four o'clock before Jimmy had finally managed to escape to Finchley. Of course he could have told Lipton about the Tom Chase exclusive, but he didn't trust him. The old sod wasn't beyond passing it on to a senior reporter, someone with more experience who'd then take all the bloody credit. No, he was going to keep it under his belt until he'd got Eden's response.

Jimmy glanced at his watch. It was ten past one and he couldn't hang around any longer. He was supposed to be on the Mansfield estate – there'd been more trouble there last night – and he couldn't afford to piss off Lipton any more than he already had. He'd have to come back later and try again.

The rain had cleared, but the sky remained ominous. As he drove towards east London, Jimmy glanced towards the heavens, sending up a silent prayer that no one would get to Eden before he did. He was looking forward to breaking the news – and wiping that supercilious look off her face. Unless she already knew. Was that possible? He didn't think so.

Jimmy had guessed he was on to something big as soon as he'd set eyes on Mrs Andrea Chase. And her story was a heart-rending one. Her son wasn't a full-grown man, a forty-one-year-old photographer currently languishing at Her Majesty's Pleasure. No, of course he wasn't. *Her* son, little Tom Chase, had tragically died at the age of two from diphtheria. The man Eden Chase was married to was a faker, a deceiver, a lowlife who had stolen a dead child's identity.

The story was sensational – in every sense of the word. He couldn't have asked for more if he'd made it up himself. Jimmy drummed his fingers on the wheel as he waited at traffic lights. So what was Tom Chase's real name? Jack Minter, perhaps, although it was more than likely that was fake as

343

well. He didn't relish the thought of another three hours down Somerset House but it might come to that if Eden didn't – or couldn't – enlighten him. But at least he had leverage on her now. If she refused to speak it would look like she was defending her husband's despicable actions.

It was a bugger that she'd disappeared. If the worst came to the worst, he could get Maurie to do the prison run again but that would mean waiting until Thursday. He shifted in his seat, scratched his neck, swore softly under his breath. He wasn't sleeping properly and his eyes felt sore; every time his head hit the pillow the story started spinning round. He needed the missing pieces. He needed Eden Chase.

Even as Jimmy approached the three tall concrete towers of the Mansfield estate, he could see the grey smoke rising into the air. It was the last place he wanted to be – a bloody jungle – and he intended to get in and out as fast as he could. Compared to the disturbances taking place in other parts of London, this was small-scale, minor, but there was always a chance things could escalate. What he didn't want was to be caught in the middle of a riot. Some reporters, the more intrepid variety, might relish the prospect, but he wasn't one of them.

He parked the car down a side street, well away from the vandals. His old Cortina might be a heap of scrap but at least it still had four wheels on it. As he entered the estate, the acrid smell of burning rubber floated on the air. Jimmy walked along the main path, following his nose. The towers loomed over him, gloomy and ominous, high-rise prisons for the poor and the hopeless. There was nothing to recommend the place. The estate was a shithole, a slum in the sky.

Jimmy scanned the landscape, alert to any signs of fresh trouble. A couple of cars stood smouldering in the central square. The ground was littered with debris, bits of wood, old pipe, and broken glass that crunched under his feet. Not a cop in sight. Not many residents either. There was the sense of something simmering, the lull that comes before the storm.

He skirted around the cars and headed for Haslow House. His intention was to find Mandy Lee, the woman who ran the residents' association, and get her views on what was happening and why. Of course everyone knew why – it hardly took a genius to work it out – but he needed someone to spell out the obvious in black and white. A few pithy quotes and he'd be on his way.

Jimmy scowled as he strode towards the door, resenting the time he was wasting when he could be trying to track down Eden Chase. He was looking forward to the moment they came face to face again, when he could show her the birth certificate of a long-dead child and shock her out of her silence. No one could refuse to comment when presented with evidence like that. She was about to find out the truth and it wouldn't be pleasant. Well, not for her at least. For him, it could be the biggest break of his career.

Jimmy was still thinking about this as he approached the entrance to the tower block. He was only a few yards from the door when it happened. He sensed rather than saw the initial movement above him, a change, a shifting in the atmosphere, but by the time his instincts told him to look up it was already too late. He had only a fleeting impression of something falling, something gathering speed, before the air was knocked out of his lungs and he hit the ground like a sack of spuds. The last thing he remembered was the dull grey colour of the concrete before everything went black.

50

Max drove into the far corner of the car park of the Fox, away from lights and prying eyes. He turned the motor around so he was facing the exit and then switched off the engine. He checked his watch – ten minutes to six – and settled back to wait. From here he could see the side door of the pub, used only by the staff. A pile of crates stood to one side, neatly stacked with empty bottles. It was in that very spot that Joe Quinn had been battered to death twelve years ago, his head caved in by a baseball bat.

Max stared over. Had Terry Street been responsible for Quinn's murder? If he *was* guilty, he clearly didn't have any qualms about returning to the scene of the crime. He was here every day; he'd even bought the damn place. It was hardly the action of a man with a guilty conscience – but then maybe Terry didn't have a conscience at all.

It was another ten minutes before the door opened. Big Vinnie Keane stepped out and looked around the car park. Max flashed his lights. Vinnie gave a nod and retreated back inside. Thirty seconds later he reappeared, followed by Terry.

The two of them walked across the forecourt, side by side, only separating when they reached the car. Vinnie went round the back and casually leaned against the wall. Terry climbed into the passenger seat.

'Max,' he said. 'How are you doing, mate?'

'Surviving, thanks. You?'

Terry shrugged. 'Getting by.' He reached into his pocket and took out an opaque plastic bag, which he passed over to Max. 'This do you?'

Max switched on the overhead light and pulled out the gun. It was a small black semi-automatic Luger. 'Anything I need to know?'

'Cleaned, oiled, loaded and in excellent condition. Only one careful owner.'

Max examined the revolver, keeping it low, out of sight of anyone who might be passing on the road. Then he nodded towards the glove compartment. 'It's in there.'

Terry opened the compartment, took out the envelope and slipped it into the inside pocket of his jacket. 'Ta.'

'Aren't you going to count it?'

'I trust you, Max.' Terry glanced towards the revolver. 'You should be careful.'

'I know how to handle a gun.'

'I wasn't talking about the gun.'

Max gave a shrug.

Terry stared at him for a while and then gave a nod. 'I'll see you around.'

Max watched as Terry and Vinnie walked back to the pub. He put the gun in his pocket, started the engine and drove out on to Station Road. At the traffic lights he turned right and went up the high street. When he'd gone past Connolly's he turned right again and began to drive up and down the side roads looking for somewhere to park. Eventually he found a place in Violet Road.

Max pulled in and cut the engine. The road was quiet, residential, a row of two-up, two-down terraces. He leaned back against the seat and gazed out into the darkness. There was an ache in his bones, an exhaustion he couldn't shake off. He wanted to close his eyes and go to sleep. He wanted everything to be over.

As he got out of the car, a black cat with sleek fur and shining green eyes ran across his path into one of the small front gardens. He couldn't remember if that was supposed to be lucky or unlucky. Terry would say you made your own luck in this world, but Max wasn't so sure. For him the fates were capricious creatures, distributing good and bad in a fashion so random it made no sense at all. You got what you were given, deserved or not.

Max noticed Eden's Audi as he made his way back to the high street. It was parked under a street lamp and the long, deep scratch along the passenger side glittered silver against the darkness of the bodywork. He wasn't proud of having done that. It had been one of those petty, spiteful acts, a lashing out, a spur of the moment thing.

As he walked on, Max rolled her name around his mouth. Eden. He refused to think of her as a real, breathing, sentient being. For him, she was no more than a means to an end. He had saved her life in order to take it. He smiled at the madness of it all. His fingers closed around the gun, the cool hard metal. There was always a time of reckoning and for Tom Chase it was fast approaching.

51

Eden gazed across the table, shocked at the state of Tammy and the story of what had happened to her on Friday. The girl's face was battered and bruised, one eye so swollen it wouldn't open properly. She had a cowed, frightened look, but there was a hint of defiance in her expression too. She was hitting back at Banner the only way she could – by telling the truth.

It was just over an hour since Tammy had called Caitlin, saying she had to talk to Eden urgently. Caitlin had given her the Kellston number – there was no need for secrecy now that Eden was moving out – and the three of them had met up at the flat.

'You should report the bastard,' Caitlin said. 'You can't let him get away with it.'

Tammy shook her head. 'And have him tell everyone I'm a grass? He would, you know. He'd make sure the entire bloody neighbourhood knew about it. And I've got Mia to think about. What if he calls the Social?'

'He won't.'

'He might. He's a shit. He does whatever he likes.'

Eden would probably have had less sympathy for Tammy if it hadn't been for what she'd learned from Tom that morning. Now the spying hardly seemed to matter; it was just one more sordid detail in the great, dirty scheme of things. She still hadn't got her head round it all. She felt like she'd been pushed off the edge of a cliff and was still falling, falling, waiting for the moment when she hit the ground and shattered into a thousand pieces.

'I'm sorry,' Tammy said for the umpteenth time. 'Honest, I am. I shouldn't have done it. I'm really sorry.'

'It doesn't matter,' Eden replied, because it didn't any more. She didn't give a damn what Tammy may have passed on to DI Vic Banner. 'But thanks for telling me. It can't have been easy.'

Tammy's hands did a flustered dance on the table, her fingers twisting round each other, linking and unlinking. 'There's something else you should know: Pete's been working for Banner too.'

'Your brother?'

'He's not my brother. That was just ... I never met him before all this.'

'Oh,' Eden said, wondering if she was, possibly, the most gullible person in the world.

Tammy, who was unaware of Tom's revelations, gave Eden a nervous glance as if wondering why she was being so reasonable. She shrank back a little, perhaps suspecting that some form of retribution would eventually be coming her way. 'You must be mad at me.'

Eden shrugged. 'I didn't tell you anything important. Well, nothing Banner wouldn't have found out about in time.'

'The stuff about Pat Lynch was true, though. Honest to God. I wasn't making it up. That guy really *is* crazy. Your old man needed to get off the wing. He wasn't safe there.'

Eden gave a thin smile. Her *old man*. Except he wasn't. Tom was someone else's husband. Poor Jackie had a shock coming her way. She wondered who'd break the bad news to her. The police, probably, as it involved a crime. There would be a knock on her door, tomorrow or the day after, and Jackie would answer it and her life would be torn apart. She must have married again after all these years, had a family, put the past behind her. But the past wasn't sleeping peacefully. Like Lazarus, Larry Hewitt had risen from the dead.

Tammy put her head in her hands. 'Banner's going to kill me if he finds out I told you.'

'Looks like he's already tried,' Caitlin said. 'Why don't you get out of London for a while, lay low until the trial is over? If you're not around he can't cause you any grief.'

'And go where? I've got nowhere to go.'

'I might be able to help you there.'

'How?'

But before Caitlin got the chance to answer, the doorbell rang. Eden stood up, guessing who it was even as she headed for the landing. There were only a few people who knew where she was staying and two of them were in the living room. She walked downstairs, opened the door and came face to face with Max Tamer again. Although she knew she should be afraid, she felt nothing as she stood aside and waved him in.

'You'd better come up.'

Tamer gave a nod and started up the stairs. As Eden followed him, she wondered why she was so calm. Or maybe it wasn't calmness, more a sort of paralysis, as if she had gone beyond feeling anything. The truth about Tom had drained all the emotion from her. She had a numbness in the centre of her heart, an odd hazy mist swirling around in her head.

Max Tamer walked into the living room and stopped

abruptly. 'Oh,' he said, turning towards her. 'I didn't realise you had company.'

Eden looked over at Caitlin. 'Why don't you and Tammy go to the caff for half an hour? We won't be long. I'll meet you down there.'

'If I'm interrupting,' Tamer said, 'I can come back later.'

Eden shook her head, wanting to get it over and done with. 'There's no need.'

Caitlin stared at Tamer for a few seconds before shifting her attention to Eden. 'Are you sure?'

'If you don't mind,' Eden said. 'We just need a quick chat.' It only occurred to her as the two women were leaving that it might have been smarter for her to take Tamer somewhere more public rather than remaining with him in the flat. But at the same time she didn't really care.

Max Tamer's face was tight and drawn. His gaze skittered around the room before coming to rest on Eden again. He said nothing until the front door had shut and he knew they were alone. 'So, did you see him?'

'Yes.'

'And?'

Eden folded her arms across her chest. 'And he says he never met Ann-Marie. I don't just mean in London, but in Budapest too. He doesn't even know what she looks like.'

Tamer's face twisted. 'Do you believe him?'

'What does it matter what I believe? I'm telling you what he said. You wanted me to ask him about Ann-Marie and that's what I did.'

Tamer reached into the inside pocket of his overcoat and removed his wallet. He slid out a photograph and held it out to her. 'This is my wife. This is Ann-Marie in Budapest.'

Eden gave a slight jump as she took the black and white picture from his hand. The photo was identical to the one

352

she'd found at the studio, the one of the couple sitting out-side a bar.

'What is it?' he asked. 'Have you seen it before?'

'Yes. There were some photos in Tom's studio and—'

'I knew it,' Tamer hissed.

Eden shook her head and passed the picture back to him. 'It doesn't mean what you think it does. The photo I saw probably belonged to Jack Minter, not Tom.' She sighed, knowing she had a lot of explaining to do. 'You'd better sit down. This is going to take a while. In fact, I need a drink. Hang on, I won't be a minute.'

She went through to the kitchen and fetched the bottle of brandy Caitlin had brought with her, along with two glasses. Until now, she'd resisted the temptation to drown her sorrows in alcohol, but she couldn't face repeating Tom's secrets without some Dutch courage. She sat down in the armchair – he was on the sofa – put the glasses on the coffee table and unscrewed the lid of the bottle.

'Not for me,' he said quickly, as if accepting a drink was like collaborating with the enemy. Or maybe he just wanted to keep a clear head.

Eden poured herself a large one. 'Suit yourself.'

'Your husband's a liar,' he said.

'Of course he is.'

Tamer, who had obviously been expecting a quite different response, gazed at her suspiciously. His lips straightened into a thin line. 'What are you up to? Don't play games with me or—'

'No one's playing games.' Eden took a large gulp of brandy, giving the booze time to warm her throat before she contin-ued. She was wondering where to start: the lies, the theft, the bigamy? 'Well, it's all going to come out soon enough so you may as well hear it from me.' She hesitated, took a deep breath and began to tell the story.

Eden did the best she could, occasionally stumbling over words, stopping and starting, trying to get everything clear in order to shed light on the darkness of Larry Hewitt's terrible deception. By the time she'd finished she'd got through two glasses of brandy and was pouring out her third. 'So you see,' she said finally, 'he's only ever pretended to be Tom Chase. He wasn't the man your wife knew. He was never her boyfriend. He's just someone who saw an opportunity and grabbed it. He's a coward and a schemer and a sad excuse for a human being.'

Tamer rose to his feet and strode over to the window. 'None of this proves anything – other than the fact your husband's a compulsive liar.'

'You've not been listening properly. He's not my husband.'

'You can't believe anything that comes out of his mouth.'

'True,' she said, 'but I still don't think he's the man you've been looking for. *That* Tom Chase is buried in Budapest. And God knows what his real name was. Jack Minter? I doubt it. That was probably a false name too.' Eden gave a hollow laugh. 'Larry Hewitt had no idea what he was getting himself into. He thought he was being clever by taking on a dead man's identity, but all he was doing was storing up a heap of trouble for himself.'

Tamer had his back to her. He was quiet for a moment and then he said, 'I don't understand why he kept Ann-Marie's letters. Why didn't he get rid of them?'

'I don't know.' She couldn't help thinking it was a good thing they no longer existed. It could only be a torment to read love letters your wife had sent to another man. 'Did Tom Chase – I mean the *real* Tom Chase – ever write back to Ann-Marie? He must have done. You could compare the hand-writing to Larry Hewitt's, make sure they're not the same.'

'I thought you were already sure of that.'

'*I* am,' she said. 'It's you I'm thinking about.'

Tamer walked back to the sofa, seemed about to sit down again but then changed his mind and started wandering around the room. As if he didn't know what to do with himself, he walked and frowned and walked some more. 'No, I never found any letters from him.'

'So she probably got rid of them. She'd moved on, hadn't she? She'd found someone else.'

'But she kept the photograph.'

'So what? It was part of her past. We all keep stuff from the past.'

Tamer stopped and heaved out a breath. 'What happens to Larry Hewitt now?'

Eden gave a shrug. 'That's down to the police. I presume they'll charge him with perjury and identity theft and whatever else they can throw in his direction. It's not my concern any more.'

Tamer gave her a long, hard look. 'He was your husband – or at least you thought he was. You must still have some feelings for him.'

Eden's lips slid into a faltering smile. 'They'll go away – in time.' And then, because she'd drunk too much and was beyond censoring her inner thoughts, she added, 'I could have forgiven him for most of it, you know, maybe even taking the money, but never for what he did to his family. He let his parents believe he was dead. How could anyone be so cruel? And Jackie too. He just disposed of her. She was an inconvenience, a millstone round *his* neck. He made her a widow and didn't think twice. What kind of man does a thing like that?'

But Tamer didn't answer. Instead he asked, 'When I was here last time, you said you thought I was the undertaker.'

'Yes.'

'Why would you think that?'

355

Eden frowned at this sudden random change of subject. She took another gulp of brandy even though she'd had more than enough already. 'Look out of the window,' she said. 'Across the road.'

Tamer crossed to the window. 'Ah,' he said softly.

'Tobias Grand and Sons. That's where you were standing the first time I saw you. I don't know . . . I thought you'd just stepped out for a cigarette.' Eden gazed at him over the rim of her glass. Something was stirring in the back of her mind, a thought that was trying to spark. Why did he remember that? Why did it matter? A throwaway comment that had somehow got under his skin. It took a few seconds before the truth finally dawned. A shiver ran the length of her spine. 'An eye for an eye. Was that what you were planning? A wife for a wife?'

He didn't look at her. He said nothing.

'Your own individual brand of justice.' The brandy gave her a kind of courage, albeit a somewhat reckless kind. 'That's what you were planning, wasn't it? Except, as it turns out, you've got the wrong guy and the wrong wife.' She gave a snort. 'Not even a wife at all, in fact. So what are you going to do now?'

Tamer turned to face her again, his eyes cold as ice. 'Someone should pay for what happened to Ann-Marie.'

'Yes,' she agreed. 'Someone should. The *right* person. But if it makes you feel better, just go right ahead. It's not as though my life's worth living anyway. It's shit, an almighty pile of shit. So why don't you just put me out of my misery?'

'You're drunk,' he said.

'So what?'

'So you don't know what you're saying.'

'I know exactly what I'm saying.' Eden gestured towards his bandaged hand. 'Are you going to tell me what happened to that?'

'I've already told you.'

'You told me *something*. You didn't tell me the truth.'

Tamer shrugged.

'It was you, wasn't it? You were the one who got me out of the flat, out of the fire. It must have been. Geoff said the guy had cut his hand. But why did you save me? Why didn't you just leave me there? If you wanted me dead ... I don't get it.'

Tamer looked away, wouldn't meet her eyes. 'It's complicated.'

'It must be. Care to enlighten me?'

'Another time, maybe.'

Eden put the glass down on the table. 'Well, never mind. Perhaps the truth's not all it's cracked up to be. I've had enough of it for one day.'

'I should go,' Tamer said.

'What will you do now?'

'Go home,' he said.

'No, I meant about ... ' Eden stopped, already knowing the answer before she even asked the question. When it came to Ann-Marie, he'd carry on looking, searching, until he got some resolution. He wasn't the type of man who would ever give up. 'It doesn't matter.'

'And you? What will you do?'

Eden had been trying not to think about it. What did a person do when their life had been ripped apart, when everything they believed to be true turned out to be one big stinking lie?

Suddenly, she found herself thinking about her father. Despite all their difficulties, all the years of sniping, he was still her dad. And she suddenly felt like a child again, weak and defenceless, needing someone to put their arms around her and love her unconditionally. A small, trembling smile found its way on to her lips. 'I don't know,' she said. 'Perhaps I'll go home too.'

Epilogue

Six months later

In the time since Larry Hewitt had made his confession, a war had been fought and won in the Falkland Islands, and a different battle – one that had been going on for years – had finally resulted in a peace treaty between Eden and her father. As she sat in the garden of the house in Edinburgh, she reflected on the journey they had made. It hadn't been an easy one, fraught as it was with so much history, so many misunderstandings and false perceptions, but they had both conceded ground and in the process come to understand each other better.

Eden raised her hand and shaded her eyes from the glare of the sun. When she'd made the decision to come home, she'd been at her lowest ebb, bereft of all hope, looking only for somewhere to shelter for a while. But what she had found was more than a sanctuary. She had formed a bond with her dad, establishing a connection that had not been there before.

Eden thought back over their recent conversations. She realised now that she'd never really considered the impact her mother's death had had on him. Widowed and grieving, he had struggled with bringing up a daughter as a single parent, his anxiety too often coming across as impatience or control.

'I didn't know how to talk to you, how to make things better when you were unhappy or upset. It was easier with Iain. I could cope with a boy but you . . . You needed your mum and she wasn't there.'

'I thought you loved him more.'

'How could you think that? I love you both the same.'

'That's what parents always say.'

'That's because it's true.'

'But you *liked* him more,' Eden insisted.

Her father had pondered on this for a while. 'He was easier to deal with, but that's not the same thing.'

Eden knew she'd behaved badly in the past, particularly as a teenager. Looking back, she could see how she'd been constantly trying to get his attention, even if it was the wrong sort. She'd wanted him to notice her, to praise her, to be proud of her, and yet had done everything in her power to provoke the very opposite response. Over the years they had both got in the habit of taking up positions and refusing to budge. Only now, in admitting to their mistakes, were they finally able to move forward.

Eden gazed up at the sky. There had been sun, rain, wind, even a few thunderstorms during the month of August. There had also been a trial, although not one relating to the Epping bank robbery or the death of Paddy Lynch. *That* had been blown out of the water by Tom Chase's confession to theft, identity theft and bigamy. The real 'Jack Minter' was dead and couldn't be called to account for his crimes.

Eden still couldn't think of Tom as Larry Hewitt. Thankfully, she hadn't been needed at court – he'd pleaded guilty to all charges – and Caitlin had called her with news of the sentence: eight years. It was a long time, but less than he'd have got if the jury had believed Archie Rudd. There had been stories in the papers, sensationalist double-page spreads about the secret life of the Covent Garden photographer. Her name had been mentioned but no reporters had managed to track her down.

Iain had proved to be a godsend in dealing with the practicalities of cutting ties. He had arranged, among other things, for the car and the keys to the two flats and the studio to be returned to Tom's solicitor. Caitlin had visited the Islington flat, but hadn't managed to salvage anything from the fire. A clean break, then, or at least as clean as it could be in the circumstances. There would be no need for a divorce because there had been no legal marriage. She had called John Connolly herself to terminate her employment and to apologise for leaving without giving notice. He hadn't sounded too disappointed; she was, she suspected, no great loss to the world of waitressing.

The practical ties were one thing, the emotional ones quite another. When you'd invested so much love in a person, it was hard to look to the future without them. And it wasn't healthy, she knew, to replace love with hate. Anyway, she didn't hate him. She hated what he'd *done*, all the lies and deceit, all the hurt he'd inflicted. It had been like falling for a mirage, for someone who didn't actually exist. She would eventually get over Tom Chase but it would take a while. A day at a time, she thought. It was the only way forward.

Archie Rudd made himself a brew, settled down in the armchair and lit a fag. All things considered, it had worked out pretty well for him, although it had been touch and go back in March. Tom Chase's revelations had turned everything on its head. With Jack Minter dead and buried in Budapest, Archie's so-called evidence had been thrown into question. He had identified the wrong man to DI Banner.

But there was a reason why Archie paid his solicitor a small fortune. Ben Curran was smart and as slippery as an eel. His client, he'd claimed, had been unsure about the photograph – after all, it was sixteen years since the robbery and the two men had only met on a few occasions – but Banner had convinced him it was the right man. There'd been no identity parade, no opportunity for Archie to take a closer look. It was a genuine mistake.

With the Epping trial dropped, Archie could have been in the proverbial if Curran hadn't already brokered a watertight deal with the police over the Shepperton robbery. In the event, he'd got a three-stretch of which he'd only serve half, minus the time he'd spent on remand, which meant he should be out in less than eighteen months.

Archie puffed on his fag, relieved he'd got away with it. Despite Banner's intensive coaching, he hadn't been looking forward to giving evidence against Tom Chase. The defence could have easily tripped him up, blowing holes in his story. And there were big holes to be found, a bleeding crater in fact, because the truth was he'd never actually taken part in the Epping warehouse job.

Everything Archie knew about the blag had come from his mate, Don Shepherd. He could remember it all clear as day. At the time, back in November '66, he had just got out of hospital. Gallstones, it had been. Bloody agonising. Even the thought of it made him wince. So he hadn't been in any fit state to be running around with a sawn-off. But Don had come over to the house and given him the low-down.

'You don't know nothin' about this guy,' Archie had said.

'I know plenty. Calls himself Jack Minter, but his real name's Tom Chase. He works for a snapper, Albert Shiner, in Chigwell. I've checked him out, Arch, followed him home.'

And then after, when it had all gone so wrong, Don had

been straight round. His old mate had been in a panic about Paddy Lynch getting shot and then, later, about his body being found in the back of the van.

'You mustn't tell no one, Arch,' he'd said. 'Not even Rose. You've got to keep schtum. If this gets out . . . '

So everything Archie had fed to DI Banner had been second-hand information. He'd never, in his entire life, set eyes on Jack Minter or Tom Chase or whatever he was really called. But when the photo had been put in front of him, he'd known it was the geezer who'd been arrested just from what Banner had said.

'This is the guy, yeah? This is the guy who called himself Jack Minter?'

And Archie had made a show of staring at it. 'Looks like him but it's been . . . you know, it's been a while.'

With two of the gang dead – Don and Paddy – and Rossi living it up in Spain, there was no one other than Ned Shepherd and Minter to challenge his claim that he'd been on the job. By keeping Ned's name out of it, there'd be no comeback there. Which only left Jack Minter. And he could hardly stand up and say that Archie hadn't been a member of the gang if he was denying having done the crime himself.

Archie sighed into the room. He'd really thought the bloke was guilty: a photographer with the right name in possession of a stolen bracelet from the Epping warehouse. What could be more damning? The guy was bang to rights. How was he to know that this Tom Chase had nicked someone else's identity?

Archie knew he'd taken a mighty risk, a gamble that might not have paid off. But it had been his only way out. It all stemmed from that night when Lee Barker and his mates had looked at him with the kind of contempt that some young men reserve for anyone over fifty. In order to try and raise his status, to save face, he had told a pack of lies about being on the Epping job. It had been sad and stupid, pathetic even, but as it turned out it had also been his salvation. After their arrest at Shepperton, Barker had grassed him up and all Archie had to do was run with it.

He grinned. He'd got lucky. Sometimes it went that way. The fates smiled kindly on you and all was sweet with the world. Of course he'd still have to square things with Vera Lynch – he didn't want that mad fucker Pat on his back for the rest of his life – but he reckoned he could talk her round. When push came to shove, all he'd actually done was lie to the police and that wasn't anything she'd care about. And yes, okay, so he'd known who had been on the job with her Paddy but he hadn't taken part himself.

Archie leaned back and relaxed. Rose was none too pleased that he hadn't been straight with her, but she'd forgive him for it eventually. She always did. At the start he'd been worried she'd remember about the gallstones, about how he *couldn't* have been in Epping, but it hadn't clicked into place. She'd known something was wrong without being able to put her finger on it. He should have come clean but he'd been too embarrassed, too ashamed, to explain how he'd been trying to impress some no-good wankers. Pride comes before a fall? Well, sometimes, but in this case it had saved him from fifteen years in the slammer. Not such a bad result after all.

Jimmy Letts limped past the colourful stalls at the St James's summer fair, his left leg still dragging despite all the physiotherapy he'd had. It was six months since he'd been on the verge of a major scoop only to have it snatched away at the very last moment. Now he was back to reporting on the sort of events that wouldn't challenge the brain of a five-year-old.

He muttered under his breath as he made his way towards

the refreshment tent. 'Why me? Fuck it! What did I do to deserve this?'

What he remembered from that day at the Mansfield estate was vivid until the point he'd looked up to see something dark, something heavy, hurtling through the air towards him. There had been a split second as it registered in his brain before he hit the deck. Now he knew he'd been hit by a piece of rusting balcony, although whether this was accidental or deliberate remained open to debate. He was more inclined towards the latter. Somewhere in the fuzzy depths of his memory, he was sure he'd heard voices, laughter, just before it had all gone black.

'Bastards!'

When he'd come round at the hospital it was to find his leg broken in two places and a lump the size of a golf ball on the back of his head. Morphine had seen him through the next few days but even that strong opiate hadn't been enough to dull the pain of seeing Bob Rich's double-page exclusive in the *Evening News*. The Tom Chase story was out of the bag. There was nothing left to tell. Jimmy had well and truly missed the boat.

From across the other side of Hackney Fields, carousel music floated in the air. He could imagine the ride going round and round, the riders getting nowhere. To his ears the music sounded like mockery, as though even the wooden horses were laughing at him. All the work he'd done, all the research, all the thinking and talking and wheedling, and for what? To have it all snatched away from him in the blink of an eye.

Jimmy walked past the raffle stall, stopped and retraced his steps. Sitting right in the centre of the trestle table, surrounded by numerous other prizes, was a large bottle of whisky, a bottle that was big enough to drown any man's sorrows. His eyes lit up. It was a sign, perhaps. Digging into his pocket, he found some change and bought a row of tickets. One day his luck had to change. Why not today?

Larry Hewitt stood facing the small window with his hands wrapped round the bars. He could deal with prison, he could adapt and adjust, but the one thing he couldn't get used to was being called Larry again. For the past fifteen years he'd been Tom Chase and had imagined that other name consigned to the bin for ever.

After his conviction and transfer to a new jail, he'd chosen to go straight on to the wing. There was no need for him to hide away in solitary now that the threat from Pat Lynch was gone. To his surprise, he'd found that the media attention surrounding the trial afforded him a certain measure of celebrity. He was the bloke who'd pulled a fast one and got away with it for fifteen years. Everyone wanted to know how.

Larry was still sussing out his fellow inmates, working out who needed to be avoided or appeased or flattered. There were three ways to survive prison – by brute force, by keeping your head down and hoping no one noticed you, or by playing it smart. He was using his brains to make sure his time inside would be as easy and as comfortable as possible. He had no intention of becoming a victim.

The trick was to learn by your mistakes. Too often the smallest thing could trip you up. In his case it had been the bracelet; without it the police would have had nothing on him other than the wild accusations of some old lag. That piece of jewellery had almost done for Denny too, albeit in a different way. It had only come to him yesterday. He'd suddenly recalled how it hadn't been Fiona who'd tried on the bracelet at the studio, slipping the gold snake over a slender wrist, but some other girl – a vapid blonde – his friend Denny been seeing on the side. If only he'd sold it to them. Everything would be very different now.

He gazed up towards the clear blue sky and wondered what Eden was doing. He tried not to dwell on her too much, to keep her at a distance. Prison was no place for regrets; if you let them worm their way in they'd burrow through your soul and leave you with nothing. What she hadn't been able to grasp was that he'd had no choice – the second the lie had slipped from his lips in Budapest, his future had been predetermined. If it had been possible to change her mind, to persuade her to stay, he'd have tried, but he'd known it was useless as soon as he'd looked into her eyes.

Eden was gone – as dead to him now as the other one. The two girls with the long red hair. Ann-Marie still walked in his dreams, the fateful moment they'd met again lodged in his mind. He'd thought he was safe, the past neatly buried in a cemetery in Budapest – until three years ago. He'd been half-way down Southampton Street, heading towards the Strand, when he'd heard a woman's voice call out the name.

'Larry! Larry!'

Not calling out to him. She couldn't be. But still freezing for a moment before casually turning, praying that another Larry was somewhere nearby. His heart dropping like a stone when he saw Ann-Marie. Already she was weaving her way through the people, manically waving at him. Too late to avoid her. Fixing a smile on his face, not having to fake the surprise. Leaning down to kiss her cheek.

'Ann-Marie. My God! How lovely. It's been for ever. What are you doing here?'

'Ah, I live here now. I live in London.' Putting out her left hand to show him the rings on the third finger. 'And married too. His name's Max. I'm very happy.'

'Congratulations.'

'How have you been? Do you have time for coffee? Oh, please say you do. I've so much to tell you. And you must tell me everything that's happened to you too.'

Although his instinct had been to run, to get away from her as quickly as he could, he knew it would be a big mistake. He had to front it out while he decided what to do next. His heart was pounding in his chest, adrenalin pumping through his body. 'Yes, yes of course. There's a café just down here.'

They had walked back to the piazza arm in arm, old friends reunited after years apart. He suggested a café on the lower floor of the shopping mall, and found a quiet corner away from prying eyes. Two cappuccinos in wide white cups. He sat and smiled while Ann-Marie talked, telling him about her life, her job, her hopes for the future. He was sweating, his thoughts in a tailspin, panic overtaking him. Try and stay calm. But every time she used his name – Larry, Larry, Larry – he felt his fear expanding, bile rising into his throat.

'So Larry, are you still in touch with Tom?'

A short hesitation. What to say?

'It's all right,' she said, laying a hand on his arm. 'I was just curious. We had that silly argument and then I never heard from him again. I tried to call but no one answered. I wrote but . . . It doesn't matter. It's the past, *oui*? We change. We move on. I hope he's happy. I hope things worked out for him.'

If she had just been passing through, on holiday perhaps, it could have all been different. But *living* in London, working at a local theatre – it was just impossible. They could easily bump into each other again or she could walk along Henrietta Street and notice the metal plaque beside the door: *Tom Chase, Photographer.*

He had spent the rest of the afternoon trying to figure out what to do. There was only one solution. He would have to tell her the truth and hope she'd keep his secret. But would she? He wasn't sure. She might guess about the money, that he'd stolen more than Tom's identity. She was bound to tell her husband. Maybe she would tell other people too. Word would get around and then . . .

By five o'clock he was at the stage door, waiting for her. She wasn't working late tonight. She had told him that while she sipped her cappuccino. Her eyes had lit up when she came out and saw him again.

'Larry! What are you doing here?'

'I've got a surprise for you.'

'What kind of a surprise?'

'If I told you that it wouldn't be a surprise, would it?' She had glanced at her watch and he'd said quickly, 'Half an hour, that's all. Come on, the car's parked just down the road.'

He had driven over to Kellston and then to the old railway arches, a dark empty place where few people ventured. What had she been thinking on the way there? That he was taking her to meet Tom, perhaps. She had tried to coax the secret from him, smiling and laughing. It never even entered her head that he was the enemy. She was too trusting, too nice.

Larry didn't like to think about the next bit. It made him feel queasy. He had bought the knife in the afternoon, from a kitchen shop on Longacre. It had a long blade, sharp, finely honed. So the purchase wouldn't stand out, he'd bought a couple of other items too, a bread board and a pair of salt and pepper shakers. He'd paid with cash and thrown the receipt in the first bin he'd come to.

Larry leaned his forehead against the cool metal bars of the cell window. It wasn't his fault. He'd never *meant* to hurt anyone. She simply hadn't given him a choice. What it boiled down to was him or her. In the event, it had been fast and merciful. She'd had no time to be afraid. The knife had plunged through her ribs, ripping open her heart, killing her almost instantly. A few seconds and it was all over.

Larry wasn't sure exactly where the body was buried. He had moved her corpse to the back seat, covered it with a rug and driven in an easterly direction out of London. It had been over two hours before he'd stopped again, somewhere in Suffolk. He'd got off the main road and wound around the lanes, searching for a spot as remote as possible, away from houses, away from any sign of life.

A shallow grave, that's all it had been. He hadn't got a spade, hadn't dared buy one in case someone remembered him. So he'd dug down into the base of the ditch with nothing more than his bare hands, scrabbling in the soft dirt, creating a space in which to lay Ann-Marie's body. He'd covered her with soil and leaves, said a fast prayer and left the rest to fate.

For the next few days, he'd been certain she'd be found. Dread filled his every waking hour. What if the waitress in the Covent Garden café remembered them drinking coffee together? What if someone had spotted him at the theatre meeting Ann-Marie? But the fates, for once, were kind. Days passed into weeks, into months, into years and still she remained undiscovered.

Larry sighed, dropped his hands from the bars and put them in his pockets. There was, he supposed, a price to pay for everything. He had lost his liberty, lost Eden, lost everything he'd worked for. But on the plus side, the worst of his crimes had gone unpunished. At the end of the day, all you could do was bargain with the Devil for the best possible deal.

Eden sat on the grass in front of the caravan and stretched out her legs. Originally she had only intended to come for the weekend, but already she'd extended that stay by over a week. The Greenham Common Peace Camp was gradually pulling her in. She liked the atmosphere, the warmth and sense of purpose that pervaded the place.

Eden had been involved in protests before – although mainly in order to provoke her father – but this felt entirely different. There was something inspiring about women coming together to make their voices heard, to take a stand. It was only a few hundred at the moment, but the numbers were swelling by the day. A few months ago the first blockade of the US airbase had taken place with thirty-four women being arrested. Then the police and bailiffs had moved in to evict them. The women, undeterred, had simply moved to a nearby site. Eden admired their gutsy determination and their refusal to be bowed.

Tammy came out of the caravan with a pail, sat down beside her and emptied a heap of potatoes on to the grass. She handed Eden a peeler.

'Here, you can give me a hand with this lot.'

Eden was surprised that Tammy had stayed as long as she had. Six months ago Caitlin had brought her and Mia here so they could escape the clutches of DI Banner, but Tammy showed no inclination to return to London. In fact she was perfectly content. She had embraced the cause and was happily contributing to the day-to-day running of the camp. Perhaps, for the first time, she felt she had some control over her life. There was no man trying to manipulate or harm her. Instead there was friendship and protection and purpose. There were even other kids for Mia to play with.

'Did Caitlin tell you about that bastard Banner?' Tammy asked.

'He's been suspended, hasn't he? Gross misconduct? I hope they throw the book at him.'

Tammy snorted. 'He's gross all right. But you know what he's like; he'll probably find a way to wriggle out of it.'

'I don't think so. I reckon he's crossed the line once too often.'

'They take care of their own, the law.'

Eden glanced around the camp, at the hotchpotch of tents and caravans and camper vans. It was a far cry from the busy streets of Shoreditch. 'You're not missing London then?'

'What's to miss? Well, only my mum, but Caitlin picks her up every other weekend and brings her down. I like it here. And Mia's happy.' Tammy grinned. 'Who'd have thought it, huh? Me at a peace camp? I'm usually the one causing all the trouble.'

'That's why you fit in so well.'

'So are you going to stay too?'

Eden had no definite plans, nowhere she had to be, nothing she had to do. She chucked a potato into the pail and picked up another. 'I'll see how it goes. I may stick around for a while.'

'You should.'

As Eden leaned over the pail, she felt the sun on the back of her neck. It was only a couple of weeks since she'd had her hair cut short and she was still getting used to it. Sometimes, when she looked in a mirror, it was like staring at a stranger – but that, she decided, was no bad thing. A fresh start, a new look, the first faltering steps towards putting her life back together.

A tall skinny girl with sunburned shoulders sauntered over and asked, 'Are you Eden?'

Eden looked up. 'Yes, that's me.'

'There's a bloke at the main gate wants to see you. Says his name's Max.'

Eden gave a start. 'Max? What? What does *he* want?'

The girl gave a shrug. 'He didn't say.'

'Okay, thanks.'

'You don't have to talk to him,' Tammy said as the girl walked off, 'not if you don't want to.'

Eden rose to her feet. 'I better had.'

'Do you want me to come with you?'

'No, I'll be fine.'

As Eden headed across the camp, she felt that familiar knot forming in her stomach. It was over six months since she'd last seen Max Tamer in the flat at Kellston, since she'd drunk too much brandy and told him everything. What now? She'd hoped she could start to put the past behind her, but Tamer clearly had other ideas. Like a bad headache, he refused to go away.

When she got out on to the main road, she saw him immediately; he was a few yards along, leaning against the side of his car and apparently studying the ground. He was wearing jeans and a shirt so white it gleamed in the sun. He glanced over as she approached and did a double-take.

'You look different,' he said, straightening up so that he towered over her. 'The hair.'

Eden frowned at him. 'What are you doing here? How did you even *know* I was here?'

Tamer ignored the second question. He didn't ask how she was or make any small talk. Instead, he reached into his pocket, pulled out an envelope and held it out to her. 'I owe you this.'

Eden took the envelope and peered inside. There was about two hundred quid in twenty-pound notes. She shook her head. 'I don't understand.'

'It's for the car, for the repairs to the paintwork.'

'Ah, so it was you.'

Tamer held his hands up. 'Guilty,' he said. 'Sorry. I've got no excuse – unless wanting to take out your frustration on an inanimate object counts as one.'

'So you came all the way here, after all this time, to try and salve your conscience?'

'It's not that far and every debt has to be paid in the end. I thought I may as well get this one over and done with.'

'You still haven't told me how you found out where I was.'

But Tamer wouldn't be drawn. He nodded towards the envelope. 'That should be enough but let me know if it isn't.'

Eden gave him back the money. 'I don't want it. It isn't anything to do with me. The car belongs to Tom.' She paused, pulled a face. 'To Larry Hewitt. I could give you the number of his solicitor if you like but I don't suppose your conscience stretches quite that far.'

'You suppose right,' he said, putting the envelope back in his pocket. 'Are you still in touch with him? With Tom, I mean.'

'No. Why would I be?'

'I thought you might have forgiven him, taken him back.'

Eden folded her arms across her chest. 'And why would I do that? We're not even legally married. Everything he told me was a lie.'

Tamer lifted and dropped his heavy shoulders. 'Some women can forgive a lot. They *do* forgive a lot.'

'Maybe I'm not the forgiving sort.'

'And if he's lied about everything . . .'

His words hung in the air, grave and accusing. Eden shifted from one foot to the other, her gaze scanning the perimeter fence before coming to rest on his face again. 'You still think he had something to do with Ann-Marie's disappearance, don't you?'

'Don't you?'

Eden remembered the photograph of the couple sitting outside the café in Budapest: Ann-Marie and Jack Minter. Someone had taken the picture and that person, although he said not, could well have been Tom. 'So what will you do?'

'Be patient. Secrets don't stay hidden for ever.'

Despite the sun, Eden suddenly felt cold. 'I hope it wasn't him.'

Max Tamer looked away. He left a short silence before speaking again. 'And you? How's it going with saving the world?'

Eden heard the mockery in his voice and glared at him. 'Why? You think women can't make a difference? I haven't noticed you men doing such a great job.'

'You're right. Maybe I just envy you – having something to believe in.'

'Bullshit.'

For the first time, he smiled. 'Well, take care of yourself. Try not to get arrested.'

'Likewise,' she said.

There was one of those awkward moments where she wasn't sure if she should shake his hand or not. Then he leaned down and opened the car door. She had started to walk away when he called after her.

'Eden? Hold on.'

She stopped and waited while he caught up with her. 'Here,' he said, thrusting the envelope into her hand.

'I've already told you. I don't want it.'

'Not for the car,' he said. 'For here, for the camp. There must be things that are needed: food, clothes, wire cutters, I don't know.'

Eden grinned even as she hesitated. Two hundred quid would certainly help to swell the coffers. It would be stupid, perhaps, to let pride stand in the way of a useful donation. 'Are you sure?'

'Just take it, yeah?'

Before she could make any further protests, Max Tamer strode back to the car, got in and quickly drove off. Eden stood on the pavement watching until he was out of sight. She realised suddenly that she hadn't even thanked him for pulling her out of the fire. Her manners had gone to pot. But at the same time she knew it didn't matter. She had the feeling there'd be other opportunities, that this wouldn't be the last she saw of him. She was sure of it.

Eden walked back to the main gate and passed through into the camp. Maybe she couldn't save the world from nuclear destruction – she couldn't even save herself from a broken heart – but perhaps all that really mattered was the trying. What had she decided when she was in Edinburgh? A day at a time. As plans went, it wasn't such a bad one. She took a deep breath, raised her faced to the sun and smiled.